The Book of Days
A Rogue Destiny Novel
Book 3

Paul Tallman

OLIVERHEBERBOOKS

Cover art by Damonza

Published by Oliver-Heber Books

0 9 8 7 6 5 4 3 2 1

To Scott
Here's to the hills we climbed, and the dreams we dreamt.
Miss you, dude.

Chapter 1
A Differing of Opinion

The air inside the tunnel smelled of moldy earth and rotting vegetation, but Ren didn't mind. The stench and darkness around him fit his mood. Ahead of him, five shadowy figures trudged down the dark passageway. Behind them lay the novel, *The Gaslight Adventures of Asher Grey*, a world they had saved from a fiery annihilation. What world lay ahead of them was anyone's guess.

The shine of their flashlights highlighted the faint greenish glow of the organic roots threading the walls of the tunnel. The internal glow had already faded since they first entered. Gone too was the familiar hum, a vibration so low it was almost inaudible to the naked ear. The silence was deafening and made Ren realize one thing. The ley-line was dying.

Raffles, a jackrabbit of Cajun Folklore, guided the party along the decaying tunnel. The circular tunnel was quiet except for the crunch of dirt underfoot. Ren watched his companions' shadows move across the walls in distorted patterns from the beams of their flashlights.

"We've been walking for a while now," Charley said. The

young tech looked up from the Echo Transponder in her hands. "Anyone have an idea how much farther? I'm still getting too much feedback to tell where we are."

"Can't be too much further," Medesto replied. The stocky gnome was the Raconteur's lead field agent. He had led the group in their search for the criminal Mordecai Davos.

"Ah still don't get what set Mordecai off like dat?" Raffles wondered out loud. "One minute, he on a hunt for da *Book o' Days*, an' da next he tryin' ta burn down da entire world. Don't make no sense."

"I think the answer to your question is obvious," Tempest scoffed. She shot an angry glare back at Ren. "B'gatti is simply not the master of subterfuge he claims he is. Mordecai Davos discovered the shape-shifter hiding among his people. B'gatti panicked and decided to burn the world down to prevent anyone from following him. Millions almost died because of the trickster's incompetence."

"What are you implying?" Ren asked.

"It's a simple accusation, B'gatti," Tempest said, her voice dripping with sarcasm. "One minute, everything is going according to plan. Then you infiltrate Mordecai's people, and the next thing we know, Mordecai Davos is about to kill the *Logos Personae* and burn the entire world to dust. So, again I ask you, what happened in the bookseller's shop?"

"It was my fault," Natascha replied, coming to Ren's defense. "The tracking compass I gave him was defective and gave away his position. I endangered the mission, not Ren."

Tempest smirked at Natascha's confession. "I don't believe for a moment the legendary Doctor Enigma, the Midnight Alchemist, would make such a mistake. B'gatti screwed up, and we almost died. I want to know why."

"You're calling me a liar?" Natascha replied.

"Yes, I believe I am," Tempest said smugly. "You defend B'gatti at every turn. I warned everyone that the trickster was not up to this job. He and Claymore Ives destroyed *The Angels of Avalon* and now he almost caused the destruction of another world."

"Leave Claymore out of this!" Ren snapped. He quickened his pace to catch up to Tempest. The compass tracker Natascha gave him had not been defective. His old partner, Claymore, turned up unexpectedly and threw him off his game. Claymore smashed the tracker and told Mordecai they were being followed to gain his trust. Ren had told no one of Claymore's involvement, but he could see Natascha had suspicions he was lying about what really happened.

Tempest stopped and shined her flashlight in Ren's eyes. "Mordecai crossed a dozen worlds, leaving no trace he had been there. You infiltrate his band of lackeys and within hours he's threating the *Logos Personae*. Nothing was different this time except you were there. That's the only thing that makes sense here. You're working both sides."

"So now I'm a spy?!" Ren replied.

"If I had proof you were a spy, you'd already be dead." Tempest growled. "I knew Gideon's plan to involve you was folly from the beginning. I don't know what your game is, B'gatti, or whose side you're on, but it ends now!"

Ren stepped closer. Tempest dropped her gear to the ground, but kept the flashlight in Ren's face.

"Mordecai sent people after Asher Grey!" Ren said. His temper flared from the accusations. "I had no choice but to let Mordecai go. I had to stop Dark Angus from killing her."

"Or your plan was to delay us long enough for Mordecai to get away," Tempest said through gritted teeth. She gripped the strap of the rifle hanging from her shoulder.

At the comment, Ren's seething anger overtook his better judgment. His body rippled, and he shifted, almost without thought. His shirt ripped open. Ren grew until his head reached the ceiling of the tunnel.

Tempest's eyes followed the shapeshifter up as Ren transformed into a misshapen mass of hair and muscle. In an instant he was no longer the lean, naked albino, but suddenly a seven-foot, four-armed crater-ape from a science fiction novel he had once passed through called *The Stars are My Co-pilot*.

Ren fell forward onto the knuckles of his two lower arms. A low growl emanated from his throat. Two ivory tusks jutting from his lower jaw flashed in the dim light.

Tempest jumped back and tossed her flashlight aside. She flipped her rifle off her shoulder, leveling it at the apish beast looming over her. Raffles and Charley backed away from the unfolding conflict. Charley's scanner flashed in her hands.

The earthen floor of the ley-line cracked under Ren's weight. He could only hold the shape of the alien crater-ape for a short time, but Tempest didn't know that. The density of the massive form could withstand a bullet or two. That would give him enough time to get at least two of his four hands around the woman's throat.

"Back down, B'gatti!" Tempest ordered. "Or so help me!"

Natascha stepped between them and drew her Peacemaker. "Lower your gun, Tempest, or this is about to get nasty."

"It's been clear from the beginning he's a threat to this operation," Tempest retorted. She held her rifle on Ren. "And yet he is given every latitude to keep screwing up."

"That's enough!" Medesto's commanding voice echoed down the tunnel. His flashlight shone on Tempest. "All that matters is that we stopped anyone from killing the Chosen One. Mordecai has left her world and there's no longer any threat. Asher Grey passed safely into her next Story."

Tempest lowered the rifle. "Why any of you continue with this folly is beyond my understanding."

Ren swallowed the anger inside him and let go of the form of the massive creature. His body shrank down to his natural shape, his chest heaving with adrenaline. He maintained a combative stance, ready to change back if Tempest threatened him again.

"Listen, we're all stressed out and tired," Medesto said. "But we need to calm down. And Tempest, stop being so paranoid. We told you Ren was no spy."

"Gideon pays me to be paranoid," Tempest retorted. She threw the strap of her rifle over a shoulder. "We almost lost an entire population of a world back there because of B'gatti's incompetence. If he's not a spy, then it's obvious he isn't up to the task he's been asked to perform. It's either that or his loyalties lie elsewhere."

"I saved Asher Grey's world from annihilation!" Ren shouted. "If I was a double-agent, I would have let it all burn!"

"All I can say is the stakes in this have changed," Tempest replied. "I say we focus on taking Mordecai out of the picture. With him dead, the search for *The Book of Days* ends."

"How are we going to do that?" Natascha said. "He's surrounded himself with professional soldiers and hardened criminals. We don't have the weaponry to take them head on."

"Then I'll do it from a distance," Tempest said, not looking at Natascha. "If I can get the man in the crosshairs of my rifle, I can end this. Then we all go home."

"I thought killing Mordecai outright was not an option," Ren said. The truth is, he had tried to kill Mordecai, although he failed when Claymore walked into the room. He still thought it would be the best solution.

"Gideon felt that way, not me," Tempest countered. "Everything changed when Mordecai attempted to assassinate the Chosen One. Looks like we won't need the trickster after all."

"That's enough, Tempest," Medesto growled, barely keeping his temper under control.

"I'm here out of courtesy to the Raconteurs," Ren said quietly. "There are other places I could be."

"Then leave," Tempest said. "The Raconteurs are about loyalty and duty to a common purpose. Fighting together for a just cause. You know nothing of these things. You're trouble, B'gatti, and you'll always be a danger to those around you. These people aren't your friends. You may think they are, but they are not. They are just using you. You're sloppy and that gets people killed. That's why you'll always end up alone."

Ren glanced at Natascha, who nodded her support to him. That was all he needed. He back away from Tempest. "I'm not going anywhere," he said. "Not until this job is finished. Gideon said we were not to kill Mordecai outright, so I'm the best chance you have of bringing him in alive."

"And I'm still in charge here, Tempest," Medesto replied. "You decided to join the party as an afterthought. We stay with the original plan. If you find that unacceptable, you are free to find your own ride back to Rogue Destiny. Understood?"

"All I'm saying is if I get a clear shot at Mordecai, I'm taking it." Tempest picked up her gear, adjusted the rifle back on her shoulder.

"Are we done here?" Medesto said to the others. "Everyone got it out of their system. Raffles? Ren? Anything to add to the discussion?"

Raffles chuckled. "Yeah, go back to da part where Temp'st accuses the skin-changer of betrayin' us all. I wanna see where dat goes."

"Shut up, jackrabbit," Medesto groaned. "Charley? You have anything to add?"

"I don't want to stop you from killing each other," Charley replied, "but I have a question." She threw Ren a wink. It was her way of diverting the tension between him and Tempest back to the mission at hand. He was starting to really like this girl. "I've read a lot about rabbit-holes. Every book said they are doorways that open directly into the connecting world. If that's true, why are we standing in a tunnel?"

"The rabbit-hole is jus' a condens'd ley-line," Raffles said. "Like takin' a metal spring an' pushin' it together until the ends meet." He pressed his hands together, imitating the motion. "Look ta me like dis machine uncoil da ley-lines when it hijack 'em, stretching 'em out closer to dere true length. It kinda like peekin' behind da curtain ta see how da sausage is made."

"That's' so cool," Charley said. "But there's no way this tunnel is the actual distance between worlds. That would be thousands of miles to walk."

"No," Natascha said. "The rabbit-hole I followed from the wintery Cossack world to Asher Grey's could not have more than a mile. So the compressed distance remains to some degree."

The rabbit nodded in agreement. "Dat why she dying. Ley-lines are organic by nature. Da strain of dat kind a manhandlin' is mo' den da poor ting can take." Raffles laid a paw against a pulsating root. "We best stop dis 'bomination of a machine 'fore Mordecai do anymo' damage."

Charley stared at the glowing screen in her hands. She wandered down the corridor and disappeared into the darkness.

"We should stay together, Charley!" Natascha called out. Her voice echoed off the tunnel walls. "Charley?!"

"Down here!" the young tech replied, her voice distant.

Ren followed Natascha and Medesto down the passageway. He kept a close watch on Tempest from the corner of his eye. Charley stood before a massive, circular steel door. Ren walked past her and regarded the metal obstacle blocking their way. The ten-foot round door sat embedded deep in the surrounding rock. A metal wheel like on a bank vault was attached to the center.

Charley whistled in astonishment. "Someone's going to a lot of trouble trying to keep people from getting in."

"Or the door's here to keep somethin' from gettin' out," Raffles replied. He scratched his chin in thought. Ren caught Medesto throwing him a concerned look.

"Mapping's coming in from the WayFinder!" Charley said, barely able to contain her excitement. The soft glow of the screen caught the grin on her face.

Ren watched over her shoulder as she started tapping buttons, losing herself in the myriad of data moving across the screen. Tempest stood off to the side, not speaking or making eye contact with anyone.

"Can you tell what Book this doorway leads to?" Medesto said. "It would be helpful to get an idea of what we'll be up against."

"Hang on," Charley said, waiting for a response to appear. "We are about to enter... *Surviving a Bad Romance at the End of the World*. The Book's described as a modern, paranormal, horror, romance novel of young love and grotesque monstrosities."

"What kind of modern, paranormal horrors are we talking about?" Natascha asked.

"I'm pulling up details now," Charley replied, not looking up. "The novel is centered in the college town of Cathedral City. The *Logos Personae* is a college student, Bree Sandoval. The Story revolves around her on-again, off-again romance with local bad boy, Ezequiel Del Toro, a former member of a street gang who is trying to improve his life. The entire Book takes place on the night of the big All Hollow's Eve party, during the university's celebration of their local sports team victory over a rival in the big Homecoming game."

Charley cleared her throat, then continued. "After the mysterious disappearance of several students, the campus is overrun by spore-based parasitic crustaceans that turn a large part of the area's population into mindless pod-people who are controlled by a hive-mind queen. Bree and her friends battle the alien spore invading their sleepy college town, while learning about loyalty, sacrifice, friendship, and the quickest ways to decapitate spore-infected fellow students. Wow, that sounds intense."

Being only nineteen made Charley Lovejoy the youngest member of the group. Their pursuit of Mordecai Davos and his outlaws was supposed to have been non-confrontational, her job being to test out new equipment that would help the Raconteurs in the field. They had already seen more action than any of them had expected, and Ren could tell the exhaustion and stress were taking a toll on Charley. She was ready to head home to Rogue Destiny.

Ren laid a hand on her shoulder. "Stay close," he told her. "Hopefully, we'll be through this one before too much can happen." Charley looked up and gave him an unconvincing smile.

Medesto sized up the steel door. "Okay, listen up," he said, turning to the others. "What's done is done and we can't dwell on it. Things have gotten more complicated since Mordecai moved from raiding dusty book archives to attempted world genocide. So I'll say it here and now. We are no longer concerned with bringing Mordecai to justice. Now we are focus on stopping him and his criminal allies by any means necessary. But we can only do that if everyone works as a team. Otherwise, we're just going to get ourselves killed, understand?"

Ren mumbled in agreement. Tempest gave a terse nod, and nothing more.

"All right then," the gnome said. "Despite the delays, we are still on the heels of our quarry."

Ren stood next to Natascha. She flashed her light on the giant hatch as Medesto mounted the three wide stone steps. His short statue made it difficult to reach, but he grabbed the handwheel with both hands and turned it. The mechanisms inside the door resounded with a loud clank and the tall circular door swung inward on rusty hinges.

A strange noise arose from beyond the open doorway. The sound of faint, but unmistakable movement could be heard heading toward them, like the rhythmic tapping of thousands of tiny taps on the hard concrete floor. Medesto flashed his light through the opening.

"Get back!" the gnome yelled. He jumped from the stoop, landing next to Ren, and drew his pistol. Natascha pulled her gas mask on and moved up alongside them, her Peacemaker in hand. Ren could still not see into the blackness that lay beyond.

The skittering sound rose to a crescendo, and a wave of tiny crablike creatures poured over the edge of the doorjamb onto the floor of the tunnel. None were bigger than Ren's hand, but they moved with frightening swiftness and purpose. He backhanded one clinging up his pant leg and leapt out of the path of the others.

As the arthropods reached Tempest, she crushed one with a boot heel. The hard exoskeleton covering the creature's back crunched under the force. An eruption of internal organs splattered across her boots. The dying crustacean gave a shrill squeal as it died. A gray cloud of spore exploded from the broken shell, floating up into the muggy air of the tunnel.

"Stay away from that cloud!" Tempest yelled, pointing at the discolored spore rising from the remains of the creature. More multi-legged organisms swarmed over her, and she frantically swatted them off. Medesto sidestepped the tiny arthropods and shot the closest one. Its carapace exploded as the bullet struck it.

Raffles gave a squeal and jumped into Charley's arms. Two arthropods climbed up the back of her legs after him. The rabbit stabbed one with his thin knife and flung it into the wall. He kicked another off as it crawled up Charley's backpack. The young tech pushed herself up against the tunnel wall to let the little monsters scurry by her.

A green mist rose around Natascha as the creatures crawled up her legs. The crustaceans dropped to the floor, unable to cling to her ethereal form. Medesto and Ren stood back to back, stomping and shooting the arthropods that emerged from the doorway. Tempest kicked another out of the way as others darted around her feet.

"Everybody, get inside!" Medesto shouted. Charley stepped around the tiny creatures covering the floor. Raffles clung to her backpack as they reached the doorway first.

One by one, the Raconteurs ran up the steps into the darkness that lay beyond. Ren watched the last of the arthropods disappear down the tunnel. Medesto pushed the heavy door closed with a loud clang and turned the handwheel until it locked. He leaned against it, breathing hard.

"Is everyone okay?" Medesto asked. "Did anyone get bitten or scratched?"

Ren shook his head. He was fine and glanced around at the others. No one appeared to be injured.

Natascha removed her gas mask. "The creatures seemed more interested in getting away than actually attacking us."

"But that's a good thing, right?" Charley asked, her voice anxious. "If they attacked us, I don't think we could have fought them off. And what was that cloud of gray gas?" Raffles stood protectively in front of her, holding long thin knives in both paws. His eyes jumped from one shadow to the next, waiting for more creatures to leap out at them.

"It looked like a spore of some kind," Natascha replied. "My guess? It may be what creates the pod-people mentioned in the Book."

"Be on your guard, people," Medesto said between breaths. "Looks like things will be jumping out of the shadows at us. That was only a taste of what lies ahead of us."

Chapter 2
School Daze

The stench of oil and grime replaced the fouls smells of the ley-line's decaying passageway. Natascha's flashlight revealed they stood in a long underground utility tunnel. She could hear the tiny arthropods scurrying through the shadows around them, always just beyond the beams of their lights.

Natascha took the lead. The Raconteurs proceeded cautiously down the maintenance passageway. Thick pipes and reinforced electrical cables ran along the walls and ceiling. Electric breaker boxes were spaced at regular intervals. The tunnel ended abruptly at a metal stairwell. Behind them, the skittering of multi-jointed legs resounded off the concrete floor, echoing through the blackness.

Natascha led the others up the stairs. They climbed the steps for two stories and emerged onto a rain-drenched street in the urban center of a sprawling industrial city. Judging by the dark streets and lack of traffic, the time was late.

"Dis look like a big place," Raffles observed. "How we gonna find Mordecai Davos?"

"I have an answer to that," Charley piped up, a bit of enthusiasm returning to her voice. "When we first entered the subway system under Old London back in Asher Grey's Story, I started picking up a low frequency signal I'd never seen before. It grew stronger as we reached the artificial ley-line. It's broken and erratic at times, but I believe it's coming from the portal machine Mordecai's using to jump worlds. It emits a residual signature that I think I can track to its source."

"Excellent work, Charley," Natascha said. "Which way do we go from here?"

The young tech pointed down a rain-slick street. She took a winding sidewalk that ran along a wide river towards the heart of the city. Raffles waddled beside Charley as the rain fell around them. Natascha walked on her other side, occasionally peeking down to watch the readouts coming over Charley's scanner. A blur of circles and vector lines crawled down the screen in a deluge of information.

"How do you make sense of all that?" Natascha asked, trying to get the young tech's mind off the potential dangers around them.

"It's a code I created myself," Charley replied. "I combined it with an algorithm from the WayFinder that interprets the descriptive words of a Book to create a basic blueprint of where we are. Then you run the program over a map of the world and see what pops."

"Where's the signal we're following?" Natascha asked.

"Wait for it," Charley said. Both women watched the screen as they continued down the sidewalk. A tiny splash of red flashed at a point north of them. It disappeared a moment later. "That is the signature the portal leaves."

The signal from Charley's scanner took them down a side street to a steel industrial bridge that spanned the river. There was no traffic, so they crossed the dark waters on a metal walkway.

On the other side of the water, they followed a concrete stairwell down beneath the bridge. The sound of music grew louder as they descended. They came out onto a wide boulevard, alive with the buzz of the city's chaotic nightlife. Loud music vibrated across the pavement as the smell of cheap perfume and bad cologne mixed with alcohol filled the air. The rain was nothing more than a drizzle now.

Natascha looked at Ren. "You might want to change into something a little less conspicuous," she said with a nod. She glanced down at the swirling pools of skin pigment snaking over Ren's naked chest and arms. Of their group, the trickster's true appearance always brought the most stares from outsiders. And questions were something the Raconteurs wanted to avoid.

"Oh, yeah," he replied. With a concentrated thought, his body morphed into a lean, shirtless youth in his late teens. An assortment of tattoos from poorly made decisions appeared across his chest and arms. Medesto dug something for him to wear from his traveling bag. Natascha often wondered where Ren found his wardrobe as the shape-shifter slipped his arms into a dark colored hoody. Now she knew.

Natascha removed her gas mask and clipped it to the inside of her trench coat. Shaking her hair out, she ran her fingers through the short, dark strands.

They passed a nightclub blaring disco funk music so loud the ground vibrated. The bar next to it was exceptionally busy, its bright lights showering everything in a spectral glow of neon. A mob of college-aged students loitered around the front entrance. The aroma of sweet smelling tobacco smoke wafted through the cool night air. The atmosphere was festive. A crush of rowdy youths lined up at a row of food trucks at the far end of the parking lot.

Natascha felt the shift in reality before anyone said anything. The strange momentary feeling of vertigo that resulted when the invisible veil into the Narrative was broken. It felt a bit jarring, but nothing she wasn't used to. They now stood inside the Story.

"Medesto, you feel that?" she asked.

"Yeah," the gnome growled through his beard. "And that means Mordecai is somewhere inside the Story too. Charley, find out what chapter we're in, then we'll push through as quickly as we can. Everyone else, do not interact with anyone if you can help it. We don't know who is crucial to the Story's Continuity and who isn't. Just talking to the wrong person could alter their actions."

Dozens of tables spread out across the chained-off parking lot, each with its own communal hookah pipes. Patrons gathered around each one, taking turns blowing smoke into the air.

Charley pointed to a young woman with long, dark hair. The girl stood on a table at the center of the crowd, holding her drink high. She wore a bright blue jacket and held up a red plastic cup to the admiring students that goaded her on.

"To the *Matadors*!" she shouted, spilling beer onto the spectators. "Go Matadors!!" The students erupted into chants of "Matadors! Matadors! Matadors!"

"That would be Bree Sandoval," Charley laughed. She tapped the screen a couple more times. "The *Logos Persona* of this world."

"Then we should avoid drawing attention to ourselves," Natascha replied. "Go the long way around so we don't risk coming in contact with her."

The Raconteurs walked around the press of students and made their way back to the river, skirting the festivities as best they could.

"We can follow the river for a hundred yards," Charley said. "And then cut back up to the road."

Intoxicated youths huddled in the shadows and paid no attention to them. Charley's scanner led them down a dirt path to a clearing at the water's edge, where several college boys stood smoking.

"Hey, sweetness!" the largest of the group yelled to Charley. "Yeah, you! The pretty blonde!" The student swayed on his feet. "Where you goin'? Come on over. Have a beer and party with us." He smiled, his white teeth gleaming in the dim light, and motioned to his buddies to follow him. They moved up the path toward the Raconteurs.

Tempest stepped between Charley and the boy. The newcomer was a head taller than her, with broader sloping shoulders. His upper body was wide and muscular. His hair was combed back, and he wore a sports jersey with the name *Matadors* over the number 23. The three lackeys behind him were carbon copies of their front man.

The young man puffed up his chest in a threatening manner, making Tempest's lean build seem small. She gave him no ground. The other students spread out behind their leader and waited for whatever was about to happen.

"You need to go," Tempest said, no emotion on her face.

"I wasn't talking to you, lady. I just want a word with the pretty girl here." He pushed close to Tempest and smiled, trying to intimidate her with his size.

"Tempest, don't." Natascha hissed under her breath.

"She's not interested," Tempest said, ignoring Natascha's order. "Move on." Natascha could see the malice behind her eyes. She needed to blow off steam after her argument with Ren inside the ley-line, but this was not the time nor the place to do that.

The larger man stood toe to toe with Tempest. "Or what?" he sneered, with a thrust of his chin. He tried to push Tempest to the side, but the Raconteur's hand shot out and knocked the assailant's hand away before it touched her.

Tempest did not break eye contact with the student, but her

expression slowly dissolved to cold purpose. "I'm not in the mood for childish shenanigans, boy," she said. "I've sent better men than you to their deaths in the cold void of space. You are nothing, little man, so walk away."

The thug threw a look at the entourage standing behind him. He was the alpha of the group and now his reputation with his buddies was at risk. That was more important to him than having his head handed to him by an ex-military deep-space flight officer.

Ren leaned over to Natascha. "You think she can take all three, or should I help?" He stepped forward, but she grabbed his arm.

"Stay back," Natascha whispered. "We don't need to make the situation worse."

The student tensed his arms. His hands clenched into fists, his knuckles cracking. Despite common sense that should have warned him against provoking a group of rough looking strangers that were obviously not a part of the festivities, he threw a punch at Tempest.

She caught his arm in a fluid practiced motion and returned a blow to his face with her other hand. Blood spurted under her knuckles and the boy's head snapped back. He tried to pull away, but Tempest twisted his wrist at an angle that forced his face down toward the ground. She stared at his three inebriated classmates until, one by one, they stumbled away up the dirt path.

"Young punks like you only understand one thing, a show of strength," she hissed through clenched teeth into the boy's ear. "You break the alpha and the rest scatter. It's the first law of the jungle."

"Let him go," Medesto said. "We have to get moving."

Tempest exerted more pressure on the man's arm until he grunted in pain, then released him. He stood up, holding both hands over his broken nose. His eyes moved over the Raconteurs one by one. Natascha could see he was deciding what to do next. Behind her, Raffles chuckled to himself.

"Maybe another time," Charley said. She smiled at the boy. Tempest remained between them until he slunk away after his friends.

"You were told not to get involved with the locals," she said.

"Hey, he approached me," Charley retorted. "I can't help it if I'm irresistible."

"You didn't do anything wrong," Natascha replied. "That was a chance encounter, out of anyone's control. The rule to survival in the field is we enter a world on its terms, not ours. Horror books of this nature can get overly aggressive to those who don't belong there."

"But didn't we just interfere with the Story?" Charley asked.

Medesto shook his head. "That was only a small ripple in events and didn't change anything of importance. The Narrative is like a river. As long as it continues to flow, we can take certain liberties before our presence actually affects events."

Raffles sniffed the night air.

"What is it?" Natascha asked.

"Don't know, but sumting ain't right," the rabbit answered. He pointed toward the water. "Over dere?"

At the bottom of the path, a person stood silhouetted against the city lights across the river. The head leaned unnaturally to one side. A second figure stumbled from the trees next to the first. Then a third. All three staggered along the dirt path toward the Raconteurs.

"Hopefully that's just more drunk students?" Charley said, her voice higher-pitched than normal.

"No, it not!" Raffles replied. "Dey smell like a dead carcass."

Natascha caught the skittering of unseen creatures in the bushes beyond the path. She pulled her gas mask on and peered through the infra-vision lenses into the darkness of the rocky terrain under the trees. A dark mass of shadows moved along the ground in their direction. The leaves quivered as the arthropods drew closer.

"We need to go now!" Natascha yelled, turning to the parking lot with Charley behind her. She looked back to see more dark shambling shapes slowly climb up the incline from the river. The sound of the scuttling arthropods grew louder. The crablike creatures poured onto the trail ahead of them, cutting off their escape.

"This way!" Medesto shouted. He crashed through the underbrush in the only direction left to them. Natascha followed with Charley, Raffles and Tempest close behind. Ren brought up the rear.

Above them, Natascha could hear the screams of the students at the celebration party. Their cries intermixed with the scurrying legs reverberating off the asphalt parking lot. She fought her way through the thick underbrush. Raffles perched on Charley's backpack, keeping a close watch on the pod-people pursuing them.

The Raconteurs emerged from the dark trees between the food carts and the storefronts of restaurants and bars. Students ran past them into the open door of a taphouse that had a sign boasting the cheapest beer in town.

The party erupted into a scene of utter chaos. Drunken students crashed into each other, trying to escape the horrors pouring out of the shadows from all sides. Some found shelter inside the businesses, while too many others writhed on the ground as the tiny arthropods swarmed over them, biting and clawing at their bodies. More humanoid shapes emerged out of the darkness. Pod-people, their heads and upper bodies coated in a pulsing mold. Splatters of blood covered the asphalt. A female student ran past her. An arthropod clung to the girl's neck.

Of all the terrible things a Raconteur faced in the field, avoiding the Narrative was probably the most difficult of all. The irony was they weren't there to save lives. They had to make sure the Story continued as written. That meant staying on the sidelines, sometimes watching people die before your eyes. Natascha passed by clusters of panicked students. She wanted to save as many of them as could. Most were still children. But she couldn't help them. She did not know who was integral to the Story and who was just Story fodder. She forced her thoughts back to the problem at hand.

"Which way?!" Natascha yelled over the din of the crowd. Medesto pointed across the parking lot to an opening in the crowd.

"Over there!" he shouted. "Stay together!" He forced his way through the crush of panicked youths. The surge of students shifted back in their direction. Natascha fought to stay with her companions, but she was separated in the chaos. Raffles clung to Charley's pack as the roiling masses pushed them away from Natascha.

The crowd suddenly parted before her. Natascha found herself facing a shuffling pod-person. By the designer clothes, the creature had once been a young, vibrant female. Now all signs of that life were gone. Sunken eyes, devoid of emotion, stared back at her. Thick gray mold covered the misshapen head and upper body. A plant-stalk protruded from its cranium, pulsating like a rhythmic heartbeat. A soft cloud of spore floated off it. The grotesque monstrosity lunged at her.

Natascha reacted instinctively. She had no time to worry about interference with the Story. This was life and death, and she needed to find Charley. She gave the monster a powerful kick to knock it back. Her boot went through bone and cartilage into the chest cavity. Dissolved internal organs oozed out onto her leg. She tried to pull her foot out, but it refused to come free. Momentary panic took her.

In desperation, she leapt up and delivered a roundhouse kick to the monster's head. It exploded into a shower of spore and liquefied brain matter. The pod-person crumbled to a heap on the asphalt. Natascha pulled her boot free. On the back of the twitching corpse, a multi-legged arthropod clung. The crab-creature retracted the mandibles embedded in remains of the student's skull and skittered away. She shuddered and searched the chaos for the other Raconteurs.

She saw Tempest and Medesto pinned in front of a taco truck, fending off a group of pod-people with open umbrellas from the vendor's tables. Charley and Raffles were among a handful of students hiding behind them. One young woman with her long black hair tied up and wearing a bright blue jacket crouched in the back, her dark eyes wide with fear.

Bree Sandoval. The *Logos Personae* of the Story.

Chapter 3
Homecoming

Natascha yanked a sun umbrella from its place at the center of a table. She fought through the invasion of pod-people, knocking aside anyone that stood in her way.

Gray spores wafted off the contaminated students surrounding them. Others thrashed on the asphalt as they struggled against the arthropods attaching themselves to the back of their necks. It was a losing battle. None could stand against their inevitable defeat at the hands of the alien organisms. Other students lay on the asphalt twitching, their minds and motor skills slowly taken from them. Once the absorption of the new host was complete, the newly born pod-person rose awkwardly to their feet to join the ever-increasing fungi army.

Once Natascha reached her companions, she pushed her umbrella open and used it to slow the growing mob of fungi pod-people. She stood shoulder to shoulder with Medesto and Tempest. Their combined efforts held the enemy back for the moment, but she knew the flimsy improvised barrier would not hold forever.

"Where's Ren?" the gnome roared over the noise. "We could use some help here!"

"I don't know!" Natascha answered. "I lost track of him in the crowd."

The crush of infected students forced her back another step. More monsters joined the horde, fighting to get past the makeshift barricade of umbrellas. Several terrified young people crouched behind Natascha, sobbing uncontrollably. She noticed Bree Sandoval staring off into space. The *Logos Personae* didn't appear frightened. Bree seemed to be in full control of her emotions, but her disposition was too calm. Natascha worried she had been infected in the chaos, as her dead classmates closed in on them.

Bree's eyes suddenly went wide, and she gagged. Once, then twice, before she vomited on the ground behind Medesto. She hadn't been infected. She was drunk.

Natascha tightened her hold on the umbrella pole, knowing it was only a matter of time before the monsters overran their defenses.

The roar of an engine rose over the chaos. Headlights appeared beyond the chained-off entrance to the parking lot. An avocado green station wagon with faux wood side-panels broke through the chain, crashing into the swarming fungi monsters. The vehicle duck tailed around, knocking pod-people out of the way and crunching arthropods under its wheels. The automobile spun around and headed back toward Natascha.

The driver slammed on the brakes, and the automobile skidded to a stop just short of colliding with the food trucks. A pod-person in a black hoody sat behind the wheel. The grotesque face winked at her. Natascha helped Bree Sandoval to her feet.

"Ooh, I love your little rabbit mascot," Bree said. Her words slurred as she spoke, pointing to Raffles clinging atop Charley's pack. Her eyes glazed over, and she still seemed unaware of the danger all around them. "He's so cute in his tiny straw hat and vest. Oh! And he has his own little backpack. That's adorable!"

Raffles harrumphed loudly, but kept any retorts to himself.

The car door opened. Ren stepped out, quite pleased with himself. His appearance had shifted from decaying pod-person back to that of a college student in a hoody. He opened the back door to let everyone in.

"Glad you could make it," Medesto rumbled.

"My pleasure," he announced with a wry grin. "Figured we needed some transportation. You know, if you pretend to be one of the monsters, it turns out they won't bother you."

Bree looked over at him. "There's my hero!" she exclaimed. "You saved us all!" She ran up to Ren and threw her arms around him, and kissed him squarely on the mouth. At first, it caught Ren off guard. Then he returned the gesture and kissed her back.

"Everyone into the car!" Medesto yelled. Ren let go of the young woman with a satisfied smile. The gnome climbed through the front passenger door, shaking his head.

"Ren, meet Bree Sandoval!" Charley said. Raffles jumped onto the front seat, and she climbed in behind him.

"Oh?" Ren lifted an eyebrow at the name. "Ren B'gatti, nice to meet you."

"The monsters were trying to eat me," Bree replied. She swayed as she spoke. Natascha grabbed her arm to steady her and helped Bree into the vehicle. Medesto and Tempest helped the other four students into the back.

Natascha noticed Ren had altered his features. His face was leaner, cheekbones higher, nose and eyebrows more symmetrical to impress the *Logos Personae* further. She smacked him on the back of the head.

"Stop that," Natascha told Ren. "Don't let it go to your head, lover boy. She's drunk and probably in shock."

"Hey!" Ren glared at her and ran his fingers through his stylish haircut.

The shuffling pod-people reached the car as Natascha pulled her door closed. Ren jumped in behind the wheel. She sat in the back seat next to Tempest while the drunken students made do in the cramped backend of the station wagon. Misshapen faces pressed against the outside windows. Ren slammed the vehicle into reverse and gunned the engine.

"Hang on!" he yelled.

The wheels spun, and the car whipped around, slamming into the monsters behind them. Ren shifted into drive and flew out of the parking lot onto an empty street.

"Charley, can you see where Bree is supposed to be right now?" Natascha asked.

"On it," Charley pulled the scanner out of her pack and turned it on. "Give me just a second."

Bree laid her head on Tempest's shoulder. "How come everyone knows my name?" she asked. "I don't know any of you."

"I told them," Charley replied. "I'm a student here, too." She raised her fist without looking up from her screen. "Go, Matadors!"

"Oh," Bree muttered. Her eyelids grew heavy, like she was about to pass out.

"Yeah, you're quite a big deal around here," Ren added. He grinned at Bree in the rearview mirror. She smiled back at him.

"Anything?" Natascha asked, looking over the front seat to watch Charley scan the details of Bree's Book as they scrolled across her screen.

"Ok, here we are. We are in chapter three," Charley announced. "It's called *The Homecoming*. The monsters attack the aftergame party and..." she paused as she scanned the next paragraph. "Bree hides out in a sports bar, named, cleverly enough, *The Sports Bar*. After that, she and her friends who survived the initial onslaught take refuge in her campus dorm as the alien invasion increases and spreads across the city."

"Then that's where we take her," Natascha replied. "It's still early in the Story and as long as she gets where she belongs, everything will be fine."

Bree, Tempest and Natascha sat crammed in the back seat of the station wagon. Bree hooked her arm inside Tempest's and leaned against the taller woman's shoulder. She closed her eyes and began softly snoring almost immediately.

"So this is the Story's hero?" Tempest stated matter-of-fact. "The one who saves everyone?"

"She'll get there," Charley replied, her eyes still scanning pages from the Story. "We're just seeing the person she is at the beginning of the Book. By the end, she's grown into the hero the Story needs her to be. It's the standard character arc you see in most Narratives. Starts out weak, grows stronger and more capable over time, before winning the final battle. In the last chapter, Bree rallies the remaining students in a last stand against the alien invaders. Then she faces the Queen of the Hive Mind alone, to save both her boyfriend, Ezequiel, and best friend, Jeni, before they become fungi pod-people themselves. It all sounds very cool."

"Where are we headed?" Ren asked as he sped down the dark street.

Charley gave Ren directions as he drove the automobile through the rain-slick streets toward the university campus. He parked halfway on the sidewalk in front of a tall building and turned off the engine. Natascha helped Bree out of the car. Charley hopped out and opened the back tailgate. The students piled out onto the street. Two ran off on their own. The other two stood looking at Charley.

"Thank you," one girl whispered. The boy next to her nodded but said nothing.

"It's what I do," Charley replied with a grin. "Go find a place to hide until this all plays out. I hear a lot of people have gathered in the clock-tower. That might be the safest place right now." Both students hugged her, then took off toward the distant tower. Natascha held Bree in her arms and smiled.

"The safest place, huh?" Natascha asked with a smirk.

Charley blushed. "I may have read something about survivors holing up there until the Hive-mind Queen's destroyed. Hope that wasn't out of bounds. I couldn't bear the thought of them wandering into more of those monsters."

"I get it," Natascha told her. "Sometimes doing what's right feels better than following the rules. Just be careful. You can only *help* up to a point. After that, you cross a line and invite disaster."

They rushed to the front entrance. Charley opened the door, and Natascha carried Bree to the elevator. The lobby was empty. Books and backpacks littered the floor. Word must have reached the dorms of the attack at the river. The elevator took them up to the third floor, and they quickly found her dorm room, number 310. Charley knocked on the door.

The girl who answered the door gasped. "It's Bree!" Her eyes were red from crying. "Thank goodness you found her! We were separated at the party when those ... those things attacked. Here, put her on the couch!"

Natascha brought Bree inside and laid her down on a shabby green couch. The dorm room was full of terrified students trying to understand what was happening. The Raconteurs said their goodbyes before making a quick exit.

On the elevator ride down, Charley seemed restless. Finally, she looked at Natascha. "None of this is going to mess with the Big Picture stuff, is it?" Charley asked. "I thought we were supposed to avoid the *Logos Personae* regardless of what happens?"

"We may have caused a small rip in the continuity by taking Bree to her dorm," Natascha said, "But as long as the *Logos Personae* continues forward in her Story, the Narrative will smooth out any minor changes. It can be risky, but sometimes we have no choice."

"Yes, we do our best," Natascha replied. "But sometimes it can't be helped. Any world we enter is only as big as the Story needs it to be. Everything in this Book takes place within the campus and the surrounding city. It's no wonder we walked right into the Story."

Charley glanced down at her scanner. "The residual signal for the portal machine is getting weaker!" she gasped. "We need to hurry!"

Chapter 4
Mystery Box

Ren started the engine as Natascha and Charley climbed into the front seat of the station wagon. He pulled out onto the street, dodging panicked students and reckless drivers zooming past them in both directions. He drove through the dark streets, guided by Charley's directions, slowing only long enough so she could recalibrate their position regarding the portal machine's invisible trail.

After a time, Ren turned onto a street across from a massive department store that stretched around the block. Charley looked up and pointed to a small area of grass in front of the store.

"There!" she shouted and jumped out of the vehicle before it stopped. She crossed the glistening street to a round indentation in the swath of wet grass.

"The portal machine sat right here nine hours ago," she announced loudly.

Ren killed the motor, and everyone climbed out. He wandered up to the large dark windows of the storefront, cupped his hand around his eyes, and peered inside.

"Looks vacant," he said. "The shelves are empty. Looks like the business closed its doors a long time ago."

"Let's see what's around back," Medesto suggested.

The other five followed the gnome around the side of the building, where they came to a set of cement steps leading down to the entrance of a pawn shop tucked away beneath the vacant department store. A closed sign hung in the dark front window. Above the barred windows, a neon sign flickered.

Money for Nothing Pawnshop
Get your chips for free with every purchase.
We Buy Anything
Gold — Jewelry — Guns
Established 1985

Before Medesto could stop him, Ren jumped down the steps and stood at the door. He grabbed the handle and turned it. "It's unlocked," he whispered.

Medesto and Tempest started down the stairs. "Wait for us," Medesto said. "We should go in together."

"No problem," Ren said. He pushed on the door. It swung in with a slow squeak and he disappeared inside before the gnome reached the bottom of the stairs.

The inside of the pawnshop was dark, the only light source filtered in from the streetlights outside. Ren saw a row of candies along the front counter. He realized he hadn't eaten in a while and grabbed a chocolate nougat bar called *Choco-D'light*.

The wrapper crinkled loudly in the silence. Ren took a bite, waiting for the others to join him. Medesto and Charley came in a moment later. Medesto grumbled into his beard and threw a nasty look in Ren's direction. Charley stayed close behind, visibly nervous.

Natascha, Tempest and Raffles entered. Tempest flipped a

switch next to the door, bathing everything in a milky fluorescent light. They stood in a long room, crammed with display racks of secondhand merchandise. It was an extensive assortment of any and everything. Glass display cases lined one wall, stuffed with all the miscellany that any contemporary society could desire. An array of watches, jewelry. They ranged from the elegant to the gaudy, and coins of various monetary values filled the first several cases.

"Spread out," Medesto said. "Look for anything indicating why Mordecai would come here."

Tempest and Natascha moved deeper into the room with their pistols drawn. Charley stayed near the front of the shop. She settled into a corner by the entrance next to a mannequin wearing a gas mask and a pink raincoat over black stockings.

Ren wandered down a row of merchandise to a display of knives and swords mounted on the wall. He studied each as he finished eating his chocolate bar, the bladed weapons a myriad of different styles and time periods.

One particular ancient sword caught his attention. He touched the handle of the three-foot curved blade before pulling it free of its scabbard. It was lightweight and perfectly balanced.

"That's Kordovian steel," Medesto said as he walked up. "See the blue-tinted pattern in the metal? I wonder if the owner of the pawnshop knows what he has. The blade is incredibly sharp and worth a king's ransom if you know who to sell it to. Wonder how it ended up here, because it certainly doesn't belong in this world."

Raffles dropped his pack next to Charley and waddled over to inspect the snacks under the front counter. But he stopped before he reached them. His long ears came up and his tiny nose twitched. He sniffed the air.

Medesto noticed Raffles' sudden change. He drew his pistol

and motioned Ren back toward the front of the store. The trickster reached the counter first and hopped over it to investigate, sword in hand. The rabbit pointed a stubby finger at a closed door behind the counter.

"Careful, skin-changer," Raffles warned. "There's blood behind dat door. I smell it."

Ren turned the knob and pushed the door open to reveal a small office with a desk and filing cabinets. Open drawers and loose papers lay strewn about. In the center of the ransacked room, the body of a man lay face down in a pool of blood.

"What do we got?" Medesto asked as he came up from behind. He got his answer when he reached the open door. He entered the office and glanced around before rolling the body over with his boot.

"Poor guy's been dead for hours," he said. "Shot twice in the chest." The gnome exhaled a deep breath. "Well, we're too late to help him," he replied, his voice tinged with regret. "But I doubt Mordecai found what he was looking for in here. There has to be more to this place."

Ren followed Medesto out and shut the door after them. He went down an aisle of clothing, watching Tempest make her way to the back of the store with her automatic pistol in hand. She disappeared behind a curtain to a backroom. Seconds later, she yelled, "Medesto, back here!"

"C'mon," Medesto said. Ren wove through the aisles, the Kordovian blade in hand. He pushed back the draped doorway to enter a back room. Natascha was already there.

In a narrow storage area, Tempest shone her flashlight on a trapdoor built into the floor. Boxes and chairs were piled haphazardly over it. She moved the light to streaks of dried blood.

"That looks like a smeared hand print," Natascha said. No one commented. Ren glanced at her. She pulled the hood of her long coat over her head and adjusted her gas mask. Her gloved hand fell to the Peacemaker Lightning gun holstered at her hip.

Ren rested the curved sword on his shoulder and kicked the closest box down from the pile. Medesto and Tempest joined in until the trapdoor was clear. With her pistol ready, Tempest jerked the hatch open, revealing a wooden staircase descending into blackness. More blood splattered the underside of the trapdoor. Everyone stood silent as they listened for any sound of movement below.

"One of us should stay up here with Charley," Tempest said. "She shouldn't be alone with those zombies running around."

"Raffles is with her," Medesto said. "She'll be fine."

Natascha descended the spiral staircase first. Tempest went next. Ren stepped forward, but Medesto grabbed his arm. "Here," the gnome said. He flipped his pistol around by the trigger guard and offered it to Ren, handle first. "Just in case."

Ren grinned and twirled the sword in his hand. "Thanks, but I'll take three feet of good steel over a gun." He descended the narrow staircase, jumping the last few feet to the ceramic tiled floor. Medesto thundered down the steps a few moments later with his flashlight.

The trickster's eyes adjusted to the darkness. They weren't in a dusty cellar as he had expected. Instead, he stood in a luxurious room filled with plush chairs and elaborately carved reading tables. The walls on one side were shelves filled with leather-bound books. Several doors lined the opposite wall.

Dusty globes, maps, and orreries mixed in with boxes of files and wooden crates stuffed with notebooks and journals. Further down the wall on the right, a portion of shelves had been emptied, their contents spilled out across the floor. Overturned crates and opened files of random papers cluttered the area.

Natascha and Tempest shone their flashlights across the basement to reveal an expansive underground sanctuary. The room measured twenty feet wide and twice that in length. Motes of dust floated in their beams of lights. Medesto and Charley searched through the piles of discarded writings for any reason why Mordecai would come to this specific archive. They found nothing.

"What is this place?" Tempest whispered. Her words echoed in the stillness.

"It's a safe house for the *Order of the Memento Ex-Libris*," Natascha replied. "They gather research and store it here for couriers to retrieve at regular intervals and take back to their headquarters in Rogue Destiny. There are thousands of hidden sanctuaries like this one throughout the Mythic Cosmos. The Raconteurs have worked with them for years. They're the good guys, like us."

Medesto ran his finger along the tabletop. "Judging by the amount of dust on everything, it appears this place hasn't been used in quite a while."

"Then let's figure out why Mordecai would bother to come here," Tempest said. "And get out of here before we find out whose blood that was upstairs." She found a switch next to the bookshelves and flipped it, but the lights didn't come on. Her flashlight beam revealed a line of broken light fixtures overhead. Fresh pock marks along on the walls and ceiling told of recent gunfire.

The ceiling above Ren had scorch marks across it. Tiny embers were still smoldering in the wooden crossbeams. The smell of plasma and sulfur hung in the air, the remnants of weaponry used by the mercenary cyborgs Mordecai employed in his quest. The battle between the airships in the pages of *The Adventures of Asher Grey* seemed a lifetime ago, but he realized it had not even been a full day yet.

Medesto switched on a reading lamp next to a plush chair. The halo of dim light revealed several wooden doors on the wall behind them. He opened the closest door. Behind it lay a small apartment with a bed, desk and a small cast iron wood stove. Ren checked the second one. It was identical to the first. He closed it with a shrug.

"Sleeping quarters for the weary traveler," Medesto said.

"Ren and I will check the bookshelves in the back," Natascha said. "You and Tempest finish searching the front. Look for anything connected to the name *Harper Bellweather*. She's an agent of the *Order of the Memento Ex-Libris* and somehow involved in all this."

In the middle of the room, stood a massive metal orrery. The highest point of the sculpture nearly reached the ten-foot ceiling. Natascha's flashlight gleamed off the decorative center piece where dozens of tiny worlds hung down on thin metal arms over a large, detailed relief map. At the base, a shallow circular bowl with a clear blue sea and an archipelago of familiar-looking islands.

"It's Rogue Destiny," Ren whispered. Natascha grinned and nodded at the obvious statement.

Two broad wooden tables occupied each side of the orrery, both piled high with stacks of books and the contents of the emptied shelves. Notebooks lay strewn across the table tops as if someone had been sorting through them.

Once they were far enough away, and no one could hear them, Natascha grabbed Ren's arm. He caught his reflection in the lens of her goggles.

"Something happened in the bookshop back in Old London," Natascha said. "What are you not telling us?"

Ren stared back at her, trying to hide any readable expression on his face. He continued walking along the bookshelves. Natascha followed him.

"Claymore was there, wasn't he?" she asked.

"Why do you say that?" Ren asked.

"Call it a hunch," she said dispassionately. "Did you talk to him?"

Ren hesitated. He wanted to lie, but couldn't, not to Natascha. They had never worked together as partners, but had learned to trust each other without question. He would handle this his way because nothing was going to prevent him from saving Claymore. Not even her.

"Yeah, he was there," Ren replied. "But I didn't get a chance to speak to him before Mordecai sent him away on some secret task."

Natascha nodded as if she understood, her expression hidden by the gas mask. "You need to be careful," she said. "I don't have to tell you what the *Paradigm Madness* will do to Claymore. He'll only get more dangerous as time passes. As the madness destroys his soul. And if he's among Mordecai and his outlaws, then he is not the person we knew."

"He's still the same man he always was," Ren replied. "Remember the man who showed up at the field house to warn you Asher Grey was in danger? Medesto assumed I sent him, but it was Claymore. He's still on the side of the angels."

"His mind is slowly being eaten away," Natascha said. "There's no known cure for what he is suffering from."

"Then I'll find one," Ren answered. He could feel his anger rising, not at Natascha, but at the helplessness he felt.

"Medesto told you about Serralto Cardus?"

"Yeah, and you confronting the Black Rose in the City of Assassins. You've been busy since you got back."

"Don't forget the dragons," Ren replied with a smirk.

"This is not a joke, Ren."

"No, it's not," Ren replied. "I let Claymore go off on his own. That was a mistake. Now I'm going to bring him home to the Raconteurs. I don't know how, but I know I can save him and make things like they used to be. I just need to handle this my way."

He had witnessed firsthand Claymore's slow descent into madness. His partner was the paragon of heroic virtue, an example to all those around him. He would never harm another unless he had no choice. Until he did.

The man, Serralto Cardus, framed Claymore and Ren for the assassination of Minstrel Cotty, the *Chosen One* from the novel *The Angels of Avalon*. A world that no longer existed. Serralto's capture would have exonerated Ren and Claymore from the crime. They chased him across worlds to Adezhda, the City of Assassins and had him in custody. Then Claymore flew into a rage before Ren watched him shoot Serralto down in cold blood.

If no cure for the *Paradigm Madness* existed, then Ren would have to find a way to do the impossible.

Ren trailed after the silhouetted form of Doctor Enigma into the darker depths of the underground chamber. Her light swept over maps, charts, and leather-bound books that lay underfoot. The ransacked room gave off the distinct smell of blood and death. Splatters of dark stains stretched across the floor. At the farthest end of the room, rows of bookshelves, like that in a library, disappeared into the blackness beyond.

His bare foot stepped in something thick and sticky. A strong stench filled his nostrils. He pointed at the floor, and Natascha followed the tracks of blood with her flashlight.

That's when they saw the bodies.

Chapter 5
Shadows in the Dark

The mangled remains of several men and women lay in a heap in Natascha's light. Each of the corpses displayed a different stage of mutilation. Ren counted seven, but thought there may have been parts of other bodies mixed into the horrific decoupage. Long streaks of blood on the floor indicated they'd been dragged to where they currently lay piled atop one another.

Ren had seen his share of death during his travels, but this carnage was not without an effect on his sensibilities. If the gruesome scene bothered Natascha, she showed no outward sign of it. She scanned her light over the bodies, then out into the darkness engulfing the rest of the aisle. There was nothing more to see.

"If we find Mordecai among the dead," she said, "We can take his body back to Rogue Destiny and call it a day." With the tip of her boot, she tilted the face of the closest corpse. "Recognize her?"

"She was in the basement of the bookseller's shop in Asher Grey's world." Ren pointed to the blood-splattered, shredded coat on one of the dead. "Mordecai had a goatee and wore a brown trench coat. No one here is dressed like that." The trick-ster tried to piece together the events in his mind. It looked as if Mordecai's people may have been sorting through the contents of the shelves when they were interrupted in a very bad way.

"I wonder how far in their search they got before they were attacked?" Natascha said as if she was wondering out loud.

Ren nodded. "What better place to hide *The Book of Days* than inside a horror world in the backwaters of the Mythic Cosmos?"

"You're right about..." Natascha put her hand up. "You hear that?" she whispered and pointed at the rows of bookshelves. "Something's back there."

There was a shuffling noise, faint but unmistakable. A scraping sound, like someone was crawling along the floor. Ren and Natascha looked at each other. Without a word, they moved toward the sound. If it was a survivor, there was a chance to get answers about Mordecai Davos and what happened here.

Natasha pointed at Ren, then down the closest aisle. She pointed to herself, then to the next aisle over. Ren agreed. She drew her Peacemaker and disappeared from sight, the beam of her flashlight swallowed up in the darkness.

Ren set his sword down, slowly unzipped the hoody he wore and pulled it off. He wanted room to shift if he needed to make a quick retreat from whatever was back there. With a thought, his skin tone blended to match the shadows around him. He picked up his blade and continued deeper into the blackness, stepping silently around the debris. The scraping grew louder.

When he reached the end of the bookshelves, he peeked around the corner. The noise grew much closer. There was movement in the layers of shadow, but all he could make out was the prone form of a body lying on the floor. His hopes rose as he watched the boot of the corpse twitched every couple of seconds.

There was a survivor. He took a step forward when he realized the body wasn't moving under its own power. The pitch black darkness around it was disturbing the dead body. Ren stepped back to reassess the situation. His foot slipped on a piece of loose paper. The scraping sound stopped.

There was a snuffling noise that turned into a high rolling purr as a shadowy form lifted off the body and searched the darkness for the source of the disturbance.

Ren backed up further, raising his sword and staying to the shadows the best he could. He held his breath. The creature's narrow head swayed, sniffing the air for a moment before dropping back down to its prize. The dead body jerked slightly as the black nightmare pulled it further away from Ren.

Despite his excellent night vision, Ren could not completely separate the grotesque monstrosity from the surrounding blackness. Its body was an undefinable shroud of darkness, ending in a long narrow head that hunched protectively over its prey.

Natasha came up behind him, flashlights on and weapons ready. In the light of their flashlights, a flat, eyeless, serpentine head came up. It hissed.

"What is that?" Natascha whispered.

Ren leaned in close to them. "I'm guessing it's responsible for all the bodies." He held the curved blade in front of him and tiptoed forward. The dark, misshapen form engulfing the body made a rutting noise followed by a repetitive pulsing sound. Ren stopped. The shadow monster was feeding.

"Leave it alone," Natascha hissed.

"But the dead guy has a knapsack," Ren said, pointing to a weather-beaten leather satchel draped over the corpse's shoulder. "I want to see what's in it."

Tempest appeared out of the darkness behind them. "We found nothing of value so far. Have you... What is that thing?"

"I need Medesto," Ren asked. "Maybe he can identify our friend."

"He's still searching the sleeping quarters," Tempest answered in an angry, low tone. "That is something we should not be messing with."

Ren braced his stance. He lunged forward, slashing at the creature's head, hoping to hit something vital and bring the creature down quickly. The blade sliced empty shadow. Ren backed away slowly, keeping the sword between them. If he could draw it away from its victim, maybe Natascha could grab the satchel.

A dark shadow detached itself from the corpse. It rose in the air toward Ren with an otherworldly grace. Its flat serpentine head bobbed back and forth. Ren stepped in to meet the monster with the full fury of his sword. The blade sliced the blackness, but struck nothing but empty air. He stumbled forward off balance. The mass of darkness whipped out, striking Ren in the chest and knocking him off his feet.

Natascha and Tempest jumped out of the way as Ren flew past them across the floor. He came to a sudden stop against another dead body. He pushed himself away in disgust.

His hand pressed down on something hard and metallic under the cadaver's jacket. He reached inside and pulled a revolver out of its shoulder holster. He climbed to his feet and stuck the pistol in the front waistband of his pants.

"Careful!" Ren yelled to Natascha and Tempest. "It materializes when it wants to!"

Both Raconteurs kept their flashlights on the shadow beast as it floated past them toward Ren. He looked for his fallen sword. The glint of metal caught his eye next to a table legs. He swept the blade off the floor and jumped up on the table.

Natascha fired her Peacemaker into the ever-changing mass of shadow. The blue, green and red electrical arc from the lightning gun lit up the area around the monster, but the beam of energy passed through the creature as if it were smoke. The shadowy monster turned toward the Raconteur. Tempest backed away as it approached them.

"Over here!" Ren shouted. He kicked the books and papers off the table as he goaded the beast. "Come on, I'm the one you want!"

Ren could hear a heavy footfall on the tiled floor behind him. He glanced back to see Medesto running up to where Tempest stood, his Thompson machine gun at the ready.

"Did you find something?!" the gnome yelled "Holy crap, what is that??"

"Stay back," Ren warned. "It's got a nasty bite."

Medesto set his machine gun down and picked up one of the massive tables. With a grunt, he flung it into the expanding shadow above them. The table flew through the blackness harmlessly. It splintered into the bookshelf behind it.

"Careful, it's only shadow!" Ren informed him. "But it can materialize when it needs to."

The shadow creature's shape expanded in size as it loomed over Natascha. Without warning, it swept down, engulfing her entire body in darkness. She disappeared from sight for a few seconds before emerging on the far side in a cloud of green mist.

Natascha appeared visibly shaken from the experience. The dark monster swirled around her gaseous form, striking out, but could not hurt her.

Ren leapt on top of another table. Tempest and Medesto backed away, guns up and ready, but neither fired. Natascha remained in her ethereal form. Green mist filled the air around her.

The shadowy creature turned back toward Ren, gliding over the open air to where he stood. The black shape grew in size. It closed the distance between them. Then it swooped down on him like it had Natascha. Ren thrust the blade into the blackness as tendrils of smoke wrapped around him in a shadowy embrace.

"Let's see you materialize now," Ren growled. He felt his blade bite solid mass as the creature's body solidified. The shadow monster twisted away, pulling the sword from Ren's grasp. It gave a high-pitched screech that was barely audible, yet pierced Ren's inner thoughts like a knife. The Kordovian blade fell to the floor, echoing as it bounced off the tiles.

The monster flowed around Ren in a blur of shadows. He felt it grab at him, ripping his skin with a thousand tiny talons. Even in the blackness of the shroud, Ren could see the eyeless face melt from shadow to nightmare clear inches from his face.

Its icy grip tightened. Excruciating pain shot down his shoulders and back. Hundreds of tiny, hooked claws dug their way into his flesh as the misshapen monstrosity moved from the immaterial to the material. Its long narrow head swaying as it considered its prey. Ren turned his face to avoid the unnatural stench it emitted.

The serpentine head tilted to the side and pulled back, preparing to strike. The gaping maw opened, revealing rows of small razor teeth. Ren grabbed the revolver from his waistband. As the mouth came at him, he shoved the gun up under what should have been the creature's chin, closed his eyes and pulled the trigger. There was a deafening blast. It's head exploded in a sticky ichor that splattered across Ren's face.

The monster thrashed about and tightened its grip on the trickster's body. Ren fired again and again into the black mass until the revolver clicked empty. The beast thrashed with each shot, then slowly the vise-like hold on Ren's back and shoulders relaxed as the tiny claws retracted from his skin. He opened his eyes, still holding the smoking gun in front of him. The headless beast dribbled down to the floor in a heap of flabby, mottled skin and lay still.

Ren jumped from the table and tossed the empty pistol back to its owner. It landed with a soft thud on the body. He thanked the corpse, but the half open dead eyes staring back at him did not reply.

"How'd you know that was going to work?" Medesto asked, keeping the barrel of his Thompson machine gun aimed at the dead monster.

"I didn't," Ren said. "The beast wouldn't stay solid long enough for me to hurt it. I had to make it think it had the upper hand, so I could get past its defenses."

"Nice strategic move, B'gatti," Tempest said. "Didn't think you had it in you."

Ren wasn't sure how genuine the compliment was, but he'd take it. He put his hands on the table and took in a deep breath. His outward appearance was bravado and ego, but not so much on the inside. He had witnessed many terrifying things in his time with the Raconteurs, but this was almost more than he could handle. He suppressed a shiver at the thought of that eyeless face staring back at him. The image was still fresh in his mind and not something he would soon forget. He couldn't shake the feeling the shadow monster was only a part of something much larger.

"Can we leave now?" Tempest said as she started for the spiral staircase. "There's nothing of value down here."

Raffle's furry face appeared in the patch of light from the open trapdoor above them. "Is everyting ah right down dere?" the rabbit asked. Charley stood over his shoulder.

"We have it handled," Medesto yelled up to him. "There was some kind of shadowy beast down here. It's like nothing I've seen before."

Raffles' eyes grew wide. "Dat not good," he replied.

"Why not?" Ren yelled from the back of the room. "It's dead."

"If it wot I tink it is," the rabbit said, "sumting like dat don't travel alone. I'd be gettin' out of dere if I was you!"

"Then we need to go!" Medesto shouted. He headed for the stairs, Tempest and Natascha at his heels.

Ren ran in the opposite direction. "Don't wait for me!" he shouted. "This will only take a second." He stepped around the seeping remains of the creature and headed back to the corpse and his satchel.

A soul-piercing shriek echoed throughout the cavernous space. It seemed to come from everywhere around him. Ren covered his ears as the cry reverberated in his head. It was a wretched, piercing cry of anger and sorrow. He looked back at the lifeless shadow monster. It remained motionless where it been killed. The sound ended as quickly as it began, and the room fell silent again.

"Throw me your flashlight!" Ren shouted.

Natascha tossed him her flashlight. "Hurry up, B'gatti!" She stood at the end of the bookshelves. "I'm not leaving without you."

Ren rushed down the aisle to the corpse. He wore a long coat, covered in so much blood its original color was a mystery. He rolled the body over, hoping against hope it would be Mordecai Davos. It wasn't. The dead man had a thick beard and wore a prisoner's shirt. Even in death, the man gripped the satchel as if his life depended on it. He could hear Tempest and Medesto shouting for him, but he ignored them.

Ren pulled the strap of the rucksack off the man's shoulder and checked the contents. There were several notebooks and journals similar to what he saw Mordecai and his followers collecting in the archive under a bookseller's shop. He pulled out a notebook covered in doodles of monsters and dragons.

The handwritten title on the front read simply:

The Months between May and August in the year 1094 per Rogue Destiny's calendar.

These looked like more of Harper Bellweather's traveling journals he had seen in the bookseller's shop inside *The Gaslight Adventures of Asher Grey*. He stuffed the notebooks back into the pack with a smile and started down the aisle, confident this could be the key to finding *The Book of Days*.

Another earsplitting screech echoed in his head. When it stopped, he could hear a hushed murmuring in the surrounding darkness. The sound followed him as he reached the end of the row. Natascha waited for him.

"Did you hear that?" he asked.

"Yeah!" she replied. "Can we go now?"

An ominous purring filled every corner of the room. It sounded like it came from a hundred different points around them. Natascha flashed the beam of her light onto the wall above them. Both backed away as another shadow creature seeped from the surface of the bricks. More black shapes joined it in silent explosions of darkness. They glided through the air toward them.

Ren's sword lay on the floor next to the body of a cyborg mercenary Mordecai employed as his guard. The soldier's armor had been torn open, a shredded uniform. He left the Kordovian Blade where it fell and picked up the plasma rifle lying beside it.

He weighed the weapon in his hands. The design was sleek and high tech, but lightweight with a short barrel and clear round magazine under the barrel full of small multi-colored balls. He had never fired the weapon before but had seen the cybernetic soldiers do it. He pulled the bolt back on the rifle. There was an audible click as a small colored ball fell into place.

Green mist rose up around Natascha again. The dark creatures dove at her, jabbing and striking out. She ran for the staircase, unharmed by her attackers.

Ren raised the rifle and fired several shots into the empty bookshelves. A soft pop, pop, pop reverberated from the barrel. The plasma balls splattered on the shelves and dripped down. The liquid sizzled for a second before bursting into open flames. He didn't know if this would do any good against immaterial shadow creatures, but figured it was worth a try.

He fired the rifle into the floor behind him as he ran. Flames burst out of the exploded capsules. The intense heat from the burning plasma felt like a hot iron on the dozens of tiny cuts on his naked shoulders and back.

The wall of fire slowed the shadow monsters enough for Ren to reach the wooden staircase. They swarmed in circles, seemingly confused by the hedge of flames. The blaze spread quickly, engulfing the massive reading tables. Ren fired indiscriminately at the bookshelves around him. The books and wooden shelves burst into sizzling flames by the time he reached the stairs.

Natasha started up, with Ren close behind. Smoke filled the staircase by the time they exited the room. Once they were up, Tempest dropped the trapdoor down.

Ren tossed the plasma gun to Medesto. "Add that to your collection," he said with a grin. "Consider it a memento from that time we fought those shadow monsters in that horror world."

The gnome caught it, but said nothing. He dropped the weapon into the blackness of his traveling bag, along with his Tommy gun, and the group rushed to the front of the pawnshop. The fire was already burning its way through the floor beneath their feet. Natasha and Tempest followed Medesto, and Ren padded barefoot after them.

Charley jumped to her feet and gathered up her gear. Raffles dug through the candy aisle, stuffing chocolate bars and bags of beef jerky into his backpack. Charley unlocked the front door and held it open as the others rushed past her. Outside the sky was a drizzle of light rain. Dawn was peeking over the eastern horizon, and it would be daylight soon.

Medesto grumbled to himself and stomped up the steps to the empty street. "You took off on your own down there, B'gatti," he growled to Ren. "That endangered the rest of us, especially Doctor Enigma."

"He told me not to wait," Natascha said in Ren's defense. "I chose to stay."

"Calm down," Ren snapped back. "I went back for a satchel. Its filled with Harper Bellweather's journals. The scratches on my back will be gone in a few hours. It's one of the perks of being me."

"You don't get it, do you?" the gnome growled. "None of us heal as fast as you do. Showboating like that is going to get someone killed. We are a team, and we have to work together to keep each alive." Medesto put his hand out for the rucksack.

"No," Ren said, pulling the bag out of Medesto's reach. "Not until I have a chance to look through it." He threw the strap over a shoulder and walked away. "I'm tired and hungry. We passed an all-night diner a few blocks back. I'm going find something to eat." Behind him, Raffles sniffed the smoky air.

"We got bigger troubles den decidin' where we havin' breakfast," he clucked.

"Quiet, bunny," Tempest said. "We don't need any of your down-home homilies right now."

"Just sayin' we got trouble comin' down on us," the rabbit said. He pointed a stubby, clawed finger at the burning pawnshop. Flames engulfed the entire store. Silhouetted in the fire's light, dozens of floating shadow creatures slithered toward them.

"Blood and thunder!" Medesto shouted. "Run for it!"

Chapter 6
Into the Night

The shadow creatures moved through the air in liquid waves, closing the distance between them quickly as the Raconteurs ran to the far side of the street. Natascha was the first to reach the station wagon.

She opened the driver's door, removed her gas mask, and slid in behind the wheel. Charley slid in the passenger side with Raffles. Medesto and Tempest climbed into the back seat. Ren stood alone in the rain as the shadowy creatures closed in.

"Get in, B'gatti!" Tempest said. "We don't have time for any grandstanding."

Ren ignored her. He stood in the path of the approaching shadow monsters. "I'll stall them as long as I can to give you time to put some distance between you and them."

Natascha could make out a couple dozen distinct dark shapes among the roiling black cloud of death coming toward them. Ren may have managed to kill one of the monsters by sheer luck, but not even his inflated ego would allow him to think he could slow down the horde of creatures descending on them.

Ren stood there a moment longer before he climbed in. "On

second thought, go!" he shouted. He sat shoulder to shoulder with Tempest in the backseat. On the other side of her, Medesto occupied the rest of the limited space.

Smoke came off the tires as Natascha hit the gas. The vehicle fishtailed its way down the predawn city street.

"Where are we going?!" Natascha yelled. She jerked the wheel to one side. The automobile skidded around a rain-slick corner and raced down the deserted streets of Cathedral City.

"Charley," Medesto said. "How far are we from where Mordecai left this world?"

The young tech pulled out her echo scanner and began tapping on the screen. "The ley-line he piggybacked on is about twenty-five miles north of here."

"The monsters are almost on us," Tempest yelled. "We'll never make it. Anyone have any other ideas?" She drew her sidearm, even though it would have no effect on the shadows pursuing them.

Natascha glanced in the rearview mirror. The swarm of shadow creatures was gaining ground. Charley turned to look out the back window.

"What are those things?" Charley asked.

"Dey a man'festation of da Muse," Raffles said ominously.

"Da *Muse*?" she asked.

"A Muse is da essence of da world," the rabbit muttered. "She everywhere and nowhere. She embodies the tone and inspiration of the Narrative. In dis case, we in a world of horror so She act according ta Her nature. She very protective of Bree Sandoval and her Story. Dese shadows may be scary, but da Muse be terrifying to behold."

"That would explain the carnage we encountered earlier," Tempest commented.

Natascha cut the next corner too tight and sideswiped a parked car. Metal scraped metal as she corrected her mistake.

The station wagon careened along the street at high speed. "Will somebody please tell me where I'm going?" she said.

"Head back inta da Story," Raffles suggested, not taking his eyes off the clouds of death trailing them.

"We can't go back there," Tempest said. "Too many innocents could get hurt!"

"Da shadows won't dare follow us dere," Raffles clucked. "It da safest place for us right now, cause da Muse alway stay clear of the *Logos Personae* and her doings. Once we back in da Narrative dey'll stop followin' us. Dey won't dare interfere with da Story."

"Charley, which way is the campus?" Natascha said.

Charley's face glowed blue in the light of her Echo Navigator. "We're fifteen blocks over," she said. "Turn left at the street coming up."

"Grab on to something!" Natascha yelled. She turned the steering wheel hard to the left onto a narrow street. The wheels spun out around the rain slick corner, and everyone flew to one side of the car. She straightened the wheel out and continued down the street at breakneck speed.

"Everyone okay?" she asked. She glanced at the backseat.

"Watch out!" Medesto yelled. He pointed out the front window.

Natascha looked back as a figure appeared in the headlights. A female student shuffled along zombie-like across the street, looking up at the oncoming vehicle with blank eyes, empty and covered in a thick film that hid the pupils. A stalk of vegetation sprouted from her head. Natascha slammed on the brakes, but the car was too close.

The vehicle hit the student head on. She erupted in an explosion of gory innards and green spore. The station wagon slid sideways from the impact. Natascha fought to regain control.

They sideswiped another parked car and went into a spin before coming to a stop.

"Hang on!" she yelled, shoving the gas pedal to the floor before anyone could answer. The vehicle skidded down the wet street. She switched on the windshield wipers to clean off the red and green gore so she could see.

"They're inside the car!" Charley screamed.

The rear windows grew dark as an ominous shadow swallowed the back of the vehicle. A second shadow creature clung to the side window. The warning came too late. Natascha watched helplessly as darkness oozed through the edges in the rear window. A tendril of smoke wrapped around Tempest's neck as an enormous wave of shadow engulfed the entire backseat.

In the front seat, Raffles opened his pack. "Hang on!" he yelled. "I got sumting dat might 'elp!" His head disappeared into his backpack, cursing as he dug through its contents. "It gotta be here sumwhere!"

"Somebody do something!" Charley screamed. Tempest, Medesto and Ren struggled under the darkness that enveloped them. Shadows engulfed the back windows and seeped inside the station wagon.

"Got it!" Raffles shouted and pulled out a small cellophane bundle of sparkling dust tied with string. "Cover yer eyes! It about ta get sparkly in 'ere and dis stuff gets everywhere."

The rabbit untied the string with his teeth and poured a pile of glittery dust into his paw. He blew it into the air above the entombed Raconteurs. It exploded in a vibrant spectrum of rainbow colors and gently floated down onto the hideous shadow creatures. The effect was immediate.

The black wave of shadows recoiled, writhing in pain at the touch of the sparkling dust. A piercing high-pitched cry of anguish rattled the inside of the automobile. The rear windows on both sides cracked, before exploding outward under the sonic force. The shadow monsters released their hold on the Raconteurs and retreated out the shattered windows.

"Take dat, ya evil bugger!" Raffles chortled.

Natascha looked in the mirror to see Ren wiping shimmering pixie dust from his eyes. Bleeding strips of flesh hung from his chest. He'd taken the worst of the attack, as if the shadows somehow knew he had killed one of their own.

Tempest had a deep diagonal laceration across her face that disappeared under her hairline. Blood dripped down her neck. Her leather vest and shirt underneath were ripped in a dozen places. Medesto came away with only minor cuts and bruises. His hair and beard glittered from the sparkling dust.

All three looked shaken by the ordeal. Tempest laid back in the seat with her eyes closed, while Ren stared down at the floor, his usual bluster and bravado gone. Blood stained the green vinyl seats from their open wounds. Medesto brushed the glittering dust from his hair.

"What was that, Raffles?" Tempest muttered between violent coughs.

"Pixie dust!" the rabbit said triumphantly.

"Where'd you get it?" Charley quipped.

"From a pixie, 'course," Raffles replied with a touch of mockery in his raspy voice. "Figur'd it might drive 'em away. Life is all 'bout good and evil. Pixie dust is good magic. Evil tings can't stand da touch o' sumting good. Its magical properties are diminished here, but it still do da job." He slapped his paws together to clean the dust off.

Natascha glanced in the rearview mirror. The monsters touched by the dust thrashed in the open air. The others continued after the vehicle, but kept themselves at a distance. She sped up, turning her attention back to the street in front of her.

"Charley, which way to the dorms?" Natascha asked.

Charley pulled her eyes away from her injured companions. "Oh, yeah, let me see." She consulted her screen again. "We're six blocks over. Take the next right at Chesterfield Boulevard. That'll take us right past the *Logos Personae's* dorm."

"Finally, some good news," Natascha said. She sped up until she felt the station wagon pass through the invisible wall separating the outer world from the Narrative. The horde of shadow monsters halted at the unseen barrier. The Raconteurs were safe for the moment, but still had to find their way out of the world. She let out a breath of relief.

Glittery pixie dust floated in the cab of the station wagon. Medesto gagged and coughed on the fine powder hanging in the air. He leaned toward his window for the fresh air.

"Good job, rabbit," the gnome choked out. His dark hair, face and scruffy beard were sprinkled with the glittery dust. "Charley, what direction is that rabbit-hole? We need to get out of the pages of this nightmare."

"The Narrative stretches another four miles up Turley Avenue," Charley replied. "That will take us around the attacks currently happening on campus and should keep the shadows at bay for as long as possible. We'll hit the highway and head north."

The car grew silent. Ten minutes later, the station wagon turned onto an on-ramp to a three-lane highway. No one said a word. Everyone stared out the windows as the miles rolled away toward the rabbit-hole.

Chapter 7
A Necessary Evil

"Look for a side road on the left," Charley said. "Our turn should be just ahead."

Natascha slowed the car and turned down a dirt road that ended in a gravel parking lot with a sign that read *Cathedral County Reservoir*. The station wagon rolled to a stop in front of a chain-link gate. She killed the engine.

In front of them, a wide valley covered in mist stretched out before them, surrounded by rolling hills. Twenty yards beyond the fence, two utility buildings sat silhouetted in the fog. Beyond them, a wide, flat concrete structure dominated the enclosed area. The early morning sun remained hidden behind somber gray clouds.

"Where's the rabbit-hole located, Charley?" Natascha asked.

"The ley-line runs under that concrete reservoir," Charley said. "The portal machine's residual signal is coming from the far side of that utility building. That's where Mordecai left this world."

"I'll get the gate," Medesto said. The stocky gnome climbed out and ambled to the fence. After a quick scan of the area, he snapped the dangling padlocked chain with his bare hands and pulled it open. Natascha rolled the station wagon through. Medesto closed the gate behind them and climbed back into the car. Natascha inched the vehicle forward to the reservoir, gravel crunching under the tires.

Raffles stood up in the front seat and stared out the passenger window. He remained there, deep in thought and motionless, for several minutes. His eyes were wide and round. The only movement was the occasional twitch of his whiskers.

"What is it?" Natascha asked.

"She here," Raffles said in a hoarse whisper.

"Who?" Charley asked.

"Da Muse," Raffles replied. "I can feel it in ma bones. Don't know where 'xactly, but She out dere. I picked up Her scent at da pawnshop, but She had gone before we arrived."

"And you didn't say anything?" Medesto snapped.

"Cause She already gone by den," the rabbit said. "She left Her little beasties behind ta deal wit us, so I figure She got better tings ta do. Most hibernate in the hollow of the world and have to be woken by some terrible event 'fore dey get involved personally. Dis Muse is different. She mo' aggressive den anyting I ever dealt with. Mordecai and his people did sumting to rile Her up. Now, we followin' in their wake."

"So what do we do?" Charley said. "Sounds like She'll be on us the second we step out of the car."

Raffles nodded. "Charley right. We off-worlders like Mord'-cai. She knew we here da moment we stepped into Her world. We need to be strategic here. Someone need ta distract Her while da others make a run for it. Odderwise da Muse kill us 'fore we get halfway to da rabbit-hole."

"So, who wants to go out there and distract her?" Charley asked.

"I'll do it," Tempest replied. She pressed a bloody towel to the side of her head. "But it sounds like a death wish."

"No, I'll go," Ren said. He scratched behind one shoulder. His ripped skin had stopped bleeding and the multitude of gashes across his chest and shoulders had started to close. "I've never tangled with an entire world system before, especially an angry one. Could be interesting. Besides, I'm the only one who has any chance of getting away from Her."

Natascha shook her head. "No," she said. "Your injuries might make it difficult for you to shift. It's too much of a risk. The shadow creatures were unable to touch me in my ethereal form, so the Muse may not be able to either. I'll distract Her so the rest of you can get to the rabbit-hole. Signal me when you're through and I'll follow when I can."

"Will your weapons have any effect on her?" Medesto said.

"I don't plan on fighting her," Natascha said with a less than convincing smile. She knew if anyone had a chance of surviving a confrontation with the Muse, it was Doctor Enigma. She would do her best to stall long enough for her friends to get to safety. What happened after that was anyone's guess.

Raffles nodded and turned to Natascha. "You mighty brave, Doct'r 'Nigma. Just remember da Muse is da embodiment of dis evil world, da spice dat give it flav'r. Most Muses are decent enuf for non-sentient personifications of a world's essence, but dis one is very deceitful and will play mind tricks wit ya. She may attack you directly or not. Who knows? She all evil. But don't doubt she will attack your mind, break through your defenses and make you see thing that not dere and think tings dat not your thoughts. Guard yourself, dear Natascha."

"I'll do my best," Natascha replied as she put on her gas mask. "Keep in contact with me through the comm." She slowly opened her door and climbed out of the vehicle, searching for any sign of the Muse. The morning air was cold and thick with a dense mist that settled over the valley. She stayed close to the round concrete structure until she found the stairs leading to the top of the reservoir.

Her footsteps echoed in the fog around her as she walked out to the middle of the circular concrete slab that covered the water reserves for the population of Cathedral City. Visibility was only about twenty yards in all directions. Any other time she would change the settings in her gasmask to infrared to pick up where her enemy might be hiding, but she doubted the Muse would give off any readable heat signature.

"I'm in place," she whispered into the communicator inside in her gasmask. "Be ready."

"Okay," Medesto replied through the comm. "When She appears, we'll make a run for the rabbit-hole."

Doctor Enigma stood silent at the center of the concrete reservoir, straight and motionless. If this was to be her end, at least she would die knowing her friends had escaped this hellscape of a world.

She straightened her stance, squared her shoulders, not quite sure how to summon forth the essence of a world. She chuckled to herself. Whatever happened here, this would still be easier than dealing with her mother.

"I just want to talk to you!" she shouted into the crisp morning air. "We are not here to harm your world or those who live in it!"

Silence.

"Raffles, are you sure She's out there?" she said into her comm.

There was a momentary silence, then a scuffling sound as the rabbit's hoarse voice came on the comm. "Oh, She out dere. Like a predator hidin' in da tall grass jus' waitin' ta pounce. Be careful, She could attack witout warning."

"Okay, just be ready to move when I engage Her."

She shifted her stance and took a deep breath. The feeling

she was being watched grew stronger. "I know you're there," she called out. "Show yourself. I promise I pose no threat to *Bree Sandoval*. I'm after the off-worlders who passed through here earlier."

At the mention of the *Logos Personae's* name, a great whirlwind cut through the mist like a wave. It grew stronger as it blew down the valley toward Natascha. A black, formless shape rode the wind and to her shock, she saw hundreds, maybe thousands of shadows monsters mixed in with the fog. Her heart pounded in her chest. The sensors in her mask could register every type of sentient beings she had ever encountered in the known universe, but they showed nothing in front of her.

The tide of mist rose high into the air when it reached the edge of the concrete. Natascha braced herself for it to fall on her, ready to activate the chemicals in her clothing that made her as a ghost.

"She's here," Natascha whispered through the comm. "Go."

The whirlwind came down with great speed, striking the concrete reservoir twenty feet from where Natascha stood. It hit the surface of the reservoir and billowed out in rolling layers of dark mist. Out of the mist walked a young woman with dark hair. Natascha recognized her from the night before. It was the girl who jumped on the table under the bridge and toasted the end of the world. *Bree Sandoval*, the central character of *Surviving a Bad Romance on the Eve of the Apocalypse*, the novel she was currently trying to escape from.

Natascha knew it was not the real Bree Sandoval standing before her. This was a simulacrum, a replica, used as bait to see if the Raconteur posed any threat. The Muse was testing her.

The young woman wore a grey sports jersey and blue jeans with white tennis shoes. She had a backpack slung over a shoulder and her dark hair pulled back in a ponytail. A content smile sparkled on her face as she walked toward the Raconteur, but her eyes were strangely vacant of emotion. She stopped in front of Natascha.

"Why have you come here?" the fake Bree Sandoval asked pleasantly. "You are like the others who did not belong here."

"I am not here to harm anyone," Natascha said, summoning every ounce of strength to force confidence into her words. "I only pursue the people who disturbed your world. I ask that you let me pass, so I might continue after them."

The comm in Natascha's gasmask crackled. "We're moving along the side of the reservoir to your right," Medesto whispered. "Buy us a few minutes to reach the rabbit-hole."

"Then why did you attack me and friends at my home-coming party?" Bree asked.

"I am not the one who attacked you," Natascha answered. "They are evil people that I am pursuing."

Bree Sandoval sized the Raconteur up and down, a mischievous grin on her face. "More outsider tricks," she said with a laugh. "I think you're here to finish what they failed to do."

"I swear to you, I'm not," Natascha said. "She is the heart and soul of this world. I would never wish harm on her." She tensed as the doppelganger of Bree walked around her, studying her long coat and gasmask.

Bree came back around to stand in front. "Liar," she whispered. A ripple ran over her body, shifting her looks, mostly in her facial expressions. "You are just like the others."

"My only wish is to leave this place," Natascha replied. "Please. Just let me go."

"No, no, silly girl," Bree giggled. "Those who came before you may have escaped, but you will not be so lucky."

The appearance of the Muse changed. Her facial expression became more strained. Her eyes and nose were not quite Bree Sandoval anymore. The illusion cracked as the anger rose in her.

Natascha whispered into her comm. "Hello?"

"We're almost to there," Medesto replied. "The rabbit-hole is beyond the utility buildings. You can't miss it."

"Good," Natascha replied. "Because I am out of time here."

"You say you were not with those who attacked me," Bree rumbled. The anger in her words continued to distort the illusion even further. "Yet you follow closely in their tracks. First at the party, then at the pawnshop, and now here, at the edge of my domain. What do you hope to find out here?"

Natascha thought about that statement. The Muse knew the borders of her domain, yet appeared to be unaware of the rabbit-hole not far from where they stood. It was a blind spot to Her. That meant if Natascha could get there, she would be beyond the grasp of the Muse.

"I told you," Natascha said. "I am only after those who would harm you."

Bree Sandoval laughed. A cruel sound full of fury, hate and sadness. "Or maybe you left your group to cause mischief elsewhere and now you cannot find them again. Either way, none of you belong here. But since you are distracting me so your friends can sneak away through the hole in my world, you get the pleasure of experiencing my wrath first."

Without warning, Bree Sandoval kicked Natascha in the chest. It was unexpected and faster than the real Bree could have moved. The attack caught the Raconteur off guard. She hit the concrete ten feet behind her and rolled backwards onto her feet. As she stood, a pressure built in her head, piercing her like a knife.

Guard your mind. Raffles' words came back to her. Natascha steeled her thoughts against the unseen forces that pressed in on her. She tried to push back, but the enraged Muse was a primal force that could not be slowed. It was like trying to hold back the incoming tide. The Muse flipped through her memories like She was perusing the pages of a family photo album.

Natascha's mind reeled. She was suddenly in the summer-house she grew up in as a child. She knew it was not real, that it was only a tactic the rabbit warned the Muse would use. Flashes of memories rolled across her mind unbidden. Each one stung like a steel needle impaled into her skull.

There was yelling coming from the back terrace. She went to the dining room window and saw her mother and father arguing outside. Each pointed at the other and shouting loudly. Her dead father. She passed a mirror and caught her reflection in it. She was young, only about seven. In her hands she clutched a rag doll of Doctor Enigma that her father had had made for her by a friend. It would be the same doll she would hold at her father's funeral eight years later.

She remembered the fight in detail. The Muse had mined it from her deepest memories. This fight was the big one, the atom bomb that destroyed her parents' marriage and everything within the blast radius. The moment that sent the young Natascha Devi into freefall.

Her parents had become more and more disagreeable with each other in recent days. Her father moved out and joined a group of international masked heroes calling themselves *The Exceptionals*. He used his scientific genius to create the gas-masked, trench-coated persona of *Doctor Enigma, The Midnight Alchemist*. Together with *The Exceptionals*, they combated threats both terrestrial and extraterrestrial across the globe. He had just returned from Shangri-La, only to tell Mother he had to leave immediately for South America to stop a mad scientist and his army of reanimated zombie monkeys. Her mother was so angry, she sided with that scientist in the end, dealing her father the greatest defeat of his professional career.

The exploits of the original Doctor Enigma and the super-group, *The Exceptionals,* had become an international sensation throughout Natascha's homeworld, but as their reputation grew, so did their list of enemies.

After several failed attempts on her father's life, their home was no longer safe. He was forced to move his family to America and a new life, despite her mother's protests. In late 1934 President Nicolai Tesla invited *The Exceptionals* to Washington, DC to accept the Presidential Medal of Valor for saving the world time and time again.

It was then their enemies attacked en mass, joining forces and striking at the moment the Presidential Medals were awarded. Natascha had always suspected her mother gave her father's enemies the needed intel for the attack.

Natascha knew in her heart she wasn't really watching the destruction of her parents' relationship, but there were tears running down her face despite that fact. She loved her father very much and to see him alive again was almost more than she could bear.

But it was only the Muse manipulating her thoughts and memories. She had to focus, change this to her advantage, or the Muse would destroy her.

The divorce was painful, so much dysfunction for a young girl to carry. But for better or worse, it was the breakup of her family that made her who she was today. Pain caused growth. If it doesn't break you, it will push you forward to greater things. Without that catalyst in her life, she would have stayed stagnant, constantly choosing between her mother and her father, and never learning who she really was.

It forced her to side with her father and move away with him to train with the *Exceptionals*. They became her family. The divorce of her parents defined her as nothing ever had or ever would. It made her strong and taught her to lean on no one but herself. When her father died three years later, there was more pain, but out of that pain came a new Doctor Enigma.

"Everyone you have ever loved has abandoned you," Bree Sandoval said. "Your father is dead. Your mother's disowned you. Your allies have abandoned you to die a horrible death inside a world where you do not belong. All that must hurt so deeply, but I understand your pain. My boyfriend, Ezequiel Del Toro, is a bad boy. He says he's changed, but does anyone ever really change?"

"Bree, please listen to me," Natascha said. She found she was shaking from the sheer intensity of Her presence. She shoved her gloved hands into the pockets of her coat.

"Do not dare speak her name!" the girl spat. "Bree is my precious child! You are less than dust to me and I will destroy any who would harm her!" The form of Bree Sandoval melted away. The young woman in front of her changed before Natascha's eyes. In her place, a dark figure of shadow and smoke walked toward her.

Doctor Enigma readied herself with the only defense she had left. The timing had to be precise because there would be no second chance. She pulled out the glass vial she hid in her pocket. The sloshing liquid inside was inert in the airless container.

Natascha threw the tiny bottle onto the concrete at the feet of the nebulous form of the Muse. The vial shattered and the liquid light inside it burst in a blinding flash of brilliance.

The Muse cried out. Whether it was from surprise or anger, Natascha did not know. She hit the button in her glove and a green mist rose up around her. The cloud of chemicals combined with the alchemy-treated clothing she wore made her entire body ethereal and ghost-like. She pressed a second button that switched off the small disks in the soles of her boots that allowed her to walk on solid ground while the rest of her was ethereal. She dropped through the concrete into dark icy waters below the reservoir.

The water did not touch her. Doctor Enigma remained completely dry as she floated weightless in the darkness, like an astronaut in space, not knowing if her trick had worked or if at any moment thousands of the Muse's shadowy minions would descend on her. She swam through the black water toward the side of the structure. The readings in her gas mask clicked down the distance until she reached the wall and pushed herself through. The gravity disks in her boots came back on and landed solidly in the thick grass outside the reservoir. Then she ran.

"Charley, send me your location!" she yelled into her comm. "Don't have time to search for it."

A moment later, the signal appeared on the tiny screen inside her gas mask. She sprinted along the reservoir's curved wall toward the rabbit-hole, expecting to run into the Muse at every step. The air was silent. She wondered what that meant.

Natascha sprinted over the open field past the last utility building. Time slowed. Every second became an eternity. The closer she got to the rabbit-hole, the higher her anxiety grew. She waited for the Muse to reveal Herself before she reached safety. But there was no sign of Her as a gaping opening in the ground came into view. She followed the slanted tunnel into the earth until she saw Medesto and Raffles waiting for her. Ren, Charley, and Tempest stood further down the passageway.

"Are you okay?" Medesto asked, his face deadly serious, before he gave her a smile of relief.

"That was an experience I do not wish to repeat," Natascha said with a nervous chuckle. She pulled her mask off and shook the sweat from her hair. They walked in silence, enjoying the momentary peace under the soft glow of the ley-line roots. Raffles nibbled on a chocolate bar and offered some to Natascha.

Raffle's ear twitched. He stopped walking and stared back

down the dark passageway toward the entrance of the rabbit-hole. Something was not right. His eyes went wide.

"What is it?" Natascha asked.

"She ain't done wit us yet!" he yelled. "Run!"

The circular passageway under Natascha's boots vibrated. A thunderous sound of wind whipped down the tunnel. It hit her with such force it threw her to the floor. The passageway rattled from the unrestrained fury. She caught a thick root sticking out of the wall that stopped her from going farther.

Raffles leapt to a hollow niche in the wall and wedged himself in to escape the winds. Medesto got knocked from his feet. Natascha threw an arm out. The gnome caught her hand in a tight, painful grip.

The strength of the gale increased, followed by an ear-piercing scream of fury and sorrow that echoed through the tunnel. Natascha couldn't be sure if the screech was an actually audible sound, or if it was only in her mind. Mixed within the chaotic winds, the shadowy monsters spiraled around.

"Watch out!" Natascha yelled. Her warning came out no louder than a whisper against the intense winds roaring past them. She saw Charley, Tempest, and Ren hanging onto what they could to keep from being blown away.

Natascha strained to maintain her grip on Medesto's hand. A cracking sound echoed over the raging winds. It grew louder and cracks appeared along the walls of the tunnel. Natascha knew what was about to happen and there was nothing any of them could do about it. She braced herself for the inevitable.

The tunnel exploded around them.

Chapter 8
Things Left Behind

Ren floated weightless as he often did in his dreams. He opened his eyes and saw nothing but inky blackness. But he was not alone in the darkness.

This was not the first time Ren had felt this other presence. The shadow had followed the trickster for as long as he could remember, but it always stayed beyond his mind's eye. Medesto told him the shadow that called itself *Rhune* had seized control of Ren's weakened body, long enough to manifest into physical form for a time.

"Rhune, I know you're there!" Ren yelled. The words echoed inside his mind. "Talk to me! I need answers!" He felt a stirring at the back of his thoughts, like old memories resurfacing. A voice spoke.

"I am here." The words had an edge to them that spoke of chaos and mayhem. Ren recognized the voice. It was his own. He still did not understand how that could be, but it was at once both familiar and strange.

"Who are you?" Ren demanded. "How are you connected to me and my past?"

"I am you," Rhune replied. "And you are me. We are the

same. It's time for you to come home. Your family is waiting for you."

"Then tell me where we're from!" Ren yelled. His earliest memories were being pulled half drowned from the waters of the Dreaming Sea off the shores of Rogue Destiny. Everything before that day remained a mystery to him.

"Mother wants you to come home," Rhune said quietly. "Our siblings are waiting. Then we can all be together again. I must go now. We will speak again soon."

"Wait!" Ren shouted. "You have to tell me more! Give me a book or the name of a city! Anything!"

"There are more pressing matters you must deal with right now." Rhune's voice sounded far away, like an echo inside his head.

"Like what?"

"You are falling."

Pain radiated through Ren's skull. He opened his eyes to find he was slowly falling in a sea of blackness. Broken chunks of dirt from the crumbling rabbit-hole fell around him. Winds whipped his body. High above him, the remains of the ley-line protruded from the great glowing orb of the novel the Raconteurs had just escaped. Rhune's voice was gone.

His mind reeled as he tried to recall what had happened. He had stood in the passageway with Tempest and Charley when Natascha reached them. All seemed good at that moment. Then a great wind rushed in, followed by some ominous presence of anger and hatred. The blast of air blew through the tunnel until the floor gave way underneath his feet. He saw Natascha holding onto Medesto's hand and Raffles hiding between rocks in the wall. Something hard struck him. Rubble from the ruptured ley-line, probably. He remembered seeing Charley and Tempest fall with him and then...blackness.

He was in the *Great Void between Worlds*, with nothing but a black abyss and slow suffocation waiting for him. His descent was not of a normal velocity. There was gravity because he was falling, so there had to be a top and bottom somewhere out here.

Ren searched for the other Raconteurs but saw no one else among the pieces of earth and roots falling around him. Then he spotted a figure far below him to his right. It was Charley. The thin air made it difficult to draw a full breath. That was going to be a problem, but he had no choice and less time to reach Charley.

He considered shifting to an angel but worried the feathered wings would not hold up well in the strong crosswinds buffeting him on all sides. Instead, he morphed into a bat-winged humanoid that he and his partner, Claymore, had encountered early in his career with the Raconteurs. Leathern wings sprouted from his back. His arms and chest became thick, gnarled muscles as his skin darkened to deep charcoal ash. He banked into the wind, pulled his wings in, and dove like a missile.

The strong gales sought to alter his trajectory, but he maintained his course with an occasional flap of wings. He focused only on his target and plunged toward her. Charley spun in a slow circle as she fell, arms and legs flailing. She looked up at him through watering eyes, twisting her head around to keep him in sight as she continued to fall.

He reached out, grabbing an arm as she spun. She stopped spinning and pulled herself in to him, wrapping herself tightly around his torso. Ren held her close and leveled off their descent, as he searched for Tempest. The winds whipped his face, blurring his vision.

Charley pointed frantically off to the side, yelling something that was lost in the deafening winds. Then he saw Tempest in freefall below them.

The Raconteur's Chief Operations Officer had accused him

of many things, including incompetence and betrayal. The thought crossed his mind to leave her, but he dismissed the idea immediately. In the end, she was still a Raconteur and only wanted to stop Mordecai, the same as him. She hated him and had told him as much to his face. After he saved her, he planned on reminding her of the fact as often as he could.

Ren dove toward Tempest, flapping his wings to increase their speed. Charley tightened her grip around his waist. The distance between them closed quickly. Ren grabbed Tempest's outstretched hands. With a great effort, he began the impossible climb back up with his heavy burden. Ren looked up at the shattered ley-line. It seemed miles away.

His lungs burned, and his head grew light. The thin atmosphere made the physical exertion harder against with the blowing winds while carrying two grown adults. Above them, the ley-line continued to crumble before Ren's eyes. Around him, hundreds of worlds watched in the silent darkness.

Combative winds assaulted them on every side. Every beat of his wings brought them higher, only to be pushed back down again. He glanced at Charley. She had a death grip on his waist, her eyes closed tight. It was only a matter of time before she would succumb to the lack of air and no longer be able to hold on to him.

Tempest held a firm grip on his wrists as he did hers. Hair whipped about her face as their eyes met, each knowing in that moment the harsh truth of their situation. In these conditions, there was no way Ren could carry them both back up.

The burden was too great, his body too weak from lack of oxygen, and he was losing the fight against these devil winds that seemed so determined to keep them from reaching their destination. He would never abandon his companions, so he consigned himself to let this play out as it would.

There had been few times in his life when the reality of the situation outweighed his bluster and confidence. If he wanted something, he made it happen, usually with no forethought or regret involved. With the extra weight of just one person, he'd be hard pressed to fly all the way back. With two, it would be impossible.

Tempest stared up at him, strangely serene despite their predicament. He saw it on her face a second before she did it. Her expression was calm. She released her hold on Ren's wrists and twisted her hands from his grip, pulling them out of his reach. There was no hesitation in her action, no second thoughts, her eyes telling him she was content in her decision. Falling backward, she nodded at him and mouthed two words as the inky blackness engulfed her.

Save her.

Charley reached an arm out for Tempest as she fell, but without the added weight, Ren's wings lifted them away from their companion. Ren held Charley tight under her arms, determined to make it back to the tunnel. There might be nothing left of the ley-line by the time they reached it, but it was their only hope. He would not let Tempest's sacrifice be in vain.

Ren banked against the fierce winds as he climbed higher and higher, cutting back and forth across the flow of the air currents. His wings grew heavy, and vision blurred. It was difficult to focus on his destination. Charley hugged him tighter, and he could feel her softly sobbing against into his side.

With the last bit of strength left in him, he climbed toward the narrow bridge of crumbling dirt and entangled organic roots. He dodged chunks of falling debris as the ley-line continued to break apart.

Charley's body relaxed, and her grasp loosened around his waist. Her head rolled to the side, and she went limp in his arms. Ren pushed himself harder, but she grew heavier with every flap of his wings. His head was light from lack of air. He felt control over his winged monstrosity slipping from his grasp.

The crumbling ley-line grew closer. He thought he saw a bearded face peer over the edge, but it disappeared a second later. Were Natascha, Medesto and Raffles safe? With one last desperate burst of energy, he tried to reach the tunnel, but the strength in his wings failed. He and Charley hovered in place for a moment before they fell.

"Sorry," Ren whispered to an unconscious Charley as the pair fell. He let go of the winged creature's shape and shifted back to his natural form as blackness overtook him.

***

Two strong hands grabbed him. Ren looked up through blurry eyes into the gas mask of Doctor Enigma. A rope tied around her waist tethered her to the ley-line above. Ren felt the cord jerk as they ascended. He knew at the other end of the rope was a gnome of inhuman strength pulling them up. He focused on keeping his hold on Charley, even as he slipped in and out of consciousness again. It felt like an eternity before they reached the edge of the broken tunnel.

Medesto pulled the three Raconteurs through the gaping opening. He took the limp form of Charley from Ren's arms and carried her to where the air was better. He laid her gently on the dirt floor. Ren rolled onto his back. His body was heavy with exhaustion. The air inside the ley-line was sweet, and the trickster savored each grateful gulp.

Natascha held out a hand to help Ren, but his mind was slow to respond. She pulled him to his feet. They stood at the precipice of the shattered rabbit-hole.

Ren looked out across the blackness, still trying to come to grips with what had just happened. All he could recall was flying back up. The ley-line had shattered out from under them and now Tempest was gone. And then there was Rhune.

He walked over to Charley. The young tech's breathing rose and fell in an even rhythm. She opened her eyes moments later and stared at the ceiling.

"Tempest?" she asked, looking up at Ren. The trickster shook his head but said nothing.

"How're you feeling?" Medesto asked Ren.

"Glad I'm able to breathe again," Ren said, taking in more air produced by the organic ley-line. Ren turned back to look at Charley. Her eyes were closed, but she was alive.

"What happened out there?" Natascha asked.

Ren took a deep breath and exhaled. "I couldn't carry both of them. I was lucky to make it back with Charley."

"Very few ever experience da outside Void like dat," Raffles said. "Wot dat like? Dey say strange tings go on out dere."

"I was too busy trying to stay alive," Ren said, staring out at the abyss beyond the hollow of the ley-line. "I didn't have time to ponder the mystery of it all."

Charley sat up, her breathing labored. Ren knelt next to her. "You okay?" he said, putting a hand on her shoulder. He was not sure what else to do but show sympathy. She pushed him away in an uncharacteristic flash of anger.

"Don't touch me!" she yelled. Tears filled her eyes. "You let Tempest fall! You had a hold of her, and you let go! I saw you!"

"*She* let go of me!" Ren protested. "I'd never leave anyone behind."

"You never liked her," Charley yelled back. She climbed to her feet. "She warned me about you, but I didn't believe her. I trusted you." Her whole body quivered with anger. She stormed off as far as she could to the other side of the tunnel and sat down against the wall. She leaned her head on her knees and began crying.

Ren turned to the others. "I would never had made it with both of them. Tempest understood that. She sacrificed herself so I could save Charley."

"I'm sure you did everything you could," Medesto said. After a moment, he cleared his throat, his voice rough. "Sometimes we face only no-win situations. Tempest was only with us for a short time, but I have to admit she will be missed. We butted heads because she had a fierce sense of right and wrong. Tempest had her doubts about you, Ren, but in the end, she trusted you with Charley's life."

"The ley-line is still connected," Natascha said. "Ren, you can get across if you go now."

Medesto climbed to his feet. "You up for that, Ren? The ley-line's unstable, but it's our only chance to stay on Mordecai's trail."

"Of course," Ren replied. He had no reason to stay there any longer. "How are you going to be able to get home?"

"Charley can send a signal out," Medesto answered. "Someone will answer, so don't worry about us."

Ren stretched his aching arms. He watched the distant world waiting for him across the blackness. Swirling colors of green and blue moved over its surface. It did not seem to be that far away, but he knew time and space were deceiving when dealing with ley-lines.

He hesitated to go back out into the dark nothingness, but this was his chance to separate from the Raconteurs and be on his own. No one else to worry about but himself. Mordecai Davos still needed to be stopped. And Claymore was out there. He looked back at the others. Medesto and Raffles were trying to console a grief-stricken Charley.

"Tell her I'm sorry," Ren said to Natascha. "Can you talk to Charley for me? Make her understand I would never leave anyone behind. Not even Tempest."

Natascha nodded. "I will. She's just exhausted and in shock. She'll come around."

"Thank you," Ren replied. He looked into her dark eyes. If he never saw the Raconteurs again, he would miss her most of all. He turned back for one last look at Charley.

Raffles ambled up to them. "Look like we can't go no further," he said. "I tink dis mission over."

"There's still time for Ren to go on without us," Natascha said.

Raffles chuckled. "You Rac'oteers don' ever stop, do ya?"

"Do we have any choice?" Natascha replied. "*In Medias Res*. Into the middle of things. That's us."

Raffles waddled out with Ren to the edge of the shattered ley-line. "Okay, den," the rabbit said. He pointed a stubby finger up to the twisted strands of roots and organic veins that held the last of the ley-line together. "Stay close to what's left of her and get across as quick as you can before she completely break apart. Otherwise you'll find yerself lost 'tween worlds. Somewhere in da Great-In-Between, not quite here, not quite dere. Dat wat h'appen to Tempes'."

The rabbit's words barely registered with Ren. He was bone tired, and his muscles were heavy with fatigue. Regardless, he knew he had to get across the chasm.

"Well, I guess I'll see you later," he said to Raffles and Medesto. Speed was what he needed. Ren shifted into the form of the raven he used so often. Taking the image of the black bird was easy for him, as natural as putting on a pair of comfortable shoes. Of all the shapes he used, the raven was the one could hold the longest, like it was a part of him.

"Good luck," Natascha said. "*In Medias Rez*. Contact us as soon as you can."

With a flap of his wings, Ren flew out of the hollow, staying along the ceiling of the narrow bridge of twisted roots. The organic ley-line wobbled in the fierce, shifting winds. Chunks of earth fell around him, but at least there was air for him to breathe. Although how long the oxygen lasted was anyone's guess.

The mystical ley-lines connected all the written worlds of the Mythic Cosmos, but they distorted distance. There was no way for Ren to gauge how far he had to go to reach the other side. He could only continue for as long as it took him.

The air became thin, and he began to get lightheaded again, but he trusted the other doorway was out there. He just had get to it before the line disintegrated completely, leaving him stranded in the Void to slowly suffocate.

Then he saw it, the white circle at the end of the tunnel, lit by the soft glow from another world. Through watery eyes, the shapeshifter focused his remaining strength on reaching the light. His tiny oxygen starved lungs made his brain fuzzier by the second.

With a final desperate sweep of feathered wings, Ren swooped down, crashing onto the floor in front of the doorway. Behind him, the remnants of the ley-line hit a crescendo of falling debris. He looked back to see the remains of it crumble and disappear in the vast windswept blackness. The trickster knew nothing about the interdimensional shifting of space and time, but he knew that he had witnessed something that no one else ever would.

He stood up, basking in the sunshine filtering through the doorway of the new world in front of him. No going back now. He was on his own.

And that's how he preferred it.

Chapter 9
The Protectorate General

Gideon Dumas could not escape the feeling that he was being watched. He sat at his desk in a cramped office at the back of the public house, the Obtuse Turtle, on the northern edge of the city of Rogue Destiny. The sensation had been gnawing at him all morning, making it hard to concentrate on his work. He knew there were eyes upon him.

Over his shoulder, a bright blue macaw perched high on its stand, its head tucked under a wing. For what felt like the hundredth time, Gideon glanced about the room, hoping to spy anything out of place.

His office was in cluttered disarray. Overcrowded shelves threatened to burst with books, charts, and maps of every imaginable place. Umbrella stands sat in every corner, stuffed with rolled up atlases and scrolls. Maps and charts filled every open space on all four walls. The window was open a crack, trying to create a cross breeze against the humid tropical air. Overhead a wobbly ceiling fan pushed the warm air around but wasn't cooling anything.

The leader of the Raconteurs was putting the final touches on a letter to a nobleman he had befriended in the novel *The*

Once and Future King. His correspondence inquired about securing a safe house on the noble's lands should Gideon's agents need a place of sanctuary while performing their duties.

Without lifting his head from the paper, he scanned the room again. Something was amiss. From the corner of his eye, he caught a tiny flash of reflected sunlight at the base of the open window. A tiny silver bug fluttered its wings, then skittered along the windowsill. Gideon rose from his chair and knelt at a bookcase under the window, pretending to search for a book. He reached for yesterday's newspaper from the wastepaper basket next to his desk. With a practiced motion, he learned from hours of fencing practice, Gideon smashed the insect as it attempted to fly away. There was the crunch of tiny gears and circuits and the bug exploded into pieces with the full force of *The Daily Inquisitor* behind it. The parrot squawked and ruffled his feathers in irritation.

Gideon examined the tiny fragments of metal before brushing them outside. "Another spy from the Common Council," he huffed. "Prying into our private affairs again, huh, Ulysses."

The Common Council of Eternal Vigilance and Public Sympathy was the ruling body of Rogue Destiny. Its authority was second only to the Protectorate General herself in the level of power they wielded.

Gideon was not always in agreement with a majority of the Council's twenty-four members. But he hoped hosting a tour of the Raconteurs' fleet of Slipstreams would help persuade the Protectorate General and a handful of select council members to support him in an upcoming vote.

He sat back down, dipped his pen in the small jar of black ink and returned to his letter. He had taken several personal visits to *The Once and Future King* over the last few months. Gideon's goal? To build a relationship with this nobleman, a secondary character in the Pendragon linage and convince him of the value the world of the young King Arthur was to his organization's ever widening network of contacts throughout the Eight Genres of Literature. He labored in securing new sanctuaries in areas where his agents currently had few places of refuge.

It was a key strategic point for the organization ever widening network of contacts throughout the Eight Genres of Literature. He labored in securing new sanctuaries in areas where his agents currently had few places of refuge.

As with most worlds from the genre of historical fantasy, *The Once and Future King* was home to a multitude of strategic doorways leading to the far reaches of the known universe that his Raconteurs could use to their advantage.

This network of rabbit-holes provided invaluable ways for quick travel to the distant reaches of the Mythic Cosmos. One jump from Rogue Destiny to *The Once and Future King* and their travel options to other points grew exponentially.

The letter should have gone out weeks ago, but the whole Mordecai Davos affair had distracted him from finishing it. The pen scraped across the parchment in deliberate strokes. His spidery handwriting showed no actual skill at penmanship, but he felt a handwritten note gave his request a personal touch. One of his agents, Artimus De Costa, had business in *The Canterbury Tales* and was leaving the next morning. Artimus could deliver it on his way.

The intercom on his desk crackled. It startled Ulysses. The parrot gave a loud squawk and shimmied across its perch. His sudden cry caught Gideon unaware, and his hand jerked involuntarily, leaving a puddle of ink across the last sentence of the letter.

A booming voice came over the comm. "Sir, the Protectorate General and her entourage have arrived."

Gideon clicked the intercom button. "Excellent, Sebastian. Let them know I will be there momentarily to greet them. Thank you." He dabbed a blotter on the page, trying to repair the damage to his letter, but it was beyond fixing. He pulled out another piece of parchment to start again, but that would have to wait for now.

This meeting was Gideon's best chance to ensure the Council's continued funding the ongoing work of his agents. If the flow of income should be cut off, he was not sure how he would continue to pay his agents. Should the vote go against them, the fate of the Raconteurs would be forever altered.

He got up from his desk, checking his appearance in the oval mirror on the wall. As cluttered as the office was, the man looking back at him was the paragon of fashion, with his pinstriped vest and crisp white shirt and black tie.

His dark hair combed impeccably to one side, was kept in place by his favorite brand of hair cream, Kovac's Vitality Suave. Gideon swore by its ability to keep his coiffure perfect throughout the day. He was delighted with the greasy product but had heard complaints that those around him thought it smelled like pungent fish oil.

He took his tailored suit coat off the rack. It fit his short frame perfectly, patterned after the 1920s style of his homeworld, *The Malcom DeQuincy Mysteries*. He slipped into the coat, smoothing out any wrinkles in the fabric, and adjusted his tie in the mirror. Pulling on black leather gloves, he dropped a handful of unshelled Macadamia nuts into Ulysses' feeding bowl and bid the parrot farewell.

Gideon left from his office, cutting through a back hall of the Obtuse Turtle and down a set of stairs across the Mezzanine landing bay to the underground maintenance garage that housed their Slipstream Runabouts. Several ships sat parked across the landing bay. He entered today's security code into the button pad on the storm doors. The tiny silver bug spying on him in his office was only the latest attempt at stealing his coveted technology. Thankfully, not every council member had set themselves against the Raconteurs, and he still had a handful of loyal allies.

Security was a priority above all else to Gideon and his organization. There were many who sought to steal the secrets that allowed a Slipstream passage through the Word Canopy that enveloped every written world they protected, not to mention the WayFinder.

When the massive doors opened, he walked down the ramp into the underground workshop where Sebastian Poe and his small crew designed, built, and maintained every Slipstream in the Raconteurs' fleet.

Dangling power cords and diagnostic equipment hung from the low ceiling of the expansive garage. Half a dozen ships sat in various states of repair. Each would range from fifty to eighty feet when fully assembled.

Sebastian waited with several important-looking diplomats at a workbench. Once Gideon reach them, the cybernetic mechanic excused himself and hobbled back to a dismantled engine he had been working on. His heavy iron leg impacted the concrete floor with every step, sending a resounding echo throughout the garage. Worn out gears in the right knee whined in protest. Gideon knew Sebastian had kept putting off replacing them because it would have taken him away from his important work.

The Protectorate General, Pahloek Zima, was an older woman with gray hair and a pleasant face. They had known each other for years, and Gideon had watched Pahloek work her way through the ranks of the Common Council to the highest political position in the Rogue Destiny. As with many denizens of Rogue Destiny, her background was sketchy. She never spoke about where she come from other than to say it had been a terrible place to live. Gideon believed it to be some dystopian novel that had left her with memories too dreadful to discuss. There were far too many worlds like that, in his opinion.

Their professional relationship had grown strong over the years. Pahloek respected the work of Gideon and the Raconteurs, and she used her influential voice in the halls of government on behalf of them.

"Good to see you, Gideon," she said, extending a gloved hand.

Gideon bowed slightly and took the offered hand. "It has been too long, Pahloek," he replied.

Pahloek motioned to the four council members standing around her. "Gideon, you know Ma Bellamy from the Fairy Tales." The cherub-faced woman remained a dogged advocate for the Raconteurs and Gideon's friend and ally. She had an infectious laugh, and dressed in the eccentric way of her stories. An oversized garden hat shaded the mishmash of colorful scarves wrapped around her neck. Her purple rubber boots squeaked as she walked. She gave Gideon a knowing smile. Their bond was close enough to require no handshake.

"And this is Osirus Spyros, a representative from the Cultural Historical Genre." Gideon did not know the man, but if Pahloek had brought him here today, she had faith he could be won to their cause. He was tall, a professional soldier by the way he held himself. The two men shook hands.

Gideon gave a polite bow to the last two in the party, Astrid Saabey and Solis Cicerone. Gideon had never met them but knew their reputations well. They were both from the Science Fiction Genre and held significant influence with the Common Council. Pahloek had indeed recruited an impressive quorum of political influencers.

"You've met our chief designer and engineer, Sebastian Poe,"

Gideon said. "He and his crew built every Slipstream Runabout in our fleet. Sebastian personally oversees the upkeep and modifications of each one."

The mechanic crouched at the rear mounting of a Cold Fire engine block. He gave a grunt and nod without looking up from the bolt he was tightening.

"As you know, most of our technology is borrowed from other written worlds," Gideon said with a laugh. "But that is Rogue Destiny after all, isn't it? We take what we need from the different worlds, retooling them for our personal needs. Shall we begin the tour?"

Osirus nodded in agreement. "I've traveled many of those worlds," he said. "They are impressive, what with their towering glass skyscrapers and interstellar crafts that travel the infinite space within the pages of a science fiction novel. Inspiring, but I always prefer the eclectic majesty of our great city."

Gideon led them past Sebastian to an aisle of diagnostic machines. He turned back to see Osirus standing over Sebastian's shoulder, watching him fiddle with an engine filament.

"Mr. Poe, I have wondered you ever considered equipping your ships with artillery or weaponry of some sort?"

Sebastian set down his wrench. With a grunt, he got up off his cybernetic knee and stood up in front Osirus, meeting his eyes. "None of my Slipstreams will ever be armed," the mechanic growled. "Not if I have anything to say about it. If they ever are, l will never design or build another one. I do not build gunships anymore."

Osirus stepped back from Sebastian. Gideon hurried over to them. "Yes, my agents use non-lethal means whenever possible to uphold the Raconteurs' Creed of Conduct," he said. "Gunships would go against our primary purpose of not interfering in the internal workings of the Narrative's Story. It's been discussed before and dismissed out of hand." He threw a quick glance at Pahloek Zima.

Pahloek took Gideon's cue to change the subject. "I understand your ships are unique among the flying vessels common in Rogue Destiny, but I have heard what makes them exceptional is the Keyhole device embedded at the front of each ship."

"Yes, the device opens a temporary doorway through the otherwise impenetrable *Word Canopy* that shrouds every world," Gideon informed them. "This allows our agents quick access to the many trouble spots that constantly come up. Before implementing the Keyhole, traveling was entirely on foot from one rabbit-hole to the next."

"How did you come by such technology?" Solis Cicerone asked. "I have never heard of such a capability before. The most advance centers of knowledge throughout the science fictional novels have no such capabilities."

"Idalia Devi designed it," Gideon said. "She worked with us in our early years and helped developed the basic technology. Idalia has the amazing ability of looking at problems from new angles and bending the physical laws of the universe. But eventually we had some disagreements and went our own ways. Her obsessions with the darker aspects of science and alchemy crossed ethical lines that I could not. Our final words to each other were not pleasant."

"Brilliant woman, but terrifying in many respects," Ma Bellamy added. "I met her twice back in the early days. Always got the feeling she was hiding her true intentions behind a pleasant façade, as though what she let you see on the outside was not the person she was on the inside."

Gideon appreciated Ma Bellamy taking the focus off his failed relationship with Idalia. He nodded and gave her a soft smile. The grandmotherly figure winked back at him.

"Wasn't Idalia Devi among those who escaped Lazaranth

prison all those months ago?" Osirus inquired. "I read they are still hunting down the escapees. Claymore Ives was also among the missing."

"Yes, both disappeared at that time," Gideon responded. "But rest assured, I have my finest agents working to unravel the details of the breakout and track down the fugitives. Half their number have been recaptured and returned to their cells inside Lazaranth by my agents. An excellent example of how indispensable we are to the safety of everyone in Rogue Destiny and beyond."

His guests bobbed their heads in agreement. Gideon hid his doubt and anxiety behind a wide smile and continued. He did not want them to see how desperate he was for their support. Their votes would bring support to his cause from the other Council members.

"Our fight has always been against those who would exploit the secrets of our existence for their own gain. Rogue Destiny is the greatest city in creation, but, sadly, it is becoming more corrupt by the day. Since our founding, the Raconteurs have maintained close ties to all previous Protectorate Generals and a majority of council members. But the Common Council has changed, and we no longer hold the influence we once did. Many newer members are less enthused by our work than previous ones. They watch us closely to see if our agents ever step beyond the agreements listed in our charter with the Council."

"Like the unfortunate events involving Claymore Ives?" Osirus asked. "I was there when he was sentenced for the destruction of *The Angels of Avalon*. And his partner, the changeling, Ren B'gatti, was never captured if I remember correctly."

"Ah, I remember that," Astrid replied. "It was dreadful for

everyone involved. I'd met Claymore on several occasions and never thought he could be guilty of such a crime."

Gideon knew the subject would come up at some point. He still struggled with his own acceptance of Claymore's situation.

"That was a dark day for us," Gideon said. "We could never prove Claymore's innocence to the Tribunal. The evidence was inconclusive and any chance of exonerating him was destroyed when the novel burned to dust. Wherever he is, I pray he has found peace. But let me say one thing. The biggest misconception about the Raconteurs is that we interfere with the Narrative's natural progression. Nothing could be farther from the truth. We protect the written worlds and keep them free from the chaos of outside interference. Please understand, Claymore's number one priority is to honor and preserve the sanctity of the *Logos Personae* and their Story. That was why we formed the Raconteurs."

Pahloek turned to address her fellow council members. "That is why we must not let the coming vote go against Gideon and his noble Raconteurs. If those of us here are unable to convince the majority of the Council to renew the Raconteurs' charter, who will continue to protect those who cannot protect themselves?"

"I make it my personal crusade to see the Council continue to pay the commissioned bounties to your agents for the exceptional work they do," Ma Bellamy chimed in. Two small birds fluttered around her, landing on either shoulder. "But times have changed. Gideon and the Raconteurs are seen more and more as a menace by certain council members these days."

"I understand," Gideon said. "That is one of a long list of things I believe the criminal Mordecai Davos is manipulating from the shadows. As our support from the Council wanes, it becomes harder to do our jobs and the criminal element gains ground. Even now, there are rumors that certain factions on the council are attempting to replace the Raconteurs. But they would need our technology first, and that will never happen. That is why I asked for this audience with you today so I could answer questions and assuage any concerns you may have."

Pahloek nodded, her eyes thoughtful. "Rogue Destiny has always been a place of sanctuary for the lost and wandering, those escaping their past and trying to build a new future for themselves. Unfortunately, there are those who have taken advantage of the freedoms Rogue Destiny offers. It's strange that Mordecai Davos, the most powerful criminal in Rogue Destiny, should disappear and risk losing his grip and influence over the mightiest city in the cosmos."

"It is, no doubt, curious." Gideon pulled out his pocket watch. "I want to personally thank you all for your support. It has made a difference since the tragedy that was *The Angels of Avalon*. I believe it is time for lunch. I've had something prepared for us at the Obtuse Turtle." He motioned them toward the large protective storm doors leading to the public house. "After we eat, we'll visit the WayFinder room, and I will show you how we monitor the vastness of the Mythic Cosmos."

Together, the group went up the stairs that led to the Mezzanine landing bay. The heavy doors slid open. Gideon found himself staring at another flying robotic spy, not unlike what he had encountered earlier in his office. The shiny mechanical device was the size his fist and shaped like a hummingbird. The silver drone fluttered in the air just beyond the doorframe. Gideon realized the threat a moment too late and pressed the button to shut the storm doors.

The drone exploded as the doors closed.

Gideon felt himself being lifted off his feet by the concussive force of the explosion. He flew back into something as the ceiling came down on the group. That was all he remembered.

Gideon opened his eyes. He had no idea how much time had passed since the explosion. The pain radiating across his body told him he was still alive. He saw nothing but blackness around him. His head throbbed. He gently touched his temple. A warm liquid oozed down his fingers.

Something heavy pressed on his chest, pinning him in place. He could not take a full breath. Even after his eyes adjusted to the darkness, all he could make out were the geometric shapes of his metal prison. He could not feel his legs.

There was an eerie silence for what seemed hours before he heard the faint sound of muffled voices. The slabs of his twisted metal tomb shifted around him. He took a deep breath, expecting his prison to collapse and crush the life from him. He closed his eyes and waited for the release of death. Instead, a sudden burst of bright light blinded him, and he looked up into the worried face of Bijou Antilles.

"I found him!" Bijou yelled and pulled a broken chunk of metal to the side. "Hurry, he's in pretty bad shape."

Chapter 10
Under a Crimson Sky

Ren stood facing a set of stone stairs carved from the living rock of this new world. The well-worn steps showed signs of frequent use. He followed them up through a rabbit-hole that came out under an ancient, gnarled tree.

He stood under the shade of the massive trunk. Its broad leaves quivered in the light breeze. Despite the damage done to the ley-line connected to it and the barren landscape around it, the tree's foliage had a strong, vibrant sheen.

The mystical *Wayward Trees* mimicked the native forests of the worlds they inhabited. The tree roots grew deep in all directions. Some eventually became ley-lines that would create new rabbit-holes to distant worlds. The more fantastical the Story, the more rabbit-holes grew within its pages. Even the most mundane world had at least a single ley-line running across it.

Ren shaded his eyes against the harsh glare of the red sky and looked out over the hard, flat land. The air was toxic and barely breathable. The heat was intense, and he coughed with each breath. There were no other trees or foliage in sight. He struck out across the dusty plain, following the footsteps in the dust of a well-worn path.

He passed pools of bubbling hot springs that dotted the endless expanse. The noxious sulfur fumes burned his throat. A hot, dry wind blew over the wastelands as he followed the tracks toward a series of low-lying hills in the distance.

Ahead of him, massive, jagged shapes protruded from the ground. As he got closer, they became clearer. He could see they were the half buried remains of massive war machines. They were once towering machines, but now nothing more than tons of twisted, broken metal. It was the graveyard of a great battle that had taken place in the past. The footprints wove through the metal husks.

Dystopian worlds like this were numerous throughout the Mythic Cosmos and while the world around him may have appeared to be in decay, it would never truly die. Every novel existed suspended within its own repeating timeframe. The Story's only purpose was to replay its Narrative over and over again. For the world's inhabitants, such a harsh, unforgiving world was an existence more cruel than death, Ren thought.

The trickster sat down on a piece of metal debris. Walking had not tired him out, but the stale, putrid air had him out of breath long before he should have been. He peeked into a gaping hole blown in the side of the machine of war. The inside was a wreckage of warped metal and shattered internal components. He climbed inside for a closer look. The cooler air made breathing easier, but still nowhere near comfortable.

Among the hanging wires and debris, he saw a mummified corpse. The pilot had been female in life. The dry heat had preserved her features well enough to tell that. She had short, cropped bleached hair, and her dusky skin stretched tight over a sunken face. The upper torso of her corpse sat directly in front of the control console. She was completely embedded in the framework around her, leaving only her torso and head visible.

Wires sprouted from her head and connected to the wall panels behind her.

The war machine seemed to have been piloted by a hybrid of human and machine components. Ren cringed, imaging what it had to feel like being grafted into the pilot seat of the giant machine of death. The thought brought more questions to mind. Had the pilot volunteered, or was her body donated for the task without consent?

Mordecai Davos had been traveling with cyborgs. Ren had dealt two of them, Cyg-Ten and Cyg-Fiver, on the airship *Sky Zephyr* in the steampunk-like world, *The Gaslight Adventures of Asher Grey*. Was this their homeworld? Made sense if it was true.

Ren could understand a conflict between two individuals. He himself was always up for a good rumble to settle an argument between disagreeable parties. What he couldn't comprehend was the concept of armies engaging in battle until one side was reduced to rubble.

There was nothing to show the dead soldier's position or rank or even which side she fought for. Next to her eye, a tattoo baring the serial number *A7-KR26*, was the only thing left identify her. She'd fought for a cause and died doing her duty for king and country. And what had it gotten her? Not much in Ren's mind. She would be forever entombed in a mausoleum of twisted metal on a desolate wasteland.

Ren searched the wreckage for anything that would protect his skin from the brutal sun. He found nothing. The torso of the corpse wore a military-looking jumpsuit. Her day wasn't going any better than his, and it would have felt like graverobbing if he cut it off her. Even he had his limits with desecrating the dead.

He'd been walking naked in the scorching heat for over two hours. His back and shoulders, as well as the more delicate parts of his body, were deeply sunburned. The skin of his face felt tight from exposure. His parched throat made it hard to swallow. He licked his cracked lips and tried to ignore his blistered bare feet.

The burns on his skin would heal quickly enough once he got out of the sun. What concerned him more was the possible exposure to unseen radiation. Past experience told him this type of world screamed that possibility, the waves either rising from the charred ground or from the mechanical wreckage he now stood in. It didn't think it would kill him, but it might slow any attempts to morph his shape.

A spindly legged insect slowly crawled up the wall to the edge of the hole. The long legs moved robotically across the surface of the charred metal. Its tiny antennae felt the way forward like a blind man tapping a cane. The bug was the only sign of indigenous life Ren had seen so far in the harsh waste-land. It was a survivor. Taking life as it came and rolling with the punches. Like him.

Ren put his finger out and let the insect crawl onto his hand to get a better look at the eyeless face. The long-legged insect crawled on the end of his fingertips, feelers reaching out for him. A thick carapace on its back split open and four delicate wings spread out. The bug lifted into the air. He watched it disappear through the gaping hole in the machine's wall.

Ren climbed out of the wreckage and ripped down a tattered banner from a pole attached to the machine. There was a styl-ized symbol of a scorpion on the thick cloth with words written in language he did not understand. Ren wrapped it over his head and his shoulders and continued on blistered feet through the graveyard of fallen war machines.

Soon he reached the low-lying hills he had seen earlier and trudged up the slope to the crest of a ridge. He found himself overlooking two great refineries, cradled in a desolate valley between two higher mountain ranges. Their smokestacks belched black fumes and soot into the red sky. There was a stale taste on the wind, the smell of ash and chemicals. Death filled the air. A large convoy of giant mechanical war machines and military transports moved along a wide roadway away from the factory.

To the east, in the facility's shadow, a cluster of twenty or more tents crowded together in a makeshift camp. Ren stood next to a patch of scrub brush and watched the movement around the tents. Convinced he'd found the hideout of the man he had chased halfway across the Mythic Cosmos, his spirits rose for the first the time since the ley-line collapsed and they'd lost Tempest.

He heard shouts and turned to see two armed sentries climbing the incline toward him. One was a woman and the other a man. He ducked down, but it was too late. He watched them through the brush as they drew closer. They stopped some fifty paces from where he hid and raised their weapons. Both had hoods pulled up, and each wore a breathing apparatus over their faces with a tube connected to a round canister on their belts.

Ren pulled the war banner down over him, shifting into the insect he had met in the graveyard of war machines. Long, spindly legs carried him quickly through the thick sage brush away from under the banner. The strain on his body was almost unbearable. Under ideal conditions, the trickster could hold a small shape for some time. But with the punishment his body had taken crossing the wasteland and the toxic air making breathing such an effort, he could barely hold on to the form.

"You in the bushes?" the man ordered. The face mask amplified his voice, and his words were clear and understandable. "Come out with your hands up."

Ren skittered behind a clump of stones to protect himself from what he knew was coming next. The sentries opened fire into the colorful war banner. Bullets shredded the banner and debris struck the dirt and rocks around him. The firing stopped seconds later, and he poked his tiny insect head over the stone.

The big man stomped forward and grabbed the shredded banner off the ground. "Where the hell'd he go?" he spat. Both looked around the open ground, confused by how their target disappeared before their eyes.

"You check over there, Domica," the big man said pointing to their right.

"I'm on it," Domica answered. "He has to be here somewhere." The two split up. The woman passed the spot where Ren hid, her boots crunching on the rocky ground. He climbed up a small branch to the top and flexed the carapace on his back. It slid apart, revealing four small wings. They buzzed to life at his command, and he lifted off the twig, flying in an erratic pattern through the air after the sentry.

Ren glanced back at the man headed in the opposite direction. Once the other sentry moved down the ridge and out of sight, he shifted back into his actual form and dropped on Domica. His bare foot hit the woman solidly in the back, hurling her forward to the hard ground. Ren dove on top of her, ripped her breathing mask off, and grabbed her in a chokehold. He held her tight until she stopped struggling.

Ren pulled off her boots off and within a couple of minutes, he dressed himself in her pants, shirt, and boots, then buckled her gun belt on. He slipped the mask over his face and enjoyed the first rush of fresh oxygen since he had left the rabbit-hole. With a boot, he rolled the woman over to look at her face. He didn't recognize her from his short time among Mordecai's lackeys in the world of Asher Grey. He studied the unconscious woman and shifted his own appearance to mirror hers perfectly.

Next thing was to hide the body. He knew he should snap her neck to prevent her from wandering back to camp after she woke up, but he couldn't bring himself to do it. He thought about what the other Raconteurs would do if faced with this situation. Neither Medesto nor Natascha ever killed a defenseless person, no matter who they were or who they worked for. Claymore had, but Ren refused to think about that.

He tied her hands behind her back with her suspenders, and pushed her down a shallow ravine. She would be hidden from sight as he contemplated his next move. Ren pulled the hood up and looked around for her larger companion. He came over the rise a moment later.

"Find anything?" he called out.

Ren shook his head and strode toward the man to keep from seeing his unconscious companion.

"We'll need to notify somebody about this," the other said. "After what happened in the Steampunk world, we can't take any chances that we're being tracked."

Ren smiled to himself and nodded, continuing to pretend to search the area for their quarry. Together, the two made their way along the steep, uneven incline to the camp below. The larger man waved to the sentries as they approached.

"We heard the gunshots, Baaklow," the guard asked. "You see anyone?" He wore the same type of breathing mask the others did and shifted the long gun on his shoulder.

"Not that we could find, Godi," Baaklow replied. "We searched the area, but came across no one. Keep an eye out, 'cause I know there was someone up there."

"We'll have the Wolf sniff them out," Godi suggested. "Could be an enemy spy from one of the Four Armies, or maybe a Raconteur tracked us through the rabbit-hole."

"It's doubtful any of the Raconteurs survived," Baaklow growled. "Not when you burn the world out from under them."

The guard agreed, scanning the hills above them. "Then it had to be a local."

"My shift's over," Baaklow growled. "I'm going to get some sleep." He strode away without another word. The remaining sentry, Godi, wandered off in the other direction. Ren watched them leave with a smile. Now he was free to explore the camp.

Chapter 11
Spies Among Us

The first thing Ren needed to do was find out if *The Book of Days* had indeed been found. If it had, he would simply take it from whoever had it and then search the camp for Claymore. Once he found his partner, he would locate the nearest rabbit-hole and get them out of this dystopian Story.

He made his way through the maze of tents, looking for anything that would give him a clue of where the *Book* might be hidden. Mordecai Davos' most trusted advisor was Tomas Demarche. From what Ren had witnessed, Tomas had been solely responsible for piecing together the writings of Harper Bellweather and getting the crime lord this far in his quest. It made sense that if anyone had *The Book of Days*, it would be either of them.

The largest of the tents had a stovepipe chimney coughing smoke into the hazy air. His stomach growled at the smell of food coming from the enclosed structure. It reminded him it had been too long since he had last eaten. Shapeshifting burned an excessive amount of calories and that, combined with the harsh environment, had him feeling fatigued. He headed toward the scent, hoping to find something edible. The tent flap flew open as he approached. A stocky man fitted his facemask over his nose and mouth and pulled his hood up against the heat.

Ren entered the dining hall tent, removing his mask and pulling his hood back. The air smelled of overcooked meat and blanched vegetables. The tables were half filled with an assortment of motley looking people, maybe a dozen in all. He scanned the room for Claymore but didn't see him anywhere.

The line for food was empty, so Ren grabbed a tray and plate. A heavy set man stood behind steaming metal dishes heaped with chunks of scorched meat and strange looking vegetables. He slopped a spoonful of each on Ren's plate as he moved down the counter.

At the end was a basket of hard bread and a barrel of questionable-looking water. He dipped a ladle in and filled a cup with water, then searched for a place to sit where he could listen in on the conversations around him. There were answers he needed, and people loved to gossip about what they knew.

Ren chose a table next to two men talking at a spirited volume. He recognized one of them from the bookseller's shop in Asher Grey's world. He had been called Verdugo by those at the table. That meant he was a survivor of the massacre that took place under the pawnshop. The other man had a scarred face that had left him with a lazy right eye. Ren listened in on their conversation as he took a bite of his food. The meat was tough as leather and almost impossible to chew.

"I'm so sick of this place," Verdugo said. 'I'm fed up with the heat and foul air." He tossed a half-eaten piece of bread onto his plate and leaned into the other man. "And the food's terrible. I'm tempted to just leave. You should come with me. There's a rabbit-hole only a few miles from here. We can avoid any War Golem patrols and be off-world by tonight."

"The boss would never allow that," Lazy Eye replied. "He'll send the Wolf after us, like he does all deserters." He lifted his head to see if anyone had heard them. His eyes stopped on Ren, but the trickster pretended to be looking down at his food.

"You're probably right, but I'd rather face the Wolf out in the open than those creeping shadows in the dark. You're lucky you weren't there."

Ren looked over the two men. "I heard about that," he said innocently. "So you were in the attack under the pawnshop back in the horror novel where the shadows moved?"

Verdugo glanced back at the trickster with suspicion. His face broke into a yellow toothed smile when he realized a woman had spoken. He jumped at the chance to tell his Story of survival to anyone who would listen. It had been a while since Ren had taken the disguise of a female. He had learned long ago that using feminine charms made extracting information from soft-headed males easy.

"Won't you join us, Domica?" Verdugo offered.

Ren smiled back. "Everyone's talking about it." He picked up his plate and glass, and joined the two men at their table. Lazy Eye shook his head and went back to eating, having heard the tale too many times already.

"That must have been terrifying," Ren said. He knew the fastest way to get someone talking was to appeal to their ego. He put a hand on the man's sleeve. "How'd you survive such horrifying creatures?"

"We lost quite a few down there in the dark, let me tell you," Verdugo muttered, almost to himself. "Saw people ripped apart right in front of me by the very shadows around us." He eyed his plate with a shudder, then caught himself and straightened his posture with a renewed bravado that wasn't there a moment before.

"The killing shadows wouldn't go near the Grimm Jester," Verdugo continued. "So I stayed close to Mordecai and his pet. It was the safest place down in that slaughterhouse. Mordecai didn't care a whit about any of us. He grabbed Tomas and left us to die. I followed them through the darkness back to the stairs. I yelled for Redi, Godard and Kley to come with me, 'cause we had to take care of ourselves. Only the four of us made it out."

At the mention of the name the Grimm Jester, Ren choked on a bite of stale bread. He took a gulp of rancid water to swallow but it still felt like sharp shards of glass going down his throat. He'd come face to face with the Jester in a dark back alley in Rogue Destiny only a few days before. The monster had saved him from torture and certain death at the hands Mordecai's gangsters, and the creature told Ren to be in its debt.

Ren had been present when Mordecai sent the Grimm Jester off to accompany Claymore on some secret task. If the Jester found out Ren was now in camp, it meant the personification of Death would call in that debt. But that also meant Claymore was back in camp.

"That was brilliant," Ren said regaining his composure.

"Yes, it was," Verdugo added with a toothy smile. "But it showed me Mordecai couldn't care less about those who died, and those of us who are still alive. We're all just pawns in some greater game he's playing. Only useful to him until we're not and then we're discarded like old boots. Mordecai cares only for his prize."

"Does that mean Mordecai's found what he's been looking for?"

"Wouldn't know anything about that," Verdugo spat. "Mordecai was all too pleased with himself when we got back to camp. He and Tomas have been holed up in his tent under heavy guard since we returned. And from what I'm hearing there's no plans to continue digging through more archives in the immediate future. But that don't bode well for those of us who have been loyal from the beginning, does it? That mean he has no use for us now?"

"I hear you," Ren interjected. "Does anyone know what we've been looking for?"

"A book," Lazy Eye said. "Not about any world, but one that's connected to the origins of Rouge Destiny itself."

Verdugo dropped his fork on the plate. "That's all the food I can choke down," he snarled. "I'm going to catch some sleep before I'm back on guard duty."

Things were finally breaking his way Ren thought. The last time he had infiltrated Mordecai Davos' band of outlaws, things did not end well. This time would be different. Ren put his oxygen mask on and left the dining tent. *The Book of Days* was somewhere in the camp, and he needed to find it.

Chapter 12
Eye for an Eye

Ren pushed the tent flap out of his way and stepped into the burning heat of an apocalyptic world. He adjusted the oxygen mask that allowed him to breathe in the harsh environment. A blood red sunset over the barren mountains to the west. In the distance, the sound of cannons and explosions filled the twilight sky. He walked across the camp, keeping an eye out for Claymore, passing drums of burning oil and armed sentries.

A sizeable crowd gathered at the center of the encampment. Ren pushed to the front to see the cause of the commotion. Mordecai Davos stood in-between two opposing groups of armed onlookers. Behind him, Ren saw many faces from Asher Grey's world. The rough group looked hungry for a fight.

Next to Mordecai, the cyborg, Silium Cinque Niner, stood engaged in an exchange of tense words with a cyborg in a similar military uniform.

"But, General Bartacchi, if you will only let me explain," Silium said.

"Silence!" the General ordered. "We warned you about getting behind on the tribute payments promised for our allegiance. You told us time and again how you were getting closer to this item you seek. Yet now the tribute you promised our Glorious Supreme Leader is due and you claim you are only able to pay a portion of it." He shook the backpack. The jingling coins broke the tense silence.

Mordecai glanced at the ground and nodded in agreement. Behind him, what remained of his motley crew of escaped prisoners stood. Across from them, the cyber-soldiers backing up the military general outnumbered Mordecai's outlaws two to one. The tension in the air was thick as both sides stared each other down.

Ren noticed a giant red War Golem standing motionless beyond the tents of the camp. Smoke streamed out of the two smokestacks jutting from its back. Massive cannons had replaced both arms on the twenty-foot-tall, bipedal war machine. A bright vertical banner of black and blue rippled in the light wind. The middle of the narrow flag featured the symbol of a desert scorpion. Ren glanced around to find three more war machines stationed at key points outside the camp.

Fire blazed up from two oil drums, distorting the shapes of the speakers on the surrounding tents. The large, unmistakable silhouette of the Grimm Jester floated in the growing shadows behind Mordecai. A tattered cloak and hood gave the monster form, but only a grinning jaw that jutted from under the hood was visible.

Mordecai looked up at the officer, his expression full of regret. "I understand I have grieved the Glorious Supreme Leader, General Bartacchi," he said. "I only wish to make amends if I can. My people have just returned from a faraway place with an item that will be of great importance to you and your cause. If the Great Leader would honor me with an audience, I shall present him with a weapon beyond any he could imagine. Something that will win this eternal war once and for all."

The general seemed intrigued by the offer. "If what you say is true, then I am sure we can come to some sort of arrangement regarding your lack of tribute. His Eminence is currently with his War Council, or he would have been here in person. I will present your offer to him and let you know if he wishes to see you. If he rejects this offer, we will immediately withdraw our military support, and order you to leave our territory."

"Thank you, General," Mordecai replied. "I will wait to hear from you."

"There is a second matter we need to discuss," the general said, his face an emotionless mask of flesh and metal. "Five of our soldiers died while under your command. Their deaths are tragic enough, but you did not even have the decency to return their bodies to their soil of birth. Now they will not rise again. You have robbed them of their dignity and denied them their destiny to continue in the sacred war of their ancestors. There must be recompense for our loss."

Ren didn't know what *rise again* meant. By the look on Mordecai's face, the criminal also understood the seriousness of the accusations made by the military officer.

"Again, I can only beg the Supreme Leader's forgiveness," Mordecai replied. He bent down on one knee and bowed in humility. "I understand the death of these soldiers is a loss of resources to your Great Cause. And as a show of my remorse, I volunteer five of my best people to replace those lost."

A wave of murmuring conversation swept through Mordecai's followers. On General Bartacchi's side of the circle, the cybernetic soldiers remained motionless, weapons held at the ready. Ren realized it was too late to leave without bringing attention to himself. Out of the corner of his eye, he saw Verdugo and Lazy Eye exit the food tent. They noticed Ren standing in the gathered crowd and wandered over.

"What's all this, Domica?" Verdugo asked.

"I'm not sure," Ren answered in Domica's voice. "But it doesn't look good."

Mordecai turned his attention to the line of followers, eyeing each one in turn. Ren counted twenty-two, including himself.

"Tadeuz, step forward, please," Mordecai requested calmly. A thin man in an oversized coat standing down the line from Ren looked around with a confused look on his face. Those on either side of Tadeuz shoved him forward into the makeshift circle, happy to offer him as sacrifice to the cyborgs rather than themselves.

"Thank you, Tadeuz," Mordecai replied. "Sabo, Genevi and Mattias, please join us up here." Two men and a woman stepped out to stand beside Tadeuz. At Mordecai's prompting, his bodyguards collected any weapons the new recruits carried.

"There is still a need for one more," General Bartacchi replied.

Ren held his breath, waiting for Mordecai to make his final choice. He averted his gaze to the small apparatus on his belt, pretending he was having trouble with his breathing mask.

"Verdugo?" Mordecai requested. "Please step forward, if you would."

"I don't think so!" Verdugo replied. He pushed his way into the crowd. Those around him grabbed his arms and pulled him back to the front. Verdugo's body stiffened, like he was gathering the courage to run. The Grimm Jester drifted to his master's side. The outlaw breathed a deep sigh.

"Well, I guess this is goodbye, Domica." Verdugo muttered through his mask. "Watch yourself. I told you we've outlived our usefulness."

"I will," Ren answered. Actual remorse for the slovenly dressed man hit Ren squarely in the stomach. He did not know Verdugo's fate, but assumed from what he had witnessed so far, whatever lay ahead for these *volunteers* would not be pleasant.

Ren patted the condemned man on the shoulder as he shuffled into the circle to join the others.

Someone from behind Ren shouted, "Good luck!" Laughter erupted at the crude remark.

Mordecai gave a grim smile to General Bartacchi. "There you are, General. Five volunteers to take the place of those who have died. Do with them as you will."

"Thank you, Mr. Davos. If you'll excuse me now," Bartacchi said with a slight bow. "I will send word if our Glorious Supreme Leader wishes to meet."

"Please assure him, he will not be disappointed," Mordecai replied.

The cybernetic general lumbered on legs of iron and alloy back to his military transport. Once aboard, he waved a hand, and the half-tracked vehicle drove through the camp. The entourage of cybernetic foot soldiers surrounded their five new recruits and escorted them after their leader.

Once the officer and his soldiers had left the area, the war machines turned toward the factories south of the camp. The ground trembled underfoot as they passed.

A murmur of unrest swept through the remaining number of Mordecai's followers. Small conversations sprang up among two or three people at a time. Ren did not join in.

Mordecai raised his hands. "My friends and fellow travelers!" he shouted to those left. "We are in the final leg of our quest. Do not lose focus on why we have come this far. Soon we will return to the accursed city of Rogue Destiny and take what we are owed! I ask for your patience and cooperation for a short time more."

The cluster of weary faces looked back at Mordecai. His words seemed to have little effect on lifting their spirits. Ren searched the assembled crowd again for Claymore. His partner was nowhere to be seen. As the people dispersed around him,

Ren saw Mordecai motion Tomas over. The two spoke in hushed tones. Ren strolled past them, close enough to catch parts of their conversation.

"Yes, I am certain this time," Tomas said in a defensive voice. "I have cross-referenced every bit of information she wrote in her journals, and I am convinced I know where she's hiding."

"And this is not another dead end?" Mordecai huffed.

Tomas gave a nervous cough to clear his throat. "Her writings mention an abandoned hideaway she stumbled across in her travels. The specific location is not mentioned, but I believe I've narrowed it down. It is the last place anyone would think to look."

"And you are certain of this?" Mordecai replied.

"You trusted me to lead you to *The Book of Days*, and I did. Trust me on this. Even if the lodestones aren't there, Harper Bellweather most likely is. If we find her, we can have the Jester persuade her to reveal where the stones are hidden."

"Very well, we will go there," Mordecai hissed through clenched teeth. "Where is this secret sanctuary located?"

Ren cocked his head to hear the location of Harper's hideaway, but the voices stopped. He turned to see Mordecai and Tomas staring at him.

"Can we help you, Domica?" Mordecai asked. His eyes narrowed. His gaunt face masked a seething anger beneath the surface. Ren listened so intently to the co-conspirators, he hadn't realized he had stopped walking. Behind Mordecai, the Grimm Jester shifted his gaze toward him.

"No...um...," Ren stammered. "There's a problem with my breathing equipment. I think there's a leak in my tube." He adjusted the plastic facemask covering his mouth and nose, then ran his fingers down the narrow tube to the filtration box on his belt, fidgeting with it to appear he was fixing some problem.

"Very well then," Mordecai replied. "Back to your duties."

Ren nodded to them before melding into the flow of the crowd. He could feel the Grimm Jester's unseen gaze on him as he disappeared around the corner of the first tent he came to. He broke into a run to circle back.

By the time Ren found a new vantage point to spy on Mordecai, the crime lord had ended his conversation with Tomas. Each man went their own way, shadowed by an armed guard. The Grimm Jester drifted alongside his master until they disappeared from sight among the tents.

Tomas carried the satchel he'd had with him in the bookseller's shop when Ren first infiltrated the outlaw gang. He and his guard made their way through the camp. Ren followed them, keeping a comfortable distance between them.

Ren passed by the largest tent in the camp, set back from the others. The sound of inhuman noises emanated from it. The stench of animals filled the air. He assumed it was where they sheltered the nonhuman minions that accompanied the mysterious lady in black. A smaller tent sat next to it. Several armed guards stood watch. Ren could only assume that the criminals stored the portal machine used to jump between worlds inside.

Tomas entered a tent at the south end of the camp. He entered while his bodyguard remained outside with a rifle resting on a shoulder. Beyond the tents, the smokestacks of the factory belched smoking ash into the darkening red sky.

As night descended, streaks of red and orange blazed across the sky. Twin crescent moons hung over a backdrop of cascading stars. The sun had fallen behind the horizon, but the temperatures remained hot and stifling.

Vibrations under Ren's feet had ceased. He glanced up to see the banner of a War Golem blowing in the harsh wind at the crest of the hill. The march of the great war machines had stopped. Curiosity got the better of him. Ren stole beyond the cover of the encampment and hid under the shadowed eave of the last tent.

Fifty yards from him, in the red glow of the setting sun, Ren watched someone run from the column across the barren wasteland. Even at that distance, he recognized the man. Verdugo had decided to make a vain attempt at freedom, after all.

A single gunshot echoed down the valley. Verdugo crashed to the ground in a splatter of blood. A soldier from the military convoy lowered his rifle and strode out to the body. He fired two more shots into the lifeless body. A second soldier joined him, pulling a nozzle and hose from the canister strapped to his belt. He sprayed a white foam over the corpse in copious amounts until it completely covered the body. The soldiers stepped back as the thick, foamy substance expanded into a hazy, elliptical bubble. The remains of Verdugo floated inside. Both soldiers lifted the entombed body and carried it to the waiting convoy.

General Bartacchi observed the scene play out with indifference. Once the soldiers had loaded the body into the back of his transport, he motioned the column forward. The soldiers fell in line and, with the War Golems, continued on as if nothing out of the ordinary had happened. The hard earth shook as the convoy continued on its way to the factory.

Ren watched the strange ritual play out. Why was Verdugo's body preserved and taken with them? Is that how they found new soldiers to fight in their sacred war? He wondered how long before the other four volunteers met the same fate as Verdugo.

Ren walked back to camp, not quite comprehending what he had just witnessed. He sat down on a bench to try and make sense out of it. Wounded soldiers could be rebuilt as cyborgs. He had dealt with two of them in the past and they had proved quite lethal. What use could this Supreme Leader have for the corpses of the dead?

He was deep in thought when a silhouetted figure walked up

to Tomas' tent carrying a tray of food with a bottle of wine. Ren could not make out the face of the person in the dim moonlight. It was the cook in the greasy apron who worked in the kitchen tent. The guard took him inside the tent. Moments later, the cook left with the empty tray under an arm, and the guard returned to his post, chomping down on a thick sandwich.

Chapter 13
Reunions

The sentry paid no attention to Ren as he walked past the entrance of Tomas' tent. He remained hidden behind the face of Domica and continued down the path before ducking between a row of canvas tents. Silently, he crept back through the shadows to the backside of the shelter.

A large squat air filter machine sat outside the windowless tent to purify the environment inside. Its loud hum would cover any noise he might make. He kicked off Domica's boots and unbuckled her gun belt, dropping it to the ground. Pulling off his shirt and pants, the trickster stood naked in the pale moonlight. He took one long breath of air from his mask before pulling it off his face.

With a focused thought, he morphed into the tiny spindly legged insect he had seen in the wasteland. His perspective of the world around him changed. The canvas tent grew to gigantic proportions. Ren climbed up the side of the chugging air purifier to a small opening between the canvas stitching and the machine.

He skittered through the hole along the floor until he was underneath a small wooden table. The only light came from an oil lamp hanging from the center of the room. From his low vantage point, Ren could not see much, but caught the soft sound of someone snoring. High above him, he could make out the hazy silhouette of a cot and a pair of stocking feet dangling over the side. That had to be Tomas. One foot twitched like he was dreaming.

Ren listened to the slow, rhythmic breathing coming from the bed. Once he was satisfied, Tomas would not interrupt him, he crawled from under the table and shifted back to his natural size.

The fully clothed form of Tomas lay sprawled out on the cot. Mordecai's advisor still wore his shoes and suit jacket. He appeared to be passed out drunk, tangled in his bedding. On the three-legged table next to him was a large tray filled with breads and meats and fruits and nuts. A single bite had been taken from a sandwich. A goblet of dark liquid sat next to a bottle of wine. The only sounds were the quiet snoring and rattle of the air filtering equipment.

Ren searched for *The Book of Days*. He had no idea how long he had before Tomas might wake up or someone entered the tent. The leather satchel Tomas carried with him lay on the table. Ren looked through it, but only found maps and more of Harper Bellweather's traveling journals. Her connection to all of this was still a mystery. A makeshift book shelf sat in one corner, made from scraps of lumber and cinderblocks. He searched through books lined up on the shelves, but none of them were the one he searched for.

Tomas appeared to play a crucial role in Mordecai's search for the ancient book. The scholar had his own tent and seemed to be left alone to work on deciphering Harper's journals. He ate well too. Ren's stomach growled. He took a handful of nuts to nibble on while he continued his search. They were spicy and salty. It made him realize how hungry he still was.

The thought struck Ren that maybe they hadn't found *The Book of Days*. He went back and grabbed a handful of spiced sweetmeat and fruit, stuffing them in his mouth. He chewed as he thought about his options. There were not a lot of places to hide anything in the cramped tent. He dug through a footlocker at the end of the cot, but there was nothing inside but clothing. Maybe the book wasn't even here. Or maybe Mordecai had it with him. Frustrated, he picked at the food on the tray some more.

A loud snuffling sound brought him around. Outside, the shadow of a great hunchbacked beast moved along the edge of the tent, sniffing the ground. It stopped at the air purifying machine where Ren had crawled through. The fur on its back bristled. A huge furry muzzle poked under the tent, nostrils flexing. A deep growl emanating from beyond the canvass wall. Ren knelt in the shadows.

As quickly as it began, the sniffing stopped, and the snout disappeared from view. Ren assumed it was the wolf he had heard the two guards mentioned earlier.

He glanced back at the table in the middle of the room. It was piled with journals and notebooks. All were slim volumes similar to the ones in the satchel. He flipped the top one open.

Handwritten notes filled the pages next to maps and diagrams of various types of landscapes. The writing had no organization to it, just hastily scribbled words recounting the observations the author, Harper Bellweather, made. He dug through the stacks of books, but didn't find what he sought.

His bare foot kicked up loose dirt next to the woven rug under the table. The rest of the floor was hard and cracked from heat and the harsh environment. He knelt and lifted the corner of the rug revealing an area of loosely packed dirt. Something was buried beneath the table.

Ren moved the table and chairs, rolled the rug up. He

scooped out the loose, dry earth with both hands until his fingers hit something solid. He pulled a small piece of plywood from under the dirt and saw a large flat package wrapped in brown paper.

The parcel was the size Ren imagined *The Book of Days* to be. Overcome with a wave of excitement, he untied the string around the bundle and ripped the paper open. He stared with an amused grin at the black embossed letters on a crimson background. The title simply read:

The Book of Days
An Apologist's Argument for the Founding of Rogue Destiny
A Brief History of My City, My Life and My Writings
By Baltazaar Gheddi

He found his fingers trembling a bit as he brushed dirt from the thick book. He thumbed through the first few pages. The words were handwritten in a bold, stylized calligraphy, every letter precise and carefully placed upon the paper. Hand-drawn illustrations painted in colorful hues adorned every third page. Besides being one of the greatest historical artifacts in recorded history, the tome was a work of art in itself. He grabbed another piece of meat from the tray and slowly chewed it as he flipped through the thick pages, flicking the crumbs off as he read.

"So this is what Mordecai had been tearing up worlds to find," he thought. Now the book was his. He only had to find Claymore, so together they could leave this place and return to the Raconteurs as heroes.

The quick perusal of the book Ren showed the highlights of Baltazaar Gheddi's early life in the royal court of his homeworld, Roskashon, then his rise to power as he became the greatest sorcerer his world had ever known. As a young adult, he overthrew his corrupt uncle to become the supreme protector of his kingdom.

Ren picked up a tin cup of water from the table and drained it. It was a start to quenching his parched throat and dry mouth. He spied a goblet next to the bed. Swirling the dark liquid around, he guessed it would be this world's equivalent of wine.

He lifted the goblet to drink when he heard whispered voices outside the entrance to the tent and saw slanted shadows moving across the doorway. He put the glass down and left *The Book of Days* where it was. Ren scanned the enclosed tent, but there was nowhere to hide. He dropped to the dirt floor and transformed back to the insect. He darted into the shadows under the cot as the tent flap flew open.

The silhouette of a tall, broad-shouldered man slipped inside, followed by Tomas' guard. The man put a finger to his lips and pointed at the cot, his face hidden by the shadows. There was no movement from the sleeping Tomas. The two men spoke in hushed whispers. Ren strained to hear their conversation through the tiny auditory orifice of the insect.

"You're right," the guard whispered. "He's dead asleep. You have ten minutes. Just as we agreed." He remained near the entrance to the tent, peering outside.

The taller man moved into the light of the small oil lantern. Ren recognized the confident demeanor and striking features instantly.

Claymore Ives.

The sentry grabbed Claymore by the arm. "My payment?" he said too loudly. Ren waited for the noise to rouse Tomas, but he did not stir an inch.

Claymore pulled out a small leather pouch from his back pocket. "Of course," he said. "It's all there." The guard unzipped the pouch and slid several gold bars into his hand. Each measured a couple of inches. The gold glinted off the lantern's glow. He returned them to the pouch, and slipped it inside his jacket.

"Ten minutes," he whispered. "No more."

"Thanks, Ruddy." Claymore patted the guard on the shoulder.

"Yeah, yeah. Just take me with when you leave," Ruddy grunted. "And don't get us killed before that." He pushed open the flap of the tent.

A rumbling growl erupted outside the tent door. A massive shape burst through the opening. Before Ruddy could cry out, a mouthful of gleaming teeth sank into the man's throat. A moment later, the Wolf lifted its bloodied jaw. Ruddy's body lay limp on the ground. The beast turned on Claymore.

"Claymore Ives?" the Wolf snarled. The hair on the beast's hunched- back stood on end. "No one is to be near Tomas or his tent. Not even you." The monster sniffed the air around Claymore. "But you are not the one I followed here."

Claymore relaxed his shoulders, and a wry grin came to his face. Ren knew that disarming smile. His partner liked to act as if he was in complete control of any situation the moment before everything exploded in chaos. He had told Ren long ago that was how you stayed alive. No matter what odds were against you, never let them think they can beat you in a fight. He claimed it was an attitude that had gotten him through every life and death circumstance he had ever faced.

"So, who were you following?" Claymore said, adjusting his gun belt.

The Wolf paced the small confines of the tent, its black eyes never leaving Claymore. "The one who came down from the hills," he growled. "The one who looks like someone he is not."

"Really?" Claymore replied, raising a quizzical eyebrow.

"There is a spy in the camp," the Wolf rumbled deep in his throat. "I have caught whiffs of him on the breeze. He has been among us before. I was told to find and kill the interloper, along with any who are not where they are supposed to be. Like you."

"Then let me help you find this spy," Claymore replied calmly. He clenched his right hand until the knuckles cracked. It was his personal *tell* that he was about to draw down on someone. He touched the handle of his holstered revolver. A foot-long knife in a leather sheath was attached to the other side of his belt. Over his right shoulder, Ren could see the butt of a saw-offed Winchester rifle. The shortened handle wrapped in tape.

"I tracked the intruder to this tent, but all I find is you." The Wolf pushed himself up on his haunches, then stood on his hind legs. His head brushed the tent ceiling as he sniffed the air. He loomed over Claymore, pointing down to Ruddy's body with a long, razor-sharp claw. "Do not attempt to draw your weapon, or you will die too."

"I'm sure we can work something out here," Claymore said. He put his hands up.

Without warning, the Wolf leapt. Claymore went for the pistol at his hip. The revolver cleared the holster, but the beast knocked it away with a swipe of a massive claw. The gun flew from his hand, and Claymore threw a forearm into the beast's neck to block its bloody teeth from reaching him. The two crashed to the floor, Claymore disappearing under a mass of fur.

Still in his insect form, Ren scuttled out from under the cot before he realized what he was doing. Adrenaline and rage took over as he ran to his friend's aid. He shifted, first into a house cat, and leapt to the table, then vaulted himself into the air toward the Wolf.

In midair, he morphed from the small feline into the monstrous crater-ape he had used to intimidate Tempest. He landed on the back of the Wolf and wrapped his upper two arms around the beast's thick neck. With the terrifying strength of the ape pulsing through his limbs, he tore the beast off Claymore.

Ape and Wolf rolled across the floor in a tangle of fur and limbs. Ren tightened his hold on the Wolf's throat to keep the snapping jaws at bay. His lower arms pinned the front legs against its body to prevent the monstrous talons from gutting him.

The Wolf was incredibly strong. It thrashed in Ren's grip, but the trickster held him fast with all four arms. The beast roared and slammed Ren back against the air purifying machine, trying to dislodge him.

The impact knocked the air from Ren's lungs, leaving him momentarily stunned. His concentration broke for only a heartbeat, but he felt his control over the crater-ape's shape faltered.

In a final desperate effort, the trickster braced his legs. The monster's foul breath hit him full in the face. Ren forced the Wolf's head back with all the strength left in him. He felt the grisly crack of bone and sinew under his grip and the Wolf's body went limp in his arms.

Ren pushed the lifeless beast away from him. Pain shot through him as he stood up. He glanced down at the deep slash across his white abdomen and grey fur where the beast's claw had caught him during their struggle. The Wolf lay at his feet in a pile of contorted limbs and fur. Its glassy eyes were half opened but there was no life in them. Ren let go of his hold on the eight-foot, multi-limbed crater-ape and slipped back to his true self.

His chest heaved as Ren caught his breath. The size and mass of the ape was difficult to maintain under perfect conditions. Fighting the Wolf, left him exhausted and out of breath. He looked up to find Claymore's pistol in his face. Blood dripped from a nasty gash on his partner's hand from the Wolf's attack. Ren threw his hands out in front of himself, hoping he wouldn't be shot before his partner recognized him.

"Claymore, don't! It's me!" he sputtered. "It's me!"

Distant eyes stared at him without any glint of recognition. Claymore was a crack shot and would never miss at this distance. The trickster froze. His partner's dark eyes narrowed for several heartbeats. Ren was not sure if he was about to die at the hand of his close friend. He braced for the gunshot that would bring the whole camp down on them. It never came.

The gun barrel quivered slightly, then slowly Claymore's eyes returned to sanity. He released the hammer on the revolver and lowered it. A familiar wry grin curled up at the corner of his lips.

"Ren B'gatti!" Claymore said and holstered his pistol. "What the hell are you doing here?"

Chapter 14
The Road Home

Medesto sat huddled with Natascha and Raffles in the hollow of the dead ley-line. No one had spoken for some time. Raffles laid back with his back against a chunk of debris. Charley stood off from the others, staring at the floor, her eyes red from crying.

He stared into the rabbit-hole leading back into the horror world of Bree Sandoval. An ominous wind continued to echo from the opening. The hairs on the nape of his neck stood up. He imagined the Muse returning, leaving them with nowhere to run but into the dark abyss of the Void to suffer the same fate as Tempest. He did not voice his concerns to the others.

In a heartbeat, the Raconteurs' situation had shifted from a momentary sense of relief to the possibility of a horrific death. The Muse and Her minions may have been the most terrifying monsters Medesto had gone up against. The experience of having the impersonal essence of a Story attempt to kill him was something he would not soon forget. He suppressed a shudder, took a breath, and returned to the problem at hand.

"What if the Muse comes back?" Charley whispered, voicing

the gnome's fear. She looked around at the tight confines of the broken tunnel. "We'd have nowhere to go."

"She won't be back," Raffles replied confidently. He sat up and scratched under his chin with a paw. "Da Muse bound ta Her Story, trapped inside it pages. All da rage and anger She can muster don't change dat. Da blast o' wind was just one last desperate effort to git at us. But steppin' out o' Her world like dat had to hurt sumting fierce." Despite his brave words, the rabbit did not take his eyes off the yawning doorway back into the horrific world of Bree Sandavol.

"Why would the Muse react like that?" Natascha asked.

"She not sentient like you and me," Raffles answered. "Da Muse more pure emotion, a mood, a zeitgeist of a place. She only get involved if Her world's threatened. Sumting riled Her up good, and I'm guessin' it was Mordecai's portal machine rippin' up da ley-lines into Her world. She saw dat as a threat and we got caught in the da wake of Her fury. Most Muses ah come 'cross keep ta demselves, but not dis one."

Medesto peeked through the sloping rabbit-hole. On the other side, he saw the tunnel that led up to the reservoir. Occasionally, the light coming through the opening would be obstructed, but none of the shadowy monsters ventured beyond the doorway.

Medesto looked over to see Charley wander to the edge of the hollow and look out into the Void. Natascha got up to go stand next to her. The gnome ambled over within earshot.

"You have to understand Ren would never abandon a fellow Raconteur," Natascha said softly to the young tech. "Even someone he didn't get along with. I know him and have staked my life on that truth many times."

"I want to believe you," Charley choked out. "I really do, but right now I can't. Tempest was hard to work with. I knew that better than anyone. She could be petty and mean, but deep down, she was a good person. I learned a lot from her about duty and honor and how you push through the pain."

"I understand," Natascha replied in a comforting tone. "Ren's belligerent and hot tempered, but so was your boss. Those kinds of personalities always clash. You and I both know Tempest was doing her job as she saw it. Without mincing words or wasting time. And she was good at it. That's what mattered in the end."

Charley gave a weak smile and wiped her eyes. "But there is no one to mourn her."

"We will," Medesto replied, laying a hand on Charley's shoulder. "Even if no one else will, we still can. But now, we need to get home, and you're the only one with the equipment to do that. We cannot go back the way we came, so it's up to you to get us out of here."

"You're right," Charley said, wiping tears away. "I'll send a distress signal out right away. Tempest wouldn't want me to be shirking my duties, even if she isn't here to yell at me."

Medesto chuckled. "Thank you." Charley straightened up and turned toward him. Her eyes held back tears, but there was a quiet stoicism behind them. She went back to her gear and dug out her scanner.

"Do ya tink Mord'cai found da *Book of Days* at dat safe house?" Raffles pondered aloud.

Medesto thought about that. "It's very possible. What better place to hide something of such great value than in a world full of death and horror," he said. "Guarded by an overly aggressive Muse that tries to kill any outside interlopers. That's pretty brilliant of Harper Bellweather, if you ask me."

"Wot we do now?" Raffles settled in, leaning back on a rock. "Jus' sittin' 'ere ain't getting' nuthin' done."

"Charley sent out a distress call for a ride home," Medesto replied. "Hopefully, someone's out there to receive it. Then we go home. Ren's on his own, so all we can do now is wait for him to contact us. He's good at what he does. Once he finds out where Mordecai's headed, he'll figure out a way to reach out."

Medesto stood up and stretched his aching back. "It's been hours since the signal went out," he said. "How long do we have before the air runs out?"

"Don' know," Raffles answered. "Da ley-line still rooted to da world. It might even grow back in time. If we run outta air, we'd have to take our chances back inside and hope da Muse don' catch wind of us while make a run for another rabbit-hole." He shuddered at his own words.

"Nope," Natascha said matter-of-fact. "I dealt with Her once. I won't do it again. She's hiding just beyond the doorway waiting. I can feel it."

Medesto watched Charley stare into the black abyss outside the shelter of their hollow. She had said nothing since her brief conversation with Natascha. Her eyes were still red from her periodic tears. The death of a mentor was never an easy thing to accept.

A beeping sound filled the broken tunnel. Charley's head came up, and she grabbed her scanner. The handheld viewer shone blue. She pressed the screen twice and then stood up excitedly.

"We have a response to our signal," she said. "It's *Braggadocio*. Valgus and Jonny are on their way."

Two hours later, a sleek seventy-foot-long Slipstream came into view. Medesto waved it over, and the ship slowed as it approached. It came to a stop at the edge. A clam-shell door opened. A lean man of Asian descent, with a pompadour hairstyle and ever-present smirk on his face, stood in the doorway. He wore a black suit and tie over a white dress shirt.

Natascha leapt the narrow gap to the ship's ramp. Charley followed, then Raffles.

"Jonny," Natascha said. "It's been a while."

"Too long, Natascha." Jonny Vega, co-pilot of *Braggadocio*, stepped aside so the Raconteurs could climb aboard.

Medesto picked up his black traveling bag, took a breath and jumped across. The space between the shattered tunnel and the ramp was not wide, but he misjudged the distance, and the heel of his boot slipped off the step. Jonny and Natascha caught him, one by his jacket and one by an arm.

With an effort, they pulled his short, hefty frame up onto the ramp. He grabbed the edge of the open door and held it tight to regain his balance. The gnome prided himself on his stoic nature. His infamous strength made him pound for pound the strongest individual in Rogue Destiny. But no amount of physical might would matter if he lost his equilibrium in the shifting realities and fell in the Void.

Medesto caught himself blushing from his clumsiness. Once he regained his balance, Jonny patted him on the back. "Valgus needs to talk to you. I'll stay here with Natascha."

The Slipstream's doors closed. Medesto ambled up to the cockpit where a large man in a leather coat sat hunched behind the controls of the ship.

Valgus Alaric was a broad-shouldered, lumbering brute of a man. Before being recruited to the Raconteurs, he had been a Visigoth marauder, whose previous life consisted of decapitating Roman Legionnaires without prejudice. These days Valgus had tamed his bloodlust, content with preserving life rather than taking it.

Claymore Ives had recruited the marauder from inside the historical novel *Across the Rubicon* and decided the barbarian invader had the attributes that might make him a good Raconteur. Claymore was gifted that way, and an excellent judge of character that helped him gain the trust of anyone he came in contact with.

Gideon never doubted Claymore's instincts when it came to recruiting new field agents. Even if the recruit was a shape-shifting trickster with little trust for anyone other than himself.

"Sit down, we need to talk," Valgus said.

Medesto slid into the co-pilot's seat. "What happened?"

"Gideon was giving several council members a tour of Sebastian's workshop when a bomb went off."

"Is he okay?"

"Too soon to tell," Valgus growled. "All we heard was there were casualties."

"Do we know who's behind it?"

"Not yet," Valgus rumbled. "The Raconteurs have many enemies." Medesto could feel the tension rise in the cabin. The Visigoth had anger issues and was getting himself more worked up by the second. If he stayed in that frame of mind long enough, people tended to get hurt. "We were on our way back when we picked up your distress call and turned around to get you."

The Slipstream pulled away from the broken ley-line and sped through the black backdrop of the Void. Medesto watched a multitude of luminous worlds fly past his window. The muscles in his neck relaxed, relieved to leave Bree Sandoval's nightmarish horror world behind.

When Medesto first met the Visigoth, he had brimmed with violent energy, intimidating all those around him. His arms were corded muscles, his jaw chiseled iron with a broad chest and narrow hips and not an ounce of fat on his body. His weapon of choice was anything he could get his hands on. He mastered any weapon with little effort and became a crack shot with firearms in a matter of a hours, even though he had never seen one before joining the Raconteurs.

Unfortunately, Valgus' time in Rogue Destiny had not been kind to the marauder. These days he was overweight, with a belly that pooched over his belt. A long mane of black hair and scruffy unkempt beard covered his face. His appearance had the disheveled demeanor of a hobo, but his physique was no less intimidating.

Valgus brought his temper under control and the cabin grew silent, except for the occasional grumble from the barbarian. Medesto turned his mind toward other things. His eyes were heavy, but he couldn't give into his exhaustion until he knew if Gideon was alive or not. Gideon and Claymore Ives had founded the Raconteurs together, but now Claymore was a fugitive who they could not locate. If they lost Gideon too, who would step up to take charge?

Gideon's new business partner, Bijou Antilles, would be the obvious choice. But she had stated many times she did not want the position. She was content to manage the public house, the Obtuse Turtle, and stay out of the problems beyond Rogue Destiny's borders.

In the last year since Bijou came onboard, Medesto had never known her to leave the City. There were rumors the Jamaican was running from something or someone, but he could never confirm what that was. Bijou never talked about her past, except to say her adventuring days were behind her. Most of the Raconteurs had their secrets and Bijou wouldn't be the first to find refuge within the City of a Thousand Moons.

Medesto had been on the run from his own problems when he first ran into the diminutive Gideon Dumas and heroic Claymore Ives inside a Regency novel of Neapolitan Wars and Fae Magic. The gnome was the first recruit back in those days, so it was always assumed he would be in line to assume leadership at some point. Basically, because no one wanted the hassle of trying to control the rowdy Raconteurs.

He prayed that day would never come, but it appeared it might have.

The main prerequisite for any Raconteur was a thirst for adventure and justice, not power. Medesto didn't want to lead anyone, even on a temporary basis. He was much happier being a senior field agent and in-house hired muscle.

With Tempest gone, there was no one else qualified that would take the job. Natascha loathed administrative work. The delicate diplomacy that it took to build relationships and connections throughout the Mythic Cosmos was not her cup of tea. Ren was out of the question. Too much of a chance he'd start a war. That left Medesto.

Maybe he'd have to lead if it came down to it. If only out of loyalty to Gideon and what the Raconteurs stood for. It would be better than letting someone unqualified lead them. It might even help him find a little redemption for the impetuous choices of his own youth. He was too tired to worry about it anymore and opened his traveling bag.

Medesto carried a traveling bag of worn black leather that he had won in a poker game from a shady member of a traveling circus that passed through Rogue Destiny years before. It wasn't until later that he discovered the lining of the bag was interwoven with its own tiny pocket-world. It opened at the top and could hold thousands of items, large and small. The gnome used it as a storehouse for the various knick-knacks, weapons and gear he'd gathered over the years. He rummaged through it for the satchel Ren had pilfered from the pawnshop safe house.

He opened the satchel and flipped through the notebooks and journals inside before choosing at random. The pages were full of watercolor studies and doodles of monsters and bizarre creatures the owner of the notebook had encountered in her travels. He thumbed through the rest of the pages and moved on to a different journal. This second one contained pages of hand scrawled writing. In the bottom corner of the inside cover, he found the name *Harper Bellweather* written in ink.

There was a bookmark in the journal. He read the page marked by the slip of paper. It talked about when Harper first entered the novel, *Surviving a Bad Romance on the Eve of the Apocalypse*. Harper Bellweather wrote:

"I'm being followed. I thought I lost him in 'On the Island of Splendor', but he's still out there. I need to reach a safe house and contact my Order. No one can be trusted with the package I carry. Not the Raconteurs and not even the scholars I work with. There's too much corruption everywhere I look. I'll have to hide it somewhere for now."

Medesto could only assume the society mentioned was *The Order of the Memento Ex-Libris*, an eclectic group of historians the Raconteurs often worked with. The organization focused on researching the entirety of the Mythic Cosmos. Harper didn't mention who was after her. He flipped to the next page.

"Been away from home too long. I miss my sister and mother. I miss the spiring towers and citadels of Rogue Destiny. But I can't slow down until the package is safely hidden. I've decided on a place no one would be stupid enough to follow me into. I dare not document in writing what any of this refers to for fear this journal falls into the wrong hands."

She classified the world with a tiny skull and crossbones. The rest of the pages detailed her journey from rabbit-hole to rabbit-hole through six novels until she reached her destination. No names were given, but Medesto knew it had to be *Surviving a Bad Romance on the Eve of the Apocalypse*. That was all that was in that notebook. He scanned the next several journals and notebooks, but found nothing connected to the package she carried. The next journal was different. At the edge of a page showing a painting of a unicorn fighting a dragon, there were words scribbled in the margin that had to mean something.

"Once the pieces are placed and the connection has been established, the wearer will regain what they lost."

"The wearer?" Medesto pondered what the words could mean. No one could wear a book. So was Mordecai hunting for something else? Gideon surmised the McGuffin was something that he could use against Rogue Destiny. That ruled out anything magical in his mind. All magic had vanished from Rogue Destiny upon the death of its founder, Baltazaar Gheddi, a thousand years before. The other pages contained painted drawings of local flora and fauna from various worlds. The last two notebooks provided no new information.

Medesto slid them in with the others and stuffed the satchel back into his traveling bag. Maybe Gideon could make sense out of them. That is if he was still alive. He sank back in his chair and closed his eyes. Valgus remained silent, but pushed the Cold-Fire engines to the edge of what they could endure.

The hours slowly passed as the miles fell behind them. Then the glow of a familiar flat world came into view. The dimensional plane that the city of Rogue Destiny sat upon resembled a great bowl of water with a chain of islands floating atop it. Valgus slowed the engines, and the ship descended.

Once *Braggadocio* passed over the outer rim of the circular world, Medesto felt the familiar shift of realities. Through his window, he watch the ship come out over a crystal clear sea that went on forever in all directions. He had seen it hundreds of times before, but it still fascinated him.

Valgus flew them out across the water to the largest island of the Sojourn Archipelago. The city of Rogue Destiny covered the majority of the island. In the middle of Prodigal Bay, a massive tower sat on a cluster of rocks. The structure rose above everything else. Legend had it, the city had been built around the black monolith which many scholars have argued was the Axis Mundi of the universe, the center of the Mythic Cosmos, and that the tower itself was like a sundial's gnomon to their universe.

The ship's engines slowed further as they entered Rogue Destiny's airspace. Valgus did not take them to the landing pads at the Obtuse Turtle. Instead, he headed straight to the medical infirmary where Gideon received medical care. He landed on a wide swarth of grass next to the hospital, much to the annoyance of citizens enjoying a pleasant day in the park.

The Raconteurs disembarked and walked across the grass toward the front of the medical sanitarium. Medesto hurried his pace to keep up with Natascha.

"Were you able to get through to the hospital?" he asked. "Any word on Gideon's condition?"

"Couldn't get past the front desk," Natascha replied. "No one is saying anything. That's making me uneasy. If he dies..."

She didn't finish her thought.

Chapter 15
The Book of Days

R en stared down at the lifeless body at his feet. The Wolf's head lay twisted at an odd angle from a broken neck. Empty, half-opened eyes stared up at him. The guard, Ruddy, lay at the tent entrance, torn up, bloody, and dead.

Claymore Ives winced as he returned the revolver to its holster. He held the injured hand up to examine the deep gash across the back of his right hand. Blood ran freely down his forearm. The Wolf's claw had sliced it open as cleanly as any blade. Red drops fell to the dirt floor.

"Well, that was an unexpected turn of events," Claymore quipped. "You showing up out of nowhere to save my hide again, B'gatti. Just like the old days."

"Do you think anyone heard the ruckus?" Ren asked, retrieving a hand towel from the water basin in the corner. He tossed it to his partner, who pressed it against his wound. Claymore stepped over Ruddy and peeked out the tent flap.

"No, I don't think so," he replied. "The camp is quiet. Mordecai's ranks have thinned to the point all the tents at this end of the camp are empty. Plus, with the continuing warfare going on, no one should have heard you. You know who that was, don't you?"

The trickster nodded. "A big, bad wolf, I'm guessing. Or one of them anyway."

"Yeah, this one looks too feral to be the *Once Upon a Time* kind. Judging from its size and the coarseness of the fur, I'm thinking he's more Eastern European. Probably from some local folktale."

Ren knew many folklore and fairy tales full of ferocious wolves that terrorized little girls in red hoods, small Russian boys, and architecturally challenged porcine house builders. There were so many worlds with many stories of big, bad wolves that it was hard to keep them straight. Now, there was one less wolf to worry about.

Not that any of it mattered at the moment. Ren was alive and his attacker wasn't. At the end of the day, that's how he preferred things. He looked over at Claymore, still a bit unnerved by his partner's initial reaction to seeing him.

"What?" Claymore quipped. He noticed Ren staring.

"I thought you were going to shoot me there for a second," Ren said. "It's like you didn't recognize me."

"Sorry about that," Claymore replied. His breathing came hard. It took a minute for him to calm down. "You appeared out of nowhere. It threw me for a moment. I wasn't sure who I was seeing. What you are doing here?"

"I was tracking Mordecai with the Raconteurs, like you wanted me to," Ren answered. "I took the place of a sentry to get into camp."

Claymore didn't seem to hear his response. He seemed too engrossed in dragging Ruddy's mauled body away from the tent's doorway. He knelt and closed the guard's vacant eyes.

"You were a good man, Ruddy Fortuna," Claymore muttered. He bowed his head in respect. A moment later, he dug through the dead man's jacket, pulled out the pouch that had exchanged hands minutes before, and stuck it his own pocket.

"How'd you find Mordecai so fast?" Ren replied.

"If you want something bad enough, you make it happen," Claymore replied. His eyes swept over the floor. "But enough talk. I came here to find something."

Despite all the carnage that had occurred, a broad smile appeared on Ren's face that he couldn't shake. He pulled the table upright. Beneath it, under a pile of papers and journals, he found *The Book of Days*. Blowing the dirt from the cover, he held it out.

"Is this what you're looking for?" Ren asked.

Claymore's eyes lit up. He grabbed it out of Ren's hands and flipped through the pages.

"After all this time," he whispered.

The fight with the Wolf had left Ren's throat parched. He picked up the goblet of wine on the table next to the cot, glancing down at the sleeping occupant. Tomas' chest rose and fell in steady rhythm.

"Is Tomas okay?" Ren asked. "Despite the noise, he hasn't stirred once. It's like he's dead."

"He won't be bothering us," Claymore replied, without looking up from the page he was reading. "How's Natascha?"

"She's doing good," Ren said. He lifted the goblet to his mouth. Claymore reacted with lightning reflexes. His hand grabbed Ren's wrist before the wine could touch his lips.

"What're you doing?!" Ren growled, agitation in his voice. He jerked his arm away. Dark red liquid sloshed down his naked chest.

"You don't want to drink that," Claymore replied.

Ren ventured a quick sniff of the goblet's content. A sickly sweet fragrance drifted out. The smell went instantly to his head. His vision blurred, and his legs buckled under him. He almost succumbed to a wave of unexpected drowsiness. His eyes grew heavy as he teetered on the edge of blacking out. Claymore caught his arm and steadied him. The intense sleepiness passed seconds later.

"That, my friend, has been laced with the nectar of the Black Lotus," Claymore said with a laugh. "A single sip and you'll be in the deepest sleep of your life. One too many sips and you may never wake up again. I slipped it into Tomas' wine when I brought him dinner. I needed time to search his tent without being interrupted."

Ren took another piece of spiced meat from the tray. "The food isn't drugged, is it?" he quipped. "Cause I have to eat something. I'm running on empty here."

"Ah, right. That insatiable appetite of yours." Claymore slapped him soundly on the back and gave him a hard grin. "Yeah, the food's fine."

Claymore ran his fingers through his dark hair like he was having trouble focusing. His broad chest rose and fell as he stared off into space. He closed *The Book of Days* and set it on the table.

"Did I tell you Gideon came to see me every week after I went away?" he said after a moment, like he was struggling to find the words. "He'd visit Lazaranth Prison to update me on what was going on in the City. We both decided there was no way I was coming back to the Raconteurs. Everything I had was taken from me." His voice trailed off.

Ren watched his partner's mind deteriorate right in front of him. They'd seen each other less than two days earlier and in that short time, the changes in Claymore's mental state frightened him. He felt helpless, and didn't know what to do, except to change the conversation.

"What does Harper Bellweather have to do with all of this?"

Claymore's head came up. "What about Harper?!" he replied. "Do you know where she is?"

"No," Ren said. "Her name keeps coming up in our pursuit of Mordecai. He'd been retracing her movements and ransacking old archives she passed through. Why does she matter now? We have *The Book of Days*."

"The Book is only a piece of the puzzle," Claymore said. He wrapped the linen washcloth around his bleeding hand in a makeshift bandage. "It's a user's manual for the real prize Mordecai is seeking. And I believe Harper knows where that's hidden."

"I told Gideon I'd contact the Raconteurs once I found *The Book of Days*."

"You don't understand," Claymore replied. He grabbed roughly Ren by the shoulders. "I don't want them involved in this. Things are in motion now and there's no time to waste. You and I are together again and that's all that matters..." He pressed the palm of his hand to his temple, his face twisted in anguish. Ren grabbed him to prevent him from falling over.

"What's wrong?"

"Nothing, it's just another spell. It'll pass." Claymore grabbed the table with both hands to steady himself and bent over in pain. Unbidden words came from his lips. They were barely audible at first, then grew louder, as if he was reading from a book.

"We're going down!" Webb yelled. "We have to abandon ship! Calypso, get the ambassador and his wife to the lifeboats! Mook and I will find Jack! We'll meet you topside!" The cruise ship shifted under their feet.

"On it!" Calypso yelled. She exited the wheelhouse at a run. The Ambassador and his wife were asleep in their cabin. She climbed down the metal stairs to lower decks where the water already reached to her knees.

The words died on Claymore's lips. He tightened his grip on the table before looking up at Ren, the internal battle he was fighting evident in his eyes. He took a deep breath and exhaled, forcing himself to stand.

"What was that?!" Ren exclaimed. "It sounded like you were reading from a book."

"I think I was," Claymore muttered, his words came in labored breaths. He lowered his head into his hands to calm himself. A moment later he looked up, his eyes full of pain. "It's the words from my world's Story. From when I was still a part of that world."

"The *Paradigm Madness* is getting worse, isn't it?" Ren replied. He knew the answer.

"Yeah," Claymore admitted. "I feel it growing inside me, Ren. It feels like another part of me dies with every new sunrise. I have to keep moving or I will go mad. It feels like words are being ripped out of my head. It comes on without warning. I don't know how much longer I have, but I'm starting to feel like an empty husk."

"What can I do?" Ren asked.

"Help me finish this one last mission," Claymore replied. "It's something I've worked on for years. Something that I thought ended in the *Angels of Avalon*. The trail stopped there, but now I'm back on it. There are three orbs, called *lodestones*. We need to get to them before Mordecai. He cannot be allowed to find them."

"What's so special about these lodestones?"

"They will change the fate of Rogue Destiny." Claymore opened *The Book of Days* and flipped the thick yellowed pages with his good hand. "This!" He pointed to a page with drawings of two different sized orbs and a bauble that opened in the middle. "Baltazaar Gheddi created them himself and named them the *Roskashon Lodestones* after his homeworld. Haven't you ever wondered why the City's founder was one of the greatest sorcerers in all of the Mythic Cosmos, yet Rogue Destiny is a magical dead zone, often referred to as *the most magical place in existence without magic?*"

"I never thought about it," Ren replied with a shrug. "I don't like magic."

"Well, now you know," Claymore said. He ran a finger along a paragraph in the middle of the page as he read the words in a low voice.

I have found a way to restore what has been lost to me in this world without magic. I left my exile and returned to Roskashon where I created the lodestones. The Sunstone for day, the Moonstone for night, and the Bloodstone for self. When set in their proper place, these lodestones create a conduit between Roskashon and the islands of the Sojourn Archipelago, where the City of Rogue Destiny would eventually be built. The transmitigation of the magical current could only be broken if one of the lodestones are removed from its place in the sequence.

Excited as a schoolboy on his birthday, Claymore turned the page to the more detailed drawing of the three orbs. The largest was labeled the Sunstone. The next one was the Moonstone. Both spheres were an iridescent color of indigo and blue that seemed to leap off the paper.

Lower on the page was a small piece of ornamental jewelry, hanging off a short mesh chain and clasp. The circular trinket opened in half on a tiny hinge. The hollow inside was empty, except for a tiny crimson stone attached to the bottom of the lower half. It was called the Bloodstone.

Claymore continued reading:

The Moonstone remained in Roskashon, hidden away beneath the earth, deep in the catacombs under my stronghold, and guarded by strong, protective magic. The Sunstone was placed in the Obsidian Monolith built at the center of the Mythos-scape. The third piece, the Bloodstone, is to be filled with dirt taken from my homeworld and kept on my person at all times. Then the connection to my magic in Roskashon will be renewed. And what was lost will be restored once again.

"And what was lost will be restored once again," Claymore repeated softly.

Ren looked at him with a furrowed brow, not quite understanding what it might have meant. "Why would Mordecai want to bring magic to Rogue Destiny? He's no sorcerer, is he?"

"Not that I've ever heard, but it won't matter when we find the Roskashon Lodestones before he does." Claymore closed the thick book. He emptied the leather satchel and slid the large tome into it. "So that's how Baltazaar brought magic to Rogue Destiny."

"Where do we find these lodestones?" Ren asked.

Claymore shook his head to clear it, his expression uncertain. "Harper Bellweather and I have been chasing the rumors for years. We learned through our contacts that Minstrel Cotty might have possession of them. Harper searched his citadel several times, but could never find them. So we figured Cotty hid them somewhere off-world. The last time I spoke with Harper was in *The Angels of Avalon*, the night before Cotty died. She had another lead to chase down. We were supposed to rendezvous later, but the murder of Cotty and loss of his world threw a wrench into that. Let's get out of here before we're discovered."

Ren headed for the tent door, then stopped. The stench of death and decay wafted over the air. Hairs on the back of his neck stood up as the canvas flaps parted inward, revealing a tall, wraithlike creature wrapped in a tattered black cloak. The monster ducked under the doorway and floated inside. All that was visible under the dark cowl was a jutting jaw of bleached bone and a hideous perma-grin. His presence seemed to fill the room and made Ren's stomach roil. He felt like he was going to be sick.

Chapter 16
One Last Thing

The Grimm Jester's black hood brushed the tent ceiling. Ren backed away as the monster approached. Claymore stood his ground, unintimidated by the sudden appearance of the physical embodiment of Death. The hooded wraith glanced down at Ruddy's corpse, then over to the dead Wolf.

Ren had dealt with this monster before. They had met for the first time, days earlier, in a hidden alleyway behind a teahouse in Rogue Destiny. The Grimm Jester had saved Ren's life from a night of torture and death, and somehow considered the trickster now in its debt.

"The aroma of death is on the air," he hissed. The barely audible words escaped through yellowed teeth, like dust blowing through an empty skull.

Ren couldn't understand how the monster formed coherent words without the proper vocal cords, but it did. The Jester pointed a crooked bony finger at Ren. "You were there at the Pithy Fool, and now you are here," the wraith whispered. "How resourceful. When last we met, I spared your life and told you that you were indebted to me. The time has come to collect on that debt."

Ren took another step back. "I'm in the middle of something right now."

The Jester loomed over him. "It was not a request, little trickster."

Claymore stepped between them. "He doesn't owe you anything," he snarled. Ren couldn't be sure, but he swore the Jester recoiled, as if it was careful not to get too close to Ren's partner.

The air grew tense. Ren readied himself to shift again, although he didn't know what he could morph into that could help the situation. He had witnessed the monster kill a man with just a brush of its hand.

He had never known Claymore to cower before anyone, but this was Death incarnate. A seemingly omnipotent entity within the confines of its own Story, yet nearly as dangerous outside its world. Ren swallowed hard. If his partner refused to back down, then he would have to stand with him.

"What do you want me to do?" Ren ventured. His voice filled with as much confidence as he could muster.

"You must kill Mordecai Davos when the opportunity arises. And do it quickly, before he commands me to stop you. Once he is dead, I will claim the body."

"Why do you need his body?" Claymore asked.

"Because that is how it must be," the wraith replied. "We are nearing the end of Mordecai's mad charade, and many things will be revealed soon."

"Do it yourself, ghoul!" Claymore snapped. "You're supposed to be Death, aren't you? That makes you pretty adept at killing."

The monster did not give an answer. The only sound in the tent was the fluttering of the tattered cloak in the currents of the air purifier.

"Okay, I'll do it," Ren replied. "If I get the chance without endangering Claymore or myself, I will kill Mordecai."

"That would be best for everyone," the Jester whispered. "Now I must go before I am missed. Dispose of the bodies in the fissure cracks on the far side of the Abattoir. And let no one see you. I will clear the area of interlopers. And it would do you good to remember, little trickster, that Claymore Ives will not always be around to protect you."

The words made Ren's skin crawl.

"What power does he have over you?" Claymore growled, unfazed by the threatening words. "What binds you to Mordecai?"

"You time grows short, Claymore Ives," the wraith hissed. The hushed words hung in the air. The hideous grin widened within the depths of the black hood.

Without another sound, the Grimm Jester glided through the tent flap into the sweltering night. Claymore stared at Ren, a skeptical smirk on his lips.

"What did he mean *he saved your life*?" Claymore asked.

"It's nothing," Ren replied. "I ran into some trouble in a back alley with Mordecai's henchmen. I didn't ask the monster to help, but it did. I had it under control."

Claymore gave him a knowing chuckle. "I'm sure you did."

"Was it my imagination or did the Grimm Jester avoid getting close to you?" Ren asked, still trying to process what had just happened. "What would Death have to be afraid of?"

Claymore laughed at the comment. "The Jester does not experience emotions like fear and doubt. Because of that, his judgement doesn't always allow him to discern what might be dangerous to him and what isn't."

"*The Paradigm Madness*?"

"Yeah, the monster must sense it inside me," Claymore replied. "Unknown variables, like the *Paradigm Madness*, are what concerns him. It's beyond his understanding. If Death can be captured and enslaved by a mortal like Mordecai, the

Jester has to be concerned about what else he may be vulnerable to."

"So when he figures out the madness isn't contagious?"

"Hopefully, we won't be around," Claymore said. "That's why we need to find the lodestones as quickly as possible. If the Jester realizes the truth, our only bargaining chip is gone. He could've killed both of us right here, but didn't. Next time, we may not be so lucky."

"So, what do we do now?"

"The Jester's right," Claymore answered. "No one can know what happened here. You and I are too close to the lodestones to let anything stop us now." He glanced around. "We can use the rug for the Wolf."

They moved the table over. After clearing the piles of Harper's journals out of the way, they pushed the dead wolf onto the thick, woven rug. They rolled the body up before tying it off with a short rope. Together, they carried it to the rear of the tent.

"Now we'll get Ruddy," Claymore said. Ren took a moment to memorize the dead man's face, then helped wrap the wool blanket over the corpse and tie it off another section of rope.

"You want Ruddy or the Big Bad?" Ren said.

Claymore bent down and checked the rope securing the blanket holding Ruddy's body. "You're stronger than me," he replied. "You can have the Wolf."

Ren shrugged halfheartedly at the suggestion. He focused his concentration until his lean frame morphed. A moment later, he wore the face of Ruddy Fortuna. But his chest was broader than Ruddy's, his arms thicker with the corded muscles he would need to carry the Wolf.

Once he settled into his new disguise, Ren dug through Tomas' chest for some clothes. He found a shirt and pants. They were tight on his frame, but would have to do. Despite flecks of blood on Ruddy's boots, he pulled them on and laced them up.

"I'm ready," Ren replied. He slipped his oxygen mask over his nose and mouth and hoisted the enormous Wolf onto his shoulders. Claymore pulled his knife out and sliced a wide doorway at the back of the room. He threw Ruddy over his shoulder, and they exited the tent. Claymore went first, heading down a sloping hill beyond the camp.

The sound of thundering cannons continued across the horizon. It had become so commonplace Ren hardly noticed it anymore. Artillery rockets lit up the dark sky. Once they were out of view of the camp, they followed a steep ravine that lead to a dry riverbed. The deafening blast of cannon fire echoed through the distant hills.

Ren watched Claymore navigate the hazardous terrain of the rocky ravine ahead of them. He wanted to trust his partner as he always had, but something in the back of his mind warned him that something was terribly off. Claymore's behavior, from plundering the gold off Ruddy's body to his inability to stay focused on a conversation for any length of time, made him worry how much of his friend remained.

Chapter 17
When Hope Fails

Ren's legs strained under him. He shifted the Wolf to a more comfortable position across his shoulders. The loose rocks underfoot were a constant hazard, but he managed to keep his feet under him. The lack of sleep and food had caught up to him, but those comforts would have to wait. In the distance, the night sky flashed with the glow of explosions as a battle raged somewhere to the west.

Ren dropped his burden to the ground with a grunt and sat down. Claymore did the same.

"Answer a question for me?" Ren asked between gulps of air from his mask.

"What's that?" Claymore's chest heaved as he caught his breath.

"Where are we?" Ren asked.

"In a dystopian novel of eternal war called *Under a Crimson Sky*," Claymore huffed. He wiped sweat from his forehead. "Basically, the Story's about four military factions — North, South, East, and West. Each is in constant warfare, trying to gain advantage over the others. Outside of those four armies, there are a dozen or so smaller ones who exist to sell their services to the highest bidder. The one Mordecai is working with is one of those outliers."

"How did Mordecai gain favor with this Supreme Leader?"

"By using the one thing that translates across all worlds. Gold," Claymore replied. "Mordecai pays tribute to the guerilla army in exchange for the use of their soldiers and land. It gives him a home base. But the gold's run out."

"So Mordecai promises them a secret weapon that will make the Supreme Leader relevant in the larger Story?"

"Exactly," Claymore said. "The rebels Mordecai has allied himself with are nothing more than window dressing to give the world depth and backstory. They play no real part in the overall Narrative. Their factories supply war machines to the four bigger armies so they can continue fighting. But Mordecai is desperate. He's promised to make the Glorious Supreme Leader a bigger player in the Great War."

"Does this secret weapon actually exist?"

"It does," Claymore replied. "I delivered it to Mordecai myself."

"The item he asked you and the Jester to acquire back in the booksellers' shop?"

"Of course, you were there?" Claymore said with a smirk. "You were the cat, right?"

"Easiest way to stay unnoticed," Ren replied. "No one suspects the cat."

"So where are we at in the Story?"

All dystopian novels looked the same to Ren, death and misery everywhere. He didn't understand why anyone would choose to stay there, because he couldn't leave the place soon enough.

"The main Narrative takes place a hundred miles north of here," Claymore said. He stood up. "We couldn't interfere with the Story if we tried. Let's go."

Ren picked up the Wolf again and followed his partner to the end of the ravine. They climbed out onto a barren stretch of land. Claymore took off across the flat open ground, staying beyond the reach of the factory lights. Ruddy Fortuna's corpse bounced on his shoulder. Ren ran after him, struggling under the deadweight of his burden. Together, they made their way around the factory.

To the east, a main road wound across the floor of the valley. Claymore stopped behind an outcropping of rocks as approaching headlights flashed on the factory's front gates.

Ren hesitated to venture into a controversial topic, but this might be the only time they were alone. And he was never known for his tact. He needed an answer to something that had been bothering him.

"So you knew Asher Grey's world was about to be destroyed, yet you didn't intervene to save it? All because you didn't want to blow your cover?"

"That's right," Claymore replied coldly. "I am still the hero and always will be. But as I constantly remind myself, I am no longer a Raconteur. After losing *The Angels of Avalon*, I decided saving worlds is best left to others. I have new purpose now. To stop Mordecai Davos from finding the lodestones. Nothing else matters to me anymore."

"And then what?" Ren asked. "Once we stop Mordecai. What will you do then?"

His partner lowered his head and closed his eyes, but didn't answer the question. Ren had to remind himself that even though Claymore may look and act like his old self, he was no longer the man he used to be. Not anymore. Ren could feel the struggle going on inside his friend. The battle between discerning right from wrong. He decided it'd be best not to push him any further.

"The Grimm Jester mentioned the word *Abattoir*," Ren said.

"Is that where the dead *rise again*?" Claymore looked up. His demeanor changed, the anguish on his face gone.

"The *Abattoir* is what they call their processing refineries," he said. "It's just a pretty word for *slaughterhouse*. The dead and dying are rebuilt inside those factories so they can continue the fight in this world's never-ending war. The wounded are repurposed into cyborgs. Lost limbs and organs are replaced with steel and hardware grafted into living tissue. The dead are sealed in a substance called *Abeyant* to preserve the body until it can be integrated into a War Golem. During the process, the mind is erased. Memories of the war and fighting are implanted to give the recipient purpose. So when they are brought back, war will be all they've ever known. They become one in purpose with the machines they inhabit."

So they could rise again and return to their proper place in the war effort. Ren recalled the words of General Bartacchi. Now he understood why replacing the five lost soldiers was so important. With the volunteers, they would build new soldiers with one sole purpose. Total dedication to the Great Cause.

"You seemed to have gained Mordecai's trust," Ren said.

"I told him I could help when the Raconteurs showed up," Claymore replied. "And I assured him they would show up. So he made me one of his bodyguards. I convinced Mordecai to expect a full frontal assault and not a shape-shifting trickster slipping through the backdoor. Say what you will about Gideon Dumas, but the man is brilliant."

Ren smiled to himself. "So, who wins the Great War in the end?"

"From what I've seen, apparently, no one," Claymore said grimly. "I think that's the point of the Story. The futility of war and all that. I don't even think anyone knows what they're fighting for anymore."

He lowered Ruddy's body to the edge of the wide crevice and

wiped the sweat from his eyes. With a push of his boot, the corpse rolled into the crevice. Ren watched the wrapped body land with a splash in the molten rock far below. The orange and red glow played off Claymore's eyes as he watched the corpse slowly sink from sight.

Hot air from the crevice burned Ren's face as he heaved the remains of the Big Bad Wolf into the chasm. The smell of burnt fur filled his nostrils. The fairytale monster disappeared into its final resting place. He couldn't help but think how many other bodies had been brought here and disposed of in the same manner.

Claymore checked the bandage on his wounded hand. "We need to get back to camp before my absence is noticed. Mordecai's getting more paranoid lately. He's ordered people shot for doing anything he considers suspicious."

As they climbed the hill toward camp, Claymore's mood lightened. When they reached the top, he clapped Ren on the back. "It's good to be back in the hunt with you, brother," he said. "I haven't felt this alive in a long time." His words were infused with more emotion than Ren had seen Claymore express before.

Now that the two were unencumbered, they made good time over the rugged terrain. Ren found himself lost in his thoughts, trying to process all that had happened in the last hour.

Without warning, Claymore grabbed his head with both hands. "No, not here!" he yelled. "The words, they won't stop!"

"What can I do?" Ren laid his hand on his partner's shoulder.

"Stay back!" Claymore shouted. He pushed Ren away and dropped to his knees. "Just give me a minute. I'll be fine." He pressed his palms against his temples, his face contorted in agony. Words began to escape his lips.

The ship rocked back and forth under the grip of the hurricane.

Water poured in through the cabin windows. Jackson fought to maintain control of the massive freighter he steered her toward the distant coastline. The ship's bow crashed through the white-capped waves.

Claymore gritted his teeth and dropped his head. "No, I will not let this happen," he mumbled to himself. Beads of sweat broke out on his brow as he strained to control his speech. "I am Claymore Ives, the first Raconteur and guardian of Rogue Destiny. I am a good man. I am stronger than this madness."

Ren watched his friend battle the insanity slowing eating away at his soul. It left him horrified, furious there was nothing he could do to help. The sound of Claymore's voice petered out, but his lips kept moving. He stared at the ground, mouthing silent words for another full minute. Slowly, Claymore brought himself under control. He looked up at Ren. His face was pale. His eyes bloodshot. The veins on his forehead evident. Exhaustion weighed down on him.

"When was the last time you slept?" Ren asked.

Claymore shrugged and stood up. "Sleeping only makes it worse, so I don't sleep," he replied, his strong legs shaky under him. "When I do, my dreams are so vivid. All the places I've ever been play out in quick succession. When I first met Gideon, before we started the Raconteurs. How I brought in Medesto as our first recruit. And how I found you running the streets with *The Gentlemen of the Open Road.*" An exhausted smile touched Claymore's lips. "Remember the first time I took you in the field as a Raconteur?"

"I remember you telling me to stop arguing with everything you'd say," Ren replied with a wry grin. "You kept reminding me I might not have what it took to be a Raconteur and how I was free to leave any time I wanted to."

"That's right, I said that, didn't I?" Claymore chuckled. "I was so mad at you that day for flying my Slipstream through a rabbit-hole."

"I told you it would fit," Ren said.

"Most of it, anyway," Claymore reminded him. "You took off an engine. We had to fly home on auxiliary power." He gazed into the sky. "But you saved my life that day."

"Of course I did," Ren said. "And more times than I can count since then."

"Which is almost as many times as I've saved your scrawny hide," Claymore replied.

The trickster stretched his sore muscles. The strain of carrying hundreds of pounds of dead wolf, while maintaining Ruddy Fortuna's muscular physique, had taxed his stamina. His stomach was empty, and the adrenaline rush from performing their grisly task had faded. His own problems paled compared to the anguish his partner was going through. But he knew he had to do something.

"*The Book of Days* states the lodestones *restore what has been lost*," Ren said. He chose his words carefully. "Why wouldn't that include the *Paradigm Madness*? What if they could reverse the effects of the madness?"

"I don't think that's how they work," Claymore said. "Once that door has been opened, it cannot be closed again. Not even Baltazaar Gheddi was brilliant enough to create something that powerful."

"You don't know that," Ren insisted. "We have to at least try." A sense of hope rose in him for the first time since finding Claymore.

His partner shot him a doubtful glance. "That's a cheery thought, but we have to find them first."

"I'm not asking permission," Ren replied. "Do you hear me, Claymore?"

His partner ignored his words. Ren watched him trudge up the moonlit path, trying to process these wild mood swings. Claymore rode one wave of emotion after another, like he was clinging to a raft lost at sea, tossed about by violent storm waters.

He didn't know how, but when the time came, Ren would do whatever it took to save his friend from a madness no one had ever come back from. And he'd kill anyone who dared stand in his way.

Chapter 18
In For a Penny, In For a Pound

Ren looked up at the cluster of gray tents as they climbed the last hill toward camp. The reddish glow of a new sunrise lit the eastern horizon. A hot, stale wind blew across the valley, carrying the smell of ash and acidic chemicals. The silence of early morning hung over the encampment, but he knew the encampment would be teeming with activity before long.

A sentry approached as they reached Tomas' tent. Ren recognized him from when he first snuck into camp.

"Where have you been, Claymore?" Baaklow asked.

"Taking care of personal business," Claymore responded. "What's it to you?" His voice vibrated with the threat of violence. Ren laid a hand on his arm, hoping to calm his rising anger.

"Mordecai's been asking for you," Baaklow answered. "He wants to see you in his tent."

"Let him know I'm on my way," Claymore replied. He waited for Baaklow to leave, then he turned to Ren. "Wait for me here and keep yourself out of trouble." He strode toward the center of the camp and Mordecai's tent.

Ren lifted the flap to the tent. Tomas lay sleeping on his cot in the same position as they had left him. His chest rose and sank in steady rhythm. Staying in the form of Ruddy Fortuna, Ren picked up the bodyguard's fallen rifle and waited out front for Claymore.

The trickster desired nothing more than to get out of the pages of this dystopian book. But first, he and Claymore had to find the lodestones. The more he thought about it, the more convinced he became that the Roskashon Lodestones were their best chance of pulling Claymore back from the precipice of madness. Staying close to Tomas would get them to the stones.

A few of minutes later, Claymore returned with a satisfied smile on his face. "Mordecai said Tomas has a possible location on the lodestones. We're going to check it out," he crowed. His body was almost quivering in anticipation. "This is where things get interesting."

"I overheard them talking yesterday," Ren replied, "But I didn't catch the details. Tomas indicated there was a secluded hideaway Harper Bellweather referred to in many of her journals, and he seemed to think it might be important."

Claymore headed back the way he had come. "Let's go, they're announcing to the camp we're leaving."

Mordecai Davos appeared in the doorway of his tent as Ren reached the common area. Silium-Cinque Niner, and two heavily armed cybernetic bodyguards followed him out on either side. The cyborg pulled a horn from his belt and blew it. The blast reverberated across the dry morning breeze.

Around them, people stumbled from their tents. Others, headed from the mess tent after another disappointing breakfast of gruel and hard bread, gathered back at the center of the camp with Ren and Claymore. Within minutes, everyone in the camp had assembled a rough circle in front of Mordecai's tent.

The last to arrive was the lady in black. Ren had seen her only from a distance in the underground rail system beneath the world of Asher Grey. She held a small wooden box in her arms, tied with a red ribbon.

Her menagerie of grotesque monstrosities trailed behind her. Ren recognized many of the beasts from the short time he'd been hiding among Mordecai's outlaws. A lumbering bear-gorilla hybrid walked on its front knuckles next to a hyena-warthog crossbreed. At the woman's side, an enormous snake creature slithered across the ground. The twelve-foot long serpent had the arms and torso of a human, along with a wedged-shaped head that no one in the crowd would look at directly.

Ren knew nothing about the woman in black, or her pets, except that she navigated the portal machine that transported Mordecai and his followers across the worlds of the Mythic Cosmos.

"I've seen her before," he whispered. "Who is she?"

"That's Natascha's mother, Idalia Devi," Claymore replied softly. "She was on my cell block in Lazaranth. Several weeks before the prison breakout, Mordecai started visiting her in the dead of night, trying to convince her to give up the location of her portal machine. She would refuse him every time. Told him only she would ever pilot the machine."

"So that could be why he staged to the prison escape," Ren said. "To break her and the others out of Lazaranth?"

"I believe so," Claymore replied. "He returned every night and the two would argue, loud enough for the rest of us to hear, until they came to a compromise. Then something weird happened. Out of nowhere, Mordecai began having long conver-sations with the man in the cell next to Idalia. They ended up talking night after night for hours on end. Mordecai would bring him books and other materials to read. Made no sense, but there seemed to be some level of trust built up between them. He completely ignored Idalia after that until the prison break."

"Who was in that cell?"

"Some insignificant sorcerer," Claymore said. "He dressed like a vagrant, walking around barefoot, wearing nothing but a dirty robe. Had a long beard and unkempt stringy hair that fell into his face. He stunk up the entire block, burning incense in his cell all the time. They called him Valgarii."

"Where is he?" Ren asked. "I don't remember seeing any sorcerers among Mordecai's followers."

Claymore shrugged. "He disappeared in the chaos of the breakout. I never saw him again. My guess is he was killed before he learned too much about Mordecai's plans. If the lodestones *return what has been lost*, a sorcerer could pose a threat. But the real question is what does Mordecai plan to do with the lodestones?"

"The night of the prison escape, the Grimm Jester released Valgarii from his cell first, even before Idalia. The three of them left together. An hour later, the rest of the cell block was let out when doorways appeared in the back of our cells that took us to Bones Martyr Island."

Claymore took a deep breath from his facemask. "All I know is we can't let anything get in the way of reaching the lodestones. Nothing..."

His voice trailed off. His expression was pensive as he stared off into space. The horn blew a second time, breaking Claymore out of his daze.

Mordecai raised his arms. "I have received word that the Glorious Supreme Leader will be arriving shortly," he announced to the crowd. "After I have met with him, we will depart for what will be the final step in our quest. So gather what you need and be ready."

Mordecai scanned the crush of people for someone in particular. His eyes fell on Ren, still hidden behind the face of Ruddy Fortuna.

"Where is Tomas?" he asked Ren directly. "Your orders were to watch him at all times."

"He is resting in his tent," Ren answered without hesitation. "He sent me to bring him breakfast, then I heard the horn blow." His response seemed to placate Mordecai's concerns because the crime lord did not push his inquiry further.

"Go and let him know we're leaving immediately," Mordecai commanded.

Ren nodded and pushed past those around him, hurrying back to the Tomas' tent. When he entered, the scholar sat on the edge of his cot, still in the rumpled clothes he had worn the day before. He wiped the sleep from his eyes and shook his head to clear it of the stupor. He could barely keep his drooping eyelids open. Ren set his rifle down, took off his coat, and walked over to him.

"Ruddy, thank goodness you're here," Tomas muttered through slurred words. He rubbed his face vigorously with both hands. "How long have I been asleep?"

"Just a few hours," Ren replied. "You had a bad dream. It's morning."

"I can't seem to keep my eyes open." He gave a painful yawn that went on for several heartbeats. "Oh, the terrible dreams! I wandered alone down dark roads where nightmarish creatures waited to devour me. People were moving about in my tent, but I couldn't wake up. I tried to yell, but couldn't. I've never felt so tired." His shoulders sagged.

"Mordecai said you know where the lodestones are," Ren told him. "I was sent to collect you. We're going to get them."

Tomas' head came up. "We're headed to *Gilgamesh*?"

"Where else," Ren replied.

Every Raconteur knew the legends. It was commonly believed *The Epic of Gilgamesh* was the very first Book with a concentration of ley-lines unrivaled anywhere. The world was said to have thousands upon thousands of rabbit-holes.

"Ha, I knew it!" Tomas said. "He finally believes me. I told Mordecai that's where the stones would be. All the writings pointed to it. It's the perfect place to hide something so valuable. Harper was always so clever."

"You know Harper Bellweather?" Ren asked, his interest suddenly piqued.

Tomas yawned again. Ren could see his back teeth and uvula for far longer than he would have liked.

"We worked together at *The Bedlam Chasers Society*," he said finally.

"What's that?" Ren asked.

"Oh, I'm sorry," Tomas said. "That's what we *called our organization*. A little inside joke between colleagues. She worked in the field. I sat behind a desk. We never dated, but I always wanted to ask her..."

His head drooped forward. The bushel of greying hair stood up at an odd angle from where he slept on it.

Ren shook him awake. "Where is Harper at?"

Tomas' head to popped up. "She went missing over a year ago. There's a sanctuary mentioned in many of her journals, a place she could get away from everything. But her writings were vague about its location. I've gone over her notes for weeks trying to narrow down where it could be."

"So you think the lodestones are there?" Ren said.

"*Monoceros* is there, I am certain of it," Tomas replied sleepily. "It's a secret hideaway Harper often spoke of, but she would never reveal its location."

"Are the lodestones there?" Ren asked.

"I don't know," Tomas replied. He stood up, but his knees buckled underneath him. Ren caught him in his arms and helped him sit down on the bed. "Thank you. I just need to rest for a moment."

Tomas De Marche seemed like a decent fellow, scientifically minded, and consumed with finding answers and documenting things, like the rest of his ilk at *The Order of the Memento Ex-Libris*. But this was Ren's chance to get inside Mordecai's inner circle. He didn't want to hurt Tomas, but he couldn't risk him interfering with what Ren needed to do. He sighed and glanced around the room.

On the table next to the bed, Ren saw the goblet he had almost drank from the previous night. The one laced with the nectar of the Black Lotus. He picked it up and handed it to Tomas.

"Here, drink this," Ren said. "You'll feel better."

Tomas reached for the cup with a shaky hand. Ren helped him hold it and guided it to his lips.

"That's it," Ren said. Tomas drained the cup and took a deep breath.

"Why does Mordecai want the lodestones so desperately?" Ren asked, trying to coax as much information out of Tomas as he could before the man drifted off again.

The scholar started nodding off. "Because *they return what has been lost*."

"What has Mordecai lost?" Ren asked.

"*The only thing he ever cared about*," Tomas muttered before his eyes drifted shut.

Ren shook him awake. "Where is this hideout located?" Ren asked. He knew he was losing Tomas.

"On the great river, Euphrates. At a waterfall overlooking the edge of the world."

"And you believe that's where the lodestones are?"

Suspicion appeared in Tomas' drooping eyes. "Why are you

asking me all these things, Ruddy?" he muttered. "You're just my bodyguard."

"Because I need to make sure I have the details right." Ren replied. He knelt directly in front of Tomas and stared into his eyes with a bemused smile. This was his favorite part. With a thought, he released his hold on the bodyguard's physical appearance and shifted to another familiar face. Tomas reacted to the sudden change as if he'd been struck.

"You... you're not Ruddy." His words slurred.

"No, I'm not," Ren said with a wry grin. "I'm Tomas Demarche."

A quizzical look appeared on the scholar's face. His brow furrowed as he tried to piece it all together. "What? No, that's... not right." His words slurred. He looked at Ren with heavy eyes. "I'm Tomas Demarche."

"Yes you are," Ren answered. "But I just need to borrow your face for a while."

Chapter 19
Visiting Hours

The front entrance of the hospital was crowded with people when the Raconteurs walked up. Natascha saw fellows agents waiting impatiently for word on Gideon. What she caught from the scrap of conversations around her ranged from deep concern for Gideon, to more mercenary interests. Several agents wondered aloud if the bounty work would dry up if the leader of the Raconteurs did not pull through, and if they should start searching for new sources of income.

Natascha pushed her way through the press of flesh to the front desk. "Gideon Dumas' room, please?" she asked the woman sitting on the other side. Medesto stepped up next to her, Raffles perched on his shoulder. The crowd parted as Valgus' mere presence cleared a space for himself, Charley and Jonny, not far from the front desk.

The nurse looked up from the chart she was reading. "I'm sorry," she said sternly. "Like I told the multitude of people behind you, no one can see him. He is resting in the infirmary after his surgery."

"Can you tell us his condition?" Medesto said. He raised his voice over the chatter behind them. His deep voice edged with exhaustion and anger.

"He's stable at the moment," she snapped. "That's all I can tell you. Now if you'll let me get back to my paperwork." The nurse threw an annoyed glare past Natascha at the crowd milling about the lobby. The noise had reached a disturbingly loud crescendo. An inadequate number of security staff stood ready in the nearby hallway.

Natascha followed her eyes. "How about we do this then?" she asked, pointing to Medesto. "You let me and him see Gideon, and we will clear these people out of your lobby."

The nurse's brow furrowed as she thought about the offer. "Get them all out first, and I'll let the two of you see Mr. Dumas."

Natascha gave her a sly grin and addressed the crowd. "Can I have everyone's attention?" she shouted. The din of noise died down and everyone looked at her.

"Our presence is disrupting the staff and disturbing patients," Natascha said loudly with as much sympathy as she muster. Her patience had reached its limit after everything she had gone through in the last few days. "If everyone can clear the lobby and wait outside, we will let you know when we have word on Gideon's condition."

Natascha sighed. "Valgus? A little help, please."

Valgus grinned. He rose to his full height and his massive frame swelled with sudden purpose. He pulled the great axe from his back and pointed it at the front doors. "The last one out gets smacked with this," he bellowed. At his words, everyone filed out except for the crew and passengers of *Braggadocio*. A minute later the lobby was empty.

Natascha turned to the nurse. "We good now?"

The nurse ushered a nearby orderly up to the desk. "Take these two up to Mr. Dumas' room on the third floor," she said in a professional manner. Natascha winked at her and stepped into the open gate elevator with Medesto. Three floors later, they were standing in front of room 356. The orderly opened the door, allowed both to file in, and then he closed it behind them.

Gideon lay on his hospital bed, his face void of color. Natascha felt like she was at his wake, instead of his hospital room. His left leg was suspended by straps slightly above the blankets, wrapped in a bandages with metal pins and screws visible to stabilize the limb. His right arm lay on his stomach in a plaster cast.

Bijou Antilles sat on the couch across from the bed reading a book. She looked up as they entered, a deep sigh of relief on her face. "You made it," she whispered. "I've been here for hours waiting for him to wake."

"We just got in," Natascha said softly. She walked to the side of his bed where the IV was attached to his arm. "How is he?"

Bijou rose from the couch. She was several inches taller than Natascha. "Hard to say," she said. "I have a feeling the doctors are not telling us everything. He has several broken ribs, a concussion, punctured lung, and possible internal bleeding. His left leg was mangled by fallen debris from the explosion. It was a wonder he wasn't killed. He's lucky to be alive."

"Yes, he is," Medesto exhaled. Natascha could tell despite their boss's injuries, the stoic gnome was visibly relieved Gideon was still with them. She felt that same relief.

"He needs his rest," Natascha said. "We won't stay long. Watch the door."

Natascha slipped a syringe from her pocket and removed the plastic cap. She lifted the IV tube and injected the needle directly into the access port.

"What is that?" Bijou asked. She took a step toward Natascha, but Medesto motioned for her to stop.

"Something I got from the first aid kit on the *Braggadocio*," she said. "It will speed his recovery and help him gain consciousness. My father developed it years ago and it's used in hospitals across a hundred of different worlds."

Gideon Dumas stirred a few moments later. "Natascha, is that you?" he murmured, his voice weak and his eyes half opened. Natascha took his hand in hers.

"How you feeling, boss?" she said, fighting to keep her emotions in check.

"Right at rain," Gideon answered, a weak smile on his lips. He did not seem to be experiencing any pain at the moment. The alchemist cocktail she had given him numbed the pain and revived him from his injuries quicker than anything the hospital would give him.

"Any thoughts as to who is behind this yet?" Medesto asked.

"My brain is still too rattled to consider all the possible theories. I have Sebastian and Pasquali gathering evidence," Gideon said in a low tone. "They'll have a report ready by the time I'm out of here."

"I'm guessing the *Black Rose* is behind this," Medesto said. "Revenge for Claymore and Ren burning down their villa in Adezhda the other night."

"That is a possibility," Gideon replied. "But the timing of this bombing was too precise." His words were stronger with each syllable now that they were discussing possible theories. Natascha could see the pistons firing in his brain. This was Gideon's wheelhouse. Deducing criminal motives and intent. He lived for it.

Gideon stared up at the ceiling, some color returning to his face. "The explosion occurred right as I was finishing up a tour of the landing bays with members of the Common Council. The explosives were delivered by a small silver drone. I saw a symbol of the Black Rose on its side as it tried to enter Sebastian's subterranean workshop. Somehow, I managed to get the storm doors shut before it exploded, or I would be dead. Three of the

Council members with me were not so fortunate. Pahloek Zima, Osirus Spyros and Astrid Saabey were killed in the explosion. Ma Bellamy had lagged behind the group talking to Solis Cicerone. She had the presence of mind to push herself and Solis down a side hall. Both sustained only minor injuries."

"So you think a member of the Council is behind this?" Natascha asked. "And the General Protectorate was the intended target?"

Gideon nodded once. "I believe that is not out of the realm of possibility."

"Isn't the symbol a little obvious?" Bijou asked. "Couldn't someone be trying to frame the Black Rose?"

"Or they wanted me to know who it was that was about to kill me," Gideon said.

"My money's on the *Black Rose*," Medesto said. "Mordecai may be off-world, but his lackeys still control large areas of the city. Whoever did this, I say we find out who they are and go after them."

Gideon gave a harsh cough and winced. He moved a bandaged hand to his ribcage. "No, we need more information before we move on anyone," he said through clenched teeth. He lifted his head from his pillow to search the room. "Where's Tempest? I need to speak to her about increasing security around the landing pads and inside the Obtuse Turtle."

Natascha and Medesto exchanged glances.

"We lost Tempest," the gnome said.

Gideon closed his eyes. "What happened?" he asked slowly.

"My mother has built a Portalith Machine that effectively hijacks ley-lines," Natascha replied. "She can redirect them to new worlds, but they become extremely fragile. They dry up and decompose in a matter of hours. We were in one that shattered when an angry Muse chased us off Her world. Tempest, Ren, and Charley fell into the Void. Ren tried, but wasn't able to carry both of them out. He said Tempest sacrificed herself so he and Charley could reach safety."

Gideon opened his eyes. "And the trickster?"

"Ren should have caught up to Mordecai by now," Medesto said. "The mission got derailed after what happened in *The Gaslight Adventures of Asher Grey* and we lost his trail. We picked it up again but when we lost Tempest, Ren continued on without us."

"Then with luck, he can still succeed with his original mission," Gideon muttered.

Natascha hesitated to say anything more. It was a lot to lay on their injured leader, but Gideon needed to know.

"There's something else." She took a breath. "Ren all but admitted to me that he saw Claymore with Mordecai. We don't know how far lost he is to the *Paradigm Madness*, but it's possible Claymore could be working with Mordecai."

"That is troubling," Gideon said. "It means we need to find Claymore before he is beyond our reach." His face suddenly looked very tired. He was quiet for several minutes before he spoke again. "Medesto, will you ask JoBucco to take over Tempest's role as security chief for time being. Tell Charley I need her to assume all of Tempest's duties along with her own. She'll be in charge of the WayFinder and all communications for now."

Medesto nodded. "No problem. I'll head over there when we're done here."

"One last thing," Gideon whispered. He coughed again and paid for it with a wave of pain that showed on his face. "There are letters locked in the safe in my office. Mr. B'gatti took them off Piqwic York. Bijou knows the combination. The letters are correspondence between York and Mordecai, and are mostly marching orders for his minions in Rogue Destiny. The Grimm Jester is being used as the courier. The writing appears to be from the criminal himself, but it doesn't quite sound like Mordecai Davos wrote them."

"So someone else is writing these letters for him?" Medesto asked.

Gideon nodded weakly. "I belief that is a possibility."

"Oh, I almost forgot!" Medesto went over to his traveling bag next and pulled out the worn rucksack. "This was found in one of the archives. It's full of journals and notebooks from Harper Bellweather. Mordecai is tracking her movements from one archive to the next, collecting her writings and journals that document her travels. We think she has *The Book of Days* or at least knows where it is. I read through them on the ride home, but nothing jumped out at me. When you're up to it you might see something I missed."

"Then we need to find out what we can about her," Gideon said. "I'll reach out to Haddy Rakewell to look into Harper Bellweather's background." Medesto laid the pack next to the bed.

"So how are we going to push back against the *Black Rose*?" Natascha asked.

"Don't do anything for now," Gideon answered. "We tighten the security at the Obtuse Turtle, and wait for Mr. B'gatti to contact us."

"Someone out there just tried to kill you, Gideon!" Natascha said her temper rising. "If Mordecai's lackeys are behind the bombing, what's to stop them from trying again? If that's not a reason for us to push back, what is?"

"Natascha," he replied. "Mordecai's business interests are tightly interwoven into the fabric of the City. If the Raconteurs go to war against the *Black Rose* many innocent people will get hurt. Please do not do anything until I know what is going to happen with the Council and we hear back from Mr. B'gatti."

"Fine, we'll wait to move on Mordecai," Natascha huffed. "For now."

"Thank you," Gideon muttered under his breath.

There was a sharp knock on the door. Bijou opened it to two official looking individuals, who walked in without being inviting.

"What now?" Medesto grumbled.

"Mr. Dumas? The older of the two men asked.

"I am Gideon Dumas. How can I help you?" Gideon said and threw a look at the other three in the room.

"I am Basalt Vole, Secretary of Record for the Common Council," the older man said. He was tall, dressed in a grey uniform with insignia of Rogue Destiny's city government on the shoulder.

The younger man next to him appeared to be a telegraph messenger. He straightened his back and spoke. "I have been sent to officially serve you with this Summons from the Common Council of Eternal Vigilance and Public Sympathy, and the City of Rogue Destiny in this Year of the Leviathan."

He bowed deeply and extended his white gloved hand with a thick envelope. After Gideon took the parcel, the messenger pulled a small notebook from his coat and checked the time on his watch. He jotted down the time in the notebook, then handed it to the Basalt Vole, who signed it and handed it back.

The older man stepped forward. "You have been ordered to appear before the Council one week from today to testify on the bombing at the Obtuse Turtle that killed the Protectorate General Pahloek Zima and council members Osirus Spyros, a representative from the Cultural Historical Genre and Astrid Saabey, a representative of Science Fictional Genre. This summons is only a formal inquiry to gather information on the events that occurred on March Twentieth."

"How can he be expected to appear before the Council in one a week?" Natascha shouted. "He cannot even get out of his hospital bed."

"Because the New Year is upon us, and all government offices are closed during the holiday. The Council wishes to hear testimony before the New Year so they can enjoy the holidays."

Gideon raised his hand. "That is fine." he said. "I will be there. The bombing needs to be investigated as soon as possible."

Basalt Vole bowed. "Thank you for your time," he said politely. "Have a pleasant day." Both men left room without another word.

Gideon tossed the summons to the small dresser next to his bed. It bounced off the corner and fell to the floor. Natascha picked it up and set it on top. She nodded at Bijou and Medesto.

"We should leave," Natascha said.

Gideon exhaled deeply. He shifted his head into a more comfortable spot on his pillow and closed his eyes. "I agree," he said quietly. "I need to rest.

Chapter 20
The Glorious Supreme Leader

Ren studied the details of the sleepy man's face to get a solid mental picture in his head. It was as simple as looking into a mirror and memorizing who looked back. Ren would be in close contact with people who knew Tomas well, so accuracy was imperative.

Tomas had sharp eyes and a large forehead. His hairline started far back on his cranium with a high widow's peak. Long, bushy hair reached his collar in the back and fluffed out in tangled clumps. Ren pulled the glasses off his Romanesque nose and put them on. He estimated the man's height from his prone position and shifted into an accurate duplicate of the scholar.

The man slumped forward, and the empty cup slipped from his hand to the dirt floor. Ren caught him and laid him back on the pillow. He lifted his legs up onto the cot. Tomas tried to protest, but his murmuring complaints died almost immediately. A moment later, he was softly snoring.

Ren found a suit coat hanging from a peg on the tent pole. Changing quickly into the clothes, he grabbed a backpack next to the trunk and checked the content. It was stuffed with folded maps, Tomas' own notebooks, along with those of Harper Bell-weather.

The ground under his feet shook. Ren came out of Tomas' tent to find several war machines lumbering over the crest of the western slope outside of camp. Behind the giant War Golems, a large entourage of armed soldiers marched in rank. At the front of the line of soldiers, riding in an open-top combat transport, sat a short, rotund individual who could only be the Supreme Leader.

The commander of the guerilla army wore elegant attire, somewhere between a military uniform and the royal decadence of an emperor. A majestic, fur-lined cloak covered his shoulders. The medals on the little man's shirt glinted in the hazy morning light. The man who held Mordecai's fate in his hands had arrived.

Ren hurried ahead of the approaching army. The backpack bounced on his back until he reached the center of camp. Tomas' satchel hung off his shoulder. He met Claymore's eyes across the way. His partner nodded. Ren gave him a confused look. Claymore frowned and tipped his head to the side, indicating where Ren should stand.

"Tomas, I hope we aren't bothering you," Mordecai said, growing irritation in his voice. He motioned to the space next to him with an outspread hand. Ren took his place beside Silium-Cinque Niner. The cyborg stood on one side of the crime lord, the lady in black on the other. Claymore stepped back to a protective position behind them.

"Of course not," Ren replied with a bow. "I apologize for my tardiness." Mordecai's eyes narrowed, but he said nothing. His stance shifted nervously as he prepared for the arrival of the cyborg army and their mysterious leader.

The armored vehicle drove down the middle of the encampment with soldiers flanking it on either side. Outside the cluster of tents, a dozen War Golems surrounded the perimeter of the camp.

"Come," Mordecai ordered. "We must greet our guests." He walked forward to meet the military procession, flanked by his inner circle. Ren stood in place until Claymore bumped him with a shoulder.

"That includes us, too," his partner whispered. Ren followed him to where Mordecai and the others waited.

One of the soldiers opened the door, and an automated set of steps slid out from underneath the vehicle. The Glorious Supreme Leader ambled down the ramp and approached Mordecai Davos.

The leader of the rebel army stood a couple of inches over five feet. His plump face, slicked back dark hair, and close-set eyes gave him the demeanor of undeserved superiority. The two soldiers at his side removed his cloak. They folded it like a ceremonial flag and placed it inside the transport.

The Supreme Leader adjusted the scarlet coat underneath. Fine stitching and large gold buttons covered the front, along with dozens of shiny medals and colored ribbons from battles he never fought in. How this person could command such a menacing army was beyond Ren's understanding.

General Bartacchi walked to the leader's side. The officer was the exact opposite of his master. In his youth, the general had been an imposing figure, both in stature and physical prowess. Now the onset of age and the horrors of war had diminished him. Everything below his neck gleamed with polished cybernetics. Only his left arm and scarred face remained flesh and bone. He wore a steel collar neck that braced his head. The dead eyes of the officer stared at Mordecai and Ren as they approached.

Silium Cinque Niner knelt on a metal knee as the leader reached them. "To the Glory," he said, raising his hand in salute.

The Supreme Leader made an upward gesture with his hand. "To the Glory," he repeated.

"Greetings, Your Most Gracious Excellency," Mordecai said with a deep bow. "How are the volunteers working out for you?"

"They have already been assimilated into their new purpose."

"That is good to hear," Mordecai replied. "Thank you for meeting with me. I'm hoping we can work through any misunderstandings. Since our first meeting, I have told you our destinies are intertwined. That your success is tied to my own."

"Let me stop you there, Master Mordecai," the Supreme Leader said with a dry smirk. "I considered killing you and your followers before razing your campsite, so no one could betray us to our enemies. But General Bartacchi informs me you have promised us a weapon of great destruction. I doubted the truth in that and assumed you were stalling for time so you could escape without giving what is owed to me. But you are still here, so I give you one last chance to change my mind." He clapped his hands twice.

The cyber-soldiers raised their short rifles. Many on Mordecai's side reached for their own weapons. "Stand down!" Mordecai bellowed. "Do not draw your weapons! We are here to negotiate, not fight!" His people checked their actions and stood down.

Ren clasped his hands behind his back as he saw Tomas often do and glanced at those around him. The lady in black held the box in her hands like she was about to present an award. Silium-Cinque Niner rose to his clawed metal feet. Claymore stood next to him, relaxed, as if he didn't care how this would play out. Ren wondered if his partner knew something he did not.

Ren met the eyes of the Glorious Supreme Leader's for a fleeting moment before he looked away. He thought it curious.

This small, innocuous man held such a frightening control over his troops.

"I understand we have fallen behind in our tribute," Mordecai said. "But we have run into unforeseen obstacles. All I wish is for you to give us a chance to settle our debt." He raised a hand. "Lady Absynthe?" The woman in black brought forward the small wooden box. She offered it to the leader of the guerilla army with a modest bow.

"Please accept this gift as a show of my complete support to you and your struggle," she said. "It will aid you in ways you cannot imagine."

The Supreme Leader untied the red ribbon and lifted the lid of the box. He stared at its contents with a quizzical look. "It this some attempt at humor?" He picked up a worn paperback book from the box and read the cover aloud. "*Under a Crimson Red Sky?*"

Mordecai smiled and nodded to him. "This will reveal to you all the hidden secrets of your world. The information contained within its pages will shift the fortunes of war and deliver to you something none of your enemies can ever attain. Victory in the Great War."

The Supreme Leader flipped through the pages, then closed the cover. "How can I be sure what you say is true? What is so special about a book?"

"If I may?" Mordecai asked politely, reaching out for the paperback book. He flipped through a few pages and read from the opening chapter.

It was mid-autumn when the Northern army overran the last of the Southern army's defenses. Thousands died within the first hour. Hundreds of the dead would be salvaged and repurposed to continue the fight in a war that would never end. But our Story starts years before, when I was a young man and there was still hope in the world.

A sudden wind picked up out of nowhere. A heavy gale shook the canvas walls of the tents. The ground trembled beneath Ren's feet as each word was spoken. The Supreme Leader stared open-mouthed at the sky. Beyond the thin stretches of crimson clouds, massive letters appeared across the sky. The letters formed words that matched what Mordecai recited from the Book.

Mordecai closed the book. The winds died down and the black letters faded behind the red-tinted clouds. "Those Words are what pulled your world into creation and control the very reality around us." He handed the book back to the military leader. "With this, you control your own destiny."

The leader of the guerilla rebels ran his fingertips down the creased cover and traced the picture of giant war machines marching defiantly across a desert background. He looked at his own War Golems that surrounded the camp. They were identical to those on the cover. "H-how is such a thing possible?" he stammered. "What magic is this?"

"The best kind of magic," Mordecai said with a knowing smile. "This book will win the Great War for you. Study every chapter and you will know your enemy's plans before they do. And when you are done crushing your adversaries, all I ask in return is the use of your mighty army in my own war. Trust me and I will show you other worlds to conquer."

"When do you require this army?"

"Only after all your enemies are laid at your feet." Mordecai said with a bow.

The Supreme Leader did not take his eyes off the book. "Then how can I help you now?"

"I need a few more soldiers for one last task I have to accomplish." He glanced at Ren. "If we are successful, all will be ready for my own conquest."

The Supreme Leader held the Book with both hands and

nodded to Mordecai. "I grant your request," he said. He looked to Silium-Cinque Niner. "Pick eight soldiers to accompany you and Master Mordecai on his task."

"Yes, your Excellency!" the cyborg replied. "It will be done!" He saluted his commander with a metal hand and scanned the soldiers surrounding them. He called out eight individuals by name to step forward.

Once all had fallen into line, the Supreme Leader gave one final command. "You will obey Mordecai as if he were myself! Is that understood?!" All eight recruits saluted as one and brought their guns to their chest in reverence to the command.

The rotund Supreme Leader clutched the paperback close to his chest and waddled back to his transport. When he and General Bartacchi were aboard, the military half-track backed up toward the crowd. Those standing behind it scattered in all directions to avoid getting hit.

The dictator's military halftrack drove off. Every cyber-soldier, except for the chosen eight, turned in unison and marched double-file after their commanding officer. The War Golems followed, lumbering across the parched earth in the direction they had come.

Mordecai watched the rebel army leave, a triumphant look on his face. Soon it was only his own people and newly acquired soldiers standing there. He looked at Ren.

"We are leaving immediately, Tomas," Mordecai told him. "Our goal is in sight, and I am counting on you to lead us to Bellweather's hidden sanctum."

Ren could do nothing but nod in agreement. He did not know where they were headed beyond his brief conversation with the real Tomas. Mordecai's forces were getting dangerously thin. His followers now numbered half of what Ren first saw in the bookshop in Asher Grey's novel. The soldiers on loan bolstered Mordecai defenses considerably, but if they ran into anything exceptionally dangerous, it could mark the end of Mordecai's quest.

"We leave within the hour!" Mordecai declared to his assembled followers. He ordered his new troops to guard the perimeter of his tent before disappearing inside. The Grimm Jester joined him. The crowd dispersed until only Ren and Claymore remained.

A contented smile slid across his partner's face. As if reading his mind, Claymore turned to Ren and whispered, "This is where things get interesting."

"Where did Mordecai get the Codex of this world?" Ren asked.

"I got it for him," Claymore answered.

"Why would you do that?" Ren didn't like where this was going.

"Mordecai had run out of gold," Claymore explained. "He was desperate, so I told him I could get him a copy of the Story's Codex. The Grimm Jester got me in and out of the Library without a problem."

"And you don't see anything wrong with that?" Ren asked.

Anger flared in Claymore's eyes. "Mordecai needed to stay in the good graces of the Supreme Leader," he spat. "I need him to lead me to the lodestones so I can finish one last mission. It was the only way to keep us moving toward them. The book increased my status within his inner circle. Now he trusts me more than ever. I had no choice. What else could I do?"

"Not give the blueprints of this world to some two-bit dictator with delusions of grandeur," Ren replied in a low voice. "Even I know that's wrong!"

"Don't be so naïve!" Claymore retorted. His expression turned hard. "Everything I do is for the betterment of the greater good. These are desperate times and compromises have to be made. All you and I need to focus on is getting to the lodestones before Mordecai. Don't worry about the Codex. Once we have the lodestones, we'll come back here to get the physical book back before anything bad happens to this world. Trust me, I know what I'm doing."

Claymore's words did not sit well with Ren. His partner's mind was deteriorating rapidly, and there was nothing Ren could do to help him.

Chapter 21
The Epic of Gilgamesh

Ren waited with Claymore at the heart of the encampment. Around him, people returned with their traveling gear for the journey ahead. Mordecai emerged from his tent with his own travel pack, shadowed by the hooded Grimm Jester. The crime lord headed toward the Lady Absynthe's tent, where her Portalith Machine sat ready. The cyber-soldiers marched in line two-by-two behind him. Ren and Claymore followed some distance back.

"M' lady, we are ready to leave," Mordecai called out.

Lady Absynthe stepped through the doorway of her tent, pulling on black driving gloves. She wore dark pants, high riding boots, and a short leather coat over a crisp white dress shirt with ruffles sticking out at the cuffs.

Judging from her dress, she could've been planning a pleasant drive on a warm Sunday afternoon in a 1920s English countryside. Instead, she prepared to leap across the empty black void to some distant world. She climbed into the pilot's seat of her Portalith Machine.

"Maquna, to my side," she said. The serpent she used as a

personal bodyguard slithered after her and disappeared into the shadows under the machine's reflective black shell, coiling up behind her seat.

"Have you located a new line for us to travel?" Mordecai asked.

"I warned you staying in one place too long would be risky," Lady Absynthe replied. "We are running out of ley-lines. My Portalith's too powerful for any single world. It eventually consumes all the ley energy a world offers. I have located one of the last lines twenty miles north of here. It is healthy enough to get us to our destination."

"We will not be returning to this place," Mordecai jeered. "So it doesn't matter anymore."

Lady Absynthe pulled her goggles down. She released a lever next to her seat before typing on the antique typewriter in front of her.

The Portalith machine rumbled to life and rose from the ground in a fury of swirling winds. Ren backed away from the stinging dirt and debris. Leaning forward, the machine drifted over the ground toward the flat barren landscape north of the camp.

Idalia's remaining hybrid pets trudged after their master, keeping their distance from Mordecai and his soldiers. Claymore took a defensive position in front. Ren and Silium-Cinque Niner walked on each side of the crime lord. The hooded wraith shadowed his master. The remaining thirteen members of the party followed.

The Portalith guided the group across a vast scorched wasteland. Ren stayed by Mordecai's side all day, drinking small sips of water in the impossible heat. There was little shade in which to rest, so the company pushed on as the day grew hotter and hotter. They reached their destination by late evening after the sun had sunk below the distant mountains.

Lady Absynthe searched the area with her machine until the glow of a soft green organic ley-line appeared beneath the Portalith. Once she connected to the ley-line, a straight line appeared stretching from horizon to horizon. The Portalith began to draw power from the mystical line beneath it.

"There is a great deal of magical interference where we're going!" Lady Absynthe shouted over the increasing hum of the machine. "I've never encountered anything like it! So much ley-line energy! There must be thousands of them, set very close together. I'll have no control where we come out. We can only hope for the best." She pulled a second lever.

A shaft of soft green light shot across the ground under the Portalith beyond what Ren could see. A strong wind picked up, swirling violently in a wider and wider circle. The earth cracked directly under the machine, creating a gaping round tunnel tinted in an emerald glow. Lady Absynthe guided her hovering machine down the opening and disappeared from sight.

Mordecai sent four cyber-soldiers into the slanted tunnel first, then motioned the other two after them before descending into the tunnel himself. Ren walked behind Mordecai, next to Claymore. His partner scratched the back of his head furiously, murmuring to himself. His demeanor was anxious, his eyes empty and distant. Ren caught the whispered words.

I am still a good person. I will not succumb. I am Claymore Ives. This will not defeat me.

"Tomas, stay close to me and the Jester," Mordecai said. "Where we are going, it will not be safe to wander off."

Ren took his place at Mordecai's side, trying to look as scholarly as he could and enjoying the freedom the face of Tomas gave him within the group. He sensed someone watching his movements and turned to find the dark hood of the Jester looming over him. The unseen eyes of the wraith bore into him.

Mordecai pointed to Baaklow and Claymore. "Both of you

will stay with Tomas," he ordered. "He is to be protected at all costs."

The ground beneath Ren's feet felt like soft dirt. The smell of freshly tilled soil filled the passageway, mixed with the unpleasant stench of death that surrounded the Grimm Jester who floated silently behind him. Twisting roots of the ley-line ran along the walls of the tunnel, bathing them in a dim green glow.

A mile or so later, the tunnel came out under the base of a massive tree. The trunk was a hundred feet in diameter. Thick, winding roots grew out of the ground around the mystical doorway of the rabbit-hole like writhing tentacles. They had entered the ancient book, *The Epic of Gilgamesh*.

Ren climbed over the roots onto the mossy ground. He brushed the dust from his coat and adjusted his glasses, focusing his thoughts on maintaining the physical appearance of Tomas DeMarche. The forest of similar trees were stretched out as far as he could see, their thick trunks twisted and gnarled with age.

"Amazing," Mordecai said, showing a genuine emotion that Ren had never seen before. "The thaumaturgy here is very chaotic. It's base elements are something I'm not familiar with. This place is very old. As old as the Mythic Cosmos itself, I would guess. Wayward Trees grow like weeds. That must be from such an intense concentration of magic. Don't you feel it, Tomas?"

"I do," Ren said. He sensed the magic on the air. It prickled across his skin. He did not like magic. He did not understand how it worked or how to control it. That made magic dangerous, so it was never to be trusted. Manipulating and controlling the primal elements of a magical world seemed more trouble than it was worth. He preferred Rogue Destiny, a place no magic ever reached. Overhead, sunlight trickled in through the thick foliage overhead.

Lady Absynthe waited for Mordecai atop her portal machine just beyond the rabbit-hole. Her hybrid monstrosities gathered at the base of the platform. Maquna's reptilian head rose from behind the pilot's seat. The serpent watched Mordecai intensely as he approached. The crime lord shifted his gaze to avoid eye contact with the creature.

The Grimm Jester floated within arm's reach of Mordecai. The embodiment of Death stared back at Maquna in a silent battle of supremacy. This went on for several seconds before the serpent broke its gaze first and turned away.

Once the remaining cyber-soldiers came through the rabbit-hole, their commander, Silium Cinque Niner, ordered them to spread out around Mordecai and the portal machine. Exhausted, the remaining fugitives from Lazaranth Prison dropped their packs and fell to the ground next to them. Despite the recent influx of soldiers, Mordecai's forces were getting dangerously thin. If they ran into any beasts formidable enough, it could end Mordecai's quest then and there. And that would not be a bad thing.

Mordecai raised his hands to address the assembled group. Ren stood at his side, disguised as his trusted advisor, Tomas. In front of them, a score of hardened faces waited for another empty inspirational speech.

"We have traveled far and lost many along the way," Mordecai declared. "But now our prize is at hand and once we have claimed it, we will return to Rogue Destiny as conquerors, taking back what we're owed. I ask all of you to persevere a little longer and remember the promises I made when I released you from Lazaranth Prison. I am indebted to each and every one of you. So let us rejoice as the last leg of our quest begins."

Ren saw Claymore walk off by himself, fighting his way through the thick undergrowth until he found a place to sit. He dropped his pack to the ground and buried his hands in his face. Ren could see the terrible battle his partner was fighting within himself, trying not to break down here in front of everyone.

Claymore had said nothing since they entered the ley-line. It seemed to Ren the madness gained ground during the long stretches of silence, when Claymore's mind was not engaged in anything else.

"Well, here we are, Tomas," Mordecai announced cheerfully. He slapped Ren on the back. "We will rest here for a short time, then you will lead the way to Harper Bellweather's secret sanctum."

Ren nodded, but said nothing. He walked through the crowd toward Claymore. Behind him, he could feel the foul presence of the Grimm Jester. He fought to control a shudder building along his shoulders. When he reached Claymore, his partner sat staring off into space like he was looking at something Ren could not see.

"Claymore?" Ren said. "We have a few minutes before we leave."

His partner turned to him slowly, his eyes vacant. He muttered something too soft for Ren to hear. He blinked. "Sorry, what?"

"I said we have some time before we have to go."

Claymore took a deep breath of the clean air and shook his head to clear it. He pushed himself to his feet and squared his shoulders before pulling the sawed-off Winchester rifle from its holster on his back. He hooked a thumb into his gun belt. He looked relaxed and in his element again.

Ren knew the stance all too well. He'd seen it enough times to know his partner was ready to erupt into a firestorm of bullets if the situation called for it.

"You sure you're okay?" Ren asked. He knew his partner wasn't, but he didn't know what else he could say.

"As ready as I'll ever be," Claymore rumbled. "Lead the way."

Together they traipsed through the underbrush back to find Mordecai talking with Lady Absynthe.

"Will you be joining us on the final step of our journey?" Mordecai asked her politely. There was a slight unease in his words.

"No, I prefer to remain here with my Portalith," the woman in black answered. "My pets will keep me company."

"So be it," Mordecai replied. "But I insist on leaving soldiers on the perimeter to protect you and the machine from whatever monstrosities may lurk out in the trees." He motioned to Silium-Cinque Niner. The cybernetic leader trundled over on heavy metal legs.

Lady Absynthe glanced over at Maquna. The tension in the air was thick. Ren found it amusing to watch the trust between Mordecai and Lady Absynthe erode before his eyes. No words needed to be spoken. Their body language said it all.

Mordecai put a hand on the cyborg's back and led him away from the portal machine. Ren followed them, imitating the walking patterns and idiosyncrasies of Tomas DeMarche. Claymore remained where he stood. Once again, they were in sync with each other, knowing when to give the other room to work and when to be close enough to assist if the need arose. There was nothing Claymore could do right now, but Ren could find out what Mordecai planned next.

Mordecai walked far enough away, no one would hear them. He leaned in close to the cyborg and whispered, "While we search for Bellweather's hideaway, I need you to stay here and prevent Lady Absynthe from leaving. She is our only way out of here. I don't want to have to walk to Rogue Destiny. Watch her closely and take two soldiers to back you up."

"She will not leave, sir," the cyborg rumbled. He hoisted his rifle up and pressed a button on his metallic skullcap. "Cyg-88 and Cyg-21, front and center." The two soldiers were in motion before he has finished speaking.

Mordecai threw an eye toward the portal machine. "And, Silium, let your people know not to make direct eye contact with the serpent. If it comes down to gunfire, the serpent should be the first one you put down. Kill them all if you have to, including Lady Absynthe. Tomas can learn to drive the machine."

Claymore watched the scene play out from a distance with a bemused smirk on his face. Ren didn't doubt he knew what was being discussed, analyzing every possible recourse if things turned violent.

Silium-Cinque Niner's cybernetic design contrasted with the sleeker technology the two younger fighters carried. Ren had not seen him up close and even though his face was half encased in metal, he still looked haggard, and world-weary.

Ren smiled to himself. *Trust among thieves*. Mordecai feared being left behind if Lady Absynthe decided things had gotten too dangerous. He couldn't blame her. No doubt the dense forest hid nasty surprises in all directions.

Mordecai gave Claymore a nod to get his people up and moving.

Claymore nodded and lightly kicked the boot of the closest person asleep on the ground. "Everyone up!" he shouted. "It'll be dark in a couple hours, and we need to cover as much ground as we can before then. Stay on guard! This place is alive with the hum of so many ley-lines it will undoubtedly attract creatures from the farthest reaches of the cosmos. Keep an eye on every rabbit-hole you pass. No telling what might jump out."

The last of Mordecai's followers climbed begrudgingly to their feet. Amid the grumbling and swearing, all of them readied their weapons and picked up their gear.

Mordecai slapped Ren on the back. "This is it, Tomas," he said. "You are most familiar with Bellweather's writings, so lead the way."

"Of course," Ren replied. He searched his memory for the sparse details the real Tomas DeMarche had told him. "We need to find the river mentioned in her journals. *The Euphrates*. But in what direction it lies from where we stand, I can only guess."

"I'll take point," Claymore said. He strode forward with a confident swagger. Ren traipsed after him under a dark canopy of leaves that blocked out the sky. Mordecai came next, with the Grimm Jester drifting after him. The eight cyber-soldiers took up positions around Mordecai, three on each side. His remaining followers of escaped fugitives brought up the rear.

The only thing Ren knew about *The Epic of Gilgamesh* was that it was very old. Possibly the oldest world in existence.

Claymore led the party through a forest of ancient trees that seemed to go on forever. There were no visible roads or paths, so they were forced to push through the underbrush at a slow pace. The tangled tree roots grew out in every direction, slowing their progress even further. Every so often, an unseen animal scurried out of their path.

Mist hung in long swaths between the giant trunks. Moss grew everywhere, on fallen trees, rocks, and open ground. Despite that, a cool breeze blew through the leaves. It was an idyllic place in its own dark, twisted way. Green and peaceful, like a snapshot of a forgotten place. Ren wondered if anyone other than Harper had ever walked among these trees that seems older than time.

As they hiked over the uneven ground, their surroundings remained unchanged. Ren could not tell one direction from another. The hum of the ley-lines vibrated on the air as they passed hundreds of rabbit-holes nestled snugly under the roots of the Wayward Trees. Every one nearly identical to the one that brought them to Gilgamesh. The soft greenish glow emanated from each, giving the forest an ethereal fairy-tale quality.

The ground suddenly sloped downward. Claymore glanced at Ren and gave him a quick nod in that direction. The coolness of the forest faded as the air became hotter. Sweat broke out on Ren's brow as they labored through the difficult downhill terrain.

They wandered through the hanging vines and thick foliage for another hour. Ren pretended to have some vague idea of where he was leading them, hoping Claymore had a better read on their location than he did. If not, he figured as long as they continued downward, they would eventually break out of the trees. Claymore offered occasional advice, which Ren happily accepted. There were no landmarks to go by or breaks in the mist covered forest.

Tangled underbrush and twisted roots blocked their way, making it difficult for the soldiers to maintain their perimeter on each side of Mordecai. As darkness fell, the forest came alive with sound and movement. Eerie cries broke the silence in the trees and the ear-piercing screeches rang out from invisible creatures hiding among the surrounding trees.

In the distance came the crashing sound of a massive beast lumbering through the moss-covered forest. A terrifying roar that shook the ground followed it. Ren caught a distant glimpse of the dark hide of some primaeval creature. Somewhere in the darkness, an identical sound answered it. Guns came up, but Claymore threw up his hand before anyone fired. Whatever the behemoth was, it slowly wandered away from them.

After a brief rest, they tromped on through the heavy under-brush. Claymore slowed his pace until he was next to Ren. He drew his revolver and held it out.

"What's that for?" Ren asked.

"We don't know what's out there," Claymore replied with a

smirk. He glanced back at Mordecai, who walked a dozen yards behind them. "You'll know what to do when the moment arrives."

Ren weighed the revolver in his hand before sliding it into the pocket of his long coat.

Chapter 22
Monsters in the Night

Mordecai Davos sat down on a moss covered log and ran a hand through his sweat soaked hair. "Tomas, did Harper Bellweather's journals mention anything specific about the location of this river?" he asked in-between labored breaths. The glow of the rabbit-holes pushed back the darkness, allowing enough light to travel by.

"No, her writings gave no clear details," Ren replied. He assumed only Tomas had studied Harper's journals, so he felt free to embellish the information as he saw fit. "She wrote that a great river lay beyond the sea of Wayward Trees. I've done my best to get us there, but I fear we are only going in circles. Harper was smart to choose this place to hide the lodestones."

"This is getting us nowhere, Davos!" Claymore rumbled. He looked around the dark forest. "It's almost nightfall and I guarantee you don't want to discover what's out there after the sun goes down. Send your ghoul up over the trees to find the river!"

There was an obvious hesitation in Mordecai's response to Claymore's request. Ren could tell the crime lord was afraid to be separated from the black-hooded wraith. While the cyber-soldiers had sworn to protect him, there was little anyone could do to prevent an assassin's bullet from inside his own dissatisfied ranks.

Ren saw Claymore smile as Mordecai found himself caught between losing face in front of his followers and leaving himself vulnerable without his favored bodyguard beside him. Claymore raised an eyebrow as if to say *now is the time*. Ren nodded.

"That might not be a bad idea!" Ren added, loud enough for all to hear. "I hoped we would stumble onto a road or an animal trail that would lead to the river, but Claymore is right. It'll be dark soon. The Jester is our best bet to locate the river."

Mordecai started to object but caught himself. "Very well," he conceded. He slipped a hand inside his long coat. It was a deliberate action, one that struck Ren as odd.

"Jester, find this river!" Mordecai ordered. "But be quick! Time is of the essence!" There was a subtle reluctance to his voice. The tall, cloaked figure gave a slight nod. He glanced over at Ren before rising through the branches to disappear into the blackness.

The stench of decay that surrounded the Grimm Jester dissipated the moment the wraith vanished among the trees. Mordecai stepped closer to Ren, glancing at his own people for any sign one of them might pose a threat to him. Ren fingered the handle of the pistol in his coat pocket and marched through the forest alongside Mordecai.

They continued forward until, somewhere in the distant trees, the piercing cry of a large feline predator split the quiet air. It came from the left side of the group. Everyone turned their attention to the dense, overgrown forest. Claymore lifted his rifle towards the sound. "We need to get to higher ground!"

Claymore led the party forward in silence. The armed cyber-soldiers spread out around Mordecai, weapons at the ready. Ren remained close to Mordecai as his followers fell in behind them.

There was a shout from someone at the rear of the group. "There's movement back here!"

An enormous beast moved swiftly through the undergrowth, making no attempt to remain hidden. Ren caught a quick glimpse of the animal, but nothing more in the dying light. He pulled the revolver from his coat and held it at his side.

"What do you see back there, Godi?" Claymore bellowed. He leveled his rifle at the darkness.

"It was there, then it was gone," came the reply.

The cyber-soldier, Cyg-51, shouted from across the group. "We've got something on this side too!"

Ren and Claymore came to a small clearing in the trees. A single shaft of dim sunlight broke through the canopy to illuminate the area. Claymore held his hand up. "Hold up, there's another one over there!" he yelled. He raised his carbine. "Just over that rise!"

Ren heard movement on their right. An occasional guttural trill drifted through the air, answered by a high-pitched growl further away. The creatures were keeping their distance but made sure their presence was known.

A scream broke the silence from someone in the back. Every weapon turned in that direction.

"Go!" Claymore yelled, pointing ahead of them. "They're trying to hem us in. Stay together, but keep moving!" He rushed forward along the clearest path he could find. Ren stayed on his partner's heels, fighting his way through the deep underbrush. Mordecai followed after him, his soldiers spread out around him.

Ren realized the presence of the Grimm Jester's vile stench kept the beasts away, but now the wraith was not with the group. It was only a matter of time before the creatures attacked in full force.

The party moved as one unit, shoulder to shoulder, watching

the dark trees surrounding them. Several predatory animals were on both sides of them now, just beyond Ren's line of sight. The company had gone another hundred yards before the path they were on descended into a wide hollow full of fallen logs and dripping moss.

Two massive cat-like beasts stalked out of the forest on a rise in front of them. They were huge, hunched-back creatures with flat heads and wide mouths, brimming with sharp teeth. Three more appeared behind them. A dozen waited in the branches above their brethren.

"They weren't trying to surround us!" Ren yelled. "They drove us to the rest of their pack!"

"Clever beasts," Claymore mused grimly.

One of the enormous cat-creatures leapt. Claymore fired his sawed-off rifle at the enormous beast. The blast echoed across the silent glade. The bullet struck the cat in the head in a spray of dark liquid. Claymore cocked his rifle as the monster continued toward him. A second shot left the fearsome animal dead on the ground.

Chaos erupted all around them. Ren couldn't tell how many cats were out there, but they had the group completely encircled. Gunfire filled the air as the beasts charged forward in the growing darkness. Others dropped from the trees behind them. Bullets tore up the brush and branches as enormous shadowy shapes closed in on the company from all sides.

Ren gripped his pistol. Under different circumstances, he would be in the thick of the fight, attacking the cats in the shape of a big, nasty monster of his own making. As it was, he stayed where he stood until someone bumped into him. He turned to find himself next to Mordecai.

"Remain by my side, Tomas, until the Jester returns!" Mordecai shouted over the gunfire.

The moment Ren had waited for had arrived. With the

Grimm Jester gone, he had the chance to kill Mordecai. His thumb cocked the hammer back. All he had to do was pull the trigger and it would be over. His death would be quick and pain-less. It was more than the man deserved. Just another gunshot lost amid the surrounding turmoil.

During Ren's absence from Rogue Destiny, Mordecai Davos had ordered the deaths of the members of *The Gentlemen of the Open Road*. An insignificant street gang, to be sure, but his loyal friends none-the-less.

A sudden hesitance stopped him from firing the gun. He couldn't explain it, but it was there, pushing past his impulsive nature to the surface. Now that the opportunity presented itself, he found himself unable to shoot Mordecai Davos. Ren had killed without remorse before. That was not the issue. Most had certainly deserved it. A few—maybe not so much.

He feared if he shot Mordecai it would only push Claymore further down the road Ren was trying to save him from. His partner had shot and killed Serralto Cardus, the only person who could prove Ren and Claymore's innocence in the genocide of an entire civilization.

Before that moment, Ren never realized how much his part-ner's moral compass meant to him. Claymore had always been the paragon of good, the one who fought evil wherever he found it. Righting wrongs and protecting the sovereignty of worlds across the Mythic Cosmos.

That's who he was, but without those moral principles, Clay-more continued to sink into a quagmire of madness. Now, it was up to Ren to remind his partner of what he once stood for. He longed for the way things used to be and if putting aside his own need for vengeance could help get back to that, so be it.

For the first time, Ren saw his own casual disregard for the lives of others in a new light. He'd always been morally lazy about right and wrong, he knew that. It's not that he didn't want to see it. He just didn't care. Maybe Ren needed to be the moral example now. He lowered the revolver.

He backed up into Silium-Cinque Niner. The gigantic cyborg glanced down at him, then returned to his aggressive, combative position, firing at the predatory cats as they bounded across the ground toward them.

The cyber-soldier next to Ren disappeared under a blur of scales, feathers, and fur. The cat pinned the soldier to the ground with four of its eight legs. Dagger-like canine teeth crunched through the armor into the soft flesh underneath.

The soldier struggled under the predator for a moment before he thrashed one final time. The cat lifted its head from the corpse, considering Ren. Its blood-spattered snout opened to reveal rows of sharp teeth behind two long canines. A low rumble grew in its throat as the muscles under its eight legs tensed.

Ren grabbed the automatic weapon next to the lifeless soldier and body-rolled as the giant cat leapt at him. He raised both his guns and fired. Bullets ripped through the thick scaled shoulders and feathered head. The creature raged in pain as it died in a heap at Ren's feet. He fired the rifle until it clicked empty. He tossed it aside and held his pistol ready. In the receding light, the dead cat-creature was bigger than it had looked from a distance. The beast was the size of a prehistoric tiger, lean, sleek and deathly quick. Its head and body vaguely resembled a feline, only with feathers, scales, and too many legs. A score of black stripes ran horizontally down its fur to camouflage its movements. Ren searched the chaos for his partner.

To his left, another soldier went down under the onslaught of the monstrous beasts. Her weapon continued firing wildly as a fury of claws and teeth tore her apart. Ren threw himself to the ground to avoid the erratic gunfire. The cyborg officer responded too slowly.

Silium-Cinque Niner shielded the organic half of his scarred face with an arm as the spray of bullets bounced off his iron frame. The impact of the gunfire forced him back until he tripped over a twisted outcropping of roots. A gigantic shadow fell on him from above.

The fallen cyborg caught the beast by the throat with one hand as it landed on him. He fired his weapon into its midsection. The cat-creature twisted in his grip as its body hemorrhaged under the high caliber gunfire. Silium-Cinque Niner climbed to his feet and pushed the corpse aside. Under his shredded uniform, deep scratches from the monster's massive claws scored the dull gray armor. Otherwise, Silium-Cinque Niner appeared physically unharmed.

Ren saw Claymore emerge from the shadows with a gigantic cat at his heels. His partner turned and got off a shot with his rifle. The beast stumbled and fell, but there was still fight left in it. It leapt at Claymore and raked a huge claw across his shoulder and chest. He staggered back, blood flying from his wounds. Somehow, he managed to stay on his feet and slammed a boot down against the wounded creature's neck, forcing it down. He fired his rifle again and again in rapid succession until the beast stopped thrashing.

The cyber-soldiers hemmed Mordecai in, protecting him and keeping the feline predators at bay while the rest of the survivors grouped together, firing at any animal that ventured too close. The cats circled around them slowly. Ren counted fourteen beasts that he could see, but suspected more hiding out of sight beyond the clearing. He found himself back to back with Claymore.

"Well?" Ren asked. "What now?"

"You should go!" Claymore replied. "One of us has to survive to finish this!"

"Not going to happen!" Ren said.

Ren felt the magic swirl in the air and crackle with unseen energy. The sensation sharpened a moment before a high wall of fire encircled them. The giant cats jumped back from the licking flames. Some of them got caught up in the inferno. Others bolted away, yowling in fear. The heat from the firewall increased in intensity. Ren dropped to the dirt and pulled his coat up to protect himself.

The center of the ring became an inferno of blazing heat. Beside him, Claymore lay with his arms covering his head. As the heat became too much to bear, the circle of flame died as quickly as it had appeared. Ren lifted his face to see nothing but a smoldering ring of ashes.

A set of boots stepped in front of him. "Come, Tomas," a voice above him said. "You have always shown me loyalty. I watch over those who are faithful to me." Ren looked up into Mordecai's face. The crime lord grabbed his hand and helped to his feet. The ground was a scorched ring of black smoke. The burned bodies of several cats lay lifeless across the open glade. Their corpses smoldered from the unearthly fire. Mordecai had a strange look in his eyes as he surveyed the damage the flames had done.

Ren checked himself for burn injuries. He patted out the glowing embers on Thomas' long coat. His face and hands felt hot from exposure to the intense heat, but he appeared to have no actual burns. He ran a painful hand through his singed hair.

"Come. We must be going," Mordecai said as he walked away. Ren watched him go, mystified by what had actually happened.

Ren heard the low growl before he saw the cat crouching in the shadows, twenty feet away. The giant feline bounded forward and launched itself at Mordecai. Ren fired. His pistol clicked empty.

A shadow fell over them in a rush of wind. The momentum

of the beast stopped as a skeletal hand snatched the cat in midair. It choked out a roar as it raked its claws across the Grim Jester's black cloak. The wraith slammed the creature down to the ground. A dark crackling energy poured over the thrashing animal.

The cat's body spasmed, and sparks flew from its fur. Smoke rose as it fought against the inevitable. The flailing slowed until all movement ended. The wraith let the smoldering corpse fall to the ground and looked around for any further threat. The display of unbridled power of the Grimm Jester scared Ren a bit, yet left him impressed.

The monster floated silently to Mordecai. Three giant cats growled and paced at the edge of the trees. They backed away, intimidated by the wraith and the foul stench that accompanied him. Ren stepped over the smoldering patches of burning debris, his ears still ringing from the gunfire.

Claymore sat on a fallen log, shirtless. He wrapped a crude bandage over his injuries where the cat had clawed him across his chest. He tied it off and pulled out a fresh shirt from his pack.

Ren ran up to him. "Are you okay?"

"I'm alive," Claymore replied. "Don't know how okay I am." He stood up to reload his rifle, then dug in his pocket for a handful of bullets. He handed them to Ren, then picked up his pack and threw it over a shoulder. "We need to find Harper's hideout soon. I can't be the only one running low on ammunition. If they attack again, we're done for."

While bandaging wounds and reloading weapons, the survivors huddled close to one another. The three remaining cyber-soldiers stood over the bodies of Cyg-24, Cyg-34 and Cyg-3-1-9. The dead soldiers lay torn open, their chest armor useless against the claws and teeth of the beats. Each, in turn, took a moment to honor their fallen comrades, while the others watched the forest for another attack. After they were done, the surviving four swiftly removed the weapons, ammunition, and supply packs from the corpses before leaving the mangled bodies where they fell.

Mordecai studied the carnage. Over two dozen cats lay dead or dying on the ground. Six Lazaranth fugitives had been killed, along with the three soldiers. He stood close to the Grimm Jester, talking in low tones. Ren listened, but couldn't hear what was being said. The wraith pointed to the east through the jungle.

"We must continue on," Mordecai commanded. "The Jester has found the river."

The remaining company pressed on in the direction the hooded wraith indicated. Claymore led the way once again under the dark trees. Ren walked by his side, watching the blackness for the giant cats' return.

Ren looked behind them. Claymore's long stride had outpaced the rest of the company. "Where'd that wall of fire come from?" he asked in a low voice.

Claymore seemed irritated by the question. "Does it matter? It means someone among us is magically capable. In the chaos, it could've been anyone. Why should I care about that?"

"Because it means someone else in the party will be going after the lodestones."

Claymore leaned over to Ren. "Then be ready for things to come crashing down very soon," he whispered with a wry grin. "It won't be long now."

Chapter 23
Monoceros

The forest grew darker the further they walked through the trees. The night became filled with noises stirred up by their gunfire. Ren pushed his way through the foliage, brushing aside the vines hanging from the low branches. The ground was uneven, and they had to find detours around the massive roots and fallen logs. Night had deepened, and he heard the stirring of creatures lurking just out of sight. The screams and cries of unknown things came from the surrounding darkness.

They marched on through the dark for several more hours, plodding up an incline that turned into a steep hill before it opened onto a wide plateau. Ren saw the twinkling stars filling the night sky for the first time since they arrived in *The Epic of Gilgamesh*. He let the gentle breeze blow across his face. In the distance, he could hear the faint roar of a river.

Mordecai held up his hand. "We'll make camp here," he announced. "Grab a few hours of sleep and once the sun is up, we will continue."

"I'll take first watch," Claymore replied. He climbed a rock that looked over their makeshift camp and sat down. He laid his rifle across his knees, staring into the star speckled night sky.

The party spread out and made camp across the flat plateau. Mordecai took a place away from the others. The remaining four cyber-soldiers took up strategic positions to watch over him. The Grimm Jester floated in the air near his master.

Ren found a spot near Mordecai and rolled out his bedroll on the rocky ground. He lay down using his pack as a pillow, but there was no sleep in him. The possibility of what tomorrow would bring consumed him. The lodestones were in reach now, and all hell would break loose once he and Claymore made their move.

Ren could not get comfortable on the hard ground. After a while, he decided to join Claymore on guard duty. He got up. Two of the soldiers turned to him, their weapons ready.

"Nothing to worry about," Ren replied, holding his where they were visible. "Just need to relieve myself."

He climbed the rocks to where Claymore had stationed himself. He found his partner speaking in low tones to himself, his attention on the sea of stars overhead. He didn't hear Ren approach him from behind.

The knife sliced the darkness. The assassin was confident he would kill Jackson Barrow with a single strike of his poisoned blade. But the killer's padded slipper gave the faintest scuff along the floor as he attacked, and Rip's cat-like reflexes reacted. At the sound, he turned and caught the wrist that held the curved dagger in mid-strike.

On the man's forearm, a tattoo of a red scorpion gleamed in the dim lantern light. The emblem of the Assassin's Brotherhood. Jackson delivered a thundering blow to the masked assailant, laying the would-be assassin senseless on the floor of the dark hotel room.

Webb burst into the room, dragging behind him a waiter from the restaurant. "I found him!" Webb declared. Jackson grabbed him by the throat and slammed the terrified man into the wall.

"Where is she?!" he demanded. His grip tightened.

"Who?" the waiter choked out through the pain. "I don't know who you're looking for!"

"Jasmina Bezadi, the heiress!" Jackson replied. He loomed over the young man.

"Two men left with her by truck an hour ago, out through the eastern gate of the city!" the man replied. His whole body was shaking under Jackson's viselike grip.

"Where are they headed?!" he roared.

"I heard them mention Constantinople!!" the waiter cried in response. Jackson released his hold on the man's throat and swore under his breath.

"Webb, gather the crew and get them back to the ship!" Jackson ordered. "Radio the Leviathan to have them ready to pull anchor! We leave immediately!"

The words stopped. Claymore's head drooped like he had reached the point of exhaustion. His breath came in short, raspy gasps.

"It's getting worse, isn't it?" Ren said. The words startled Claymore, but brought him out of his stupor. He grabbed for his rifle, then he slowly glanced over his shoulder.

"Yeah," Claymore muttered. "Give me a moment to clear my head." He took a deep breath. Ren sat down cross-legged on the flat boulder across from him. Conversation seemed to keep Claymore grounded to reality, so that's what he would do. Keep him talking.

"You ever miss your homeworld?" Ren said.

"Not really," Claymore replied. "After a while, one place looks like any other. All the genres blend together. The people of any given world are pretty much the same, wrapped up in their own petty problems, never realizing what lies beyond their doorstep. What's the point anymore? What does any of it mean?"

"Who knows?" Ren replied. "Once we have what we came

here for, we can discuss the deeper mysteries of the universe. How are your injuries?"

"Sore, but the bleeding's stopped," Claymore replied. "Tomorrow is going to be a big day. You should try to sleep if you can. No telling what might happen. We both need to be sharp."

"I'll be fine," Ren insisted.

They sat together in silence for hours. Ren dozed off and on, resting his head on his knees. The world appeared quiet and peaceful from the escarpment. Behind them, the forest of Wayward trees stretched as far as the eye could see. He stared out across the raw beauty of *The Epic of Gilgamesh* until the eastern horizon was aflame with the light of a new day.

Claymore's eyes stared off into space. His face appeared more gaunt than it had before the prehistoric cats attacked the party. The Paradigm Madness continued its insidious consumption of his mind, slowly eating away at his soul. Ren watched helplessly as his friend slipped further from reality with every moment. He knew they had to get the lodestones soon, or Claymore would not survive this.

As the daylight increased, Claymore scanned the landscape with a small pair of binoculars. He had not moved the entire night. He mumbled to himself from time to time, but too softly for Ren to pick up what he said.

Claymore handed the binoculars to him. "Look out toward the horizon. You see it?"

Ren stretched his aching muscles and took the binoculars. Through the glasses, the harsh desert terrain came into clear view. The rocky, barren ground extended all the way to the horizon. In the distance, he could make out the thin blue strip of a winding river.

"Is that the Euphrates?" Ren asked, handing the binoculars back.

"It has to be," Claymore replied, climbing to his feet. "It'll be a hard day's march to reach it, but if we hurry, we could be there by afternoon." They climbed off the plateau to join the rest of the camp. A fire had been lit and the exhausted troops sat around it.

After a cold breakfast of dried fruits and meat, Ren helped Claymore break camp, and they started what he hoped was the last leg of their journey.

Ten hours later, Ren traipsed the rocky shore of the Euphrates River, his hands behind his back imitating Tomas' distinct plodding gait. Claymore walked beside him, looking out at the water as it surged by them in a torrent of fury. They had encountered no more threats throughout the day. The only signs of life they came across were insects, birds, and a few small animals.

Once the river was in sight, Claymore marched forward with sudden purpose. His long stride made it difficult for Ren to keep up without breaking the nuances of his disguise. His partner had been getting more agitated and unpredictable as the day wore on, but his sour disposition vanished into a determined savage grin when he saw the Euphrates.

"We have found the river, Tomas!" Mordecai announced. "Which way is Harper's hideaway?"

"Monoceros sits at the top of a waterfall," Ren told him. "So we need to go downriver."

The sun hung in the sky over the western mountains. Mordecai nodded and assumed the lead with his entourage of soldiers flanking him. The Grimm Jester drifted not far from his Master. The handful of Lazaranth fugitives trudged along behind. Many looked like they were ready to collapse on the ground at any moment.

"You ready for this?" Ren whispered.

Claymore didn't answer. Either he hadn't heard the question over the sounds of the river or something else dominated his thoughts. A moment later, he fell in line behind the others. Ren could only follow. The company marched along the rough shoreline.

"There!" Mordecai announced. "Harper Bellweather's private sanctuary, Monoceros!"

Ren's gaze drifted over the swirling waters to an odd-looking building that sat in the center of the river, downstream from where they stood. A house of Victorian architecture had been built atop the overturned hull of a large wooden sailing ship. The bow of the vessel sat low enough in the water that the roaring river surged around it. Beyond the house, a dense wall of mist rose up.

Harper's hideaway hung precariously over the precipice of a great waterfall. The structure was two stories of high-peaked roofs and a rickety watchtower. It was the perfect getaway to hide from the dangers of this world. And the perfect place to hide the artifact they were searching for.

Beyond the house, a shroud of misty vapor stretched to the sky. The dense veil stretched to the horizon on either side. They had reached the edge of the world, where all maps ended. Ren had never ventured past the veils of mist he had encountered in his travels and often wondered what lay beyond them.

Mordecai hurried the party along the riverbank to the point closest to the sanctuary. The company spread out and explored the rocky river bank for a way across the surging waters, but they found no hidden boat or any way to cross. Mordecai stepped out onto the rocks overlooking the swirling river.

"If Harper gets across this, so can we!" he shouted over the roar of the river. "Spread out! Maybe there's a hidden tunnel that leads under the water!"

Ren caught his partner's eye. He gave a head bob toward the

house and made butterfly gestures with his hands. He could fly over and locate the Roskashon Lodestones before Mordecai could get to them. Claymore could play dumb, and they could meet up later before leaving Gilgamesh together. There were hundreds of rabbit-holes to choose from and no way anyone could follow them if they were careful.

Claymore gave a nod toward the shrouded form floating next to Mordecai and shook his head. The Grimm Jester would chase after the trickster and without Claymore there to keep him at bay, the encounter would not be pleasant.

Ren shrugged and wandered to the cusp of the cliffs where the thundering river disappeared into the mist covered abyss that marked the end of this world. An idiom commonly used by the Raconteurs came to Ren's mind.

A world is only as big as the Story needs it to be.

It was an easy descriptor to explain what constituted the size of a world. An epic Story spanning continents would be infinitely larger than that of a Story set entirely inside a small college town like the apocalyptic world of Bree Sandoval.

The glint of sunlight flashed off something metallic in the mist below him. He squinted in the afternoon light and looked down into the mist. Twenty feet below him, in the shrouded haze, he could make out a thick steel cable running along the cliff face, held aloft by brackets intermittently attached to the sheer rock. He walked to the edge, following the cable's path out over the waterfall until it disappeared under an outcropping of rocks beneath the sanctuary. Ren motioned Claymore over.

"There's something down there."

Claymore laid flat on a rock and peered over the ledge. "So that's how she gets across!" He jumped to his feet.

Ren walked along the precipice for fifty yards before he came to a set of rough steps carved into the rocks of the cliff face.

"Claymore!" he yelled. "Down here!" His partner ran over. Ren started down the steps first, but Claymore caught his arm.

"I'll take the lead, *Tomas*," he said with a wicked grin. "You remain in character and stay behind me." Claymore scratched the back of his head furiously, but stopped himself and ran his fingers through his thick, dark hair instead. He navigated the narrow stairs with Ren at his heels. The flimsy handrail proved useless.

The steps descended fifty feet down the side of the cliff, stopping at a crude wooden platform that protruded from the wall. A metal handrail lined the scaffolding to guard against falling off into the misty depths below them. The overhead cable threaded around a large metal wheel and stretched across the abyss to the sanctuary. The platform creaked as Claymore stepped onto it. Ren remained on the last earthen step.

He flipped open the metal panel of a control box mounted on the rock wall to reveal a dial set all the way to the left. Insulated wires ran along the stone from the box to the small flywheel that held the cable aloft.

Claymore twisted the knob to the right. Gears clunked above them, then the sound of a motor started. The wheel turned slowly, pulling the steel cable taut. Ren followed the moving steel line to where it disappeared from sight under the waterfall.

"Have you found something, Claymore?" Both looked up to see Mordecai glaring down at them over the cliff's edge.

"We'll know in a moment!" Claymore shouted, unfazed by the anger in Mordecai's voice. The criminal descended the steps, staying close to the wall until he reached the platform. Behind him, two cyber-soldiers carefully navigated the slippery steps. The Grimm Jester drifted from the clifftop, but kept a respectable distance from Claymore.

"Mr. Ives, you forget your place," Mordecai said sternly. "I am leading this expedition, not you." He shot a hard glare at Ren, too. "That includes you, Tomas."

"I wanted to make sure it was important before we bothered you," Claymore replied. He threw a wry grin at him.

A crackle of electricity erupted from the control box. The cable above them dipped as if weight had been added at the other end. Moments later, an open air gondola moved slowly along the steel line toward them. As the basket grew closer, Ren saw a look of eagerness return to Mordecai's eyes.

When the dangling cage reached them, it stopped with a clank, swaying back and forth in front of them. Claymore opened the gondola door and stepped in. The platform was only wide enough to fit a couple of people, so Mordecai and his retinue waited on the narrow stone steps.

"Mr. Ives? If you please." Mordecai stepped down onto to the wooden platform next to Ren. "You have been a valuable asset to me but remember who is still in charge."

Claymore stepped out of the gondola to let Mordecai slip by him. "Sorry, boss. Getting a little ahead of myself." He glanced at Ren.

"I will cross first with Tomas," Mordecai instructed. "His expertise will be necessary once we are inside. Claymore, you and the soldiers will follow next. I ordered the rest of our party to wait for us out of sight until we return."

Ren joined Mordecai in the gondola's basket and shut the gate. A handle hung from the cart's motor box. Mordecai pulled it down. The metal cage jerked forward and surged away from the platform over the abyss, pulled along by the tiny motor above them.

"Jester, come!" Mordecai shouted. Ren felt goosebumps rise on his skin as the monster's vile stench of decay drew closer. They hung out in the open air, the spray from the waterfall hitting their faces.

The wooden floor creaked under their weight. Mordecai shifted his feet, fighting his impatience. The cage left the cliff face on the single steel cable, swaying above the misty abyss.

"You and Claymore Ives have become quite chatty of late, Tomas," Mordecai remarked. His dark eyes studied Ren with an uncomfortable intensity. "Why is that?"

"Claymore told me where he went with the Jester to steal the book you offered to the Supreme Leader so he could win his war," Ren replied without hesitation. "I have always been fascinated by the Library, where the Books of the universe are safeguarded. I asked him for details and came to find Claymore Ives has lived a rather fascinating life."

"Good enough, but do not bother getting to know Mr. Ives." Mordecai gave him a cruel smile. "His knowledge has been invaluable to our mission. Without him, we would never have maintained our relationship with the cyborgs. But his time with us is coming to its end. Once the lodestones are in my hand, the Jester will have him."

Ren's eyes were drawn to the wraith floating alongside the gondola. The Grimm Jester stared at him silently. His hideous grin stretched wider than usual, like he understood the irony of the statement. He wondered if Mordecai would feel so smug once he learned his flying ghoul held an irrational fear of Claymore. He took a deep breath, eager to get to the end of this job.

Chapter 24
Thrill of the Hunt

Natascha's agitation rose as she exited Gideon's room. Now they had the Common Council to worry about. No doubt this *inquiry* would lead to blaming the Raconteurs for substandard security that failed to protect the Council members so they could accuse Gideon of letting the bombing occur. She hated government politics, and the Common Council was among the worst she had personally encountered. Everyone on the council had personal agendas and pockets filled with bribe money.

The Raconteurs had the *Society of the Black Rose* coming at them from one side, and now the Common Council assailed them from the other. She worked herself into quite a fury by the time she finished her thought, but was already formulating their next step.

There was a ruckus in the hallway. She looked over to see Valgus pushing his way through a dozen orderlies, with Jonny, Charley and Raffles following in his wake. Two of the largest guards blocked Valgus's way. He grabbed each of them by the throat and continued forward. Both men stumbled back, trying to break free from the barbarian's grip.

Medesto held up his Raconteur badge. "They're with us," he

said. The rest of the security personnel stopped where they were at the sight of the badge. The Raconteurs still held sway in some parts of the city, Natascha thought.

Raffles waddled up to Natascha. "Gideon goin' be okay?" he asked, almost choking on the words.

"He's badly injured," Natascha told him. "But the doctor said he should pull through."

"That's good news then," Valgus rumbled. He released the two men he held and strode over.

"I want someone here with him every minute," Natascha ordered. "Whoever did this may come back and try to finish the job. After losing Claymore, we won't lose Gideon too. Jonny, you mind staying here and watch over him?"

"No problem at all." Jonny slicked back his pompadour with a comb and adjusted his custom-tailored black suit. "Let them come."

"You armed?" Natascha asked.

Jonny lifted the sides of his black suit jacket to reveal a double shoulder holster with two pearl- handled automatics. "Don't go anywhere without them."

Jonny Vega had arrived in Rogue Destiny a year earlier from a distant, futuristic novel series called *On the Streets of the Neon City*. He'd worked on a police task force that hunted illegal genetically mutated humans that roamed a metropolis called *Hong Kong*. His proficiency in hand to hand combatant was unrivaled, and no Raconteur was a better shot.

"Thank you," Natascha said.

Jonny glanced up and down the hallway. "So, where are you going?"

"After the *Black Rose*," Natascha replied. "We won't attack anyone directly, but I have some ideas how we can hurt them. With Mordecai out of town, this may be the perfect opportunity to bring them down financially."

"Raffles, you're welcome to join us," Natascha said.

"Love ta, Doct'r, but Ah need to be goin'," the rabbit chuffed. "I been gone from home too long as it is and have ta get back 'fore my Story start ta ferget me."

"So this is goodbye?" Charley asked. She bent down to give him a hug. "I'm going to miss you, rabbit."

"Ah'll miss you too, darlin'," Raffles said, returning the embrace. He stepped back and wiped a tear from his eye. "You did good out dere. Now just go easy on da skin-chang'r, 'kay'? He doing 'is best. I tink he tellin' da truth 'bout wat happen'd ta Temp'st. Dey didn't like each oth'r, but he would't let 'er die like dat."

"Maybe you're right, bunny," Charley said with a sad smile. "When will I see you again?"

"Nev'r know when I might blow back inta town." The rabbit tipped his straw hat to the others and waddled away down the hall. Charley watched him leave.

"He'll be back before you know it," Medesto said. "No one stays away from Rogue Destiny for long."

Charley continued staring after the rabbit. "Do you think I was too hard on Ren?" she asked. "He could have been telling the truth about what happened."

"Ren's difficult at the best of times," Medesto replied. "He's rash and hardheaded, but I couldn't image he'd let anyone die without trying to save them. Tempest was a strategist, guided by sheer logic no matter where it took her. It's possible she determined the three of you would never make it back. So she sacrificed herself to give Ren a chance to save you."

"I want to honor that sacrifice," Charley said. Her voice dropped to a whisper. "She was a good leader and I think she would appreciate it."

"Fair enough," Natascha said. "We have other agents that need to be remembered for what they sacrificed in this fight."

"Then let me go with you after the *Black Rose*," Charley pleaded. "It can't be worse than what we just went through. Rogue Destiny has no angry Muses."

Medesto grinned, but shook his head. "Gideon asked that you take over all communications, including the WayFinder."

"I'll get on that right away," Charley said. The corners of her eyes watered, but her face remained stoic. Natascha hadn't considered the impact this sudden shift in responsibilities might have on the young tech now that Tempest was gone. This was a dream promotion for Charley, but under the worst possible circumstances.

"Thank you," Medesto said. He seemed relieved they had an excuse to leave Charley behind on this run. It was going to be another long night.

"Thanks again for everything," Charley said. "I need to get back to the shop and see what needs doing. Huxley's been all by himself for days now. He may not even know what happened yet."

She turned to leave, but hesitated. "So you're going to hit Mordecai hard, right?" she asked with quiet conviction. "Tell me there's no more tiptoeing around, and you're going after everything he holds dear for what he's done to us? Like the trickster said, *If he's dead, he can't hurt anyone else.*"

"So what are you asking?" Medesto inquired.

Charley's eyes went cold. "We lost Tempest and almost lost Gideon. He tried to burn a world out from under us, not to mention a rampaging Muse. So I don't think revenge is too much to ask for."

"That road to revenge only leads to heartbreak," Natascha said. "It can change you in ways you won't like."

"Then how about justice?"

"We're working on that," Natascha replied.

Charley's expression softened. "And if Mordecai ends up dead by the time this is over?"

"Then you'll have both," Medesto answered with a nod.

With that, Charley walked away with a satisfied look in her eyes. Everything the young tech had witnessed in the last few days left her jaded beyond her previous youthful optimism. Revenge was a powerful motivator, but if you weren't careful, it could make you careless. Nothing wrong with bringing down the bad guys. Field work had a way of wearing a person down. Not everyone was cut out for it. Natascha would have to wait and see if Charley was.

Chapter 25
Rollo Pennymaker

The gondola passed behind the waterfall and came to a stop at a flat stone landing hidden beneath an overhang of the rocks directly under the boathouse. Mordecai opened the gate and stepped out onto the flat surface. Ren climbed off the cage behind the criminal.

The Grimm Jester floated past him, close enough his black cloak brushed against him. Ren involuntarily jerked his arm away and shuddered at the momentary contact. He glared at the ghoul, knowing that was a deliberate attempt to intimidate the trickster.

They stood in an underground grotto, carved out of living stone. The roar of the waterfall filled the small cavern. The cascading water created a wall between them and the outside world. Solid rock formed two other walls, leaving the gondola the only way in or out. The doorway at the back of the hollow opened to a spiral wooden staircase leading up to the floor above.

"We are under Monoceros," Mordecai said, searching the open space around them. He saw a control box built into the rock wall, identical to the one at the other end of the cable. With a turn of the lever, the cart rumbled out across the chasm, back toward Claymore and the others. Ren leaned over the railing to watch the waterfall cascade into the infinite mist below them.

Minutes later, the tram appeared with Claymore, Cyg-51 and Cyg-6-1 aboard. Claymore threw the gate open and jumped to the stone landing before the gondola reached it. The cyborgs stepped off once it had stopped. Not waiting for the last three in their party, Mordecai hurried up the winding, spiral staircase. Hand carved images of dragons and unicorns covered the thick wooden handrail and balusters. Ren stayed close to him. The stairs brought them to a dusty cloakroom.

Several weathered coats, heavy with mud and dirt, hung on pegs fastened to the wall. A cushioned bench sat against one side for removing muddy footwear. Mordecai continued down a short hallway that ended at a large door trimmed in fine wood. He waited for Claymore to catch up with them. When he caught up, Mordecai stepped aside and motioned to the door.

Claymore drew his sidearm, put his hand on the doorknob and nodded to Cyg-51, who stood right behind him. The cyborg returned the gesture and Claymore turned the knob. The door swung open silently. With their guns ready, Claymore and the cyborg entered the adjoining room. Ren waited for Mordecai and the Jester before entering a room full of knick-knacks and gew-gaws.

The flotsam and jetsam of a rabid collector filled the walls. Shelves of eclectic items, weapons, jars and oddments from across all the Eight Genres. The bookcases along every wall held not just books, but carved jade, decorative pottery, and more paraphilia of mythical creatures. The one recurring theme was that of dragons and unicorns, like the sketches Ren had seen repeated many times in Harper's journals.

Intricate statues of bronze and porcelain dragons or unicorns sat in glass display cases. Another glass case was filled with children's plastic toys. Further into the room, many of the shelves were empty where it appeared items had been taken.

Across the room, a strange little man in a white dress shirt and suspenders stacked boxes and crates. He kept referring to an inventory page on a clipboard. The group watched him for several moments before he slowly turned his head toward them. His eyes went wide. Cyg-51 and Cyg-6-1 leveled their weapons. The little round man set down the vase he held and raised his hands. Ren recognized him.

Rollo Pennymaker.

He wore white pinstriped pantaloons, and highly polished black shoes with white spats. A black top coat and tails hung across the back of a chair near him, along with a top hat and white gloves. Ren thought he would have made a reasonable Master of Ceremonies in some sideshow carnival.

Beads of sweat rolled off his matted hair, down his face to his goatee. His breathing was heavy, like the act of physical exertion was a foreign concept to him.

Wooden crates stuffed with straw and cardboard boxes filled the far wall. Many were open, while most were sealed shut with tape.

"Who are you?!" Rollo cried.

"That is not important," Mordecai replied. He motioned for him to take a chair.

Rollo plopped into a red velvet chair, his expression one of utter defeat. He fidgeted as Mordecai roamed from box to box, finally pulling a two-foot tall statue from the straw of a crate. It was a porcelain unicorn rearing up on its hind legs, carved in an Art Nouveau style, slender and graceful. He weighed it in his hands. "And what are these?"

"Valuable antiques I've acquired over the years," Rollo replied.

Mordecai threw the statue against the wall. Rollo cringed as the figurine shattered into tiny bits. The small man sat up in his chair, only to be shoved back down by Cyg-51.

"What is this?" Mordecai asked. He pulled a short black rod from an open box. The large crimson gemstone at the top gave off a soft red glow as he held it.

"That is the Scepter of Azmodus Doom," Rollo answered, "from the Book *The Seven Sheiks and the Handmaiden*."

"And why are you hastily packing all these treasures up?"

Rollo gave an exhausted sigh. "Because they have monetary value," he stated. "They are worth a king's ransom if offered to the right people. Take it! Take all of it, just don't hurt me."

Mordecai set the scepter back into the crate. "We are looking for three round stones of varying sizes. They are called the Roskashon Lodestones."

Rollo seemed visibly shaken by his words. "I don't know where they are," he replied, licking his dry lips. "Do you think I'd be here wasting my time selling off these little baubles, if I had something as priceless as Roskashon Lodestones? I would have sold them long ago and bought myself a kingdom inside some mundane world where no one would ever bother me again."

The criminal mastermind of Rogue Destiny's underworld hesitated. He looked at the stacks of boxes. "I suppose that could be true," he said. "So tell me where I can find Harper Bellweather. She will know where they are."

"Harper?" Rollo replied. "I haven't seen her for months."

"That, I do not believe," the crime lord spat. "But where are my manners? We've not been formally introduced. I am *Mordecai Davos*. And you are?"

Mordecai spoke his name with a grandiose elocution, as if he expected Rollo to fall to his knees, quaking in fear. Instead, a small, almost indiscernible smile touched the diminutive man's lips. It was there for only a moment as the two stared at each other, like they were sharing some secret joke known only to them.

"Jester, if you could loosen his tongue, please," Mordecai smirked. The wraith drifted toward their captive. A skeletal hand reached out for him from beneath a cloaked sleeve.

"His name is Rollo Pennymaker!" Claymore announced from across the room. He raised his pistol at Rollo for emphasis. "He's a grifter and a thief. Now just give us the lodestones, Rollo, and you may still get out of this alive."

Rollo looked over at Claymore, then shook his head and buried it in his gloved hands. "I told you I don't know where they are," he whimpered.

"But you know where Harper Bellweather is, don't you?!" Claymore shouted. The pistol in his hand trembled slightly. Ren reached up and gently lowered his arm. His partner didn't resist.

"Easy," Ren whispered. Claymore stared at him with vacant eyes before he holstered his weapon.

The Jester reached skeletal fingers out for the little man. "She's dead, okay?!" Rollo screamed. "She died last year. And only she knew where the lodestones are hidden. Now they may be lost forever." The wraith pulled his hand back.

Mordecai's eyes filled with rage. "Tear this place apart until we find the lodestones!" he spat. He grabbed a stack of crates and pulled them over. "Search every corner! They must be here somewhere!"

Cyg-51 and Cyg-6-1 stood guard over Rollo as the others proceeded to break open every sealed box and crate. They dumped the contents out onto the floor, much to Rollo's chagrin. Ren and Claymore scoured every closet and room on that floor. They found nothing to indicate where lodestones might be or if Harper was still alive.

"How do you know that guy?" Ren whispered to Claymore as they went through the cramp kitchen area.

"Only by reputation," Claymore mumbled. "He's a smuggler who deals in stolen magic artifacts and relics. The authorities in Rogue Destiny have been hunting him for years. He and Minstrel Cotty worked together back in the day until they had a falling out."

Ren could tell his partner knew more than what he was saying. He saw the gleam of recognition in Claymore's eyes the moment he saw Rollo.

When their search downstairs proved fruitless, they wandered up the stairs to the three small rooms on the second Story. The first was a bedchamber with clothes thrown haphazardly around the room. The two Raconteurs rummaged through the dresser and closet, and every nook and cranny of the room. Satisfied they had missed nothing, the two moved to the two remaining rooms. Ren took one, Claymore the other.

The room Ren entered looked like a private study, strewn with more of Harper's journals, dozens of watercolor paintings stacked on a drawing board, and an extensive collection of poetry books. He lit the lantern on the desk with the matches next to it and scanned the room for any clues, searching through a file cabinet in the corner.

Books that appeared to be for personal reading filled a short shelf behind the desk. Among the titles were pulp mysteries, *Down the Old Mill Road* and *The Day after Tomorrow I Die*, mixed in with several children's books, *The Cat Came Back*, *Spooky Stories for Brave Children*, *There's No One on the Moon*, and *What the Goblin Wanted*. No clues indicating where the location of the lodestones might be.

After a frantic search, he convinced himself this was all a waste of time. A corkboard on the wall covered in quickly jotted down notes caught his attention. Some were quotes from the passages of books or doodles of random fantastical creatures beyond dragons and unicorns. There was a loveseat in front of a small television. On top of the machine, a picture of two girls sat in a small frame. Ren picked it up. It appeared to be Harper and maybe a younger sister.

Ren had seen the boxed device before, in many technological worlds he had wandered, but he'd never understood the appeal of it. Zombie-like viewers watching fake lives being acted out for entertainment purposes. He'd rather be out there living life as it should be lived, than living vicariously through pretend actors. Next to the television was a flat machine with a VHS tape sticking out. Ren was familiar with this device, too. He pushed the tape in and switched the box on with its remote. He sat on the sofa to watch what was on the tape.

At first, nothing but static appeared on the screen. Then a scene of a young girl playing in the snow flashed onscreen. The young girl joked back and forth with whoever was holding the camera. She squatted down and scooped up snow to pack into a lopsided snowball.

"Don't you dare throw that at me, you little brat!" the unseen voice behind the camera said with a giggle. "Don't do it!" The little girl threw the snowball. The camera jostled as the operator ran after her. Ren watched the scene play out. The camera showed the young girl being chased around a swing set until she fell back onto the snow laughing.

The picture on the screen shifted from a clear blue sky to the faces of the two girls laying in the snow. One held the camera up over them, and the younger girl next to her stared into the sky. The two matched the girls in the picture on top of the television.

They lay there for a moment in the white powdery snow, before sitting up. The younger one giggled, then dropped a handful of snow down the back of Harper's parka neck and ran off laughing.

"Oh, I'm so going to get you for that, Calliope!" Harper shouted.

"You find anything?" Claymore asked from the doorway.

"Nothing," Ren replied. He stopped the video and turned off the television. "Just some old videos and a few more of her journals."

"Grab the journals and come see this."

Ren stuffed several of the journals from the desk into his shoulder satchel next to *The Book of Days*. He knew they would prove fruitless in their hunt but joined Claymore in the last of the three rooms. A wide table filled the small space, covered with charts and atlases from the many worlds Harper Bellweather had visited. She had pinned larger maps from all different genres across the walls.

"Any one of these could be where she hid the stones," Claymore rumbled, his temper flaring for a moment before he caught himself. "I'm at a loss here." He vigorously scratched the back of his head. His disposition was getting worse by the minute. They began sifting through the maps on the table when Cyg-51 appeared on the stairs outside the door.

"Mordecai wants you downstairs," she said. They traipsed back down to the main room. Mordecai emerged from the narrow stairwell that led to the tower.

"Did you find anything upstairs?" Mordecai asked, barely containing his anger.

"We searched the tower thoroughly and found nothing," Claymore growled, shaking his head.

"There's a map room and a study on the second floor but nothing to indicate where the lodestones may be," Claymore replied. "I say we focus on Pennymaker."

"I was just about to do that," Mordecai said. "Jester, if you will."

The cloaked wraith drifted across the room and loomed over the rotund little man. Rollo fidgeted in his chair as the dark hood stared down at him. Rollo bunched up into a ball and covered his face with his arms. The surrounding air grew thick with the stench of decay and the open grave.

"I will ask the questions," Mordecai declared. "And you will answer them, Mr. Pennymaker. If you do not, you will discover what true pain feels like."

Rollo sank deeper into the chair, not daring to look up.

"Where are the Roskashon Lodestones?"

"I don't know," he cried. "I swear. Harper never trusted me with their location."

"He's lying!" Claymore yelled.

"Jester," Mordecai said. "Persuade our guest to enlighten us about all the places Harper Bellweather might have hidden the lodestones."

The Grimm Jester picked up Rollo by the neck, lifting him out of the chair. Rollo grabbed the skeletal arm that choked him but pulled his hands away as if the touch burned him. Smoke rose off Rollo's face. He cried out in desperate pain.

"All right!" Rollo screamed. "Stop! Stop! You're killing me!" The wraith held him a moment longer, then released his grip on the small man. Rollo crashed to the floor, coughing and sputtering. He pushed himself away from the wraith and looked at Mordecai.

"Harper Bellweather is alive," the Grimm Jester hissed. "And I believe he knows where she is."

"So, you lied to me?" Mordecai stated calmly. "Where is she?"

"Did I say dead?" Rollo sobbed. His whole body was shaking, tears dripping down his face. "I meant she's captive. She's a prisoner in the city of Ur. I honestly don't know if she's still alive, but that's where she is. I can take you to her!"

"Where is this city?"

"Far up the Euphrates," Rollo whimpered. "If you push yourselves, it will take a day of hard marching to get within sight of Ur."

"Finally, some truthful answers," Mordecai replied. "You will take us to this city where Harper Bellweather is being held. Jester, bring our guest. We are done here."

Rollo scrambled to his feet. He pulled on his black coat and tails, then placed the top hat on. The Grimm Jester reached down with one hand and picked Rollo up by the collar of his coat, carrying him towards the door.

The return trip across the abyss was done in silence. Mordecai, Ren, and Rollo went first, much to the dismay of Claymore. His partner didn't want to let Rollo out of his sight now that he was their only link to Harper Bellweather and the Roskashon Lodestones. The Jester drifted alongside the gondola.

Ren noticed Rollo recovered rather quickly from his encounter with the Grimm Jester. His own first encounter with the ghoul had taken place in a dark alley on Rogue Destiny's waterfront. While the wraith never touched actually touched him, the experience has stayed fresh in his minds for days.

A few minutes earlier, Rollo had been thrashing about in the grip of the Jester's bony hand, crying and wailing for his life. Now the little man appeared unperturbed by having been touched by the hand of Death. He stood at the rail, looking out into the mist, like he didn't have a care in the world.

Ren risked a quick glance. Rollo wore a mask of determined resolve. A fierce intensity burned in his dark eyes. What that meant, the trickster did not know, but he knew that Rollo Pennymaker was not to be trusted.

Chapter 26
City of Whispers

Ren walked down a dusty road beside Claymore under the unforgiving heat of the desert sun. Rollo Pennymaker trudged reluctantly between them, directing the party toward the ancient city of Ur. He appeared despondent and showed no desire to escape, seemingly consigning himself to captivity by shuffling along silently.

Mordecai Davos walked some distance behind them, hedged in by his cyborg soldiers. His remaining followers trailed after him. The Grimm Jester brought up the rear to ensure no one tried to run off.

The company had hiked continually through the night and well into the next day. Mordecai rarely let them stop to rest, and everyone was beginning to reach exhaustion. Claymore's attention seemed focused, in complete control of his emotions. There was an urgency in his step as he guided them on. About midday, Rollo turned inland, away from the Euphrates.

"So tell me about your partnership with Harper, Rollo," Claymore rumbled. "Why would she work alongside a lowlife such as yourself?"

"I was merely her assistant," Rollo mumbled, "not her partner. We worked together on many dealings before. She needed my knowledge of the illegal underground market to help her find hard to locate items of interest. I needed her skills to obtain said objects. It was a peculiar but profitable partnership."

"That doesn't explain how Harper ended up with both *The Book of Days* and the lodestones," Ren replied quietly. He glanced back to see if their conversation could be overheard. Claymore's unyielding gait had outpaced the rest of the party. They were far enough ahead no one could eavesdrop on their words.

Rollo mopped the sweat from his face with a handkerchief. "Rumors began to circulate *The Book of Days* had resurfaced after being lost for centuries. Every dealer, collector and buyer in Rogue Destiny was eager to obtain it."

"How did Harper end up with it?" Ren asked.

"We got word there was going to be an auction hosted by Minstrel Cotty in *The Angels of Avalon*," Rollo replied with a sly smile. "It was going to be the largest of its kind in many years and would include a vast array of magical artifacts and relics. Although it was never stated outright, *The Book of Days* was rumored to be among the items to be auctioned. I gained entrance to the event for Harper and myself as buyers. Mordecai Davos sent representatives there also. Needless to say, between my illusionary talents and Harper's raw chutzpah, we stole *The Book of Days* before the auction even started."

"How long ago was that?" Claymore growled.

"About a year back," Rollo replied. "Right before Harper disappeared."

"And the lodestones?" Claymore asked. "You still claiming you don't where they are?"

"I wouldn't be here if I had them or knew their location," Rollo said. Sweat continued to drip from his brow. "Harper hunted for them obsessively for over two years, but always swore she'd never found them."

Ren knew anything Rollo said would never be the complete truth, but he wasn't about to argue the point. Claymore strode beside him, lost in deep thought, like he'd stumbled upon some forgotten memory. His partner had never mentioned Harper by name before, but she seemed to be more than a causal acquaintance.

"You alright?" Ren asked. His partner gave no response.

"How did Harper end up in Ur?" Claymore asked.

"She insisted on exploring every world she dragged me through," Rollo responded. "I told her how dangerous it was to explore the cities of Gilgamesh, but her mind was made up. She was always too curious for her own good, if you ask me. And sure enough, when we entered Ur, the denizens of the city attacked us."

"Why would they attack you?" Ren asked.

"*The Epic of Gilgamesh* is an ancient Story," Rollo replied. "Maybe the oldest written world in the cosmos, but its foundations are crumbling. The inhabitants, including Gilgamesh himself, are little more than phantoms now. Their minds are gone, leaving only their base natures behind. Harper insisted the lodestones were in *Gilgamesh*. We found an abandoned house sitting at the edge of the world and set it up as a base so we could search for them."

"You abandoned Harper to save your own skin, didn't you?"

"Yes, I left her there!" Rollo confessed, his voice filled with shame. "We were exploring the city of Ur when we were separated. If I had stayed, we both would've been captured. I've always meant to go back for her, but I was just too scared."

Claymore cuffed Rollo across the back of the head, knocking his top hat off. "Liar," he growled. "You're too busy stealing everything of value from her hideaway. If anything's happened to Harper, you will answer to me!" Rollo went scurrying after his hat as it blew down the dirt road.

Ren leaned toward Claymore. "Something about his story's not right," he whispered. "Rollo's leading us into a trap."

"I've no doubt he is." Claymore's face went hard. "He may look nonthreatening, but he's more treacherous than Mordecai."

"So what do we do?" Ren asked.

"We play this out, as always. Be ready for anything."

They continued inland for miles, past silt flats and reed marshes, until signs of civilization began to appear. Fields of wheat and barley grew next to orchards of figs and olives. Ren scanned the sparse, low-lying hills for any evidence of life.

Since leaving Harper's sanctuary, they hadn't come across any other living beings. The road they traveled remained empty of carts or caravans. Ren had expected the surrounding terrain to be filled with herds of goats and sheep. Other than the occasional lifeless mud hut, the landscape was empty of people.

Finally, an ancient city rose in the distance.

Claymore grabbed Rollo by the shoulder to hold him until Mordecai and the others caught up.

Rollo bent over, hands on his knees, gasping for air. "I give you the city of Ur," he announced. "Harper Bellweather is somewhere inside."

"Good," Mordecai ordered. "How do we enter the city without arousing the local populace?"

"There is a bridge on the northwest side of the wall," Rollo said. "That will be our way in."

"Then let us go," Mordecai replied. He shoved the small man forward and kept walking, suddenly full of energy after the exhaustive march from the edge of the world. Rollo led them through a maze of narrow pathways across the marshlands toward the massive walls of Ur.

As they drew closer, Ren saw a large ziggurat that reached

high above the walls. The marshes ended and the company took a narrow dirt road to a wooden bridge and mud arch that would lead them into the city. Rollo stopped before crossing.

"What is it?" Mordecai asked. At his side, Ren readied himself for any unseen attack, but the entrance to Ur remained silent.

"I thought I heard something," Rollo hissed. "If we're lucky, there should be no living souls in this part of the city." After a moment, he took an exaggerated breath and continued over the bridge. Ren eyed Claymore before following him.

The city gates stood open before them. The party crossed the bridge to a dirt street that wove between buildings in various stages of deterioration. Rollo hurried them down the narrow empty street that zig-zagged among the mud structures. He would stop from time to time to get his bearings before ambling forward again.

The soldiers with Mordecai watched the buildings and rooftops for movement. An eerie silence filled the deserted streets. Mordecai moved closer to Rollo, prodding him to go faster. The avenue turned onto a wider lane. Living quarters mixed in-between the empty shops and vender stalls along the street. Ren walked next to Mordecai. Claymore trailed behind the group. Ren took in everything around him as they went, never knowing what small piece of information would prove invaluable later.

The windows of every building remained empty and dark. The dirt streets lay undisturbed, free of footprints or wheel tracks left from carts. To their right, they could see the giant ziggurat on the far side of the city. The squat temple rose several stories high. Long, narrow steps led up to its entrance.

Rollo stopped with his back to everyone. He raised a hand and looked around the empty streets, before motioning them to a dark side street.

"Down this way!" he called out. "I'll show you where the attack occurred. Then we can search for Harper."

"Rollo, stop!" Mordecai ordered. His voice hung in the silent air. The company had no choice but to follow.

At the far end of the avenue, a ghostly shape appeared from the shadows. It was a warrior, tall and broad shouldered, dressed in a knee-length tunic and long white cloak. The figure seemed to melt in and out of the surrounding shadows. A thick squared-off beard reached to his chest, and a large bronze sickle sword hung from his belt. In his hand, he held the severed horn of a bull.

"Claymore?" Ren said.

"I see it," Claymore replied. He pulled his shortened rifle from the holster on his back and cocked a round into the chamber.

"Pennymaker, who is that?!" Mordecai yelled, pointing at the otherworldly phantasm.

"I don't know!" Rollo cried. He was breathing in short, heavy gasps. The cyber soldiers stepped past Ren to protect Mordecai as the rest of the company held their weapons ready. Claymore remained at Ren's side. Only the Grimm Jester seemed unconcerned by the sudden appearance of the apparition. Ren noticed the wraith held back from interfering until ordered to by Mordecai.

"That's Gilgamesh!" Claymore growled. "The demi-god king of the Sumerians."

"No! That's impossible!" Rollo cried. His body shook with fear. "The Narrative takes place far north of here, at the city Uruk. It's late in the Story-cyclE. Enkidu has died, and Gilgamesh should be searching for Utnapishtim to learn the secret of everlasting life. At no point in the Story does the *Logos Personae* ever travel this far south. The city of Ur is only a place marker on the map, its inhabitants merely props to populate the world. They are never involved in the Narrative of the Epic."

"Perhaps our presence has changed the flow of the Story," Mordecai wondered aloud.

The shimmering figure in front of them lifted the horn to his lips and blew a long, deep mournful blast. It echoed down the street and reverberated off the clay buildings. A second ghostly phantasm appeared in a doorway off to their left. The sandaled figure shuffled out into the street, dressed in a short tunic with a sash over one shoulder and copper bands on his arms. He sported a thick beard that tapered to a round flat bottom.

Ren was struck by the lack of color in the man and his garments. The building on either side of them were a deep, rich blend of brown and umber, matching the dirt of the streets. Even the massive physique of Gilgamesh held a hazy white glow. But the man approaching them seemed drained of any color, only a fading image of what he once had been.

Several more shadow-people, both male and female, appeared in other doorways. A handful at first, then more and more, until dozens emerged from the buildings. They carried no weapons and moved in slow, fluid steps, as if they were passing through deep water. The horde came at them from all directions, encircling the entire party. Although the phantoms' feet seemed to move along the ground, they left no impressions in the dirt.

Ren glanced back to where Gilgamesh had stood. The figure in white was nowhere to be seen. He searched for a way through the mob, but their escape had been cut off. The horde of ghostly forms hedged them in from all sides.

Claymore grabbed Ren by the shoulder. "Go!" he whispered. "Find Harper!"

"No, we stay together!" Ren argued. He knew he could fly

himself to safety in an instant, but he would never leave his partner behind.

Claymore struck Rollo in the face with his free hand and knocked him to the dirt. He pressed the little man to the ground with his boot.

"What are you trying to pull, Pennymaker?!" he shouted. "You said there was no one left in the city!"

"I said *no one living!*" Rollo sobbed. "They are what remains of this accursed city's inhabitants!" He was visibly shaking. Blood dripped from his lip. "I knew we should not have come here!"

Panic ensued among Mordecai and his followers. Even the normally emotionless soldiers showed a nervous level of agitation. They held their guns high, backing into each other as the apparitions closed in. Mordecai yelled for the Grimm Jester.

"Cyg-6-1, Cyg-1-11!" Cyg-51 shouted. "Cover the rear flank! Cyg-8! Opposite me!" All four soldiers opened fire into the horde of approaching ghosts. The rest of the group followed suit. Their bullets passed through the shuffling figures, tearing chunks of clay and bricks out of the structures behind them, but the discolored apparitions continued on.

Claymore removed his foot from Rollo's chest to join in with the shooting. The little man remained on the ground at their feet, covering his head. "Why did you bring me back here?" he wailed.

One of the dead came at Ren, reaching out for him. The trickster ducked out of the way, but the empty eyes of his attacker did not follow him. The phantom's hand buried itself in the man directly behind him.

Someone at the outer edge of their circle let out a bloodcurdling scream. Ren turned to see the guard named Baaklow with a translucent arm embedded in his chest. The fugitive emptied his pistol into the monster. The bullets had no effect on the ghostly form. The apparition ripped its hand free. Baaklow's body shuddered violently as he fell to his knees, even though he had no visible injuries.

In the ghost's open palm, a vapor of pale smoke swirled. The delicate wisps wrapped around the slender fingers as the hand closed. The vapor dissipated in the creature's grip. Baaklow's body stiffened. He gave the final choking gasp of a dying man and collapsed like a rag-doll. The hollow eyes of the phantom stared at Mordecai.

"Jester!" Mordecai bellowed. He stumbled away from the outstretched hand.

A bony claw sliced through the apparition in a wide, arching swipe. Bullets may have been useless against the otherworldly horde, but the grisly touch of the Grimm Jester slit the ethereal monster through the middle. The severed halves separated and dropped to the dirt street before dissolving into nothingness.

Claymore fired into an approaching phantom. His rifle thundered, but the bullet passed through the ghost with no effect. He swung the butt of his gun across the bearded face, but the features only blurred momentarily in a smokey haze.

The monster shoved a colorless arm through Claymore's shirt into his chest cavity. The Raconteur gritted his teeth and struggled to stay upright, before dropping to one knee. His face twisted in agony.

Ren reached for the apparition's arm, but his hand grabbed only air. A rush of icy numbness rushed up his fingers like an electrical charge. The agonizing tingling sensation reached up to the shoulder.

A moment later, the monster jerked its hand free and backed away from Claymore. The expression on the undead face remained void of emotion, but Ren could tell its demeanor had changed. Whatever sentience remained in the dead creature must have sensed the growing malignancy flowing through his partner's veins. Claymore clutched his chest.

"Are you okay?" Ren asked, standing in front of him.

"No, but I will be in a moment," Claymore replied. His legs wobbled under him, almost falling before Ren caught him. "Where'd Pennymaker go?!"

"He's gone!" Claymore swayed on his feet. "Did you see which way?"

"No, but we have to get you out of here!" Ren moved without thought. He shoved Claymore through the mass of shadowy figures surrounding them, keeping his own head pressed against his partner's back.

Claymore offered no resistance. The encroaching phantoms parted like water before Claymore. Cold hands grabbed for him, but Ren shook them off. Once they were free of the crowd, he and Claymore broke into a run.

"How are we going to find Rollo?!" Claymore yelled. "He's an illusionist with all the magic from this world to draw on. We're going to lose him."

"Trust me," Ren replied. "He's the only one who can lead us to Harper! I will find him."

Chapter 27
A Fly in the Ointment

Ren glanced over his shoulder as he ran. Screams and gunfire rose behind them as he and Claymore ran. The silhouette of the Grimm Jester cleaved the air, making quick work of the apparitions encircling Mordecai and his people. Several fell to the ground as he watched. Claymore stumbled, clutching his chest. Ren grabbed him by the arm and helped him stand. His staccato breathing showed he had not yet recovered from the brutal attack. Had the phantom's touch worsened Claymore's condition? Ren had no idea.

"Come on," Ren urged. "We need to keep moving!"

"How are we going to find Pennymaker?" Claymore groaned.

Ren had first run into Rollo Pennymaker at the Obtuse Turtle, a public house in Rogue Destiny, only days earlier. He'd been caught off guard when the little man turned invisible to escape a beating for cheating at cards. His only take-away from their initial confrontation was that Rollo Pennymaker was a devious little devil who had the ability to throw illusions around, even in Rogue Destiny, a city without magic.

Fortunately, for whatever reason, Ren could see through his invisible illusions then and hoped he could do so again. He stopped at an intersection to look down the street on either side. Claymore came up after him, more out of breath than he should have been.

"Over there!" Ren yelled, pointing at a wavy distortion of air the size of the short, round Rollo Pennymaker. The hazy image turned down a street ahead of them.

"I don't see anything!" Claymore growled.

"Just trust me for once," Ren said. The anomaly disappeared through the doorway of a dark building.

The question running through Ren's mind was Rollo's connection to the whole affair. The mysterious little man had shown up out of nowhere in the middle of the Raconteurs' search for the Roskashon Lodestones. That could not be a coincidence. There had to be a reason, and Ren sensed Claymore knew more about Rollo than he was saying.

Ren took the lead as they ran to the spot where the wavering form had disappeared. Inside the corridor, he found a set of wide earthen steps leading beneath the surface. By the time Ren reached the bottom of the stairs, Rollo was nowhere in sight. Three separate passageways vanished ahead of them. Claymore stood before the three-way juncture, visibly befuddled what to do next, as if the choice of multiple corridors was some unsolvable puzzle to him.

"Why is it so difficult to think?" Claymore grumbled. He clutched his shirt where the ghost had touched him. The wounds from the prehistoric cat's claws began bleeding again.

Ren pointed to the one on the left. "Go that way," he said. "I'll go down the other corridor. Keep an eye out for Harper! And be careful!" Claymore nodded and disappeared into the dark tunnel.

The air became cooler as Ren moved down the corridor. Darkness swallowed everything. He turned on a flashlight from Tomas' pack, and found himself in a crudely carved dirt passageway. He listened for any sounds. The silence unnerved him. He walked on further until he caught the faint sound of distant footfall. He headed in that direction.

The dark catacombs were a maze of twisting corridors. Most of the rooms he passed seemed to be used for storage. He took a set of stairs down to a deeper level. The floor was full of what looked to be prison cells with bronze bars on the doors. Ren walked on for several minutes until he saw the soft glow of a light and heard a low voice.

He crept forward, turning off his light, and peeked around the corner to find Rollo Pennymaker standing on tiptoes outside a wooden door. The source of illumination came from a tiny fey light that floated a foot over his head. He spoke to someone through a narrow slit in the wood.

"I brought the key to let you out," he said sweetly. "Tell me where they are."

A weak but defiant voice answered him from the cell. "Go away, Rollo. I'd rather die than see you have them."

"Harper, love," Rollo cooed. "I have water and food for you, but we don't have much time. The city is being overrun by those who also seek the lodestones. They'll be here any minute. Tell me where you hid them, and we can leave this horrible place together."

"No one should have them," Harper answered. "Not you, not anyone." Her voice was weak and barely audible. "In the wrong hands, Rogue Destiny would be doomed. They are too powerful to control."

"You should be more appreciative of my efforts!" Rollo spat, his patience waning. "Your strength is running out. You won't last another day without my help. But you can save yourself if you just tell me."

"No." Harper's voiced wavered.

"Then you'll die here," Rollo hissed. The once soft-spoken

man in the top hat suddenly reached the limits of his temper. His frightened, helpless demeanor fell away. Ren could see everything about him was a deception. "Your bones will rot here, and you will never see your sister again! Goodbye, Harper." He stomped away, but stopped just beyond the door.

"Rollo!" Harper called out. "Please." An evil grin spread across Rollo's round face. The short man stepped back to the slit in the door and rolled his eyes in mock frustration.

"What?," he sneered. "I have to get out of here before they find me."

"Who's out there?"

"*The Society of the Black Rose*," Rollo replied. "Mordecai Davos himself is here and will stop at nothing. Do you want them to torture the location of the Roskashon Lodestones out of you? Imagine staring into the face of Dmitri the Confessor from atop his Table of Pain. If you won't tell me, there's nothing more I can do. But remember, I tried to help you!"

"Okay," Harper conceded. "But I'm so thirsty. Give me water."

Rollo moved his hands in a series of deliberate motions that escalated with his arms widespread. The door unlocked with a click. He pushed it open and went inside. Ren crept forward to the edge of the door. He saw Rollo offer Harper the canteen from his pack. She took a long drink before he pulled it away.

"Okay," Harper whispered. She muttered something too low to hear. Rollo leaned in close to her. Ren heard Harper whispering, but could not make out what was being said. When she finished, he stood up, no readable expression on his face.

"That is anatomically impossible!" he yelled. "So you will die here! I'll figure out another way to locate the lodestones! They cannot stay hidden forever."

Ren removed the satchel that contained *The Book of Days* from his shoulder and dropped it to the ground. Shrugging out of the heavy coat, he threw it aside and with a thought, his disguise of Tomas DeMarche disappeared. He was Ren B'gatti once again. Still wearing the dusty suit and tie, he stepped into the doorway as Rollo turned to leave the small cell.

Ren caught him with a punch across the face. Rollo stumbled back, blood gushing from his nose. His eyes went wide when he saw the trickster. Ren grabbed him by the shirt and dragged him out of the dry, musty room.

"You were at the Obtuse Turtle...!" Rollo gasped. "With that Raconteur!"

Ren cut him short with another blow to the nose, fueled by all the anger and frustration he could summon. He hit him a third time, harder still. Rollo fell back onto the dirt floor outside the cell. The Fae light floating over his head went out, throwing everything into darkness. Ren fumbled for his flashlight and switched it on. The little man didn't move again.

"Rollo? Are you still there?" Harper moaned. "Is someone with you?" Ren picked up the canteen of water and turned his attention to the cell's occupant, but hesitated before entering the room.

Harper had been adamant that no one should have the lodestones. He was a stranger to her, so she would not reveal where she hid them. He could wait until Claymore found him. Maybe he could convince her. Then an idea struck him. He decided to approach the problem from a different angle. One that might get her to drop her guard a little.

Ren felt guilty for what he was about to do, but he had no other choice. Claymore could find him at any moment and that would only complicate his plan to rescue his partner from the madness consuming him.

But first, he had to get Harper out of there before Mordecai's people reached her. Rollo was right. If Mordecai found her, they would torture her until she revealed the lodestones' location. Ren was a trickster, after all. This is what he did.

Stepping away from the door, took off the suit coat and flung it aside, along with the dress shirt and tie. In only a white undershirt, pants and boots, he focused on the image of a particular young girl he had seen in the video the night before. Once the transformation was complete, he grabbed the long coat and went back to the door.

Harper Bellweather lay on a pile of straw in the far corner of the room. She looked younger than she had in her pictures. Her shoulder length hair was now a matted mess falling down into her eyes. Every inch of exposed skin was covered in tattoos of mythical creatures. An Asian dragon coiled around her right forearm and a brightly colored unicorn dominated the left arm.

Ren flashed the light in the cramped cell. An overturned jug lay in one corner amid a large pile of empty food tins. Harper's face was sunken from malnutrition. She had been here a while. She was dehydrated and barely alive. Mud and straw covered her clothes. He could tell she was near delirium. As he approached, Harper gazed up at him through hollow, unfocused eyes.

Ren set the light in the straw and unscrewed the top of the canteen. He knelt in his new form, lifting the water to her lips. Harper drank deeply until Ren pulled it away.

"It's so good to finally find you," Ren whispered in a voice familiar to her.

"Calliope?" Harper murmured, trying to focus her vision. She grabbed Ren's hand. "How'd you get here?"

"I've been looking for you, silly," Ren replied in the child-like cadence of Harper's younger sister.

"I don't understand. Did Rollo bring you here?"

"I've come to take you home," Ren said, choosing his words carefully. "We've been so worried about you. What are you doing in this nasty place?"

"I'm sorry I didn't write," Harper replied. "I've been busy with work." Her head dropped back onto the straw.

"That's okay," Ren replied. "I know it must have been very important, if you didn't write. Did you tell that wicked man where you hid the rocks everyone is searching for?"

Harper muttered something inaudible, then she fell silent again. Ren gently patted her cheek and gave her another sip from the canteen. Most of the water dribbled down her chin.

"Harper?" Ren said. "Stay with me. I'm going to get you out of here."

"Do you remember when you were little, and I'd read to you every night?" Harper whispered. She lifted her face to Ren, her eyes sad and distant. She touched his face with her fingertips. "I've missed you so much."

"I missed you, too," Ren replied, taking her hand. It was obvious Harper wasn't in any shape to talk more about the location of the Roskashon Lodestones. She was going to die if he didn't get her help. He went out of the cell and picked up Tomas' coat. Lifting Harper to a sitting position, he wrapped it over her shoulders and lifted her from the dirty straw.

Ren retained his natural physical strength, even in the disguise of a small child. Harper was not that heavy, but awkward because of the differences in size. Harper began humming as Ren carried her from the room.

"*There's no one on the moon. No one I can see*," she sang. "Remember when I used to sing that to you? It was your favorite book."

"Yes, I do," Ren replied. He took her out to the passageway and set her down against the wall. Rollo lay flat on his back where Ren had left him. A trickle of blood ran down from his broken nose. Ren glanced over at Harper.

He felt bad for deceiving her, but he was not sure where the guilt was coming from. He had a job to do, just like she did. His need to get to the lodestones before Mordecai outweighed being nice, regardless of what he had to do to get his hands on them.

The pounding of heavy boots echoed down the tunnel behind him. Claymore appeared out of the dark, stopping just before he stepped on Rollo's prone body. "What happened to him?" he asked with a smug grin.

"He was in my way," Ren replied.

"You're not Tomas anymore?" Claymore said, stating the obvious. The fire in his eyes had returned.

"The time for hiding is over," Ren answered. "Help me with Harper."

"Harper!" Claymore exclaimed. He knelt and patted her face gently. "Wake up, we need to talk." Harper stirred but didn't open her eyes. She softly continued singing her song.

There's no one on the moon, no one I can see, there's no one at the bottom of the deep, blue ocean sea. Only when you're home will I miss you no more.

"Claymore, there'll be time for that later," Ren advised.

"It's all that matters!" Claymore snarled. "She can take us to the lodestones! We need her to wake up." He stopped as if the outburst surprised him and glanced back down the passageway.

Ren ignored his partner's erratic behavior. It was not the time for them to lose focus. Harper was safe, and now they needed to get out of the city.

Claymore leaned closer, stroking her cheek with the back of his hand. "Harper, it's me, Claymore."

Harper stirred. "Claymore? What are you doing here? Where'd Calliope go?"

"Calliope's not here," Claymore whispered softly. He brushed the hair from her eyes.

"She's been hallucinating since I found her," Ren said with a careless shrug. No need to go into further details.

"Did she say anything to you about the lodestones?" Claymore asked.

"No," Ren answered. "But I don't know if Rollo tricked her into telling him their location."

"You're right. We need to get Harper out of here!" Claymore admitted. "We'll figure out the lodestones once she's safe." He lifted the unconscious Harper from the ground with ease. She appeared small and fragile, wrapped in Tomas' coat.

Ren picked up his satchel and they started down the passageway when the glow of an eerie light filled the tunnel. A moment later, a shimmering figure bathed in white walked toward them, blocking their way.

The warrior stood taller than Claymore. His massive physique filled the corridor. His face appeared to be carved in stone. He wore a knee-length tunic and a long cloak that hung off his shoulders. A thick beard protruded from his chin, cut square at the base. A sickle sword hung from his belt, and he held a severed bull's horn in a gauntleted hand. The smooth metal breastplate under the cloak glittered in the darkness.

"Gilgamesh!" Claymore spat. He shifted Harper in his arms to put his body between her and the illusion.

Ren glanced back at Rollo. The little man was awake and sitting up. Blood dripped from his nose as he made cryptic hand gestures through the air in front of him.

"It's only a trick!" Ren yelled to Claymore. "It's one of Pennymaker's illusions!"

"You're sure it's not another dying revenant of Ur?" Claymore growled.

"Don't be fooled by his games!" Ren insisted. "The armor is not from this time period! And the phantoms are colorless! Gilgamesh's glowing white."

Ren reached out a hand to prove the figure was nothing

more than an illusion. His fingers pressed against the cold metal of the warrior's armor. Gilgamesh was solid.

A backhanded blow from a metal gauntlet sent him flying into the side of the passageway. He dropped to the ground, gasping for breath.

Rollo climbed to his feet, still throwing strange hand signals into the air. The little round man backed down the dark tunnel. Ren shook his head to clear his head.

Claymore laid Harper down against the wall and pulled his sawn-off rifle from his back, ready to face the manifestation of the world's *Logos Personae*.

The warrior drew his curved sickle sword from his belt. Claymore dodged to one side as the blade slashed at him and fired point blank into the giant's face. The corridor reverberated as Gilgamesh staggered back from the force of the blast. By the time the giant recovered, Claymore scooped Harper from the floor and sprinted down the passageway. Ren ran alongside him.

"Where's Rollo?" he said. They both looked around, but he was gone.

"That way!" Ren replied. He threw the strap of the satchel over his shoulder and flashed his light down the corridor Rollo used to sneak away.

"You find Rollo!" Claymore ordered, his demeanor suddenly hard. "I'll get Harper to safety. Meet me on the ridge where we camped the first night we arrived here!" There was a haunted look in his eyes Ren had never seen before. Claymore disappeared down a side corridor with Harper in his arms.

Ren hesitated to let Claymore out of his sight. Physically, his partner seemed as formidable as ever, but Ren could see the madness that was growing stronger with every passing minute. Time was running out for Claymore. The trickster cursed under his breath, snatched up the leather satchel from the ground and took off into the darkness after Rollo Pennymaker.

Chapter 28
Into the Great Unknown

Ren sprinted down the underground corridor after Rollo. He knew he could outrun the little man's short legs and expected to reach him at every turn in the passageway, but somehow he failed to catch up. The further he continued, the more frustrated he became at the thought of losing his quarry.

The ground vibrated faintly beneath his feet. He stopped to listen. In the heavy silence, he caught the sound of horse hooves on dirt somewhere in the tunnel ahead of him. There had been no signs of horses anywhere within Ur, so it had to be Rollo. He turned a sharp corner and saw the glow of sunlight ahead.

The soft light illuminated the dirt floor ahead at the next bend. Ren quickened his pace, running up the shallow steps and out into the scorching heat. The city streets were deathly quiet. He continued down the avenue, listening for hoofbeats. They were faint in the distance.

Ren pulled off his boots and shirt. Rollo was too far ahead to catch him on foot. With a thought, his naked back sprouted feathered wings.

The flying monkey ran forward on his knuckles into the sunlight. His wings spread out and with a strong flap, Ren lifted off the ground. He searched the maze of streets below him for any sign of survivors from Mordecai's party, but saw no evidence of anyone, alive or dead.

Once he cleared the city walls, he headed south toward Harper's sanctuary, climbing higher into the sky. The monkey's fur was stifling hot under the burning sun, but Ren ignored the discomfort.

On the dirt road beneath him, he saw Rollo Pennymaker riding on a great white stallion. The little man bounced comically on the back of the shimmering horse, one hand clutching his top hat and the other tightly gripping gold reins. A full saddle and bridle rig adorned the steed. Rollo glanced down the road behind him every couple of minutes to see if he was being followed. After a while he stopped looking, confident no one could have kept up with him. The thought never occurred to him to look up.

Ren flew high over the arid landscape, keeping pace with the line of dust kicked up by the horse. If Rollo somehow knew the location of the Roskashon Lodestones, the trickster would be there when he went to retrieve them. Harper would die rather than reveal their location to Rollo, but in her befuddled state, she might have said something that gave Rollo the clue he needed. Was there something he missed in Rollo's conversation with Harper?

Once Ren reached the lodestones, he would go back to find Claymore and Harper, and together they could get out of *The Epic of Gilgamesh* forever. His only fear was Claymore's rapidly deteriorating mental state. Every minute brought Claymore one step closer to the ever encroaching madness.

The road ran along the Euphrates for many miles. Ren pushed to keep up with the speed of the steed. The luminous horse was incredibly fast, much more than any horse Ren had ever ridden. The miles fell behind them until, in the distance, an endless sea of Wayward trees came into view.

Rollo slowed down to a trot as he approached the forest. Ren veered to the side to avoid being seen and circled back. He landed in the top branches of a giant tree. Rollo reined the horse to a stop and dismounted next to an incline of rocks. He stood there unmoving for a long time, glancing in all directions. He swept his hand across the air in front of the giant steed. The horse faded from existence.

The sun began to set in the west and the shadows grew long. The trilling of insects filled the dense forest and the occasional roar of enormous beasts echoed deep among the trees. In the coming dusk, the organic emerald glow of countless rabbit-holes bathed the forest floor.

Rollo made another motion with his hands. A small flame appeared at the tips of his fingers. He tossed the light above his head. The light was identical to the one that floated over Harper's cell door. The illuminating glow moved with him as he waddled into the opening of a black cave wedged in between the cleft of rocks.

Ren flew down across from the cave entrance, hiding behind the twisted roots of a tree. Rollo came back out of the cave, the small light still hovering above him. Behind him, two faceless humanoids shimmered in the dying light, as Gilgamesh had. The illusionary figures pushed a wooden flatbed four-wheeled cart covered with a drop cloth.

The manservants rolled the wagon to a flat area of ground. Rollo jerked the canvas tarp off. Underneath, a large gondola tied by a tangle of thick, corded ropes to a pile of red silk-like fabric. The two humanoids lifted the basket out of the wagon. With the aid of his helpers, Rollo pulled the fabric off the back of the cart. They stretched the red material out over the open ground. Ren realized he was looking at a hot-air balloon.

Rollo looped a rope around a nearby tree root and tied it off. He opened the gate to the basket and climbed in. Kneeling before a metal cylinder in the center of the gondola, he fiddled with several knobs. After a moment, there was a loud pop and fire appeared at the top of the cylinder. Hot air began to fill the mouth of the red balloon. Rollo waved away the Fae light above him as the giant tear-shaped balloon took form.

The two faceless servants returned the wagon to its hiding place within the cave. They ambled to the balloon, standing beside the wicker basket. Rollo looked up, clapped his hands twice and made a sweeping gesture in the air. The two shimmering figures faded into oblivion as the power that created them was severed.

A few minutes later, the bright red balloon reached full capacity. Rollo turned the fire down and jumped to the ground. He untied the anchor rope and climbed into the basket as it rose, shutting the gate behind him. Dangling ropes dragged across the ground as the balloon lifted into the air.

Ren did not know Rollo's destination, but believed he headed toward the prize everyone had been searching for.

The balloon floated out over the Euphrates River, past Harper's sanctuary. It caught a current of strong winds that pushed Rollo toward the veil of mist that led beyond the edge of the world. Ren took to the air, desperate to stay with him. He flew over the peeked roof of Harper's hideaway as the Rollo's balloon approached the dense mist. He stayed below the gondola to avoid being seen as it drifted into the heavy mist and disappeared. Ren followed.

The thick fog made visibility difficult. Rollo's balloon was nothing but a dark shape fifty yards in front of him. The strong winds hampered Ren's progress as he continued through the shrouded air. Ren fought to keep up. He flapped his wings harder, closing the space between him and the rocking basket.

Gales buffeted Ren from every direction, throwing him head over heels through the air and pushing the basket further from his reach. When he got himself upright, Rollo had drifted out of sight. Ren fought the torrent of winds and headed in the last direction of the balloon.

The giant red balloon came back into view, its gondola swinging violently under it. Ahead of him, the mists cleared, but the skies darkened into a whirlwind. Rollo directed the balloon directly toward the darkest part of the storm. A funnel of swirling wind formed a massive tornado at the heart of the raging maelstrom.

Where could he be heading? Was there something he missed in Rollo's conversation with Harper?

Ren closed the gap between them. He realized if the balloon entered the tornado before he reached it, he would lose Rollo for good. He redoubled his efforts, flapping his wings desperately as exhaustion crept into his limbs. Several ropes dangled under the basket, whipping in the wind. He reached out for the closest one, only to have a torrent of air pull it out of his reach.

The winds tore at him. He tried again and caught the flailing rope, dangling from the end as the wind funnel sucked them in. The whirlwind tossed the balloon around like a toy. Ren slammed against the gondola. He morphed back to his true shape so he could concentrate entirely on holding onto the side of the wicker bucket. The wind pulled at the satchel on his shoulder. The satchel's flap flew open. Ren closed his arm and held it tight.

Dim lights appeared at the center of the whirlwind. The balloon rode the edge of the tornado like water circling a drain. Another dozen revolutions and they reached the everchanging lights. The trickster held in his nausea and closed his eyes to fight the sharp reality shifts happening around him.

Ren tightened his grip on the basket with all of his

remaining strength when the violent winds abated. The air calmed, and once again Ren found himself surrounded in thick, dense fog. He adjusted his hold on the rope and breathed easy now that the winds had died down.

The balloon broke through the wall of fog and came out over a crystal clear sea under a multitude of glowing orbs the sat in a vast black void overhead. They came out of the storm over an archipelago of islands. Somehow, Rollo had guided them through the maelstrom to a doorway leading to the world of Rogue Destiny. Ren shook his head to clear it of the aftereffects of sliding through the reality-shifting journey Rollo had just taken them on.

Ren dangled from the end of his rope. His hands started to cramp, but he kept his hold on the rope. He looked back at the storm they had passed through. The mystical veil collapsed in on itself and, a moment later, it was gone. He'd heard rumors of hidden rifts in time and space used to reach Rogue Destiny from outlying worlds. Secret ways beyond rabbit-holes and Slip-streams. This was the first time he had seen one of them.

He climbed up, hand over hand, before grabbing onto the ropes tied to the wicker gondola. He peeked over of the rim of the basket. Rollo had his back to him as he guided the balloon toward the city.

As if he sensed he was being watched, Rollo turned. His disfigured face, swollen from the broken nose and bruises he had sustained from Ren only hours before, tightened into a spiteful sneer. With deceptive speed, the little man picked up a walking cane from the basket floor and swung it at Ren.

The metal-capped wood stick struck Ren in the side of the head. He fought to maintain his hold on the gondola. The satchel slipped off his shoulder and slid down his arm before he caught it.

Rollo lifted the cane to strike again. Ren hung off the basket by one hand and reacted instinctively. He swung the satchel into Rollo's head, knocking from sight. The flap flung open, spewing papers and notebooks in the air. They slapped Ren across the face as he climbed over the rim of the gondola. Rollo lay curled in a heap against the far side of the basket, cradling his broken nose. *The Book of Days* lay next to the burners supplying hot air to the balloon.

Rollo spied the ancient tome and picked it up. "Where did you get this?!" he cried. Ren grabbed it out of his hands.

"Sit there and be quiet," Ren ordered. He bent down to gather what remained of the scattered journals and notebooks. He stuffed the journals back into the satchel, never taking his eyes from Rollo for more than a moment. Among the random notes written on scraps of paper and napkins that were strewn over the floor, a bookmark caught his attention.

He picked it up. The illustration on the bookmark showed a small boy looking out a window of his house at the moon. It was from a children's picture book. The name written in colorful letters on the cover read:

There's No One on the Moon.

"Could the answer be that simple?" Ren thought.

Harper had been delirious when Rollo pressed her for the location of the Roskashon Lodestones. She refused to tell anything. But when Ren appeared hiding behind the face of her sister Calliope, she began singing *There's No One on the Moon*, her sister's favorite children's book. Did Harper subconsciously give away the lodestone's hiding place when she thought she was talking to the only person she trusted? It might be worth looking into.

Ren pulled Rollo to his feet by front of his coat. "Take us to the Obtuse Turtle," he demanded. The dejected little man skillfully navigated the winds toward the great city on the horizon.

Below them, on the calm waters of the Dreaming Sea, Ren watched sailing ships carry adventurous travelers to the distant shores of faraway worlds. Rogue Destiny wasn't held to the natural laws of physics that bound the other worlds floating overhead. If the ships sailed long enough over the waters, they would reach many of those worlds.

The balloon floated over long stretches of water, passed tropical islands toward the fabled City of a Thousand Moons and her five million denizens. A warm, calming wind blew across Ren's face. A half hour later, the red dew-drop shaped balloon descended on Rogue Destiny. Eclectic structures of every imaginable architectural design passed beneath them.

Twenty minutes later, the giant red hot-air balloon landed gently on the well-manicured lawns in front of the popular public house, the Obtuse Turtle. A crowd of curious spectators watched the large basket hit the ground. Ren, now in his natural bleached bone-colored persona with dark streaks of pigment snaking across his naked chest and arms, dragged a struggling Rollo across the grass to a side entrance.

The lighter-than-air balloon started to float away. A three parking attendants ran, grabbing the dangling ropes to stop it's ascent. They struggled but managed to tie the balloon down to a small tree.

Ren forced Rollo across the grass, past the crowded front entrance of the public house, heading toward a back entry used by the kitchen staff. Ren thought it may be time to get the Raconteurs involved. Natascha, Medesto and the others would bring Mordecai down once and for all. That would have ramifications across Rogue Destiny. He stomped down a hallway that led to Gideon's office and opened the door without knocking. The cluttered room was empty. The trickster swore under his breath.

"All right" Rollo hissed. His beady eyes glanced up and down the hallway. An underlying fear of being seen by the wrong people evident. "Get me out of here and I'll tell where the lode-stones are."

He pushed Rollo inside the office, shut the door behind him and slammed the little man against it.

"Listen to me, you nasty little grifter," Ren spat. "If you knew where they were you would gone straight to them. That's why I followed you. But now I don't need you anymore." He tried, but failed to hold back a devious smile.

Both of Rollo's blackened eyes narrowed to slits. "You lie," he growled. "You don't know where they are."

"Keep telling yourself that," Ren replied. He could tell Rollo wanted to believe him, which further proved the little man did not know where they were.

"Then why did you chase after me?" Rollo paused to think, then his eyes went wide "Unless you just learned their location!"

Ren gave him a wry grin. He couldn't help it. It was too fun to watch him squirm. The little man's scowl disappeared into shock. The look on his face proved so comical, Ren almost laughed.

"Of course! The answer was in *The Book of Days* this whole time!"

"Maybe," Ren replied. He released Rollo and stepped back. "Too bad you'll never see them, because you'll rotting away inside a Lazaranth prison cell."

Rollo threw his hands up. "Hold on a moment!," he cried. "I'm sure we can work something out. How about a partnership? We go get the stones together and then we sell them, splitting the profits. I know a dozen buyers who would pay any price for them. Kings, sorcerers, demigods!"

"So they can use their magic to conquer Rogue Destiny?" Ren replied. "I don't think so. I know a better use for them."

Rollo cleared his throat and glanced down at his feet. "Like trying to save Claymore?"

It was Ren's turn to be visibly shocked.

"It's the Paradigm Madness, isn't it?" Rollo said quietly. "I'm just guessing from his erratic behavior."

"What do you know about that?"

"It's sad, a story I've seen too many times before. The effects of the madness are a slow painful slide to insanity, and, then, horrible death. He's pretty far along, isn't he? Suddenly recites words out of nowhere, doesn't he? Like he's reading from a book."

"Yeah. Claymore doesn't even know why."

"They are the words from the Narrative of his homeworld. Once he reaches the end of the story, his mind will empty, and he will suffer horribly before the madness kills him."

"That's why I want the lodestones, so I can save him."

"But do you know how to properly use the lodestones? Time is running out for Claymore and any mistake could prove fatal."

Ren knew what was coming next.

"Let me help you save him," Rollo mewled sweetly.

Ren felt the rush of new feelings out of nowhere. An emotional response as seductive as any Muse. Rollo was using glamour to influence his decisions, despite standing in a world that was a magical dead zone. His sudden anger overpowered the pleasant emotions. He slapped Rollo.

"Stop it!" Ren said. "I know that trick, remember?"

Rollo persisted. "Then bind my hands and keep me prisoner. All I ask is that when Claymore is saved, you set me free."

Ren tapped the side of the satchel hanging from his shoulder. "I have *The Book of Days*" he replied. "I don't need your help."

"That's true," Rollo said. "But the Sunstone must be set in its proper place inside Baltazaar's Tower. Do you know where? They say no one has been inside the monolith since his death nine hundred years ago. Do you know how to get past the protections set up to keep intruders out? I do."

Ren thought about that. He wasn't fooled by Rollo for a second, but he wasn't scared by him either. Rollo Pennymaker was a liar and hustler, unpredictable and dangerous. The Black Tower was inside Rogue Destiny's borders and Rollo's illusionary powers would be greatly inhibited compared to inside *Gilgamesh*. Unlike Ren's shape-shifting gifts, which remained with him wherever he went.

Between him and Claymore, they could accomplish anything. Ren was confident they wouldn't have a problem dealing with the small rotund man. Now that he knew where the lodestones lay, all Ren had to do was go get Claymore. And he had no doubt Harper Bellweather would have a few choice words for Rollo, too.

"Okay," Ren said at last. "I'm only going to tell you this once. You try anything, and I will beat you senseless. Then I'll dump you by the side of the road. Got it?"

"I understand," Rollo answered. His humble demeanor returned to the submissive act he had played for Mordecai. "But we have to move. Time grows short for your partner."

Ren had made deals with the Devil before and always came out on top. But this time it was different. He wasn't gambling with just his own life. Claymore's fate hung in the balance. He concluded he had no choice in the matter. He didn't have time to waste finding a way into Baltazaar's tower and if Rollo knew how to get in, he would have to let him show them. He just couldn't let his guard down or let the grifter out of his sight.

"Will your balloon get us back to *Gilgamesh*?"

"No, the trip back would long and arduous," Rollo replied meekly. "It would us take days to return. Do you have access to other transport?"

"No," Ren replied. "But I know where I can get us one."

Chapter 29
Home Again

Natascha took a floating, horse-drawn Hansom cab from the infirmary to an abandoned part of the industrial district near the Bayfront. The carriage stopped at a tiny shop hidden in the shadows of Hightower bridge at the center of the City. She paid the driver and stepped out onto a dark, desolate street in front of a shop badly in need of repair. The sign read *The Apothecary Blues*. She had always been curious about the significance of the name, but the subject never came up with the shop's owner regarding why he'd decided on that particular name, so she let it lie.

A shingle slid off the roof and landed in the tall grass as she strode up the sidewalk to the front of the establishment. The bell rang, announcing her arrival as she pushed open the creaking door to the cramped shop. Tall shelves covered every wall from floor to ceiling. Apothecary supplies, mostly contained in clouded glass bottles topped with white stoppers, filled every shelf.

The owner of the shop sat on a stool behind an ancient wooden countertop that was worn and stained from many years of use. Natascha couldn't recall ever seeing him anywhere else in the store.

Slevin Hardrus had long, raven-black hair that ran down his back and skin the color of bleached bones. To say the man was gaunt was an understatement by anyone's standard. He wrapped himself in black clothes and wore a long silver scarf.

Natascha did not know what brought Slevin to Rogue Destiny, or even where he came from, but he had the finest selection of apothecary materials she had ever seen. A unique combination of chemicals and natural herbs found nowhere else in Rogue Destiny. And he was her landlord.

She grabbed a small notebook next to the cash register. "I need this list of ingredients," she said as she wrote them down. "And I would appreciate any suggestions you may have to maximize their potency and effect."

Slevin eyes came up from the book he was reading. He slipped the thin wire glasses to the edge of his long nose and read the list. "Another of your non-lethal remedies to disable your enemies. Would it not be quicker to kill them outright?"

"No, it would not," Natascha responded. "You know I won't kill unless given no other choice."

Slevin shrugged and set the paper down. "Just saying," he croaked. "In my experience, they don't attack you again if they're dead. I know someone who could get you the highest grade explosives that you won't find elsewhere in the City."

It was Natascha's turn to shrug. "Killing takes no skill, but it's an art form to take someone down and keep them alive. How long before this'll be ready?"

"Couple of hours at most," he answered. "After my assistant, Sacca, returns from his errands." He went back to the page he had been reading.

"Good enough." Natascha started for the backroom then

stopped. "And I need one of the spare fobs I gave you for safe-keeping."

Slevin looked up from his book. His clear crystal eyes sparkled in the kerosine lamplight. He opened the register and pulled out a small, oval-shaped fob, dropping it in her hand.

"Another argument with your mother?" he purred. "How is Idalia? I haven't seen her since she went to Lazaranth Prison."

"On the run from someone again. She goes by the moniker *Lady Absynthe* these days."

"Lovely name," Slevin said with a wink. "I always liked your mother. Never understood why you two don't get along better."

"She started it," Natascha muttered. She felt her face flush in embarrassment. "I was caught unaware, and she brought her pets with her. That's why I need the things on this list. And stay out of my head."

Natascha wasn't sure how he did the mind game thing. Slevin may have been a psychic or a seer of some skill or even a powerful Oracle. She didn't know. But she always had the feeling it had more to do with reading her emotional state rather than her thoughts.

"Have Sacca leave my order out on the dock when it's done." Natascha headed toward the backroom. "Thank you."

"Don't forget the rent is due," Slevin said dryly.

"I'll have it to you by the end of the week."

"Of course," he chuckled. "Oh, I see there are spices on the list this time. Interesting."

Slevin smiled at her. His teeth were unusually long and oddly squared, but somehow fit in with the rest of his appearance. He reluctantly got up from his chair. Slevin was extraordinarily tall, well above the size of any normal human, yet skeletal-thin. He moved with a slow gracefulness that was hypnotizing, but Natascha wasn't in the mood to be beguiled by it. She'd been caught in the hypnotic eyes of a great serpent all too recently. She shuddered at the memory of her mother's pet, Maquna.

For some reason, Slevin's peculiar idiosyncrasies did not creep her out. He was more of an oddity to her than anything. They were acquaintances beyond the landlord and renter relationship. She kept to herself and so did he. But Natascha could never figure out how Slevin always seemed to know things about her personal life that he shouldn't. Things she never spoke about to anyone.

Natascha left through the backroom. She went down the rear steps of the shop to a garden area overgrown with brambles. The once beautiful fountain was covered in moss and had thorny weeds growing out of its stagnant green water. She stepped out onto a rickety dock that extended to the Ampersand River and hit the button on the fob in her hand.

The water at the end of the dock rippled. A round opening formed on the surface below where she stood. She climbed down a metal ladder attached to the wooden dock, and entered the collapsible tunnel that led to her underwater laboratory in the depths of the river.

The trust between Natascha and Slevin was absolute. He would never betray the location of her secret lab because he was forever indebted for services rendered involving Doctor Enigma dealing with a gang of cyberpunk vampires that hunted him.

Natascha stepped off the ladder into the muck that had collected on the floor of the artificial tunnel. In front of her, a dry, circular tunnel disappeared from sight into the murky water. She walked down the tube, watching sea life swim past the clear walls of the seven-foot-high passageway. The tunnel continued on for fifty yards until it reached a squat stone structure. She typed the passcode onto the keypad and the security door clicked open.

Doctor Enigma maintained a hidden lair deep under the

waters of Rogue Destiny's largest river. The underwater bunker was big enough to house her sixty-foot Slipstream *Nevermore*. The watertight structure provided her a large workshop and spacious living facilities, complete with a kitchen, two private sleeping quarters, and a small study. Natascha could think of nothing more than crashing for a few hours in her own bed until she had to regroup with the Raconteurs and begin their systematic dismantling of Mordecai's criminal empire.

With a press of the fob key, the tunnel collapsed, becoming invisible on the floor of the bay. The soft hum of the bunker's air filtration system soothed her exhausted mind. She left the nightmare of the last few days outside. This was her sanctum, and nothing could touch her here. The familiar scents of jasmine and motor oil hit her as she closed the door. She was home.

Exhaustion washed over her as she tossed her gloves and gas mask on a workbench filled with beakers, decanters, and Bunsen burners. How much time had passed since she and Medesto had left to find Ren playing outlaw in a dark fantasy novel and brought him home? Her brain was too foggy to think about that.

"Gustav? I'm home," she called out. A small fly-bot popped up into view from the back of the garage.

"Welcome back, boss," Gustav 7 said in his synthesized inflection.

Natascha pulled off her trench coat and hung it up in a closet next to a dozen identical ones. The closet door was from her old bedroom, one of the last remaining remnants of a chaotic childhood. She unholstered both her Peacemakers, and fitted the handles into their chargers on the workbench.

Despite her exhaustion, she wanted to check on the updates Gustav had added to her beloved ship. Then she could sleep. She walked around one of the Cold-Fire engines mounted at the rear of the ship, then down the pilot's side to find her droid companion welding the front grill of the Slipstream.

Nevermore was her pride and joy. They had been through too many harrowing adventures together, fighting everything from star ships to evil Fae Queens to fiery dragons. The sleek design of her ship resembled the pulp fiction technology with a twist of alchemy. Sebastian Poe had built it for her off of Natascha's specs and design.

Slipstream pilots often decorated their rigs with flames or racing stripes. Natascha preferred glossy black. A simple, dominant image among the Raconteurs' fleet.

"How did the mission go?" Gustav asked.

"It was a rough one," Natascha answered. "We lost Tempest."

"Only one?" Gustav 7 said. "That better than last time."

Natascha designed and built the fly-bots herself. She'd imagined a handful of assistants to help her with her workload. The first of the robotic companions were given a full range of artificial emotions for Natascha's benefit. Long hours alone in the lab, proved to be a lonely existence.

Not all of the companions survived the brutal existence of working beside the Raconteurs. The ones that did proved too emotionally unstable from the experience. Natascha adjusted their internal circuitry to dial back on their emotive responses. Even with fine tuning, it never quite worked out the way she'd hoped it would. The crying and gossiping about each other, as well as the Raconteurs got on her nerves. So, in a moment of desperation, she had decommissioned the remaining prototypes and reconfigured them all into a sixth generation.

Valor 6, the last iteration of what would eventually become Gustav 7, was given a logic chip and long list of rules. She immediately blew a circuit and came at Natascha with a kitchen knife for leaving a Bunson burner on.

Gustav was the seventh generation and had no negative

emotions to speak. Everything he said sounded happy and logical. Even bad things. It made him sound cruel in context to Tempest's death. But he was only an artificial fly-bot, after all, still learning how to interact with the world around him.

"But I am glad you're okay," Gustav 7 added.

"Thanks." Natascha replied. She stifled a yawn. "I'm gonna catch some sleep. Make sure I'm awake by eleven. It looks like this whole mess is just getting started."

Chapter 30
Subterfuge

Ren led Rollo to the landing bays behind the back of the public house. Several ships sat prepped and ready for the next time they would be called into service. Construction barriers blocked their way. An extensive amount of damage had taken place to the front of Sebastian Poe's underground workshop. A set of massive doors directly between the building and the Obtuse Turtle appeared to have been damaged by an explosion. Mounds of concrete and twisted metal lay piled on one side of the entrance. Something terrible had taken place in the short time Ren had been away.

Dragging Rollo with him, he reached the next entrance down the way and pressed his open hand on the sensor next to the storm door. Ren hoped he was still allowed entry into the subterranean garage. The heavy doors slid opened. Ren descended the ramp to Sebastian Poe's dimly lit workshop, where the cyborg mechanic designed and built the Raconteur's fleet.

Ren wandered the aisles of the expansive shop with Rollo in tow. They wove their way in-between the workstations, diagnostic equipment and dangling power cords, looking for Sebastian or one of his assistants so Ren could ask about securing a ship. He wasn't sure if the Raconteurs' chief mechanic would simply let him take a Slipstream because he asked for it, but Ren thought it would be worth a try. If the answer was no, there were other options open to the trickster.

They passed the massive fuselage sitting on hydraulic lifts, waiting for their Coldfire engines to be installed. Rollo gaped at the internal workings of the Sebastian's workshop. Ren pulled him along, not giving the rotund little man too much of a look at the secret technologies of the Raconteurs.

"Hello?" a voice called out behind him. "Can I help you?" Ren spun around to see B'Tori Poe, the youngest daughter of the Poe clan, staring at him.

He pushed Rollo into a chair next to a workbench. "Stay here," he told him, poking his finger into his chest.

"Oh, Renny!" B'Tori laughed. "What are you doing back in town?" The young woman stood as tall as Ren but was skinnier, with grease-stained overalls and a headful of dreadlocked hair like her older sister, Danique.

"I'm still undercover," Ren replied. "Just on my way out again. Is your father here?"

"He's not here right now. Whatcha need?"

"When will he be back?"

B'Tori shrugged. "Not sure. He's visiting Gideon at the hospital. After the explosion, everything's been chaos around here."

"I saw the damage outside. What happened?"

"You didn't hear?" B'Tori said. "There was an attack on our workshop. Three council members died in the explosion. Gideon's still hospitalized from his injuries."

Ren felt his heart drop. "How is he?"

"It was scary at first, but father says he's going to pull through."

"Any idea who's behind the attack?"

"Everybody's got their theories," B'Tori replied. She returned to scrubbing grease and oil from a giant coil inside the ship's engine with a heavy bristled brush. "I don't pay attention to politics, but the word is it has to do with the Common Counsel. I think *The Black Rose* is responsible. What can I help you with?"

"I need to borrow one of the slipstreams."

"I don't know," she replied. "Did Father give you permission to use one of the ships? He's really fussy about people touching his precious babies. He and Medesto go around and around about it all the time."

"Of course," Ren answered. The words escaped his lips without thought. Lying came too easy to the trickster, and if he needed something desperately enough, it came even faster. "But that's okay. I didn't think you had the authority to help me. I'll just wait until Sebastian gets back." He found a stool, pulled it up next to Rollo and plopped himself down.

"I can help you," B'Tori said. The teenager straightened her posture. "Father says I'm in charge when he's gone. Did you have any particular one in mind?"

"Last time I was here, your father had refitted Claymore's old rig, *Righteous Indignation*. Is that one still here?" The thought of saving his partner with his own ship made the guilt building up in Ren a little easier to swallow. It was Claymore's after all? How was that wrong?

"Yeah, it's out back on the landing bay," B'Tori replied. "Father's been taking it on test flights when he thinks no one notices. It's one of his favorite builds."

"Gideon said I could use it if I needed to." Again, he said what was necessary in the moment with no concern for the consequences of his actions.

The statement rang true in his mind. Gideon said he'd consider giving Ren a Slipstream of his own as payment once he stopped Mordecai from reaching the *Roskashon Lodestones*. Ren had *The Book of Days* and would soon have the lodestones. So, technically, he had finished the job. Mostly. It wasn't Ren's fault Gideon wasn't there to confirm their agreement.

"Do you have the keybox for the ship?" Ren asked.

"Wait here," B'Tori said. "Father thinks he's so clever, but I know where he keeps everything." She disappeared into a side room. The light inside went on, and moments later, B'Tori reappeared holding a large keyring.

Ren felt guilty lying to the sweet young woman adored by everyone. But he was in a desperate situation and told himself what he did was for the greater good. Time was running out for Claymore, so one little white lie wouldn't hurt anyone. While he hated deceiving B'Tori, he wasn't sure what disgusted him more, lying to her face or the fact that the dishonesty bothered him. He had too many questionable things left to do to grow a conscious now.

B'Tori went to a six-foot tall cabinet with a steel door and punched in several digits on the security pad. The cabinet door clicked open.

"The pass code is my mother's birthday." She gave him a coy smile. "Father always uses that."

Ren watched the B'Tori fumbled with the keyring, looking at the numbers on each key, her lips moving ever so slightly. After scanning the labeled drawers, B'Tori hooked her foot around a stepstool and pulled it over to her. Climbing up, she slid the shiny key of a lock into the drawer and opened it.

"Here we go," she said, jumping down and handing the keybox to Ren. "Father just finished downloading the navigation information from The WayFinder a couple of days ago, so she's ready to go."

Ren studied the black keybox in his hand. It was slightly

larger than a deck of cards, and part of the new security protocol to prevent the unauthorized use of Sebastian's precious ships. The annoying twinge in the pit of his stomach increased, but he ignored it. He was in too deep to turn back now. He'd apologize later, once this was over, and Claymore was safe.

"Thank you," he said. "I appreciate your help."

"No problem," she answered. "Father says you're one of the good ones, and I can trust you." Her fresh face, oil smeared, stared up at him with a wide grin. "Where are you headed?"

"Back to work," Ren replied. "Not quite finished with the job yet."

"You going after bad guys?"

"Always," Ren said with a forced grin. "In fact, you may have just saved the day." He felt a strange remorse. What was that? Guilt.

B'Tori beamed with pride at the remark. It surprised Ren that the lie actually troubled him. He was doing what had to be done, and Claymore's old Slipstream would be his compensation when he completed his mission, so why not take it now? What annoyed him most wasn't the feeling of regret, but that his deceptive words bothered him at all.

"Is he a bad guy?" she asked, throwing a thumb at Rollo. "He doesn't look too scary."

"He's mixed up in the middle of this mess. I need to keep to him close, but when I'm done, it's off to Lazaranth Prison with him."

The ship, once known as *Righteous Indignation*, sat in the shadows near the ramp on the stone floor of the Palisades Landing Bay. The sleek polished ship carried Coldfire Coil engines on each side. Its design was a strange blending of exotic sports cars and aerodynamic spacecrafts.

The carbon alloy body made the fuselage lightweight but

stronger than iron and gave the Slipstreams their lightning speed. The ship stood sixty-feet long from nose to tail, the last twenty feet all engines. Ren laid a hand on the cool, smooth surface. She was beautiful.

"Thank you for your help, B'Tori," Ren told her. He hit a button on the key-box and the hatch on the side of the craft opened. A short set of steps slowly descended to the ground.

"Always glad to help when I can," B'Tori replied. Her bright eyes shone out from under the thick mop of dreadlocks. The guilt bothered him, but not strong enough to stop him from doing what he needed to do.

Ren grabbed his prisoner by the coat collar, and they climbed into the cabin. He forced Rollo into the co-pilot's seat and slid into the pilot's chair at the front of the ship. B'Tori stood next to him.

"Anything I need to know about these new models?" Ren asked. "I haven't been behind the wheel for a couple of years."

"The navigation is quicker than it used to be." B'Tori pointed to a rectangular screen that dominated the front dashboard. "You punch in the destination there. Drop a Book's name in the Wayfinder's data banks and you'll get the coordinates. She's fully stocked with supplies and medical kits. There are no weapons onboard yet. Is that a problem for you?"

"No. I won't need any weapons. But what about prisoner restraints?"

"Yeah, over here."

B'Tori opened a panel on the wall where a variety of firearms would be stored. It was empty. She pulled open a drawer inside the cabinet. Inside were a row of physical restraints used to transport fugitives back to Rogue Destiny.

Ren chose a set designed to restrict the hand movements of those who dealt in the magical arts.

"I've heard you stole your glamour magic from a Fae Prince," he told Rollo, "so we're going with the iron infused shackles."

The manacles Ren chose completely encased Rollo's hands and fingers, restricting movement. He locked them and wrapped the attached leather belt across Rollo's thick waist, buckling it tight. He slid the key into the pocket of his baggy pants. The trickster didn't know if the place they were heading would be magical or not, but he wasn't taking any chances with Rollo. He returned his attention to B'Tori.

"One last thing," he asked. "How do I turn off the tracking system?"

A quizzical look came over B'Tori's face. "Why would you want to do that?" she asked. "It's there for your safety."

"This is a special circumstance," Ren said. "I'll need to keep a low profile out there. Where I'm going is dangerous, and I don't want to risk anyone following me."

"I don't know," B'Tori replied, her voice suddenly crestfallen. "Father is very strict on safety protocols. If you crash or need us to locate you, we won't be able to if the tracking is off."

"This is on Gideon's orders. Tell your father I'll explain everything when I get back. Please help me with this, B'Tori. Remember, you can trust me."

"Okay, but only because it's you. I know you wouldn't lie to me." She disappeared down the ramp into the garage.

"My, you are a wonderful liar," Rollo replied quietly, once B'Tori was out of sight.

"Shut up!" Ren growled, not bothering to look at him. "Or I will punch you again to shut you up." B'Tori returned before he could make good on his threat.

She carried an odd-looking tool with her. "This is the corkscrew key. It's the only way to get to the new tracking circuitry." She knelt down and crawled under the dashboard. Ren knelt to watch her work.

B'Tori inserted the end of the tool into a slot on a panel under the main screen and turned the handle. A thick metal bolt slowly unscrewed until there was enough room to stick her hand through the opening.

"There's a knob you have to turn," B'Tori said. Her fingers felt around until there was an audible click. "There, got it." She screwed the panel shut and crawled out. "Well, good luck with wherever you're going, Renny. What are you doing that's so secretive?"

"The usual. Sneaking into places I don't belong and causing trouble."

"That's so cool!" B'Tori exclaimed. Her trusting eyes bore into his conscience.

Ren put a hand on her shoulder. "I'll take all the responsibility myself. I'll bring her back as soon as I can."

"It's so good to see you!" She hugged Ren tightly. "It's gets boring without you around."

Ren returned the sentiment, hugging her back. "I should get going," he replied. "Thank you again, B'Tori." He motioned Rollo to the Slipstream with a nod.

"Wait!" B'Tori shouted, throwing her hand up. "She doesn't have a name yet! It's bad luck to fly a ship without a name. You have to think of one!"

Ren shrugged. "Okay, how about *Righteous Indignation* 2? In honor of Claymore."

B'Tori shook her head "No. Father says it'll bring misfortune if you use a name on the same ship twice. If you're flying her, then it should be something that fits your personally... like *Sneaky Pete*. Or *Trickster's Delight*. Or *Chicanery Row*."

"Have anything a little more subtle?" Ren responded.

She furrowed her brow in thought. "How about *Subterfuge*? Its sounds sneaky, like you."

"*Subterfuge*?" Ren replied. "It's perfect."

B'Tori stepped away. Ren grabbed his prisoner and walked him up the steps into the cabin of the ship, now called *Subterfuge*. He hit the button that closed the hatch. B'Tori smiled and saluted him as the doors closed.

As they entered the cockpit, Ren forced him to sit in the co-pilot's seat. He fastened the seat belt around his round belly and slid into the pilot's chair next to him and inserted the key-box into its slot on the dashboard. A dozen lights flickered on. He fired up the Coldfire Coil engines.

Ren hadn't flown a Slipstream since that terrible night in *The Angels of Avalon* when the *Paradigm Madness* fell on Claymore. But he hoped it would come back to him quickly. The floor-boards vibrated beneath his feet. He double-checked the controls before easing the route thrusters to quarter strength. Outside, B'Tori waved one last time, before returning to her duties in the garage. Dirt and debris blew up as the ship lifted from the ground. He checked the radar for other ships in his air space before opening up the engines and shooting into sky.

He knew he might be burning bridges that he could never rebuild. But everything he was doing, he did for Claymore's sake. Gideon had once told him trust was the only way the Raconteurs could successfully work together. Sometimes it was the only thing to hold on to, knowing their fellow agents had your back.

Once that trust was broken, it would be hard to regain. Ren knew stealing a Slipstream and planning to activate the most powerful artifact in existence could constitute a betrayal of that trust, even if it was to save Claymore.

His allegiance to the Raconteurs had always been precarious at best. He enjoyed the life and death struggle to keep the worlds of the Mythic Cosmos safe and the satisfaction he felt when lives were saved. But something occurred to him. This time he may have finally crossed a line from which he could never return.

The islands of Rogue Destiny disappeared beneath them as the Great Void loomed ahead. Ren typed the title of their destination into the ship's navigation system.

Subterfuge sped toward the children's picture book, *There's No One on the Moon*.

Chapter 31
Moonboy

As the unending miles of the Great Void fell behind him, Ren struggled to stay focused on the task that lay ahead. It may have been sleep deprivation, or the fact that, despite all his efforts to save Claymore, it could prove worthless in the end. He guided *Subterfuge* past hundreds of floating worlds, following the ship's navigation to a place he believed hid the relic that would bring his friend back.

His thoughts weighed heavily on him. His exhausted mind played through every likely outcome he could think of. Could the lodestones actually reverse the madness? What if they didn't? He glanced at Rollo sleeping in the co-pilot's seat and smacked him in the arm.

"Wake up!" he snapped. "I need you to tell me everything you know about the Paradigm Madness!"

Rollo's head popped up. He blinked several times before he spoke. "The Paradigm Madness is one of the greatest mysteries there is," he said. "It's an insidious sickness of the mind that corrupts a person's soul from within."

"I know that!" Ren replied. He swallowed the impatience

building inside him. "So can the Roskashon Lodestones save Claymore?"

Rollo's expression grew somber. "Their sole purpose is to reestablish the lost connection between the user and their homeworld across the Void. They say the power they command is unlimited. So, yes, I believe they can save your friend."

"Good," Ren replied. "Now all I have to do is find them."

"You must realize what will happen if the lodestones work on Claymore," Rollo added, expressing what appeared to be genuine concern. "If they can restore his mind, he will be forever bound to them. They won't heal him. They will only ward off the effects of the madness for as long as the lodestones remain in place. He can never be free of them."

"At least he'll be alive to complain about it," Ren mumbled. He wasn't sure if anything the little man spoke was true or if he was being told only he wanted to hear. He hadn't forgotten that Rollo was full of trickery and deceit and almost killed Mordecai's party in Gilgamesh. But Ren needed some shred of hope to cling to, and this was all he could find at the moment.

The navigation screen flashed to show they were approaching their destination. Ren leaned the ship toward a small, luminous world. As they drew closer, he pressed a button on the dashboard. A ping filled the cabin, and a tiny ball of scintillating light shot out from the ship's grill. It struck the outer layer of the world, and a keyhole appeared amid an explosion of rippling waves.

Subterfuge passed through the artificial opening into the world of *There's No One on the Moon*. The misty veil of words disappeared a moment later. The Slipstream collided into the treetops of a small forest grove. Tree boughs shattered against the sides and undercarriage of the ship. Ren pulled up on the controls to avoid plunging to the ground.

The ship veered to the side and burst from the branches over a single two-story house with a perfectly manicured lawn. The minimalistic words of *There's No One on the Moon* created an extremely tiny world in which to navigate. Ren had never been inside a world so small.

Behind the house, a solitary tree stood at the center of an open field that stretched to the edge of the Story. Ren slowed the ship and landed *Subterfuge* near it. He pulled the key-box out of its slot and escorted Rollo to the main cabin. Ren shoved him into a passenger seat and fastened the crash harness over him.

"I'll be back," Ren told him. He checked Rollo's manacles to make sure they were secure. With his hands locked inside the restraints, and the harness preventing him from leaving his seat, Rollo was going nowhere. Ren hit the button that lowered the ramp and walked down into the tall grass.

The shady Wayward Tree loomed over him. Its colorful green leaves were a more natural earthy shade than the glossy field of grass around him. The tree was young, not yet having reached its full height. A soft emerald glow radiated from the rabbit-hole at its base. He found traces of a campsite and the remains of a small fire near its base. Harper Bellweather had been there, and this was how she entered the world.

He moved across the field through the small group of trees until he stood in the backyard of the two-story house. The scene was idyllic. Vivid colors of greens, blues, and reds covered everything from the grass to the sky. The lawn was immaculate, with rows of beautiful rosebushes along one side and a wooden gazebo in the middle of the yard. A patio butted up to the back of the house with a picnic table and umbrella, gas barbeque and lawn chairs spread across it. A full moon hung low in the sky above the trees, bathing everything in a soft glow.

A strange, childlike wonder overcame him. For a moment, the anxiety of finding the lodestones and saving Claymore melted away. The scene filled him with the feeling anything was possible. The grass under his bare feet was lush, but he left no footprints behind. His movements felt slow and weightless, like he walked through a veil of dense air. He reached out, but no resistance met him as he closed his hand.

The temperature was perfect, neither cool nor warm. A calm feeling of serenity washed over Ren as he crossed the yard to the house. The colors were vibrant, with geometrical designs that did not quite match reality. The hues of the grass, the roses and the moon were too vivid to be real. He realized what that meant. Unlike a world constructed only of words, this was a child's picture book and he stood inside an illustration.

"Hi," a tiny voice said. Ren looked up to a second-story window. A small cherub face smiled down at him.

"Have you come to play with me?" the boy asked.

"Yes, I have," Ren replied, thinking quickly for a response. "I heard you might be lonely."

Ren crossed the patio to a sliding glass door and pulled it open. The kitchen inside was spotless of dust and as colorful as the outside. He smiled. Harper Bellweather could not have found a more out-of-the-way hiding place for something as valuable as the lodestones. He walked through the pristine living room and mounted the stairs to the second floor.

The small boy stood waiting for him at the end of the hallway when he reached the top. He was about five years old and wore dark blue footie pajamas. His head was a little large for his body, giving him an unnatural doll-like quality. He stared at the shapeshifter with big, wide eyes. His smile seemed genuine, but there was a vacant look in them.

The moon-eyed boy put a finger to his lips. "Shhh!" he whispered. "We need to go into my room, or we might wake my mommy. I'm supposed to be asleep, but I have to wait for daddy to get home."

Ren followed the little boy into his bedroom. Toys and

stuffed animals filled the room. A red biplane hung from the ceiling along with a whimsical colored blimp. Wallpaper covered the walls with animals and ice cream cones. His bed sat in the corner, the blankets thrown back to reveal bedsheets with dinosaurs printed on them. Everything a five-year-old would want.

The boy stood in front of him, oversized eyes looking up at Ren. "Are you from the moon?"

"No, I'm not."

"That's okay." The boy looked at the floor. "The other lady wasn't either."

"The other lady?"

"The one with the pointy horse picture on her arm. She comes and visits me sometimes. We play catch." He darted over to a toy box and dug out a blue striped rubber ball, holding it up for Ren to see.

"How long ago did this lady visit you?"

"I don't 'member," Moonboy said. "It was forever ago. I miss her. Is she coming back again?"

"I don't think so," Ren replied as he glanced about the room.

His innocent face beamed up at Ren. "Will you play catch with me?"

"I'm sorry, but I'm kind of in a hurry."

Moonboy threw his head back dramatically and slumped his shoulders. "Please? I'm so bored," he pleaded loudly. "I never have anybody to play with. Mama's sleeping and daddy won't be home for a long time. Please!" His voice rose again. Ren worried the noise would wake his mother. He gave a deep sigh of resignation.

"Okay, I'll play catch," he replied. "If you answer questions while we do, okay?"

Moonboy jumped up and down. "Okay, okay!" He threw the ball. It went straight up in the air, then back down, bouncing off his head. He looked flabbergasted, then grinned when he saw the ball rolling to Ren.

"Throw it to me!" he said, clapping his hands together.

"Okay, but answer a question first," Ren said. "Did the lady ever leave anything behind when she visited you?"

"I don't know," Moonboy replied. Ren rolled the ball to him. The little boy bent over to grab it, but it went right between his feet. It rolled across the room and disappeared under the bed. Moonboy crawled after it.

"Did the lady go anywhere else in your house?" Ren asked. Moonboy gazed about his room, pausing for a moment to stare at a poster of brightly colored dancing vegetables on his closet door.

"She sat on my bed," he said, "but I really don't 'member if she walked around."

Ren opened the closet door. Hanging clothes lined the wall on one side. The other had shelves filled with shoes and more stuffed animals. Everything in the closest was the same colorful illustrative style as the rest of the world, slightly off and unreal.

At the back of the tiny closet, next to a small pair of cowboy boots, Ren saw an old suitcase that was neither illustrative nor brightly colored. Travel decals from places like Paris, Shanghai, Marrakesh, and Singapore covered the worn surface of the suitcase. Ren grabbed it and brought it to the bed. His heart skipped a beat.

He undid the leather straps and popped the latches on the front. Inside, two cloudy glass globes stared up at him. One was the size of a grapefruit, the other was twice as large. Both shone with an eerie glow of swirling colors. Next to them, a small round bauble of intricate metalwork. All three pieces lay nestled in soft black silk. The Roskashon Lodestones of Baltazaar Gheddi sparkled in the low light. He'd found them.

Ren stared down at the elusive pieces of Rogue Destiny's

ancient history. How many had died trying to find them, he could not guess. He did not care how Mordecai planned to use the lodestones, but he needed them to save Claymore.

Ren pried the larger of the two orbs from its black satin nest and weighed it in his hand. The polished stone felt solid and heavy. He held the globe up to the light. The inside was translucent but cloudy, swirling magicks and scintillating bursts of tiny colors flashed at the point where his fingers touched its surface.

Could the lodestones show him who he was? He stared at the orb and waited for it to do its magic. To give him some burst of memory or flash of transmitigation in his mind, or to reveal how he and Rhune were connected. Nothing happened. No flood of knowledge, no revelations of anything new.

Of course, it wouldn't be that easy. Nothing ever was. The lodestones needed to be set in proper sequence for them to work.

He sighed and placed the orb back in the black satin space, shut the suitcase, and snapped the lid tight. Part of him was relieved nothing happened. Maybe it was for the best. He didn't need more complications in his life right now. He might not be ready for the truth.

"I have to go," Ren said. The boy didn't answer him. "Did you hear me? I have to leave."

Moonboy stood in the middle of his room. His back straight, his arms at his side.

"It's time to say the words," he said.

"What *words*?" Ren wondered. The air pressure in the room changed. He felt a vague anticipation that something strange was about to happen.

Moonboy turned to him, his eyes glazed over and empty. "The words that bring my daddy home," he said.

The small boy became fixated on the full moon outside. The ball slipped from his hands and rolled across the floor. He walked to the window and began reciting the words he was fated to say every night.

There's no one on the moon,
No one I can see.
There's no one at the bottom of the big, deep, dark blue sea.

The boy's voice thundered across the night sky. His words echoed so loud Ren had to cover his ears. Moonboy climbed onto his bed.

"C'mon, or you'll get wet," he said ominously, his voice strangely devoid of emotion. He sat down at the foot of the bed.

I once took a trip,
On a purple pirate ship.
I traveled the world, far and wide.
With my favorite snacks by my side.

Water flooded into the room from all sides. It came from nowhere. The swirling waves knocked Ren from his feet before he realized what was happening. He threw the suitcase onto the bed and pulled himself up after it. A moment later, the ceiling faded to blue sky.

Winds picked up around them. A golden sun appeared in the sky. A flock of seagulls flew under fluffy cotton candy clouds. Ren found himself on the deck of a tiny sailing ship. An endless sea filled the horizon in all directions. The colors of the illustration were so bright he had to shade his eyes.

The deck heaved in rhythm with the roiling waves. Moonboy stood at the giant wheel of the ship, dressed in a pirate outfit.

Ren jumped to his feet. Harper's suitcase slid down the deck and he dove after it. Moonboy put a telescope to his eye and looked out over the water. Ren saw a whimsical sea serpent heading toward them.

Then a sea serpent appeared and tried to swallow me up.
I offered her a cookie and poured tea into a cup.
She ate the cookie, as we drank tea.
And the sea serpent paid no more attention to me.
With a flick of her tail, she stirred up the waves.
And just like that, I sailed away.

The scene shifted as the words pulsated through the air. The pirate ship disappeared under him, and Ren stood on a forest path. He saw Moonboy on a white steed in glittering armor. His sword raised as a huge scaly dragon charged down the path, fire spewing from its mouth.

Then I went to fight a dragon with my sword.
But the dragon scared me with a fiery roar.
So, I tickled it with a feather.
Until he was rolling on the floor.
Then we roasted marshmallows over his fiery breath,
And I made s'mores because he liked them best.

The picture book had no slow, meandering plot for Ren to keep pace with. Instead there were ever-shifting scenes, filled with dinosaur-riding cowboys, sneaky ninjas, spaceships and fast race car. His mind reeled with every turn of the page. He almost blacked out more than once from the chaos and disorientation.

I miss you whenever you go away,
I sit by my window and wait for you all day.
Only when you're with me, am I no longer alone,

And only then will I miss you no more.

The Story ended. Ren found himself lying on the floor in Moonboy's bedroom. His head spun from the shifting realities he had just experienced. Once the vertigo stopped, he looked around the room. Everything was exactly as it had been before the waters rushed in. Nothing was wet or out of place. He decided right then he did not like children's picture books.

Ren climbed to feet and looked for the suitcase. It lay on the boy's bed, undisturbed. He felt the air pressure change. His ears popped, and he heard vibrations in the distance like rolling thunder. Moonboy sat at the window, unfazed by all that had just happened. His head rested on his arms at the windowsill. He stared up at the moon in the dark sky.

Outside, a car door slammed shut.

"Daddy's home," Moonboy said. "I have to go. Will you come back to play with me again?"

"I don't think so," Ren told him.

"Ah," Moonboy said with a pout. "If you see the nice lady, tell her to visit me." Without waiting for an answer, he disappeared out the bedroom door.

Ren stared after him and sighed. He grabbed the suitcase and ran from the room, down the stairs and out into the backyard. A rush of energy swept over him as his feet hit the grass. He sensed the pull of the Muse's influence.

Part of him felt compelled to stay, to protect the boy from any others that might intrude upon this world and threaten him. The childlike innocence of this place completely overwhelmed Ren. His mind filled with thoughts of a carefree childhood he would never know. He ignored it and kept running.

He sprinted across the field, up the ramp, into the main cabin of *Subterfuge*. Rollo remained in his seat where Ren had left him. The grifter's eyes followed the suitcase to where Ren set it down.

"Are those the Roskashon Stones?" Rollo asked, the slightest waiver in his voice. "Tell me you found them?!"

Ren couldn't resist showing off his hard won victory. He opened the suitcase and flashed the lodestones. Rollo gasped when he saw them. The light of the stones shone in his dark eyes.

"I found them," Ren grinned. He snatched Rollo's top hat from his head and placed it on his own. "Now shut up before I leave you here."

"Very well," Rollo grumbled under his breath. "Where are you taking me now?"

"To save my friend," Ren replied.

Chapter 32
The Black Tower

Subterfuge reached the Sojourn Islands as twilight hung over the city of Rogue Destiny. Overhead, a thousand floating worlds reflected off the clear ocean waters. Ren switched the route thrusters on. The sleek Slipstream slowed and descended over Prodigal Bay toward the great black monolith.

The black tower of Baltazaar Gedde sat ominously on a windswept pile of desolate rocks, two hundred yards off the southwest shore of the city. The structure appeared to be constructed from a single piece of black stone. Even in the dim twilight its shiny surface reflected off the dark waters. Large cut stones formed the foundation of the tower.

Ren piloted the ship around the pinnacle of the tower. From his vantage point, there seemed to be no way into the monolith. Windows speckled the smooth surface of the tower, but they looked to be tightly sealed and impassable. He assumed protective magicks were in place to prevented entry.

"Wake up," Ren said. "We're here. How do I get inside?"

Rollo stirred in the co-pilot's seat next to him. "The only way inside is through a crack in the structure's foundation."

"Where do I set down?" Ren asked. He extended the landing gear and brought the ship around.

"There's an outcropping of rocks on the far side of the tower. You can land there," Rollo replied with a yawn. He rubbed his tired looking eyes with a shackled hand. His polished shoes tapped the floor in rhythm, trying to calm his apparent anxiousness.

Ren set the ship down at the base of the immense tower overlooking the clear crystal waters of the bay. He shut off the engines and pulled the key-box from the ignition, then dropped it into the satchel hanging off his shoulder.

"There's an outcropping of rocks on the far side of the tower that the ship will fit on," he replied with a yawn. His polished shoes tapped the floor in rhythm, trying to calm his apparent anxiousness.

"You said you've been here before?" Ren asked.

"Once," Rollo replied. "Long ago. It's forbidden by law to go near the tower, but, of course, there are those of us who must try. I spent years searching for ways to get inside and finally located one."

Ren unfastened the harness holding Rollo to his seat, but left the restraints confining his hands locked. Rollo stood up to look out the side window. "The tower is said to be built at the very center of the Mythic Cosmos, a point where time and space collide. Strange things happen inside. The tower does not take kindly to intruders. There are rumors that some nights you can see a lone figure standing in a highest window of the monolith. It's said to be Baltazaar watching over the City."

"Let's go," Ren replied. "I want to get this over with so I can get back to Claymore." He grabbed the suitcase containing the lodestones and set it down on an empty seat in the main cabin. Opening a storage cabinet, he laid *The Book of Days* inside, then dumped everything else from the satchel into the compartment and shut the door.

He lifted the Sunstone from its velvet resting place. It was much heavier than it looked. Rollo peeked around him. The glow of the Sunstone reflected in his eyes. Ren set it in his empty satchel.

"Back away!" Ren ordered. He closed the suitcase and shoved Rollo toward the hatch, hitting the button with his palm. The clamshell doors yawned open. The bottom half of the hatchway came to rest on the bare rocks at the edge of the water. He led his prisoner down the ramp.

He knew he couldn't leave Rollo alone in the ship with *The Book of Days* and remaining lodestones. But he also knew bringing the conniving little grifter into the tower created a whole new set of problems. The iron restraints that bound him were supposed to dampen Rollo's access to his magic. The trickster had to take his chances on how well they worked.

He considered his options a moment longer, before deciding he had no choice but to take his chances, keep Rollo in sight at all times, and wait for the inevitable betrayal that would happen once he put the Sunstone in place.

The fresh air reinvigorated Ren's mood. He had been to many worlds during his time with the Raconteurs, but the smell of the islands and the City of a Thousand Moons was unlike anything else. He closed his eyes and let the warm wind wash over him. His keen senses picked up the faint aroma of the food venders in Beggar's Row, mixed with the stench of the textiles factories south of them. It all blended into a rich tapestry that made Rogue Destiny unique. He opened his eyes to see Rollo watching him.

"What?" Ren growled. "It's just good to be home."

Rollo smiled, but said nothing.

A sudden surge of sympathy washed over Ren. He felt an

unexplained pity for the helpless little man standing next to him. After all, wasn't Rollo the victim of circumstance in all this. None of what happened in *The Epic of Gilgamesh* had been his fault. This had all been a tragic misunderstanding.

Rollo held out his shackled hands. Ren dug in his pocket for the keys to the restraints, then caught himself.

"Stop it!" he ordered and smacked Rollo in the back of his head, knocking his top hat off. "No amount of enchantment is going to make me feel sorry for you. You almost killed Harper to get to the lodestones, then came after me and Claymore in *Gilgamesh*."

The wave of sympathy coursing through his mind dissipated as quickly as it began.

"My apologies," Rollo replied. "I didn't know you or your partner. When you threatened me, my survival instincts kicked in. Self-preservation is a powerful motivator to one's actions."

"Drop the martyrdom act," Ren growled. "You knew who Claymore was, and he knew you."

Rollo nodded. "I'm sorry for overstepping. I will watch my tongue from now on."

"How are you tapping into your magic?" Ren asked. He picked up Rollo's top hat and flung it the open hatchway. "Rogue Destiny's a magical dead zone."

"You are correct," Rollo replied. "These islands have no natural magic of their own. But Baltazaar's tower is a powerful conduit and oozes residual magic like a sieve. When I'm in proximity of it, I regain a proportional control over some of my various gifts. Who knows how it all works or where the enchantments of a world originate?"

"The magic isn't even yours," Ren replied. "You stole it."

"That's only a rumor," Rollo said. He gave the trickster a smile that did not quite reach his eyes. "The rules of magic never make sense. Iron may inhibit Fae glamour in one world but not another. If you hope to reach the top of the tower, you'll need my gifts to deal with what awaits us inside."

Ren shook his head. "Just show me how to get inside."

Rollo shrugged. He tottered forward over the uneven ground, searching the rocks at the structure's foundation. "The protections surrounding the tower have weakened over the centuries since the sorcerer-king's death."

He picked up a small red stone on the ground in front of a pile of rocks at the base of the tower.

"Here is the marker I left the last time I was here!" he cried, holding the colored stone up.

"Where's the entrance?" Ren asked.

Rollo pointed at the large pile of boulders. "I'll need full access to my magic if we are to get inside." He raised an eyebrow and held out his shackled hands.

"I don't think so," Ren replied.

"Please!" Rollo begged, "Just remove the restraints long enough for me to clear away the rocks."

Ren reluctantly pulled the key from his pocket and held it up in front of Rollo. "If I remove these," Ren said, "and you try to move against me. I will break you in half, understand?"

Rollo stared at the key, nodded and raised his bound hands. Ren inserted the key into the restraints. There was a click. Rollo pulled his hands free.

Ren held the shackles, ready to slap them back on his prisoner once a clearing was made.

With an exaggerated wave of his hands, Rollo conjured two large faceless humanoids from nowhere. Both stood taller and more massive than anything he had brought forth in Gilgamesh. The phantasms immediately began to sift through the massive pile of rocks, tossing each one aside with frightening ease. The little man seemed impressed with his work.

Hidden behind the stones, Ren saw a narrow crack running

up the side of the base of the tower. The entrance was so well concealed, he would have never found it on his own, even if he had days to search for it. Once the apparitions cleared the rocks, Rollo waved his hands across the air like he was clearing away smoke. The spectral figures faded to nothingness.

"Come on!" Rollo shouted. "The game's afoot!" The small, round man wedged himself through the thin crevice and disappeared from sight. Ren followed him in.

The narrow crack in the stone foundation continued beyond what the outside light could reach. The rock widened in some areas before narrowing in others. Ren felt his way through the darkness until he came upon Rollo wedged between the rocks at a particularly tight point. Ren took great pleasure in giving him a swift kick in the backside to force him through.

A high-pitched yelp filled the passageway and Rollo flew forward. Ren followed, his guard up, ready for the unexpected. A dim light came through a hole that had been chipped out of the stone fifteen feet above him. Visibility was limited in the narrow tunnel, but Ren could make out a tall ladder standing in the shadows under the opening.

Rollo glared back at the trickster, but said nothing. Instead, he scrabbled up the ladder, quicker than Ren would have thought possible. The trickster climbed after him and emerged into a large open area that had been used as a kitchen.

"Stop!" Ren yelled. Rollo halted in the doorway to the next room. He raised his hands and turned around. Ren locked his wrists and hands back into the iron restraints and shoved him forward.

The stone and wood fixtures appeared strangely free from the ravages of time. Pots and pans hung from a wall rack above a countertop used to prepare food. Nothing in the place had dust or cobwebs to indicate it had been unoccupied for centuries.

"Baltazaar kept a very tidy house," Rollo said.

The adjoining room revealed a modest dining area with a wooden table and high-backed chairs. Overhead, a wrought iron light fixture hung from the ceiling, covered in melted candle wax. A giant oval mirror filled the space between a tall hutch full of dishes and a credenza.

Rollo glanced around the fixtures of the room. "These are simple living quarters for someone as mighty as Baltazaar Gheddi."

Ren noticed it, too. The opulence of royalty was nowhere to be seen. The expensive tapestries and trinkets those with great wealth flaunted to impress others and reenforce their own self-importance were missing. Nothing in any of the rooms they passed through indicated a king had once lived there.

Tall cupboards and a wooden hutch with glass doors lined one wall. A serving trolley stacked with porcelain cups, a tea kettle and wine glasses sat on the opposite wall. Rollo picked up a bottle of wine from the cart and examined the label.

"This is a vintage I've never seen before," Rollo gasped. "The name of the winemaker is a family that has not been around since the great purges that followed in the wake of Baltazaar's death. This would be worth a prince's ransom to any collector."

"Put it back," Ren growled, his temper coming through. "We're not here to take anything. Where did you go the last time you were here?"

Rollo returned the bottle to the wine rack. "That was a time long ago," he muttered. "I wandered the rooms, but couldn't shake the feeling I was being watched. The sensation grew stronger the further I went. Then I found a hallway lined with mirrors. At the end, I stood before a massive looking-glass. A shadowy figure stared at me from within the mirror. I approached cautiously, before realizing it was not my reflection. I was looking at Baltazaar Gedde in the distant the past."

"How is that possible?"

"Like I told you, the tower fractures time and space," Rollo replied. "Baltazaar was in his time. I was in mine. His ghost told me to leave his tower. I did not argue. I left and have never been back."

"Show me this hallway," Ren ordered.

Rollo looked around the room, a confused look on his pudgy face before he seemed to get his bearings. "This way!" he shouted, pointing to a side passageway and took off out of the room.

Ren broke into a run to keep the little man in sight. They passed through several rooms, each with a large oval mirror on the wall among the curiosities and knick-knacks that filled the shelves and bookcases. After several turns and several staircases, Rollo halted at an arched passageway that was swallowed in darkness.

"Down there is where I saw the ghost of Baltazaar Gheddi," he whispered.

Ren pushed past him into a hall filled with large mirrors that lined both walls. The reflective surfaces gave off a soft glow that cast the corridor in low light. He pressed his hand against the surface of a mirror to see if it might be a rabbit-hole. His fingertips touched a hard surface. The reflection blurred but cleared a moment later. It was not his reflection he saw.

The mirror showed an elderly lady in a blouse and peasant skirt. A handmade apron wrapped around her waist. She stood at an iron potbelly stove, stirring a large cooking pot filled with thick stew. Ladling the pot's contents into wooden bowls, she carried them, two at a time, to four occupants of a small kitchen table.

The old woman ambled back to the stove and prepared another bowl. She headed toward the door with the bowl in hand. One of the occupants of the table jumped up to open the door for her.

"Is he really out there, mother?" the green-faced young female asked. Her fishy eyes blinked back tears.

The elder woman stopped and gave her a pensive smile. "I believe he is," she said softly. "We'll find him. Be sure of that." She hobbled out the door down the rickety stairs of a ramshackle cottage to the edge of dark swamp.

She knelt and set the steaming bowl of stew down on the damp, spongy earth. Next to it lay a discarded, empty bowl. Picking it up, she stood and stared into the thick tangle of moss-covered trees.

"Rhune," she whispered. "Come home to us, my son."

The old woman climbed the steps and disappeared inside. A moment later, the cottage rose from the ground on giant chicken legs and waddled away over the brambles and thorns covered the ground.

Ren staggered back. The scene struck him like an unexpected wave capsizing a small boat. The face of the old lady stirred memories buried deep within the recesses of his mind. Nothing else mattered in that moment. Not Claymore. Not the lodestones. He remembered the words of his shadowy alter-ego, Rhune, when he fell through the darkness of the Great Void alongside Tempest and Charley.

"Mother wants you to come home," Rhune had said. *"Our siblings are waiting. Then we can all be together again."* The weight of those words were almost more than he could take in. He'd wondered for so long where he came from and how he ended up in Rogue Destiny. Now he had seen a small part of the answer to those questions.

He shook his head to get the images out and turned to see Rollo's reaction. The little man was not looking at him. Instead, Rollo stared into the mirror across from the trickster.

The reflection in Rollo's mirror showed a dark, rain soaked dirt road. A caravan of circus wagons sloshing through the mud.

The lead wagon turned onto a backroad that led to a barren field in the middle of nowhere. The rest of the caravan followed.

Slowly, the glassy surface of the mirror shifted. A new image appeared. A dozen workers struggled to raise a magnificent red and white striped tent. Another group fought the rain to assemble a mechanical carousel of swans and prancing horses.

The scene blurred to a bright sunny afternoon over an open field. The circus was up and running. Bustling patrons walked amid the massive tents as a Ferris wheel rose over the crowds. Flimsy wooden booths speckled the open field. People lined up to play games of coin toss, darts and other contests of skill. Young children ran through the crowds, holding tight to the strings of helium balloons while devouring hot dogs and cotton candy.

The span of time within the mirror sped up. The sun passed overhead at a rapid pace. Shadows lengthened until the daylight disappeared. Night descended on the carnival. Raucous music blared from speakers mounted high on wooden poles. Dancing colored lights filled the air as the crowds wandered the carnival grounds.

The music faded and a voice came over the speakers. "Come one, come all," the voice proclaimed. "Come now and witness the greatest spectacle to be found anywhere throughout the Mythic Cosmos. The excitement is about to begin inside the big top."

The throngs of excited spectators rushed toward the largest of the circus tent. Inside, the assembled audience crowded onto the bleachers that surrounded the circular performance arenas.

Moments later, a short, round figure in a crimson tuxedo with gold fringe appeared from a side entrance into the main spotlight riding a great white stallion. He leapt to his feet atop the shimmering saddle, before doing a magnificent backflip, landing lightly in the center of the ring. The crowd went wild.

The diminutive man removed his top hat and bowed to the approving roar of the spectators. He spun around on his heel where Ren caught a look at his face. The ringmaster was Rollo Pennymaker.

A shiny bulbous microphone on a thin wire lowered from the rafters in front of him. Rollo took hold of it. "Ladies, gentlemen and children of all ages!" he shouted. "Welcome to the Phantasmagoria Extravaganza! Prepare yourself for an evening of sheer delight. Tonight you will see things your bedazzled eyes will not believe. We have creatures of unimaginable beauty and mystery bought here from the farthest reaches of the Mythic Cosmos. You will witness impossible displays of ariel acrobatics and magicians of the highest caliber. And clowns! So many clowns! Open your minds for the impossible! For this will be a night of unforgettable wonderment!"

A small group of tall, richly dressed individuals entered the tent. Their stand-offish, aloof appearance caught Ren's attention. The five looked like royalty, quite different from the rest of the rustic spectators around them. He decided they were most likely Fae. A member of the circus staff led the entourage of Faery folk to a section at the front row of bleachers cordoned off by velvet ropes.

Ren's gaze seemed to be pulled deeper into the mirror. A strange sensation came over him. His viewpoint shifted until he stood on the floor of the circus tent, watching each entertainer perform to the roar of the crowd. He watched one circus act after another perform before his eyes. He had no idea how long he stood there. It was as if time itself had stopped. Beside him, Rollo stood mesmerized, too.

Once the final act ended, and the boisterous cheers of the audience died down, the crowds began to disperse. A large, rotund man with a dominating mustache and curly goatee walked upstream against the press of the crowd, stopping in front the Fae. He wore a gaudy prismatic tuxedo that shifted colors as he moved. He took his top hat off, placed it over his heart, thanking the royal entourage for coming. Small talk commenced until the crowds were gone and the tent was empty of witnesses.

The spotlights overhead went out and the tent was pitched into darkness. The man in the prismatic tuxedo raised his hand. The sound of metal scraping metal filled the air. A round cage with thick bars suspended by a steel cords crashed down over the Fae.

The leader of the Faeries leapt to her feet. Her hands lit up with a radiant light. Her retinue did the same. The cage shook and flashed with a brilliant glow from the Fae's magic. The counterattack died immediately.

The Rollo Pennymaker within the mirror ran in with a long metal pole. Several circus hands rushed in with him. Each carried the same type of pole. They poked them through the bars into the captives within. Sparks flew from the forked tip of the poles as they made contact with the trapped Fae.

One by one the powerful supernatural beings within the cage collapsed to the bleachers.

"The cage is made of iron," Rollo said softly. He winced as if he had been struck himself, but his eyes did not move from the imagery playing out before them. "It's the Fae's greatest weakness. It robs them of their immortality. Makes them vulnerable to things such as cattle prods."

"What happened to them?"

Rollo turned his face away as if he was embarrassed. "Their glamour was stripped from them by the most diabolical means possible. Whatever was left of them after that was sold to their enemies at a great price. You can guess their fate."

"Why would anyone do that?" Ren asked.

"Money, of course," Rollo replied. He glanced at Ren as if he was an idiot. "It always goes back to money. The stolen glamour is stored in containers of cold iron, sealed with salt and a sprig of holly. It's value is more than can be calculated. But I left that life behind long ago, so none of it matters now. I no longer work for that employer. Their methods were too repugnant, even for me."

Ren smiled to himself. "I notice you still kept the Fae's magic."

"I didn't take anything from the Fae," Rollo spat. He continued walking. "I simply took it from those who stole it from the Fae."

Ren followed him. He found it interesting that even someone with a heart as corrupt as Rollo Pennymaker had limits to what he was willing to do.

Chapter 33
Echoes of the Past

Ren continued down the hallway behind Rollo. Mirrors on both sides flashed shifting images as they passed them. The reflection in the next mirror revealed a tall, lanky youth playing in a walled-off courtyard with a hunched-back beast that resembled a jackal the size of a dog. The boy's youthful face beamed with delight as he wrestled his grotesque pet to the ground.

The next mirror showed Baltazaar in his prime, tall and muscular, clad in gleaming armor. He rode a massive white steed into battle, leading a horde of charging horsemen across a field of battle toward a distant enemy. The ground shook from the thunderous hooves. Beside him, the fully grown jackal creature sprinted to take part in the coming carnage.

Rollo stopped to watch the scene playing out.

"There's no time for this," Ren fumed. He shoved his shackled prisoner forward. "We need to get to the top of the tower."

Rollo turned to him. "This is the history of Rogue Destiny," he said. "How are you not fascinated by it?"

"Because I don't care what happened in the past," Ren replied. "I care about saving Claymore."

"Don't you understand what we're looking at?" Rollo replied. "These are reflections of different periods in Baltazaar Gheddi's life. Forgotten moments that have been lost in time."

Rollo moved down the row of mirrors to where Baltazaar stood before an enormous assembly of citizenry, both military and civilians. He knelt at the foot of a throne. A priestly figure in flowing robes set a crystalline crown of shimmering light on his head. Everyone bowed as the new king rose. The elaborately dressed woman next to him took his arm in hers.

"And that's the Lady Jacquetta Kismet!" Rollo pointed wildly at the reflection. "Together they reined over the kingdom of Roskashon," Rollo said, "and saw years of peace and prosperity. Until a close advisor betrayed them both to the barrow-lich, Ghulgoth the Ever Dying. The monster led its allies on attacks to the surrounding cities to draw Baltazaar's forces from his castle. In the heat of battle, Ghulgoth suddenly flew off. Baltazaar knew where the monster headed, but he made it back to his stronghold too late to save her."

Rollo turned to the next looking-glass in line. His excited expression changed to dismay. Ren stepped next to him. The image in the mirror showed the shattered side of a castle stronghold. Amid the rubble, a heartbroken Baltazaar held the limp body of his only beloved. Tears rolled down his cheeks as he lifted his face and vowed revenge to the storm-filled skies above him.

"Baltazaar pursued the monster with an unrivaled fury," Rollo continued. "He battled Ghulgoth time and again, killing the monster with both sword and magic. But, like the fabled phoenix, the unnatural creature always rose again from the ashes. Baltazaar's obsession consumed him to the point it ripped his kingdom apart.

"In his quest to destroy the unholy monster, he betrayed both friends and allies until even his most loyal generals plotted to overthrow him. The great armies of the east saw the chaos taking place in Roskashon and marched against Baltazaar's armies. The greatest sorcerer-king in history had first lost his only love and would now lose his throne.

"Baltazaar wandered his world as a vagabond, pursued by hordes of enemies. Then, as the legend goes, he stumbled upon a rabbit-hole in the southern wastelands at the edge of his world. The doorway came out onto the shores of the Sojourn Archipelago.

"Crushed under the weight of his grief, he lived in seclusion on a world where his magic was beyond his reach. His kingdom had been taken from him, but, even worse, the monster that killed his beloved queen still lived.

"The exiled king spent years plotting revenge and figuring out how to kill something that refused to die. Ghulgoth had destroyed his life, but without his magic, how could he hope to bring the monster down? He realized the path to victory lay in the fact that if he had no magic, then neither would Ghulgoth. He built a tower and created the lodestones to be a conduit to his lost magic.

"Baltazaar goaded Ghulgoth into chasing him through the rabbit-hole to the magical dead-zone that is Rogue Destiny. Atop Mount Perdition, they fought their last battle. With his magic returned to him, the sorcerer-king vanquished the monster. Separated from his regenerative magic, Ghulgoth could not save himself this time. The monster fell, never to rise again.

"The defeat of his mortal enemy did nothing to replace his lost love and only left Baltazaar despondent. He never returned to his homeworld again. Instead, he began to build a city. One unlike any in the Mythic Cosmos. A place where the lost and wounded can come to forget their past tragedies. He named it Rogue Destiny."

The hallway ended abruptly. The way was blocked by a wall of black stone. A single mirror, larger than any they had seen before, hung in front of them.

Ren's reflection slowly morphed into a darkly lit study. A man in long robes sat at a desk before a roaring fire, writing in a large book. Bookshelves cover the walls, filled with the oddities only a sorcerer would treasure. There were two doors on opposite walls.

The man seemed to sense Ren's presence and looked up. Rising from his chair, he approached the mirror, his multicolored robes shifting hues. He towered over Ren, separated only by the dimensions of the looking-glass.

"How have you gained access to my tower?" the man asked in a low tone. His eyes held a deep intelligence.

"You are Baltazaar Gheddi, are you not?"

"Yes," the man replied.

"My name is Ren B'gatti, and I am a Raconteur."

Baltazaar's eyes narrowed in suspicion. "I do not know what that is."

Ren pulled the Sunstone from the satchel hanging on his shoulder and held it up. "The Raconteurs protect the written worlds from danger. We're the good guys. I'm here to save my friend, Claymore Ives. To do that, I have to place the Sunstone at the top of the tower."

Baltazar's eyes blazed with anger. "Where did you get that?!" he roared. He pressed his hands on the glass surface separating them.

Ren pulled *The Book of Days* from his satchel. "You wrote this to justify the existence of Rogue Destiny." He flipped through the pages and pointed to a diagram of the tower. "This documents how you protected the written worlds from outside corruption. Claymore created the Raconteurs to continue your work. He is a good man and fights to protect Rogue Destiny to this day. He deserves to live."

A bitter sadness appeared in Baltazaar's eyes. "How long have I been dead?" he asked.

"For almost a thousand years," Ren replied. "But what you built has continued to this day. Rogue Destiny has endured the ages and is the crown jewel of all the Mythic Cosmos."

"It's been that long, huh?" Baltazar dropped his hands from the mirror. His eyes softened, and the anger melted from his face. "Why do you think the lodestones will aid your friend?"

"He's consumed by a madness that is tearing his mind apart," Ren said. "He doesn't have much time left. *The Book of Days* says your lodestones *return what has been lost*. I need to reach the observation deck to put the Sunstone in place." He pointed to the top of the tower in the drawing.

"I sense your sincerity in your desire to help a friend," Baltazaar replied. "But the lodestones cannot be allowed to be used by anyone but myself. They are simply too dangerous. No one person should wield that kind of power. If magic is controlled by a single individual, it could mean the end of Rogue Destiny."

Ren's temper exploded. "Claymore's not magical!" he yelled. "He doesn't desire power, but he's going to die without my help. If there's any chance to save him, I'm going to do whatever I have to. Either with your help or without it."

"Leave this place now," Baltazaar warned. "Before your life is forfeit." He turned away from them.

Ren pounded on the glass. "Come back here! You have no further use for them! You're already dead!" He dropped his head, trying to clear his mind and unravel the puzzle he faced. If the room existed in the mirror's reflection, then logically, there should be an identical room somewhere in the tower. He bet that's where he would find the way up the tower.

"Baltazaar!" he yelled. "I'm going to find a way to the top, even if I have to tear this place apart room by room. I'm sure your home is full of priceless relics and artifacts. I will bring everyone I know back here to plunder your tower until it is empty. The choice is yours."

The sorcerer-king stopped and turned around. Ren had his attention now.

"Very well, Raconteur," he said. "But there is something I need you to do for me first."

"I don't have time for pointless tasks," Ren growled.

"This will take no time at all," Baltazaar replied. "If you ever wish to reach the observation deck, you will do as I ask. There is a simple item I need you to retrieve for me."

"Why can't you get it yourself?"

"I am only a reflection trapped in the past. The physical tower you stand in is beyond my reach. This room is my prison."

The statement took Ren by surprise. "Where it is this item you want?"

"Under the kitchen there is a wine cellar," Baltazaar said. "On the southern wall of the cellar, you will find a stone door." He held up a brass skeleton key. "This will unlock the cellar door. Inside the inner room, you will find a sarcophagus. I need you to bring me the leather scroll case inside the casket. Once I have that, I will tell you the secret to reaching the observation deck."

The request made Ren angry, his patience exhausted.

"What could be on a rolled-up piece of parchment that is more important than Claymore?!" he growled.

"That is my business," Baltazaar retorted. "If you wish to save your friend, then you will do as I request." The sorcerer-king touched the tip of the key into the mirror. It passed through the solid surface, causing a ripple that distorted the reflection for a moment.

Ren took the key. It was ice cold to the touch.

"Fine," he said. "We'll be right back." He shoved Rollo down the hall of mirrors, and they made their way back to the kitchen.

"I think I saw a staircase back here," Ren said, pointing to a pantry. In the back of the room, he found a set of steps carved into the tower's foundation that led down to a wine cellar. Rollo raised his bound hands and made a sign in the air with a finger. The same faery light he conjured in *The Epic of Gilgamesh* appeared above his head.

Ren glanced at the flickering light. "How're you doing that?"

Rollo shrugged. "Like I said, the tower pulsates with magic," he replied, "It allows me to override the restrictions of my shackles enough to throw a few lights around."

Cool, damp air clung to the rough-hewn walls lined with wooden racks filled with dust-covered bottles. The fae light threw long shadows over the vaulted ceilings. Dark casks of aged wine, weathered from centuries of use, filled the far corner of the cellar next to a rough-hewed door cut into the stone wall. Ren took out the large brass key and inserted it in the keyhole. There was an audible clicked when he turned it. With an effort, he pushed it open.

The door opened to a dimly lit octagonal room. A stone sarcophagus sat on a raised platform at the center of the inner chamber. Long slats cut high in the walls allowed a minimal amount of sunlight to illuminate the sarcophagus. Shadows clung to every corner of the room. Four of the eight walls had oval mirrors mounted on them. Ren felt an eerie, foreboding presence he couldn't explain.

Four large stone knights, ten feet high, stood watch over the tomb at the other four walls of the chamber. Ren noticed they wore the same armor and helmets as the riders in the battle scene inside the mirror upstairs. Each held a massive sword, the pointed tip resting on the pedestal where they stood.

Ren approached the platform. Every surface of the stone casket had intricate carvings. He placed his hands on the edge of the lid and pushed. It didn't budge.

"Help me get the lid off," he ordered.

Rollo ambled up the steps to his side. He held out his shackled hands. "I'll need my hands free first."

"Not happening," Ren replied. He took a step back, morphing into a tall, overly-muscled man with a bald head, and leaned into the task again. The muscles in his back tensed and the veins on his arm popped from the strain. Slowly, the sound of stone scraping stone filled the room, and the lid of the sarcophagus slid open.

Inside, the richly dressed corpse of Baltazaar Gheddi lay in his final resting place. The founder of Rogue Destiny appeared untouched by the ravages of time. Ren half expected his eyes to open at the disturbance.

The sorcerer-king wore polished armor under a magnificent white surcoat that bore the crescent moon and compass symbol of Rogue Destiny. He wore metal gauntlets on his hands. They clutched the prize Ren sought. A weathered scroll case lay across the chest of the deceased ruler.

Ren pried the cylindrical leather case from the grasp of the lifeless gauntlets. Curiosity took over, and he examined the tube, wanting to know what could so important to a man that died a millennium ago. The ends were sealed tight, and he saw no way to open it.

"This has to be it," he said. "Let's go."

Behind him, Rollo let out a startled yelp. Ren wheeled around to see the four stone statues move under their own power. One by one, they stepped from their pedestals and brought their swords up.

"How do we fight stone?" Rollo cried. He leapt out of the way as a giant sword slammed down. The fae light over his head extinguished.

"Use your glamour!" Ren shouted back.

"I can't do anything until you let me out of these!" Rollo yelled, lifting his bound hands. "Throw me the keys!"

Ren hesitated. He knew the little thief would turn on him as soon as he was freed. That is, if they survived the next few minutes fighting the stone knights, hemming them in on every side. The closest statue approached with its sword raised. A second statue came up behind him. He pulled the keys from his pocket.

"Catch!" Ren shouted.

The stone knights moved with surprising agility. One stepped between them as Ren tossed the keys to Rollo. They careened off the statue and disappeared into the shadows at the edge of the room. Ren caught Rollo's glare and could only shrug. They looked at each other for a brief moment before Rollo ambled into the dark shadows after the keys to the restraints.

There was nothing Ren could morph into that would help him fight stone adversaries. He could only transform into organic creatures. Flesh and blood would do little against the might of the stone statues.

Ren slung his satchel across his back and tucked the scroll case under an arm. The closest statue stepped toward him. He rolled under its legs and moved to the far side of the sarcophagus. He pounded his hands on the lid, hoping the false threat to Baltazaar's body would draw their attention and buy Rollo time. It worked. All four statues turned toward him.

A massive sword cut through the air. Ren ducked out of its way. The blade struck the wall. The entire room shook under the force. Debris spilled down from the ceiling.

Ren backed up to put distance between him and his opponents. Out of the corner of his eye, he saw the open door. A thought came to mind. He had what they had come there for. Would leaving Rollo there to fend for himself be such a bad thing? The little grifter wouldn't hesitate to abandon Ren if their roles were reversed.

Rollo Pennymaker was nothing but a lying, conniving, back-stabbing grifter. No one would miss him, and the worlds would be a better place if he was dead. Ren had no doubt of that. But he was trying to do better, and yet, somehow, always seemed to fall back into his old ways.

A compact figure stepped from the shadows. Rollo fumbled with the keys before unlocking the bindings encasing his hands. He shook his himself free of the restraints and thrust his hands out in front of him, carving jerky patterns in the air.

The form of a hairy four-legged beast with a hunched back and massive curved horns appeared next to him. The creature's hair was so thick, Ren could not tell if it was a wild mountain goat or some sort of woolly beast from Rollo's imagination. Rollo pointed at the closest statue. The animal slammed itself head-first into the stone figure like a battering ram. The creature bounced off the thick stone leg with a resounding thud.

"Again!" Rollo ordered. The beast crouched and flung itself into the statue again. This time, the stone leg gave an audible crack. The knight turned toward Rollo, shifting its weight onto the fractured leg. There was a grinding of stone at the point of the break. The statue swayed before falling back into the stone knight behind it. They both crashed to the floor.

"Pennymaker, we got what we came for!" Ren yelled. "Let's go!"

Rollo wove his way through the chaos, dodging the remaining stone knights, only to stumble and sprawl headfirst across the floor as he reached the door.

Again Ren considered leaving Rollo there. The little grifter had outlived his usefulness and was now nothing more than deadweight. Any insight he might offer, Ren could figure out on his own. He pondered the idea a moment longer, then shook his head.

Instead, Ren grabbed Rollo by his lapels and flung him through the open doorway, unsure what compelled him to do so. Was he just going soft? He pulled the stone door closed behind him.

Rollo lay on the floor in the breathing hard. "I feared you would leave me in there to die," he muttered.

"It never crossed my mind," Ren replied. He held up the scroll case. "Let's get back to Baltazaar."

Chapter 34
A Matter of Trust

They raced up the steps to the hall of mirrors. Ren easily outpaced Rollo's shorter legs, reaching the mirror at the end of the hall long before Rollo.

The sorcerer-king looked up from his chair as Ren approached. He jumped to his feet when he saw what was in Ren's hands.

"You have it?" he said, doubt punctuated in his words.

"Of course," Ren retorted. "Right where you said it would be. But you didn't expect us to survive those guarding your tomb, did you?"

It was only a blind guess on Ren's part, but he could tell from Baltazaar's expression he'd guessed right. But none of that mattered right now. Only Claymore mattered.

"Where is your companion?"

"He's on his way," Ren replied. He grinned and held up the scroll case. "Ready to tell me how to reach the top of the tower?"

"Give me the scroll first," Baltazaar said. "And I'll tell you what you want to know." He stepped closer to the window and put out his hand. Ren backed away, not knowing if the sorcerer might reach through the reflective glass.

"Tell me first," Ren replied.

"How can I trust you will give me the scroll case if I tell you?"

"I guess you can't," Ren said. "Just like I don't know if I can trust you."

Baltazaar shrugged, his expression unchanged. "Then it seems we are at an impasse," he said.

"It would appear we have," Ren replied, holding the leather scroll case up. "I'm beginning to think this holds more than just a scroll."

Rollo stumbled into view. He stopped short of reaching the mirror and leaned over. He put his hands on his knees, trying to catch his breath.

"So, tell me what this really is," Ren said turning back to the image in the mirror. "Or I will sell it on the black market. Then you'll never see it again."

"Very well." Baltazaar sighed. "It's a map."

Rollo's head came up. "A map?!" he asked. "Of what?!"

"Of Rogue Destiny," the sorcerer replied. "And the surrounding islands and cities of the Sojourn Archipelago."

"So?" Ren asked. "There are lots of maps of the islands."

"No, this is not just any map!" Rollo exclaimed. "It's the *map*! The Terra Carta Mundi! Baltazaar's dream of the Ideal World Made Real! That's what this is, isn't it?"

Baltazaar did not answer.

"There was a picture in *The Book of Days*," Rollo shouted, barely able to contain himself. He jerked the tome from under Ren's arm and flipped through the thick pages. He pointed to a drawing of the map near the end of the book. "Here it is!

Ren was confused. "I don't follow."

"Every world within the Mythic Cosmos is a Book, a story that plays out over and over in a never-ending cycle. Rogue Destiny is not like any of those worlds. The map inside that scroll case is Rogue Destiny! Do you have any idea how much that would be worth? Its monetary value is unimaginable!"

"We're not here to pilfer anything," Ren said. "Rogue Destiny's a map. What do I care? I just want to get to observation deck."

Rollo shook his head. "You're not listening to what I'm saying, B'gatti."

"Your friend understands the value of what you have," Baltazaar said.

"He's not my friend," Ren replied. "So, tell me what I'm not understanding."

"The map is much more than its monetary value," Baltazaar said. "Rogue Destiny exists only as long as the map is safe. Harm the map and you harm the city. Destroy the map and you destroy the city. The map *is* Rogue Destiny."

Ren tried to make sense of his words. He had experienced many strange, illogical things during his time with the Raconteurs, but the city literally being a map pushed the limits of credulity. He glanced down at the scroll case in his hands.

Why would anyone make up such an implausible story? The *Book of Days* seemed to confirm the authenticity of the map, so it had to be true, right? Even Rollo believed that Rogue Destiny and the map were interconnected.

Ren realized he had forgotten his number one rule regarding Rollo Pennymaker. Never take your eyes off of him. He glanced around. The little man had set *The Book of Days* down on the floor and was backing down the hallway. His hands moved through the air in quick arcane patterns. Two phantasmal figures appeared in the hallway between them.

"Bring me the scroll case," Rollo said, a malicious smile on his lips.

By now, Ren had dealt with Rollo and his illusions enough times to know the pattern. The sudden turn of events did not catch him off guard. Before the two muscled servants completely solidified into physical form, the trickster sprinted past them.

He tossed the scroll case into the air. Rollo instinctively reached for it. Ren smashed a fist into his nose again. Blood spurted and Rollo's eyes rolled into the back of his head. He fell backward onto the floor. Ren stood over the unconscious man with the scroll case and *The Book of Days*. Rollo wasn't getting up any time soon. With his glamour interrupted, Rollo's two goons faded into nothingness.

"An impressive display of skill," the sorcerer-king said.

Ren shrugged. "It's what I do."

"Your companion appeared to be some sort of illusionist?"

"More or less. His magic is stolen."

"So what do we do now, you and I?" Baltazaar asked. His eyes flashed.

"I have not been in Rogue Destiny long," Ren said. "And I'm just beginning to find answers about my origins and where I come from. I've heard stories that the great Baltazaar Gheddi was an honest man. A good man. Someone who aided people in their darkest moments. I only want to save my friend from a madness that's eating away at his soul. So I'm going to trust that good man still exists."

Ren touched the end of the scroll case to the mirror as he had seen Baltazaar do with the bronze key. The sorcerer pressed his palm to the surface on the other side with the glass. With little effort, Ren pushed the map through the solid surface of the looking-glass. The sorcerer grabbed the case and pulled it through.

"The city you built still gives hope to the lost," Ren said. "The Raconteurs continue the mission you began. Claymore has dedicated his life to that mission."

"Thank you," Baltazaar said, a look of great relief on his tired face. "Not even my closest disciples knew the map's true importance. I ordered them to bury it with me, so it would never fall into the wrong hands. It was my deepest held secret. Now that the lodestones have surfaced after all these centuries, I knew the map would only be safe here with me, in a time no one can reach."

"I understand that now."

Baltazaar put out his hand. "And the key?"

"Oh, yeah," Ren said. He pulled the bronze key out of his pocket and pushed it through the mirror.

"Thank you," Baltazaar replied. "So your friend, Claymore, protects my city?"

"And countless other worlds of the Mythic Cosmos," Ren replied with pride in his voice.

"And he is no wizard?"

"No, he's not," Ren replied. "Like me, he doesn't care for magic. I think you would like him. He's a lot like you. Stubborn and hardheaded."

Baltazaar let go a laugh. "I'm sure I would. The only wizard Rogue Destiny will ever need is me." He reached beyond Ren's sight to something on the wall. There was an audible click and the escape of trapped air. An unseen doorway in the stone wall cracked open next to the mirror.

Baltazaar Gheddi bowed to Ren. "Go save your friend," he said.

Chapter 35
The Devil You Know

The circular room at the top of the black tower measured thirty feet across. In the center, stood a large octagonal platform. A shallow bowl cut from black, reflective stone sat upon it. Ren circled the platform, still breathing hard from running up the steps to the observation deck. He lifted the lodestone out of his bag with both hands.

The Sunstone had grown heavier the higher he carried it up the tower. With a grunt, he placed the lodestone over the center of the stone bowl. The weight was suddenly taken from him. Ren pulled his hands away and the Sunstone floated in place under its own power. He stepped back, waiting for something amazing to occur. Nothing happened.

The center of the Sunstone sparked, followed by a pulsating light that Ren could only image was magic. Tendrils of electricity inside the lodestone blazed to life. The radiance filled the room. The loud clank of mechanisms falling into place reverberated all around him. Eight horizontal storm windows slowly opened on each wall. A gust of ocean air rushed through the room from outside, sweeping out the stale, musty stench.

The Sunstone spun faster and faster. The light grew brighter.

Ren covered his eyes with an arm against the blinding glare. A moment later, the piercing brilliance faded, but the lodestone continued to spin at a slow rhythmic speed.

Outside the storm windows, Ren could see the lights of Rogue Destiny across the bay. His face to face encounter with Baltazaar left him with a different perspective. He saw the city through new eyes and found he missed her. She looked somehow vulnerable and innocent, and worth saving from anyone who threatened her. The distant sounds of the night and the glare of lights comforted his uneasy thoughts.

Ren stared transfixed at the radiant Sunstone for a moment longer. It was time for him to go get back to Claymore. He'd already taken too long.

His eyes came up to find Rollo Pennymaker staring at him from the far side of the bowl, his face lit in the spinning light.

"You should have closed the door behind you," he said.

Ren heard the sound behind him. He twisted his body just enough to prevent having his head taken off. A massive two-handed sword struck the stone bowl.

The sword may have missed him, but the metal boot did not. It struck him in the chest, sending him flying away from the stone table. He climbed to his feet, the room spun as he fought to get his bearings, only to find himself facing three more swordsmen. Each one identical to the others. Beyond them, out of his reach, Rollo stood with an indifferent look on his face.

"Set the satchel down," Rollo growled. "And you won't get hurt."

Ren slid the bag from his shoulder and set it on the floor. Even though it contained *The Book of Days*, he was more concerned that his Slipstream's ignition box was also inside. If Rollo took *Subterfuge*, he would have *The Book of Days*, the two remaining lodestones and the freedom to go anywhere he wanted.

"Kill him," Rollo ordered, pointing his minions in Ren's direction. The conjured phantoms advanced forward as one unit, forcing Ren back until he was stopped by the open storm windows. Far below, the waters lapped the rocky shore.

The phantom swordsmen formed a half circle around Ren. He thought about shape-shifting, but their swords would cut him to ribbons. He risked a glance back at the Sunstone. Just as he had hoped, Rollo was completely focused on digging through the contents of the satchel. Instead of fighting, he sidestepped a sword swing and dove out the narrow window into the night air.

As a general rule, he wore loose fitting clothing, when he was forced to wear clothing at all. He pulled an arm free of his shirt. The rocks below him drew closer as he struggled to pull the other arm free.

Ren shifted into a black raven as he fell. With a flap of his wings, he reversed his descent. His abandoned shirt and pants fluttered to the rocks below. He flew around the tower and through a storm-window on the other side.

Rollo stood to his feet, the key-box in his hand. He threw the strap of the satchel over a shoulder. The entourage of knights stood silent behind him. Ren darted across the observation deck, changing midway from the raven to a black panther. Momentum carried him into Rollo before the grifter could react. The little man looked up and screamed as the panther collided with him.

Ren dug his claws into Rollo's shoulders and pinned him to the ground. Rollo yowled in pain, his eyes as wide as saucers. Ren roared in his face hoping to break his hold on his creations. The four swordsman closed in on them. He shifted back to his natural form, punching the little man in the face.

"Release them!" Ren shouted. He punched him again to break Rollo's concentration.

The attack had the desired effect. The four phantasms

slowly faded to mist and vanished, leaving the two alone in the room.

Ren pulled Rollo off the floor. "I told you what would happen if you tried any tricks!" he spat in the man's cherub face.

"Mercy!" Rollo cried, but Ren had none left.

"It's too late for mercy!" Ren dragged him bodily across the floor to the storm window. He peeked out the window and saw *Subterfuge* directly below him. He lifted Rollo up by the scruff of his tuxedo and threw him through the window.

"No! No! No!" Rollo screamed. He caught himself on the window ledge with both hands and held tight. Ren stepped back and delivered a hard kick into his chest. Rollo toppled out the window.

Ren watched the flailing figure fall to the rocks far below. To his disappointment, Rollo missed the rocky shoreline completely and landed in the water. He didn't like cruelty for cruelty's sake, but he was willing to make an exception in Rollo's case.

He picked the key-box off the floor and threw it into his bag with *The Book of Days*. They were both still inside. Throwing the strap over his shoulder, he shifted into a flying monkey and leapt through the storm-window. He flew down in a wide spiral, his wings spread wide.

Rollo thrashed in the water, too far from the tower to draw on his magic for aid. His face disappeared beneath the waves before fighting his way to the surface again, gasping for air. Ren landed on the rocks by the Slipstream, watching the small man struggle.

"I thought you said you could swim," he asked with a wry grin. He found his discarded pants among the rocks and pulled them on.

Rollo lifted his face as far as he could out of the water. "I lied!' he sputtered. "Don't let me drown!"

"All you do is lie, Rollo!" Ren replied. "You're a conniving, backstabbing grifter that no one would miss if I left you to die."

"But you are a Raconteur!" Rollo cried. "You can't do that." His arms slapped at the water in vain, a dozen feet out from the rocks. Ren knelt down and dug the key-box out of the bag and opened the hatch of Subterfuge.

"Am I?" Ren answered. "Don't remember ever saying I was. Like you, I may have done terrible things in the past, but unlike you, I'm trying to do better. No one can say that about you."

"Then if you're trying to do that, you can't let me die!"

Ren stared down at the drowning man. He thought it would be a fitting to leave him after what he'd done. Vengeance was the same as justice to the trickster. On the other hand, it would be nice to see the little toad rot away in Lazaranth Prison, his magic crippled and beyond his reach, as he lived out the rest of his miserable life in solitary confinement for his innumerable crimes. Rollo flailed helplessly in front of him before disappearing under the waves one last time.

Cold vengeance was one thing Ren understood, but if he and Claymore were going to start up a new band of world protectors, he would need to learn to choose justice over revenge. He didn't necessarily agree with that. Vengeance had its place, but it's what Claymore would want him to do. He dropped the key-box into the bag and threw it through the open hatch of the Slipstream, then dove into the water.

Rollo Pennymaker had stopped thrashing. His limp body slowly sunk into the depths of the bay. Ren grabbed him by the arm and swam back up. He pulled the lifeless body up onto the rocks. Rollo lay on the ground unmoving, water dripped off him. Then he coughed violently once and vomited. The coughing and sputtering resided after a time. Rollo rolled over and sat up with his head down.

"You okay?" Ren asked quietly, handing his top hat to him.

"Thank you for saving me," he answered, placing the hat on. Ren punched him in the face for a third time in the last hour.

Rollo's head snapped back, and he fell onto the rocks. Ren dragged unconscious man into the cabin of *Subterfuge* and hoisted him into an empty passenger's seat. He grabbed a second set of iron infused restraints and locked the grifter's hands into them. The he pulled the straps of the seat harness over his head and fastened them tight. Rollo was going nowhere.

Ren lifted Rollo's face to better see his injuries. Fresh blood oozed from his swollen nose over the crusted blood from previous blows, his eyes blackened. Ren bent down and picked up Rollo's fallen top hat and set it on his own head. Sliding into the pilot's seat and fired up the Coldfire engines. He eased *Subterfuge* off the ground and gunned the engines, shooting into the sky.

He punched the coordinates to *Gilgamesh* into the console on the dash and brought up the route to Gilgamesh. It was time to rendezvous with Claymore and Harper.

Hours later, *Subterfuge* approached a decaying world. Ren hit a button on the dashboard. An audible ping resounded in the cabin. A tiny spark of light shot out from the front of the ship and streaked forward, striking the outer veil of the world. The swirling green and blue that covered the surface rippled. An opening appeared. Ren gunned the engines and shot through the keyhole.

Subterfuge flew through the Word Canopy that shrouded *The Epic of Gilgamesh*. Giant words and sentences flashed past the front windows. The Slipstream followed the raging Euphrates River until he spotted the ridge where he and Claymore had camped the night before. At least, he thought it had just been the day before. Traveling in and out of worlds always messed with his inner clock.

Descending toward the ridge, he spotted a figure standing at the edge of the forest of Wayward trees. Claymore. He dropped the landing gear and brought *Subterfuge* to a soft landing on the hard rocks of the ridge.

Ren opened the side hatch, grabbed the suitcase from the co-pilot's seat. Rollo stared at him through blackened eyes and dried blood. Ren smirked. How many times had he broken Rollo's nose? Claymore met him as he stomped down the steps of the ramp.

"Where have you been?" Claymore growled.

"Finding what we came here for," Ren said. He lifted the suitcase containing the lodestones. "Where's Harper?"

"I asked you a question." Claymore's voice hardened. "Where were you? I've been waiting for two days."

"Why are you angry?" Ren replied. "I chased Rollo down like you wanted, all the way to Rogue Destiny."

"Did you catch him?"

"Of course, I did," Ren replied. "Then I found the lodestones and came straight back here."

"You went to Gideon, didn't you?" Claymore asked. "I thought we agreed to leave the Raconteurs out of this!"

"I never talked to Gideon." Ren saw Claymore's demeanor had gotten worse in the short time he had been gone. The madness was winning.

"That's because he wasn't in his office when we went there," Rollo said.

"Shut up, Pennymaker!" Ren snapped.

"I thought you were on my side." Claymore stepped toward him.

"I have always been on your side," Ren replied. His body

tensed. "I got us a Slipstream and I'm standing here with the lodestones!"

Claymore stormed past him. "I need to talk to Rollo," he rumbled. He stomped up the steps into the Slipstream. Ren rushed after him.

"What do you need with him?"

"Give me the keys to the restraints," Claymore ordered. Ren did so without thought or question. Claymore led. He followed. That had always been the order of things.

"Give me your hands," Claymore said. Rollo lifted his restraints.

"What are you doing?!" Ren shouted. "He's tried to kill us! The restraints prevent him from using his magic." He grabbed Claymore by the arm.

"You had your chance," Claymore snarled, pulling his arm away. "I trusted you. You betrayed that trust."

"I didn't talk to anyone. I took *Subterfuge* and left. I got the Roskashon Lodestones! We have everything we were after!"

"Don't forget the young girl, B'Tori," Rollo interjected. "You talked to her. She helped us steal the ship. She could have told anyone."

"I said shut up!" Ren backhanded Rollo across the face. He raised his fist to hit him again, but Claymore grabbed his arm.

"That's enough, Ren," Claymore said. He knocked Rollo's top hat from Ren's head. "And stop messing around! I'm getting tired of your shenanigans."

Claymore unlocked Rollo's binders. The small man slid his hands from the metal restraints and rubbed his wrists. He slipped out of his chair and stepped away from Ren.

"Claymore, don't you think we should go?" Rollo said, his voice soft, yet commanding. The reopened wounds around his nose bled down his face.

"Yeah, I think you're right," Claymore answered.

Ren realized what was happening. Somehow Rollo used his Fae glamour, even in iron restraints, to influence Claymore's fragmented mind. His partner's compromised condition would easily fall under Rollo's influence. Ren jumped forward and kicked Rollo in the chest with every ounce of strength he could muster. Rollo flew back in to the wall of the cabin. He cracked his head against the metal bulkhead and crumbled to the floor. Ren turned to Claymore.

"He's using magic on you!" Ren yelled.

Claymore stared into space as if he was trying to gather his thoughts. He looked down at Rollo's unconscious form, then back at Ren.

"No, he isn't," Claymore rumbled. He drew his pistol, lightning fast. "Hand me the suitcase. And don't try shifting. Not even you are that fast."

Ren set the suitcase on the floor between them. "What are you doing?" he asked.

"Gideon can never have the lodestones," Claymore replied. "I thought we were going to rebuild the Raconteurs together. Start fresh, do it right this time. Just you and me. Now I'll have to do it myself."

"I came back to get you," Ren said. He stepped back toward the open hatch. If he could keep Claymore talking for a few more moments, he might have a chance to escape.

"You lied to me," Claymore said in a low rumble. "I told you to leave the Raconteurs out of this, but you didn't. The first thing you did was run back to Gideon. We were brothers in arms once, but now that's over." His voice was even, but undermined by growing rage.

"You're not thinking clearly," Ren said. "That's the madness talking! This isn't you!"

"This is me," Claymore replied. "I'm seeing clearly for the

first time. You betrayed my trust. Just like Gideon, just like the Raconteurs!"

"How have I betrayed you?" Ren asked. "I've brought you the lodestones. With them, the madness doesn't have to be a death sentence. They can save you."

"I don't need to be saved," Claymore growled. "We're all dying, just at a different pace. We're only given so many days before Death comes for us. Did I ever tell you how no one wanted you in the Raconteurs? I fought to get you in and made excuses every time you screwed up. And this is how you thank me?"

"I'll always be on your side," Ren replied softly. He backed up another step.

Ren could see the pain behind Claymore's eyes. His friend stood teetering on the precipice of the abyss. The Raconteurs meant everything to him, and he'd lost everything in an instant. He understood Claymore's anger. He'd founded the guardians of Rogue Destiny, recruited the first agents himself. To be tossed aside was something Ren would not have forgiven either. Now it seemed every past affront, real and imagined, bubbled up to the surface of his memories.

Claymore's mind was gone, eaten away by a madness that Ren could not stop. He had failed his friend.

"How can I ever trust you after this?!" Claymore bellowed. "You're a trickster. You live your entire life in falsehoods and deceit! Your entire existence is one big lie. I trusted you and you go running back to the Raconteurs at your first opportunity!"

He leveled the gun.

Ren shook his head. "Claymore, don't," he begged.

The pistol fired once, then twice. The sound of each shot echoed in Ren's head. He staggered back from the impact and grabbed the edge of the doorway to stop himself from falling out of the ship.

"I'm sorry it had to come to this, Ren," Claymore said, a touch of sadness in his voice. "The truth is, I could never take you in a fair fight."

Claymore fired again.

Ren fell backward, tumbling down the steps to the ground. He landed hard, blood gushing from his midsection.

Claymore appeared in the ship's doorway, a canvas backpack in his hand. He holstered his gun and threw the pack to the dirt next to Ren.

"Can't have you following me, buddy," Claymore said, his voice strangely devoid of emotion. "There's an Echo Transponder inside, so you can contact the Raconteurs. There's a revolver in there too. If you're lucky, someone will get here before you bleed out."

"W...what did you do to Harper?" Ren stammered. Each word burned in between searing breaths of air.

"She's safe. I wrapped her in a blanket and left her in a cave near the forest. She has a burning fire and food and water."

"Where are you headed?" Ren asked. It wasn't like he could follow, but he figured it was worth a shot.

"I've been asleep for so long," Claymore said. "But now the curtains have been drawn back and I see things as they truly are."

"What do you see?" Ren replied.

"The Words, my friend," Claymore declared. "I see the Canopy that covers the sky from horizon to horizon. Everything is visible to me now. And it tells me we're all merely ink on a page, created to live out our roles in a Narrative we have no control over. It's all just an illusion, an endless cycle that plays out over and over again. Now I'm an empty husk of who I used to be. At the end of the day, we're all just lost souls in an unconcerned universe. I've lost any greater purpose that I thought I had. I'm sorry things had to go down like this. I truly am."

Rollo appeared next to him. "Claymore, it's time to go," he cooed. "It will take time to round up buyers. Then you can start the Raconteurs over again, from the beginning."

Claymore disappeared into the ship. Rollo tipped his hat to Ren. A moment later, the hatch closed. The engines started. Dust blew up, shrouding the ship from view. Ren choked and coughed. The ship slowly rose from the ground. Claymore glanced down from the cockpit window. His face showed no emotion. The roar of *Subterfuge's* engine grew fainter until only the sounds of the jungle remained.

Ren's breathing came in short, painful gasps. Blood seeped between the fingers he pressed to his stomach. He closed his eyes and laid his head back in the dirt.

The End of Book Three

GLOSSARY OF MAJOR PLAYERS

The Good Guys

Ren B'gatti — Shape-shifting trickster of dubious morals and mysterious past.

Claymore Ives — Founder of the Raconteurs and Ren's partner.

Natascha Devi — aka — Doctor Enigma — Senior field agent for the Raconteurs.

Medesto Bodenhammer — Senior field agent for the Raconteurs.

Tempest Vondersteen — Security Officer for the Raconteurs. Oversees general operations.

Charley Lovejoy — Tech specialist for the Raconteurs.

Gideon Dumas — Director of the Raconteurs.

Sebastian Poe — Head mechanic

Raffles Bonhomme — Cajun Rabbit — Mythic Folk Hero of the Bayou. Expert in the lore
of ley-lines and rabbit-holes, and deep knowledge of the Mythic Cosmos. Always helps out the Raconteurs whenever they call on him.

Valgus Alaric — Visigoth barbarian marauder turned Raconteur.

Jonny Vega — Police officer from a futurist Hong Kong

Rollo Pennymaker — Grifter and smuggler of rare antiquities and artifacts of great price.

Harper Bellweather — Field agent for the Order of the Memento Ex-Libris, an organization obsessed with documenting the Mythic Cosmos.

B'Tori Poe — Slipstream designer and mechanic in training. Youngest daughter of Sebastian Poe.

The Bad Guys

Mordecai Davos — The shadowy overlord of Rogue Destiny's criminal underworld who has kept his true identity hidden, even from his innermost circle.

Tomas Demarche — Mordecai's right-hand man and scholar from the Order of the Memento Ex-Libris.

Idalia Devi — Natascha's mother. A brilliant scientist whose inventions have revolutionized travel throughout the Mythic Cosmos.

The Society of the Black Rose — A secret society controlled by Mordecai Davos whose influence extends throughout the Mythic Cosmos.

The Grimm Jester — Mysterious wraith under the control of Mordecai Davos.

Piqwic York — The overseer of Mordecai's vast fortunes. He uses his financial expertise to increase the Black Rose's wealth and help them maintain their dominance over Mordecai's criminal underworld empire.

Odd Bod — Mordecai's Grand Enforcer.

Maquna — Idalia Devi's serpentine bodyguard.

GLOSSARY OF PLACES AND TERMINOLOGIES

Rogue Destiny — The fabled City of A Thousand Moons that stands at the crossroads of the Mythic Cosmo.

The Mythic Cosmos — A universe filled with the mythos of every fable, myth, legend and fairy-tale.

The Raconteurs — A self-appointed band of world-hopping troubleshooters who protect the Mythic Cosmos from the corruptive influence of Rogue Destiny's criminal element.

Ley-lines — The mystical pathways that grow from the roots of the Wayward Trees and connect all the written worlds of the Mythic Cosmos.

Rabbit-hole — A doorway between worlds created by the ley lines.

The Word Canopy — The mystical veil of words that surrounds every world.

The Narrative — The continual progression of a world's Story that must remain uninterrupted and free of outside corruption. If that narrative flow is broken, the consequences will be catastrophic.

The Logos Personae — The main character of a world's Story. The individual who is intertwined with the Narrative and the linchpin to the world's survival.

The Muse — The zeitgeist of any written world. An intangible, impersonal force, She gives the Story its essence and vitality, and the Narrative its soul.

The Crucible Event — A catastrophic event that burns a world to ash. Occurs at the death the Story's main character, the *Logos Personae*, or when the flow of the Narrative is altered beyond what can be repaired or restored.

About the Author

Paul Tallman lives in the wet and wonderful Pacific Northwest with his long suffering wife, Tina.

After having worked for far too many years in the insurance industry, he finally broke away from the security of a steady paycheck to pursue writing.

A geek by birthright, he has spent his life in the social awkwardness of his calling, ever since reading *The Lord of the Rings* for the first time in middle school.

Paul can be found holed up away from the society, working on his next book.

He still mourns the cancellation of the TV show *Firefly*.

To find out more about the Rogue Destiny universe visit: paultallmanauthor.com

Also by Paul Tallman

A Rogue Destiny

Rogue Destiny: Beginnings

Ley Lines and Rabbit Holes

The Book of Days